Ten years ago, the passion was ignited...
And it's only gotten hotter with time!

Blaze

Join the editors in celebrating
a decade of wonderful authors,
irresistible stories...and great sex!

Look for all six
Special 10th Anniversary Collectors' Editions
from The Original Sexy Six authors.

Check out:

THE BRADDOCK BOYS: TRAVIS
and *THE PLEASURE PRINCIPLE*
by Kimberly Raye

HOTSHOT and *GOING FOR IT*
by Jo Leigh

UNDENIABLE PLEASURES and *YOU SEXY THING!*
by Tori Carrington

COWBOYS LIKE US and *NOTORIOUS*
by Vicki Lewis Thompson

TOO HOT TO TOUCH and *EXPOSED*
by Julie Leto

EXTRA INNINGS and *IN HIS WILDEST DREAMS*
by Debbi Rawlins

Harlequin Blaze—
Celebrating 10 years of red-hot reads!

Blaze

Dear Reader,

They're baaaaaaack....

Travis Braddock is a wild and wicked cowboy with a ripped bod, a knack for horses and enough sex appeal to melt even the toughest woman's resolve. He's also a 150-year-old vampire dead set on revenge...until he meets wedding planner Holly Simms.

A three-time loser when it comes to men, Holly has given up on finding her own happily-ever-after. The last thing she wants is forever. Luckily, the sexy cowboy who arrives in Skull Creek to attend her latest wedding has *temporary* written all over him.

I hope you enjoy reading Travis and Holly's story as much as I enjoyed writing it! As a writer, the Blaze line has always been near and dear to my heart. I love intense, powerful stories that push limits and unearth the sensuality buried deep down inside all of us. For me, love and lust go hand in hand and it's been a dream come true exploring them both for the past ten years. Whether it's cowboys or vampires, I've been able to portray my characters with real passion and true emotion, and that means the world to me. My heartfelt thanks to Harlequin for allowing my stories to be a part of such a wonderful collection of books.

Cheers to another ten years and happy anniversary from deep in the heart!

Kimberly Raye

Kimberly Raye

THE BRADDOCK BOYS: TRAVIS
THE PLEASURE PRINCIPLE

 **Harlequin**®

TORONTO NEW YORK LONDON
AMSTERDAM PARIS SYDNEY HAMBURG
STOCKHOLM ATHENS TOKYO MILAN MADRID
PRAGUE WARSAW BUDAPEST AUCKLAND

ISBN-13: 978-0-373-79631-1

THE BRADDOCK BOYS: TRAVIS
Copyright © 2011 by Harlequin Books S.A.

The publisher acknowledges the copyright holders of the individual works as follows:

THE BRADDOCK BOYS: TRAVIS
Copyright © 2011 by Kimberly Raye Groff

THE PLEASURE PRINCIPLE
Copyright © 2001 by Kimberly Raye Rangel

Recycling programs for this product may not exist in your area.

CONTENTS

ABOUT THE AUTHOR

Bestselling author Kimberly Raye started her first novel in high school and has been writing ever since. To date, she's published more than fifty novels, two of them prestigious RITA® Award nominees. She's also been nominated by *RT Book Reviews* for several Reviewers' Choice awards, as well as a career achievement award. Currently she is writing a romantic vampire mystery series for Ballantine Books that is in development with ABC for a television pilot. She also writes steamy contemporary reads for the Harlequin Blaze line. Kim lives deep in the heart of the Texas Hill Country with her very own cowboy, Curt, and their young children. She's an avid reader who loves Diet Dr Pepper, chocolate, Toby Keith, chocolate, alpha males (*especially* vampires) and chocolate. Kim also loves to hear from readers. You can visit her online at www.kimberlyraye.com.

Books by Kimberly Raye

THE BRADDOCK BOYS: TRAVIS

This book is dedicated to the real Holly
and her hubby Tim.
Thanks for being such great friends!

1

THERE WERE WOMEN EVERYWHERE.

That was the first thought that struck as Travis
Braddock pulled up at the front gate of the CB Ranch.
The lawn in front of the sprawling two-story house
had been set up for an outdoor ceremony, complete
with a red carpet for the bride, huge flower arrangements and lots of free standing candelabras because
it was an evening affair. He'd expected a small shin-
dig, but there were at least a hundred people crowded
into the rows of white chairs that flanked either side
of the aisle. Mostly females.

Hungry females.

A mix of perfume, lush sensuality and raw need
wafted through the open window of the Land Rover
and teased his nostrils. His groin tightened and he
stiffened.

An overabundance of women was usually a good
thing.

Particularly for a one hundred and fifty year old vampire who fed off sex as ravenously as he did blood. But Travis wasn't here because of the beast that lived and breathed inside of him.

Tonight was all about revenge.

He'd spent the last one hundred and fifty years blaming his three brothers for the massacre that had killed their family while they'd been off raiding for the Confederacy. He pointed the finger at his youngest brother Cody because he'd run off and joined the army in the first place, forcing the rest of the brothers to leave home just to keep an eye on him. He held Brent responsible because he'd refused to call it quits a week early when the war had been all but lost anyway. And he resented his oldest brother Colton because he'd forced them to detour to Austin to file an official report about their last raid before heading home to discover the carnage.

He'd blamed his brothers. But the real blame lay with his sister-in-law. Rose was the one responsible.

A traitor.

A *killer*.

He ignored that tiny niggle that told him he was jumping the gun. That maybe there was some crazy explanation for what had happened. That maybe, just *maybe*, Rose Braddock hadn't set fire to the Braddock spread and fed her own family to the wolves all those years ago.

His nephew had died in that tragic fire. So had his

mother. A half dozen ranch hands. And Rose herself, or so they'd all thought. The entire place had been a blazing inferno when Travis and his brothers had ridden in.

They'd been too late to save anyone that fateful night, even themselves. One minute they'd been trotting along, making plans for the future and the next, they'd found themselves smack dab in the middle of a fiery nightmare. Before they'd had a chance to figure out what was going on, much less rescue anyone, Travis and his three brothers had been attacked from behind and left for dead.

They'd died that night. But they'd also been reborn. Thanks to an ancient vampire who'd happened upon the scene and given the Braddock brothers a second chance.

He'd done the same for Rose.

That's the story Cody had recently uncovered when he'd tracked down their maker right here in Skull Creek, Texas. Rose hadn't died in the fire as originally thought. Rather, she'd fled the scene with a man. The pair had been attacked a few miles away by Indians. Garret Sawyer had arrived after the attack and done the only thing he could to help the innocent couple who'd been left for dead by a band of Commanches. He'd turned them, just as he'd turned the Braddocks.

Innocent?

Like hell. Rose wasn't the loving sister-in-law,

the caring mother, the perfect daughter-in-law they'd thought. She'd fooled the entire family. Every damned one of them.

But not for long.

Cody had sent a letter explaining the truth about Rose and the all-important fact that he now knew her whereabouts.

The news had chased Travis around a few weeks before finally catching up with him at the Bar T Ranch in Montana. He'd been hired on to break some horses for the owner and was smack dab in the middle of a midnight session when one of the hands had flagged him down with the frayed envelope.

Inside had been a brief description of the incriminating evidence Cody had on Rose, the news that he'd finally found her and—much to Travis's astonishment—a piece of engraved cardstock requesting his presence at tonight's event.

A bonafide wedding *invitation*. After all the bad blood between them.

He still couldn't believe Cody had invited him. Any more than he could believe his brother was fool enough to think he would ever be satisfied with just one woman. He needed sex as much as he needed the blood. It was a need that was fierce. Intense. All-consuming. The hunger didn't lend itself to monogamy, that was for damn sure. No matter what delusion Cody was operating under, he wasn't the marrying kind. None of them were.

Travis knew that firsthand. He'd tried to settle down with one woman. To pretend he hadn't changed that fateful night, that he didn't yearn for sex the way a man craved his next breath. He'd tried, all right. And he'd failed. And Amelia, his childhood sweetheart, had gone to her grave hating his guts because he'd cheated on her.

He wouldn't do that to another woman. He wouldn't make promises he couldn't keep.

But Travis wasn't here to warn his baby bro about the nature of the beast, and he sure as hell wasn't here as a guest. He was here for information.

For forgiveness.

The thought struck and he drop-kicked it right back out of his head.

Even if he did regret the fallout with his brothers—which he didn't—there were too many bad feelings between them to make amends now. He'd turned on them and they'd turned their back on him. That was that.

Travis stared through the windshield at the lavish spread. His hyper sensitive sight zoomed in on the rose archway where his youngest brother stood facing a petite blonde. To his left, stood his other brother Brent. That sucker-punched Travis right in the gut for a long moment. Brent was the last person

Travis expected to see standing next to Cody. Brent wasn't the stand-up type. He was wild. Free. Selfish.

Then.

But now?

There was no denying that he was here. Cody's best man. His friend. His *brother*.

Travis's chest hitched as he watched Brent hand over the ring. The gold band slid into place and Cody sealed the deal with a kiss. And just like that, the ceremony ended.

Which meant Travis was too late once again.

If he'd come to see the exchange of vows, that is, which he sure as hell hadn't. He was here for Rose. To find out her whereabouts.

Nothing else mattered.

He swallowed against the tightness in his throat and climbed out of the Land Rover. Walking through the gate, he crossed the massive lawn. It seemed his baby bro had done pretty well for himself riding bulls on the PBR circuit. Travis had kept tabs on him and knew Cody had won a few championships, but he hadn't realized the size of the payouts.

Obviously they had been big. Real big.

He closed the distance to the throng of guests and made his way toward the archway where the bride and groom stood amid a shower of camera flashes.

Just before he reached his target, a group of elderly women pushed in front of him to admire the bride's dress. He tried to slip through, but the women were intent on getting an eyeful!.

"Doesn't she look lovely?" one woman said.

"That dress must have cost a small fortune."

"I heard her new beau took care of the tab AND bought her this place as a wedding present."

"Can we stop all this lollygagging and go find a seat? My bunions are killing me?"

"Excuse me," Travis said to one blue-haired woman as he tried to make his way past her.

She turned a pair of cataract-clouded gray eyes on him and smiled. "My, my but you're a strapping young man." *"You remind me of my dear, sweet, departed Walter before he kicked the bucket."*

The last thought echoed loud and clear in Travis's head as he made eye contact with the woman and his chest hitched.

Her name was Gladys Martin and she lived at the local senior's home where the bride worked as the activities coordinator. Miranda had personally invited all of the ladies at the home and had even taken them to Austin on a shopping trip so they could all buy something special to wear on her big day. She'd also promised to take a picture with each and every one of them, which was why Gladys was waiting in line.

Travis tipped his hat and grinned. "I hate to trouble you, ma'am, but I need to scoot by you and have a quick word with the groom if you don't mind."

She looked as if she wanted to protest, but then Travis stared deep into her eyes for a long moment and acceptance sparked. She smiled. "Of course, dear."

She started to move, but then an ancient little man with a bald head and a mean expression stepped in front of her and broke the temporary spell Travis had cast.

"Hold your britches there, sonny." Arbor Crabtree poked Travis in the chest with a bony finger. "We all want our picture taken with Miranda and we're not about to be sideswiped by some young buck who cain't wait his turn. You'll get back to the end of the line lickety-split if you know what's good for you."

While Travis's charm worked with the females, he was out of luck when it came to men. Particularly Arbor. He was a two-time decorated war veteran who'd carved up an enemy sniper with his witling knife in a one-on-one battle back in 1942. He still had the knife to this day, carrying it in his pocket for bragging rights.

He also had a hemorrhoid that was making him even crankier than the fact that he'd lost at checkers to Milton Decker earlier that afternoon.

The point? Arbor was not about to be crossed by man or vampire.

Travis held up his hands in surrender. "I'm not trying to put any one out, sir. I've just come a long way is all."

"So did I. Do you know how far away we had to park? Why, this place is busier than the Dairy Queen on senior citizen night."

"They give free ice cream to anyone over sixty-five," one of the women added.

"And whipped cream."

"That sounds real nice," Travis said. "But I just need to talk to my—"

"Is there a problem here?" The soft, feminine voice slid into his ear and cut him off mid-sentence. He turned toward the female who appeared on his left, her hands on her hips, her blue eyes drilling into him.

She was at least a head shorter than he was, with long, blond hair that had been swept up into a tight, no frills ponytail. She wore a knee-length black skirt and a plain white button up blouse. Sensible black pumps. *Boring.*

That's what he told himself. No legs up to here or breasts out to there.

At the same time, she had the most incredible eyes he'd ever seen. Pale blue with just a hint of green around the edges. Color so translucent that, for a split second, he saw only his own reflection in their sparkling depths.

No thoughts. None of her personal stats. Nothing. Not even her name.

Before Travis could delve deeper, she shifted her attention to the old man.

"What's going on, Mr. Crabtree?"

"This whippersnapper is trying to cut in line," the man declared. "But Miranda promised me I could have the first picture. I cain't stand for long without my arthritis acting up."

"Mine, too," a woman added. "I've got seconds."

"And I've got a corn on my big toe that's aching something fierce so I get to go third."

The pale blue eyes darkened just a hint, killing the reflection that had him so mesmerized and opening the door so that he could see straight into her thoughts.

Her name was Holly Simms. Mid-twenties. She was a wedding planner who loved dogs, Reeses' Peanut Butter cups and her job. Except when she had to deal with stubborn guests or a lying, cheating, line-cutting cowboy.

Ouch. "I wasn't trying to cut in front of anyone." He shrugged. "I'm just here to talk to the groom."

"And we're here to talk to the bride," Arbor added. "She promised us pictures and I'm not moving 'til I get my picture."

"Me either," a woman added.

"Neither am I."

"You'll all get your pictures. I promise." Holly turned on Travis. "Excuse me? What did you say your name was?"

"I didn't say, but it's Travis. Travis Braddock."

When her gaze sparked, he added, "I'm the groom's brother."

Her mind seemed to rifle for a memory before recognition dawned and she frowned. "The one who didn't RSVP?"

"My job keeps me really busy."

Too busy for your own brother's wedding?

The question rang loud and clear in her thoughts and guilt niggled at him.

"We're not very close." He wasn't sure why he told her. The words simply tumbled from his lips before he could stop them and he stiffened. "Listen, I don't want to cause any trouble. I just wanted to say a few words to my brother."

"He and Miranda are going to host a receiving line when they're finished with pictures. I'm sure you can wish him well then. In the meantime, you should move on to the reception area." *Otherwise these seniors are going to kick your firm, tight, totally amazing buns all over this ranch and I'm going to let them.*

Her thought echoed through his head and a strange sense of warmth stole through him. A grin tugged at his lips.

She motioned toward the massive tents set up just beyond the barn. "You can have something to drink and a bite to eat while you're waiting."

His groin tightened at the suggestion and his gaze

shifted to her creamy white throat. He could see the faint pulse beneath her skin and his fangs tingled.

"There's a full menu," she continued. "Swedish meatballs. Pigs-in-a-blanket. Mini chimichangas. Southwest egg rolls. I'm sure you can find something you like."

"I already have," he said, staring deep into her eyes.

He expected to see passion flare in the blue depths, her lips to part, her body to lean toward his. Particularly since she thought his buns were firm and tight *and* totally amazing. That's the way it always was when he focused his complete attention on a woman. She couldn't help but fall under his spell.

Her eyes widened and then she blinked. Once. Twice. As if she couldn't quite believe she'd heard him correctly. "What did you just say?"

"I said I already found something I like." As anxious as he'd been to talk to Cody, he knew he wasn't getting anywhere near his baby brother for the time being. Which meant he might as well slow down and kill a few minutes.

On top of that, he really *was* hungry. And it wasn't a Swedish meatball or any of the other things she'd just rattled off he was craving. He'd been in such a hurry to get to Texas that he hadn't even stopped to feed. "I like you, sugar."

You.

Now he would see the flare of desire, the physical proof that she wanted him...

She stiffened and Travis knew in a glaring instant that she wasn't going to fall all over him the way other women did. She was stronger than most. Determined. *Different.*

And damned if he didn't like it.

2

WAIT A SECOND.

Wait just a cotton-pickin' *second.*

Holly Simms shook her head and tried to clear the cobwebs from her brain. No way had she heard this cowboy say that *he* wanted *her.*

A real, balls-to-the-bull *cowboy.*

Her brain snagged on that all-important fact as she noted the worn tips of his black boots, the soft, molded jeans holding tight to his thighs, the smell of leather and fresh air that clung to him. She knew cowboys. She'd almost married one. But then her very own Mr. Tall, Dark & Irresistible had stood her up in front of God, the Skull Creek Cattleman's Association and the entire Ladies Bingo club. The wedding had been called off and she'd been stuck with a six tier red velvet wedding cake to eat all by her lonesome.

She'd gained ten pounds thanks to her low-down

sneaky rat of an ex-fiancé and learned a valuable lesson. Namely, that she was more cut out to plan a wedding than actually participate in one.

She'd spent the past three years as Skull Creek's resident wedding planner. She'd orchestrated over one hundred ceremonies, overseeing everything from seating charts and bags of birdseed to sit down dinners and cages of live butterflies. She'd booked disc jockeys and ordered cakes and she'd even called in Marty and Serena, the 2010 Texas brisket cooking champions, to make an appearance at the Morgan reception last June. Marty and Serena had cooked all the food on-site over a live grill—much to the bride and groom's delight—and handed out bottles of homemade Serena Sauce as wedding favors. The event had been a huge success and she'd even got a mention in the *What's Up Y'all?* section of the *Skull Creek Gazette.* A huge coup that had doubled her business. Well, that and the fact that Eliza Mac-Donald, the eighty-eight-year-old owner of her only competition, From Courtin' to Cuddlin', had needed a double hip replacement and been forced into retirement.

Holly had been busy ever since, giving the couples of Skull Creek the happily-ever-after she, herself, would never have.

Her great-aunt Tootie had tried to warn her.

The old woman had always said there were only two types of women in the world. The kind who were doomed to settle down, get married and have babies and the lucky few who were actually meant to avoid all three and have some real fun. Tootie's definition of fun involved lots of wild parties, single cowboys and plenty of one-night stands.

The Simms women? They tended to fit into the second category. Aunt Tootie had avoided matrimony like the plague and spent her life sowing one wild oat after another. The few Simms women who tried to break with tradition and go the happily married route ended up divorced like Holly's own mother (five times as a matter of fact) and her three aunts. Not one of Holly's female relatives had ever had a long lasting relationship except Holly's Aunt Celia, but that was with a pet poodle named Sassafrass.

Bottom line, Holly simply wasn't the marrying kind. She had a pre-determined path. One that didn't involve his and her monogrammed towels.

She knew that now. She'd accepted it. She'd even joined an online group of women committed to overcoming their addiction to falling in love. As a full-fledged Love Buster, Holly had given up her childhood dreams of wedded bliss and decided to focus on living out her most wild and wicked fantasies.

But that was a little hard to do all by her lonesome.

She was a *wedding planner*. Translation? She scared the bejesus out of every bachelor in town.

They were convinced she only had marriage on her mind and so they all kept their distance. Since her moment of public humiliation at the altar, the only *fun* Holly had involved a case of batteries and a vibrator named Big Ben.

Which meant that no way had she heard this hunk of testosterone correctly.

She licked her lips and noticed the way his gaze followed the motion. Her stomach hollowed out and her heartbeat thundered in her ears.

"Would you, um, mind repeating what you just—" she started to ask, but Evan chose that moment to rattle over her headset.

"I hate to tell you this, but we've got a tiny little problemo with the PA system in the reception tent."

Evan Valentine was her twenty-six-year-old protégé and a die-hard romantic. He'd come to her last year after a hand full of various temp jobs and a six month online course on how to be a party planner. He was young, creative and hopelessly in love with his high school sweetheart, a once-upon-a-time quarterback named Bob.

"I like—" the hunk of testosterone said, but he was drowned out when Evan jumped in. "I told you not to hire that DJ. Seriously, what sort of lunatic plays the Chicken Dance at a PETA event?"

"Could you excuse me for just a sec," she held up a quick finger to Hot and Hunky before turning to blurt into her headset, "What are you talking about?"

"The disc jockey that yours truly *told* you not to hire is incompetent. His PA system doesn't work. It's completely dead and the natives are getting restless."

"And that's a *tiny* problem?"

"When you compare it to the fact that there are people starving in Third world countries, the ozone layer is slowly depleting and Bob's parents refuse to include me in the family Christmas card. Not that I'm crying over it, mind you. I know that if I just hang in there, they'll eventually see how hopelessly in love we are and welcome me into the family with open arms. Why, I bet they even ask me to pick the background for next year's card…"

Evan went on about red versus green while Holly tried to calm the sudden pounding of her heart. She stiffened, determined to ignore the fingers of heat dancing up and down her spine. She could feel Mr. Testosterone behind her, his gaze on her back.

Watching.

Waiting.

Wanting.

She ditched the last thought, gave her hormones a quick shake and tried to concentrate. "Where's the DJ now?"

"The last time I saw him he was running for the bathroom. He said he ate the enchilada special for lunch at the diner and now he's regretting it."

Her heart jumped into her throat and she swallowed it back down. Easy. Calm. She'd been down this path before. Unexpected situations were par for the course when it came to wedding planning. The key was to keep her head and think. "Get him an Alka Seltzer and meet me in the reception tent."

"You think that's going to help?"

"It can't hurt." She clicked the off button and turned back to face the megalicious cowboy standing behind her. She would talk to him, get everything straight and if he truly had said what she thought he'd said, then maybe…

The thought faded as she found herself staring at the empty spot where he'd been standing.

Her gaze swept the crowd, but he was nowhere to be seen. Proof beyond a doubt that her imagination had kicked into overdrive thanks to her deprived hormones.

I like you.

Yeah, sure.

She gave herself a great big mental shake, turned on her heel and went to find the MIA disc jockey.

"I'M SURPRISED YOU had the balls to show up," Brent said as he shoved Travis up against the backside of the barn.

Travis blinked and stared at his younger brother. One minute he'd been admiring the very attractive rear end of Cody's wedding planner, and the next, he'd been gripped by the collar and whisked away at preternatural speed by the vampire in front of him.

Green eyes so much like his own stared back at him. "Hello to you, too."

The green shifted and Brent's gaze fired a bright, vivid red. "If you're here to start trouble, you can forget it. I'm not letting you screw this up for Cody. No arguing tonight." The red flickered and anger sizzled in the air surrounding them. "I mean it."

"Easy." Travis held up his hands. "I'm not here to start anything. I just came to talk."

"You really expect me to believe that?"

He didn't. The last time he'd been face to face with his brothers, he'd blamed them for the massacre that had taken their family.

But he'd been wrong.

Travis eyed his brother. "Where's Rose?"

Silence stretched between them for a long moment before Brent relaxed his grip just a little. "Your guess is as good as mine."

"What's that supposed to mean?"

"That I don't know."

"You're lying."

"Believe what you want." He shrugged. "I don't know jack about her. That's Cody's bomb to drop and he'll drop it when he's good and ready. And I can promise you it's not right now. We're in the middle of pictures, for Christ's sake." Agitation washed over him as the photographer's voice echoed in the distance. His grip loosened. "Listen, if you want to talk, we'll talk. But later."

He wanted to argue, but then Brent disappeared as quickly as he'd first appeared, leaving Travis no choice but to bide his time until the photographer finished.

He straightened his shirt and started back around the barn. His attention shifted to the huge white tent that towered in the far distance before he chanced a glance at the spot where he'd last seen Holly Simms talking on her headset. She was nowhere in sight and damned if that didn't bother him. Not that he expected her to hang around, waiting for him. She undoubtedly thought he'd ditched her on purpose.

A damned fine idea.

That's what his head told him. There were too many women to choose from for him to set his sights on one who obviously didn't have the time to get up close and personal. She was the wedding planner after all, and busy as all get out. He needed a guest to kill some time with. Or a bridesmaid. Someone who wouldn't be missed for a few minutes.

Someone who would actually respond when he looked deep into her eyes and willed her to get naked.

The thought conjured a vision of long blond hair trailing down his bare chest. Feathering over his abs. Brushing his thighs. Swirling around his cock.

His stomach hollowed out and his mouth went dry. He picked up his stride, his boots kicking up dust as he headed for the tent and the bar that had been set up along one length. Sliding onto a bar stool, he ordered a beer and took a long swig. The golden liquid went down smooth, but it didn't quench the thirst that yawned in the pit of his stomach.

The tent filled up quickly. The sound of laughter echoed around him. Glasses clinked as the bartenders shifted into action. The scent of vanilla candles wafted through the air, blending with the sugary-sweet smell of the stacked wedding cake that sat center stage on a nearby table.

Travis tried to focus on the women surrounding him. A tall brunette with a purple dress. A shapely redhead wearing a pink suit. A blonde in a hot, tight, red number with lips to match. There were plenty. All his for the taking.

All except for Holly Simms.

The thought struck and he signaled for another beer. She was just one woman, he reminded himself. A damned infuriating one at that since she didn't seem susceptible to his vamp charisma. No falling into his arms or rubbing her soft curves up against him. Nothing. Just that crazy disbelief.

As if his thoughts had conjured her, she rushed around the bandstand toward the pale looking man who'd just taken his place behind a large mixing board. Static cracked open the steady chatter of guests and in a split-second, a slow, twangy Jason Aldean song spilled from the speakers.

Jason sang about big green tractors and taking a

ride, and relief seeped into Holly's expression. She actually smiled and his chest hitched. It was the damndest thing, considering his response was always centered below the belt when it came to women.

He took a swig of his drink and watched as she touched her headset and informed the person on the other end that the music was on and the dancing could commence. Disaster averted. Or so she thought until she got the news that the champagne was missing. Her smile faded in the blink of an eye and he had the sudden insane urge to cross the distance between them, haul her into his arms and do any and everything to bring the smile back to her beautiful face.

Her tight skirt pushed and pulled, hugging her shapely ass as she made a bee-line for the house. His groin tightened, throbbing to the point that a growl worked its way up his throat.

She was different, all right.

But not *that* different.

While he hadn't wowed her with his vampness, he'd still read every thought that had flashed through her pretty blond head. He knew she was sexually frustrated and that she had a thing for cowboys, that she'd been hurt by one. She'd sworn off love and relationships, and had resigned herself to brief, meaningless, one-night stands.

Exactly what he needed at the moment.

Not an entire night, mind you. In the deprived

state he was in, a good fifteen minutes would do him just fine. He was already *this* close to the edge. Pain twisted at his gut. His hands trembled. His throat tightened. His fangs tingled.

Travis downed the last of his drink, set the glass on the bar and went after Holly Simms.

"I CAN'T BELIEVE they misplaced the Cristal," she murmured into her headset as she entered the house through the back kitchen door and glanced frantically around the large room. Platters of food covered every available granite countertop. Boxes sat stacked against the walls and in front of the custom cherry cabinets, but not one had the familiar name she was looking for. "How do you lose ten cases of ultra expensive champagne?"

"I love Cristal," Evan declared. "Bob ordered it on our first date. After dinner, we went up to Lucky's Point and watched the sun set. Say, maybe someone snuck off with the champagne because he wants to propose to his girlfriend. Why, they could be sitting on the tailgate of a pickup truck as we speak, bottles in hand, watching the stars dance across the sky."

"Are you on medication?"

"It's called love, dearest. In case you've forgotten."

If only.

But she remembered all too clearly the pounding

heart, the rush of excitement and the pie-in-the-sky notions—

"The bartender said all ten cases were supposed to be delivered to the bar," Evan cut in, effectively killing her spiral down memory lane. Thankfully. "I called the delivery service and they said someone in the kitchen signed for it."

"Which means it has to be here somewhere." Holly moved out into the massive hallway and headed for the walk-in pantry a few yards down.

The Braddock spread was one of the newest and biggest ranches in the area. The house itself was over nine thousand square feet with tons of closets and way too many places to stash several cases of the bride's favorite beverage.

"Maybe it's in the barn," Evan offered.

"Who would move it all the way from the kitchen to the barn?"

"A loony tune who needed more room to craft her masterpieces." Evan referred to Millicent Dupree, the one and only gourmet chef in Skull Creek, Texas. Millicent was temperamental, stubborn and very focused when it came to her work. "I asked her, but she told me she couldn't listen because she was in her pigs-in-the-blanket zone. She also said if I bothered her again, she would come after me with a pair of cooking shears."

"You check the barn," Holly told him, "and I'll look in the house." She pushed open the door to the walk-in pantry area which rivaled the size of the small bedroom she'd grown up in. A ray of light pushed back the shadows and illuminated stacks of catering boxes, crates of fresh fruit and vegetables, and the empty white boxes that had carried all the petit fours and cheesecakes over from the bakery. Shadows hid the rest and she reached for the light switch.

She was just about to flip it on when she felt the presence directly behind her.

"I've been looking for you." The deep, familiar voice slid into her ears and stirred every nerve in her body. And then a hard wall of muscle urged her forward, the door shut and she found herself standing in the darkness with Travis Braddock.

3

HE'D PROBABLY GOTTEN lost on the way to the men's room.

No way was he in this closet with her on purpose. Because he wanted her and she wanted him and it was meant to be. Definitely a great, big, fat *no*.

That's what she told herself but then he turned her around, his mouth descended on hers and just like that, he was kissing her, his lips covering hers, his tongue thrusting deep. *Yes*.

He tasted like cold beer and hot, decadent thoughts and the air stalled in her lungs.

Stop!

That's what her head said.

Wrong time.

Wrong place.

Wrong man.

If only he hadn't felt so *right*. Like a cold drink of water on a blistering hot summer day. She couldn't help herself. She kissed him back and kept kissing him. Longer. Deeper. His hands were everywhere, trailing down her back, tugging up her skirt.

It was the best thing that had ever happened to Holly.

And the worst.

Not because it was exciting. Heaven knew she needed a little *oomph* in her life. A little wild, mindless sex with no second thoughts. But it was the *worst* because she was smack dab in the middle of a wedding reception for two hundred guests. And the champagne was missing. And Evan kept repeating as much over the headset every few seconds, in between humming the tune from "Unchained Melody." And she was wearing a pair of heavy duty Spanx to keep her tummy flat and her thighs shapely. *And* it was just too friggin' dark.

"Please tell me you found it," Evan declared.

She managed to tear her lips away. "Not yet, she gasped, her lungs struggling for air, "but I'm getting warm." Boy, was she ever.

A slow, chuckle rumbled over her lips and goose bumps chased up and down her arms.

Evan's voice, along with the sound of music and laughter, faded into the sudden pounding of her heart as she became acutely aware of the man standing in front of her, surrounding her. His fingertips seemed to melt through her skirt and the dreaded Lycra smoothing her thighs.

Okay, so dark was good considering the last thing she wanted was for him to see her struggle out of her modern day version of a girdle. But the thing was, *she* couldn't see *him*.

And despite all the extra baggage on her hips, she really wanted to see him. The broad shoulders and muscular arms rippling beneath her touch. The long, hard thighs braced on either side of her own. The prominent erection pressing just below her belly button.

She reached out a hand to her left to feel for the light switch, but he caught her wrist and pinned her arm above her head. He went stiff in the next instant and if she hadn't known better, she might have thought he was purposely trying to keep her in the dark. But just when his grip grew a little too tight, he eased his hold and drew the palm of her hand to his lips.

His lips pressed against her palm. The kiss was soft, tender, *loving* and for a split-second, she actually forgot this was meaningless sex.

"Exactly how warm are you?" Evan's voice pushed past the frantic staccato of her heart and yanked her back to reality and the fact that she was getting naked in a storage closet with a man she'd met less than five minutes ago.

Romeo and Juliet it wasn't.

"I think it's here somewhere—" she offered, but

then strong hands plucked off the headset. A heartbeat later, it clattered to the floor.

"But I'm working—" Strong, sensual lips silenced the rest of her protest in a fierce, determined kiss that scrambled her common sense and drew her full and complete attention.

He tugged the blouse from her skirt. Long, determined fingers worked at the buttons until the silk parted. A flick and her bra clasp opened. The cups fell away. Thumbs rasped her nipples and her breath caught.

Before she had a chance to drag some much needed air into her lungs, he dipped his head and drew the aching tip deep into his mouth. He sucked her so hard that she felt the tug between her legs.

She shuddered as he slid his hot, wet mouth to her other nipple. He caught it with his teeth and flicked her with his tongue, over and over, making her squirm until he opened his lips and suckled her again.

Heat spiraled through her body and pleasure gripped her for several sweet, intoxicating moments before she felt the sharp prickling sensation on her sensitive skin. His teeth, she knew. But it felt different. Sharper.

Just as the thought struck, he pulled away. His mouth closed over hers, drawing her tongue deep. She thought she felt the same sharp sensation against her bottom lip, but then he plunged his own tongue deep and the floor seemed to tremble.

Desire welled up inside her and suddenly she couldn't help herself. Since she couldn't see him, she needed to feel him.

Now.

Frantic fingers grappled at his shirt, pulling and tugging until she found her way underneath. Soft, silky hair met her hands and she trembled. Muscles rippled beneath her palms as she trailed them over his chest and down to the waistband of his jeans.

She unbuttoned him with several fierce, frantic tugs. He sprang hot and huge into her hands and she stroked his length. Her fingers slid back and forth, tracing the bulging head, the hard, smooth shaft. She cupped his testicles and massaged them, and his arousal pulsated against her.

He reached for her skirt then, tugging it up and hooking her underwear. He pushed them down her legs until the lycra sagged around her ankles and she stepped free. He reached down, dragging a finger over her sex in a smooth, sweet rhythm that made her moan.

For a fierce moment, she thought she saw a flash of blue in the darkness, like twin laser beams aimed directly at her.

Eyes. His eyes. Staring back at her.

A red alert went off in her brain. His eyes were green. She'd seen them herself.

She blinked and the bursts of color faded into the nothingness that surrounded them.

Still, something wasn't right.

She reached for the light again, but then he caught her hand and guided it around his neck. "We're not finished yet, sugar. Hold on tight," he murmured, his voice deep and raspy. And then he was inside of her and her thoughts scrambled as exquisite heat flooded her body.

He moved in and out in a fierce rhythm. Pleasure needled her brain with each thrust until she couldn't take any more. She closed her eyes as her orgasm crashed over and consumed her entire body. Tremors racked her and her knees buckled. She went limp, but Travis was there, his strong arms around her, holding her as he plunged deep one last time.

He followed her over the edge, his body rigid. A growl rumbled in her ears and she saw the pinpoints of blue light again. Brighter this time. Fierce.

Gone.

She blinked, but there was nothing there. Just the consuming darkness and the tiniest sliver of light underneath the door that illuminated her discarded Spanx and the forgotten headset.

She became keenly aware of the noise and Evan's frantic voice buzzing in the earpiece.

"I have to find the champagne," she said, but Travis had already stepped back to give her some space.

Cool air washed over her and a strange sense of loneliness crept through her. It was an absurd reaction. She should be feeling anything but lonely. Relieved. Satisfied. Smug.

The sex was over. It was time to get back to work and forget all about this yummy cowboy.

No strings.

The thought stirred an expected rush of disappointment and she stiffened. Not that she wanted the past fifteen minutes to mean something. No sirree.

She'd been there, done that. Not once, but three times as a matter of fact. Each time she'd inched a little closer to wedded bliss. Allen had been her first serious boyfriend. They'd dated exclusively for six months, but he'd bailed before popping the question. Ben had been number two. They'd dated a year and a half and he'd gone so far as to give her an engagement ring. But then he'd asked for it back the next day so he could run off with a waitress from some truck stop. Chad had been number three. They'd dated for two years before he'd asked her to marry him. She'd spent the following year planning her dream wedding.

Third time's a charm.

That's what everyone had said, but in Holly's case, the third had been the last and final piece of evidence that she just wasn't the marrying kind. Chad had literally left her standing at the altar.

Which was why she'd joined Love Busters and decided to fall into lust instead of the big L.

Sex was easy. Fun. Satisfying.

Over.

Still… It had been awhile.

A long, *long* while.

No wonder her fingers tightened around the doorknob and she paused. Meaningless sex was hard to come by for Holly. It stood to reason that she wouldn't want to turn her back on her sudden good fortune.

"We could try for round two if you're game," Travis's stirring voice slid into her ears as if he'd read her thoughts. "But I think we might be doing it in front of an audience."

She became aware of the distinct footsteps that grew louder with each moment that passed. A steady click of leather on tile that told her Evan and his new Feragamos had given up on the barn.

She bent down and snatched up the headset. "Meet me on the back patio," she blurted. "Now."

"Where have you been? I've been calling you *forever!*"

"I was busy going through all the boxes the caterer left on the back patio. Stop with the twenty questions and give me a hand."

"But we found the champagne already. It's being served up now. That's what I was coming to tell you. I figured you had a malfunction on the headset and—"

"We have extra on the back patio," she blurted. "Lots of extra. I'm practically drowning in the stuff. Help!" The footsteps turned abruptly and then a fading clatter signaled that Evan had bought the distraction and was heading to the opposite end of the house.

"Does that mean you're staying?" Travis asked when the footsteps finally disappeared and Holly could actually breathe again.

"He'll be looking for me again when he realizes I'm not on the patio." She turned the knob.

"Wait." Before she could pull open the door, he stepped up behind her and pressed her up against the wood.

She could hear his voice distinctly, his lips feathering over her ear. But there was no warm rush of breath against her temple. No heartbeat pounding against her shoulder blade.

He was there, yet he wasn't there.

Just as the strange thought struck, he murmured "Thanks." The knob seemed to turn beneath her fingers and suddenly the door was open and she was free.

She resisted the urge to turn and catch a glimpse of him standing in the shaft of light from the hallway. His hair mussed. His shirt hanging open. His pants still undone. His eyes still gleaming with passion—

She stiffened and ignored the image whispering through her head. Sure, it was a purely sexual image. But that was beside the point. If she turned around now, they would have sex again. And possibly again. And then before she knew it, she would be hopelessly in love. A repeat offender.

These boots were made for walking.

She squared her shoulders, stepped forward and went to intercept Evan.

4

TRAVIS MANEUVERED HIS way through the crowd gathered on the front lawn just in time to see Cody follow his bride into the back of a black stretch limousine. It was barely nine-thirty, but there was no mistaking the birdseed in the air and the shouts of congratulations. The crowd waved goodbye and panic suckerpunched him smack dab in his gut.

"They had to cut the reception short to catch an early plane," Brent's deep voice sounded next to him just as the limo door closed, "otherwise they won't make it to Colorado before sunrise. They're going to Aspen for the honeymoon."

Travis glanced at his brother. "You're kidding me, right?" When Brent shook his head, he ran a hand over his face and damned himself a thousand times for following Holly Simms into that storage closet and wasting precious time. What the hell had he been thinking?

But then that was the point—he hadn't been able to think. Not with the lust raging through his veins, the hunger gnawing at his gut. He should have stopped to feed before he left Wyoming, but he'd been in a hurry to catch his plane. He'd figured on holding out until after he talked to Cody.

But then he'd seen Holly—her soft lips and lush body and those sparkling, surprised eyes—and all his *figuring* had gone to hell in a hand basket. Now it was too late to talk to Cody. To find out the truth.

Like hell.

He shoved a hand into his pocket to retrieve his keys. "Which airport?"

"They're flying out of San Antonio."

"If I leave now, I can catch him before he boards the plane—" The words died as a vice grip tightened on his arm. His gaze swiveled to his brother and he saw the steely determination in his eyes.

"You're not going after him," Brent told him. "It's his honeymoon, for Christ's sake."

"I just need five minutes. He'll tell me what I need to know and that'll be that."

"No." The grip tightened and Travis knew he wasn't budging a step without a fight. "He's not talking until Colton gets here and that won't be until Saturday. Cody will be back Saturday night and we can all have a sit down."

"That's a week from tomorrow."

"That's the way it is. Rose was Colton's wife. He should be the first to know."

"We all have a right to know."

"Damn straight we do, but not until Colton gets here and we're all together."

Which meant he was stuck here for the next seven days.

The truth sank in as he stood there, staring at the crowd that walked past him. People laughed and smiled as they headed back to the reception. While Cody and Miranda had cut the evening short, their guests weren't inclined to do the same. The DJ had kicked up the music and the promise of a great party hung in the air.

Brent clapped him on the shoulder. "Seeing as how you've got a little time to kill, why don't you come on back inside and have a drink."

Travis shook his head, his mind still trying to wrap itself around the fact that he would be forced to hang out in Skull Creek if he wanted to find out Rose's whereabouts.

And he *was* going to find her. He owed her and he intended to see that she got what was coming to her for destroying his family.

"It's just seven days," Brent added. "Think of it as a vacation."

"I don't take vacations."

"Think of it as work then. I could use some help out at my place." When Travis arched an eyebrow, he added, "Skull Creek's not a bad place. The people are nice and there are even a few vampires to keep things interesting." At Travis's surprised look, Brent added, "Garrett Sawyer and his buddies own Skull Creek Choppers. They live just up the road from me."

"Since when did you become the settling down type?"

The last Travis had heard, Brent had been making his fortune as one of the most sought-after guns-for-hire. He went from job to job, guarding the rich and famous and doing his damnedest to not get too attached to any one person or place.

"I'm tired of living out of a suitcase." He gave Travis a pointed stare. "Aren't you?"

"I like moving on. It keeps things much more interesting."

"I can't imagine anything more interesting than Abby, that's for damned sure."

"Abby?"

Brent glanced at a petite brunette who stood talking to a nearby group of women. As if she felt him, her head snapped up and their gazes locked. She smiled and a strange expression lit his brother's eyes. "I bought a hundred acres just down the road from here. I'm going to try my hand at ranching."

"How much does she know about you?"

"How much doesn't she know? Abby is ex Special Forces. Nothing gets by her." His attention shifted back to Travis. "Take you for instance. She knew you were a vampire the moment she saw you. She also knew you were my brother. She said we have the same eyes."

"And the same fangs."

Brent grinned. "There are some people who aren't bothered by what we are. Abby's one of them. So is Cody's wife Miranda. Garrett's business partners are both married to humans, too, though Garrett himself is with another vampire."

"He's smart. Meanwhile, you're playing with fire."

"Maybe, but I like the heat." A wistful look twisted his features. "That's the one thing I miss the most about being human. Being warm from the inside out. When I'm with Abby, I feel it again, bro. Deep inside my bones." He must have noticed Travis's *get real* expression because he added, "Don't knock it until you've tried it. You don't sit still long enough to meet anyone, let alone warm up to them."

"I like moving."

"That or you're just so used to it you don't know how to stop."

"You buy a spread and suddenly you're a shrink."

Brent shook his head. "Just a rancher. Speaking of which, I've got three mustangs that might make damn fine cutting horses if I could ever get close enough to them."

"And?"

"And since you're sticking around for the next seven days, I thought you might help me out."

"Horses don't like vampires."

"They like you," Brent argued. When Travis cut him a glance, he added, "Ranchers talk. You've become a hot commodity." When Travis shrugged, Brent added, "I could really use the help."

But the less time Travis spent with Brent, the better. Already, he felt the strange pull he'd once felt with his brother. The camaraderie. The sense of *family*.

But his was gone. Rose had seen to that.

She'd destroyed them all and there was no rebuilding what was permanently damaged. They'd turned on each other and gone their separate ways, and that was okay.

It was better than okay.

Out of sight, out of mind.

That had been his motto all these years. He'd done his damnedest to forget his brothers and his life before. And he'd managed to do just that. Hell, it had been easy. The farther away he stayed, the less he thought about them. No doubts. No regret. No remorse.

Just the hunger.

Until Cody's invitation.

His little brother had stirred it all up, reminding him of the man he'd been, of the injustice he'd dealt out and the fact that the real culprit had yet to be punished.

Travis knew now that he couldn't forget again.

Not unless he spent the anger inside of him and dealt it out to the real murderer. Then he could move on again. He *would* move on. And forget.

His gaze shifted to the woman standing several feet away, herding people back to the reception tent. Her cheeks were pink, her eyes bright. A few tendrils of hair had come loose from her ponytail. His fingertips tingled and he had the crazy urge to cross the lawn, tug her hair loose and run his fingers through the long, blond silk.

He stiffened. He wasn't here for sex, despite the past half hour. He was here for information.

For vengeance.

Just as soon as Cody returned and Colton arrived and the Braddock boys were back together once again.

"So what about it? You gonna help me out?"

Travis shook his head. "I can't."

"Can't or won't?"

"Does it matter?"

Brent looked as if he wanted to say something, but then thought better of it. "If you change your mind, my place is just a few miles north of here. I could use you." And then he turned and headed toward the petite brunette.

She smiled and Brent smiled and for a split second, Travis had the crazy thought that his brother had found the real deal. One man. One woman. *Love.*

If there'd been such a thing.

But Travis knew better. There was no such thing for their kind. Sooner or later, the hunger would get the best of Brent and he'd grab the first woman that crossed his path.

That's what had happened to Travis tonight. He'd gotten hungry. Holly had been handy. And bam, he'd satisfied that hunger in the storage closet.

He watched her gather up a group of seniors and steer them toward the dessert table, and the familiar pang hit him hard and fast. Hunger. Because he'd only partially fed.

He'd drank in her sweet energy, but for Travis it wasn't enough. He'd grown accustomed to taking sex *and* blood. While most vamps leaned more toward one or the other, Travis was a fan of both. It made him feel more alive. More in control. More in touch with his senses. For a vamp who made his living by being in tune with each of the five senses, a double whammy was essential.

But he hadn't bitten her.

He wasn't sure why. He'd wanted to more badly than anything else. At the same time, he'd felt a moment's hesitation, as if drinking her in would make it impossible to get rid of her. She'd be under his skin. In his head. His heart.

Crazy.

While drinking and having sex with the same woman often created a bond for most vampires, that wasn't the case for Travis. He was too much of a hard-ass. That, and he kept moving. The distance weakened the connection until, eventually, it snapped altogether and there was nothing. He'd learned that early on with Amelia. She'd been his girl before he'd gone off to war and she'd been more than eager to rekindle the fire in the weeks after his return.

But the night of his return had changed him. He'd been hardened by the war and devastation at the ranch. Insatiable thanks to the beast that lived and breathed inside of him. The hunger had been all-consuming and he'd quickly learned that he could never go back to being just a man.

And one woman would never be nearly enough.

The hunger had driven him into the arms of another and Amelia had been devastated. Thanks to the sex and blood they'd shared, he'd been completely in tune to her feelings. He'd hurt the way she'd hurt. But then he'd left town and the farther he'd gotten from her, the less he'd felt her sorrow and angst. No hitch in his chest. No knife twisting his gut. No piercing white hot pain when she'd finally ended it all and pulled the trigger. Rather, the news of her death had caught up to him months later in the form of a letter from her parents.

We just thought you should know...

But he hadn't known. Not even a clue. Because he hadn't felt a thing. He was a vampire now and incapable of feeling anything other than lust.

He knew that. He'd accepted it.

Which is why he should have bitten Holly and gotten it over with. The attraction would have ended, and he wouldn't be standing here at the entrance to the tent, as hot and horny as a cowpoke about to crawl into bed with his first saloon girl.

That was the only reason.

Damn straight it was.

And if he downed enough Jack Daniels over the next few hours, Travis might actually start to believe it.

IF TRAVIS BRADDOCK looked at her one more time, Holly was going to dunk her head under the nearest champagne fountain.

She forced her gaze from the man standing at the bar and busied herself replenishing the dessert table for the remaining guests. The newlyweds had departed, but the party was still in high gear. The band cranked out a lively Kenny Chesney tune and a sea of Stetsons bobbed across the dance floor. Waiters moved here and there, passing out glasses of the newly discovered champagne. The sweet smell of cake infused the air.

"Methinketh this is one more fabulous set of event pics for our Facebook page." Evan's voice sounded behind her. "I think the worst is over."

She turned to see her assistant balancing a platter of chocolate covered cheesecakes. "Don't count your chickens yet. The DJ doesn't wrap up until midnight."

"By then people will be too drunk to even notice if something goes wrong. As long as the champagne is flowing, everyone's happy. You can lose the worried look."

"I don't look worried."

"You look flushed, which means you're in panic mode, which means you're worried and headed straight for a Prozac prescription if you don't lighten up. Girlfriend, you need to slow down and enjoy the moment. Don't sweat the small stuff. *Carpe diem* and all that."

If he only knew.

But he didn't and she wasn't about to broadcast to the world that she'd spent the last fifteen minutes seizing not only the day, but one ultra hot cowboy. Not that she cared if everyone knew that Holly Simms had had her first of many one-night stands. She would welcome a little notoriety. Maybe then available bachelors would stop treating her like she had some deadly disease.

At the same time, she was on the clock, and more than an active sex life, she valued a good work reputation.

"Take a load off and enjoy." Evan handed her a plate of chocolate ganache cheesecake and a fork. "I'll make sure the rest of the desserts get put out." He handed her another piece of cake.

"What? One for each hip?"

He wiggled his eyebrows and stared past her. "That one's for the hot cowboy checking you out at three o'clock."

She chanced a glance at Travis. Her gaze met his and heat rippled through her body, from the soles of her feet, to the top of her head. Time pulled her back and suddenly she felt his strong arms around her, his hands on her back, his body pushing into hers.

The urge to grab his hand and haul him back into the storage closet hit her hard and fast. Her nipples tingled and her hands trembled and she stiffened.

Hello?

She had a mortgage to pay and a gluttonous St. Bernard to feed, and that meant controlling her impulses.

For now.

"I think he likes you. Why don't you walk over and offer him a dessert. You'll sit down and the two of you will stare longingly into each other's eyes over bites of decadent cheesecake. One thing will lead to another and bam, I'm planning the event of the century and you're playing the difficult bride."

"You've been watching too much Oxygen."

"Actually, it's the Soap Opera Channel. Mitchell just proposed to Loren on *The Sands of Time*." He let out a deep sigh. "He gave her a ring on top of a piece of cheesecake. Do you think Bob might do that?"

"I think you need to ditch the cable TV."

"Don't be such a hater."

But she wasn't a hater. She was an official Love Buster and she had the t-shirt and screen saver to prove it. Holly was through setting herself up for heartache. From here on out, it was all about busting the myth and having fun.

But not with Travis Braddock.

The entire point of what had happened was that it wasn't supposed to happen again. That's why they called it a one-night stand, even if they hadn't technically had a full night together. It was the principle of the thing.

She didn't want more.

Okay, so she wanted more, but she wasn't giving in to it.

She forced her attention back to the buffet table and the all important fact that the clock was ticking. Two hours to go and she would be home free.

Travis free.

She set aside the duo of cheesecakes in her hands and reached for Evan's platter. "Maybe you could worry about refilling the coffee urn while I finish setting out the desserts?"

"Fine." Evan turned to stomp off. "But don't blame yours truly if you never get the opportunity to register for his and her tray tables."

5

THERE WASN'T MUCH that surprised Travis Braddock. He was a vampire, after all, with super charged senses. He could feel the moisture in the air before the first raindrop fell. He could smell the lightning when it struck clear into the next county. And he could hear a clap of thunder from fifty miles away.

Honestly, though, he had to admit he was damned surprised when Holly Simms walked into the Iron Horseshoe bar later that night after the wedding.

After several hours of watching her rush around and worry over everything from desserts to punch to a guest who'd misplaced her purse, he'd called it a night and headed for the most crowded bar he could find and some real sustenance. A warm woman, a quick bite and he could quench his thirst and forget a certain wedding planner with silky blond hair and big blue eyes.

At least that had been the plan.

But here she was, screwing things up and surprising the hell out of him.

Despite her lush body and long legs and full lips, she wasn't the last call type. She was the sort of woman who headed home after a hard day's work, to a hot bath, a steaming cup of tea and a good man.

But Holly Simms didn't want a good man. She wanted a good time.

At least that's what she was telling herself.

Mission accomplished and now it was over. She didn't do seconds any more than he did.

And truthfully, he wouldn't have considered a round two if he'd finished what he'd started in the first place. But he'd only had sex with her. No sinking his teeth into her sweet neck and drinking in her delicious heat. No feeling the rush of energy and the swell of satisfaction.

He'd missed his shot, but here she was, ready to give him another opportunity.

Obviously she wasn't as immune to him as he'd first thought.

To think he'd actually entertained the notion that she was different from all the other women he'd met over the years. She was one and the same. She'd gotten a taste of the beast and she couldn't help herself. She wanted more.

He saw it the moment her gaze locked with his. Heat swept through her, firebombing several key targets along the way—the backs of her knees, the insides of her thighs, her nipples. Her breath caught. Her heartbeat revved several frantic beats. Desire flooded between her legs and filled the air with a sharp, sweet, succulent scent that stirred his hunger even more.

A vision rushed through her head—of him dragging her into the nearest restroom, lifting her up onto the counter and plunging into her over and over while his fangs sank so deliciously deep.

Bring it on, baby.

He sent out the thought and expected the usual. Her eyes to glaze. Her lips to part. Her chest to heave.

She stiffened and he heard the words echo in her head.

Love's a bitch.
I'm not falling for this guy,
I'm keeping my head and avoiding the lie.

Love's a bitch.
I'm not falling for this guy.
I'm keeping my head and—

"Hey there, cowboy." The voice pulled him out of Holly's thoughts and back to the neon lights, the crowded bar and the Lady Antebellum song playing on the juke box. "Can I get you anything else?"

Travis turned his attention to the waitress who set a beer on the table in front of him. She looked like all the other women packed into Skull Creek's only hotspot. Big hair. Big boobs. Too much eye make-up. Too little clothes.

Her tongue swept her bottom lip and her heavily-rimmed eyes flashed suggestively. "Some salt? A lime?" *Me?*

Okay, now this made sense.

Women wanted him. All women. He had mucho sex appeal. A by-product for any vampire. Add a dose of Texas charm and semi-decent looks and the females were powerless to resist.

A grin crooked his lips as he held up the beer he'd been nursing. "I'm good right now."

"You sure? It's no trouble. I'm here to serve." He shook his head and disappointment chased across her expression. She shrugged. "The name's Amy. Holler if you need anything." She smiled and lust shimmered in her eyes. "Anything at all."

"I'll keep that in mind." He tipped his hat and she reluctantly turned away. He turned back toward the door and caught Holly staring at him as if she were about to jump into the deep end of a swimming pool and all she could do was dog paddle.

He winked and she stiffened, and he knew then, beyond a doubt, that she hadn't come begging for seconds. She seemed to gather her courage as her gaze went past him, to the adjoining room over-flowing with people and pool tables. The clack of balls split the air. Holly squared her shoulders and started forward as if she were power walking her way through a marathon.

He didn't mean to reach out. If she could bolt past him as if he hadn't just loved her within an inch of her life, he could certainly do the same. Hell, that's what he did best. Move on. To the next town. The next woman.

He didn't do the territorial thing.

At the same time, Travis Braddock didn't do half-ass either. He never left things unfinished, and he sure as hell didn't sleep with a woman without biting her.

He reached out and caught her warm hand in his.

"WHERE'S THE FIRE, sugar?" came the deep, familiar voice.

Right here.

The notion struck before Holly had a chance to think. She was too deep in sensory overload with Travis Braddock so close. His strong fingers held hers. The intoxicating aroma of leather and fresh air and a touch of wildness filled her nostrils. Her gaze collided with his. Eyes the color of lush green grass stared back at her and her breath caught.

For a split-second, she was mesmerized before the thump of a cue ball hitting its pocket jarred her from the sudden daze. "No fire," she finally managed to stammer, determined to keep her perspective. "I'm meeting someone."

"It's a little late for a date."

But not for a booty call.

That's what she should have told him. Make him think the worst. That's what she wanted in the first place, wasn't it? For everyone and their Chihuahua to believe that Holly Simms had gone from being the proverbial good girl to becoming Skull Creek's biggest good time girl?

And how.

But Travis wasn't everyone. He was a total stranger from out of town and so it didn't really matter if he considered her the latter. That and there was just something about the sudden flash of jealousy in his gaze that warmed her heart and made her open her mouth and tell him the truth. "I'm meeting my aunt."

A grin tugged the corner of his mouth, but it didn't quite touch his eyes. "And here I thought you might be following me."

"Oh, I would never do something like that," she blurted. She'd followed Chad home from work one night with a picnic basket stocked with all his favorite foods. Meat loaf. Mashed potatoes. Fried pickles. Sweet potato pie. The goal had been a romantic picnic under the stars in his backyard. But Chad hadn't gone home that night. He'd driven to the next county to meet with one of his ex girlfriends.

Nothing.

That's what the rendezvous had meant, or so he'd

told Holly when she'd confronted him in the parking lot. He'd had a long relationship with his ex and he'd wanted to break the news to her that he was getting married before she heard it through the grapevine. End of story.

Obviously, though, instead of letting his old girlfriend down, he'd decided to patch things up. A week later he'd left Holly at the altar and taken off with the ex.

Holly had learned her lesson then and there. No following a man home. No cooking him dinner. No putting herself out there. No falling in love.

Never again.

The minute the thought struck, Travis's gaze flickered and his lips thinned even more. If she hadn't known better she would have sworn he was disappointed.

But she knew better. Boy, did she ever. Her own wishful thinking had turned her into a three-time loser in the first place, a die-hard romantic that kept reading more into each and every situation, firing her hope, urging her to fall for men who didn't fall back.

She stiffened and the clack of pool balls echoed in her head. Her gaze shifted to the next room and through the crowd she caught a glimpse of a snow white beehive, bright pink lipstick and silver blue eye shadow. Another clack of pool balls, a familiar shriek of "Hot damn," and Holly knew there was a room full of truck drivers getting their butts kicked at that moment. "My great Aunt Tootie plays pool here every Friday night and I'm her designated driver."

"Too many Cosmos?"

"Too many fender benders." When he arched an eyebrow, she added, "She's had ten in the past six months and is now sitting at the top of the DMV's Most Wanted list. The doctor gave her a prescription for glasses, but she says they make her look old, so she refuses to wear them."

"Contacts?"

"Her vision is so bad she can't see well enough to put them in."

"That's nice of you to help her out."

"I owe her." She wasn't sure why she told him. She shouldn't have. But when he stared at her so intently—as if he actually cared about what she had to say—the words seemed to come on their own. "My mom was always MIA with whichever cowboy paid her the most attention and so I spent a lot of time with Aunt Tootie. She was more of a mother to me than my own mom, though she'll be the first to deny it." She shook off the sudden sadness that niggled at her and forced a smile. "She likes to think of herself as the older, wiser, hotter sister."

"She'll have to settle for two out of three." A grin crooked the corner of his sensuous mouth and her stomach hollowed out.

"So what about you?" she asked, eager to distract herself from her body's traitorous reaction. "Shouldn't you be on your way back to whereever it is that you came from?"

"Cody and I have some unfinished business, which means I'm in town until he gets back from his honeymoon." He toed the chair next to him. "Sit down."

She entertained the idea all of five seconds before the reality of what was happening hit her and her chest tightened. "Listen, you don't have to do this."

"Do what?"

"Be nice to me."

"You want me to be mean to you then?"

"Yes. No." She shook her head. "I mean, I don't want you to feel obligated to be nice to me just because of what happened between us. I had a really great time in that closet, but I have no intention of making more out of it than what it was."

"And what was it?"

"A little harmless fun. The last thing I'm looking for is a serious relationship." When he gave a pointed stare at the pink button that read *I Love Happily-Ever-Afters* pinned on her collar, she added, "It's my job. Personally, I plan on staying single for a really, *really* long time."

"Sugar, I'm offering you a drink and a little conversation, not a marriage proposal."

The deep timber of his voice echoed in her head and coasted along her nerve endings, bringing them to full, tingling awareness. She had the sudden image of the two of them sprawled in bed together on a bright, sunny morning, arms and legs intertwined, his lips moving against her ear as he whispered sweet nothings.

"You feel obligated after what we did," she rushed on, determined not to let herself get caught up in the fantasy. That's all it was. Her own crazy imagination blowing things out of proportion, trying to turn a physical connection into something more. Something real. "You shouldn't. I don't have any misconceptions about what happened. I don't need you to be nice to me or try to get to know me. I know I look like that kind of girl, but I'm not."

Not anymore, she reminded herself. Even if she did have the urge to slide into the seat next to him and ask him how he'd gotten that scar on the back of his hand. Her gaze lingered on the tiny strip of white that ran from his thumb to his wrist. Her finger itched to trace the path and feel the rough skin beneath her own.

She stiffened and pulled her hand from his grasp. "I really need to go. It was nice seeing you again."

And then like any devout Love Buster committed to non-committal sex, she gathered her courage, turned and walked away.

6

"NICE DOING BUSINESS with you boys," Aunt Tootie told the two red-faced men holding pool sticks. Years ago, Tootie had been one of the most beautiful women in town. At eighty-one, the looks had long since faded, but not her personality. She was still as big and bold and outlandish as ever.

She tucked a twenty dollar bill between the overflowing cleavage visible above her low-cut pink knit blouse. Grabbing Holly's hand, she yanked her front and center. "Say, have you boys met my niece?"

"We went to kindergarten together," Holly told her great aunt. "And middle school. And high school."

"Really?" Melvin Meyers exchanged glances with his twin brother Cecil. "Were you in one of our English classes? 'Cause we sat front row so we never really got to see who else was in there. Mrs. Jenkins watched us like a hawk."

"It was Mr. Wolinski's biology class. I was lab

partners with you and your brother. For three years in a row."

"Oh, yeah." Recognition seemed to dawn. "You were the one who brought the bridal magazines to class every day."

"That was back then," Aunt Tootie said. "But she's totally given up that nonsense, haven't you, dear?" Before Holly could respond, she rushed on, "She's my running partner now. We're happy to be single and ready to mingle, ain't that right, sugar?"

Before Holly could utter an enthusiastic *yes!*, Melvin asked, "Didn't you plan my older brother Jim Bob's wedding last year?"

She had half a mind to deny it, but as the only wedding planner in town, she didn't exactly blend into the woodwork. "I might have made a few arrangements—"

"She's a beauty, ain't she?" Tootie cut in, effectively killing the walk down memory lane. "It's all the good genes that run in our family, ya know." She winked. "All the women are lookers."

"I'm married, Miss Tootie," Melvin offered.

"Me, too," Cecil added.

"That don't make no never mind. You can still admire a woman's attributes, cain't you?"

The twins exchanged glances. "If we say she's a looker, will you stay a little longer so we can win back our Justins?"

"If I stay here another hour, the both of you will

likely end up naked and broke." She picked up the two pairs of cowboy boots sitting on the ledge of the pool table. "While I've got nothing against getting naked, I won't be the cause of either of you starving to death. Think of your families, boys." She hooked an arm through Holly's free one. Excitement twinkled in her eyes as she turned to her niece. "Now then, why don't you tell me who that cowboy is that you were just talking to?"

"What cowboy?" Holly followed Tootie toward a nearby table where her purse sat, careful not to glance in Travis's direction. She could feel his gaze brushing up and down her skin. Awareness skittered along her spine and her nipples throbbed.

"The one sitting over at that table." Tootie waved a hand and Holly stiffened. "Watching us."

"I doubt he's looking at us."

"Why, I'll be first in line for a colonoscopy if he ain't." Tootie pulled out a tube of pink lipstick and touched up her already bright lips. "I'm telling you, honey, his eyes are practically eating us alive." She glanced into her compact mirror and rubbed her lips together. "Then again, I cain't really blame him. When there's this much eye candy, even the strongest man turns to mush." She smoothed her hot-pink blouse over her black and white zebra striped pants. "It's that there Darwin's theory, ya know. Strong, virile, handsome men cain't help themselves. They're just pre-wired to gravitate toward the most attractive females on account of good looks scream fertility."

Holly had half a mind to remind Tootie that at eighty-one, the only thing she screamed was *Where's the Metamucil?* But her aunt looked so excited that she heard herself say, "You *were* the Cherry Junction Dance Hall Queen six years in a row. A man can't help but look when you walk by. Speaking of walking, I really think we should go." Holly helped Tootie gather up her things. "It's Saturday tomorrow. My busiest day of the week."

Awareness rippled over Holly as she navigated toward the door. A few seconds later, she stepped outside into the sultry night air and sent up a silent *thank you.*

"I've always been the charitable sort, honey. Maybe I should waltz back in and give that boy a little thrill." Tootie stalled just a few feet shy of the exit and glanced over her shoulder. "I bet that would sure-as-shootin' make his day—"

"No," Holly cut in. "I mean, you wouldn't want to get his hopes up, now would you? It's not like you're actually going to hook up with him or anything like that." When Tootie frowned, Holly added, "Not that you couldn't hook up with him if you wanted to. You're a mature, vivacious, intelligent woman. You could have any man that you want."

"You forgot sexy."

"That, too. But while you've obviously still got

it," Holly went on, "you really shouldn't be using it, what with the dangers associated with high blood pressure."

"High blood pressure?" Tootie stiffened. "Why, I'll have you know that my pressure's just fine, thank-you-very-much. That was a bad reading. I told the nurse she ought to get a new one of them doohickeys. Hers was obviously broken."

"Not *your* high blood pressure," Holly rushed to smooth Tootie's ruffled feathers. "His. That cowboy could be a walking cauldron of boiling cholesterol for all we know. You wouldn't want to be the fire that sends him rushing over the edge of the pot, now would you?"

"He did look a little red in the cheeks," Tootie finally agreed, letting Holly steer her back around. "Men are more inclined to have high blood pressure than women. I saw that on Discovery Health when I was flipping channels, looking for the latest *Jersey Shore* episode. At the same time," she added, digging her silver glitter heels into the gravel parking lot and stalling again, "he might be perfectly healthy and eager for some company." She patted Holly's arm and cut her a glance. "I know he had his sights set on me, but if there's one thing I've learned about men over the years, it's this—they ain't picky. Especially when it's close to last call and they haven't a prospect in hell."

"Please don't tell me you're thinking what I think you're thinking."

Her pale blue eyes twinkled. "You should mosey back in there right now and be his rebound woman."

"Don't most rebound women generally end up miserable and alone?"

"That's 'cause they're wanting a happily-ever-after. But if the only thing you're interested in is a little rub-a-dub-dub, you're sure to be one hundred percent satisfied. Why, when I was your age, I used to waltz right up to whichever man caught my fancy and drag him into the nearest broom closet. That's exactly what you ought to do."

"And have him run the other way?" The comment came from one of the waitresses who pushed through the door behind them. "A man that hot isn't the least bit interested in a woman like Holly." Amy Harold was only twenty-three, but she'd been around the block so many times that she looked a good ten years older. Add a pack-a-day habit and she could be the poster child for *Just Say No*.

Tootie's gaze narrowed. "Are you sayin' my niece is a loser when it comes to men?"

"I'm saying she's the marrying kind when it comes to men. And there isn't a man out there who doesn't know it."

"I am not."

"Girl, everything about you screams *take me to*

the altar from those cover-everything-up-clothes,
to your minivan." Amy's gaze shifted to the white
Honda parked a few feet away, *Here Comes the
Bridal Consultant* in blazing pink letters on the side.

"It's my profession."

"It's the total package, which is why I chased you
out here. See, my cousin Jeanine is thinking about
getting hitched next month. I'm the maid of honor
so I told her I'd take care of stuff for her, but I don't
have a clue. I know I'm supposed to do the bachelorette party, which I've totally got covered, but I've
never planned a shower and I don't know shit about
flowers or cakes or…" Amy went on about being
nuptually challenged while Holly's brain launched
into major denial.

Maybe once upon a time she'd been the marrying kind, but those days were long gone. She was a
wild woman now. The sort of woman who had sex
with strangers in storage closets on the spur of the
moment.

Not that anyone knew that little tidbit of information, which presented her problem in a nutshell.
Every available man in town saw her as wife material and they always would.

Unless she could prove them wrong.

"So can you help me?" Amy asked.

"Stop by the shop on Monday. Wait here," she told
her aunt. "I think I forgot something."

"Atta girl," Tootie called after her as she headed back inside the bar. "See?" she said to Amy. "I told you she was a chip off the old block."

Which is exactly what Holly intended to show everyone in Skull Creek. She was a Simms through and through. Sexy. Fun-loving. Uncomplicated. And ready for action.

If Travis Braddock agreed to cooperate, that is.

Drawing a deep breath, she gathered her courage and started toward his table.

"LET ME MAKE sure I'm hearing this right." Travis leveled a stare at Holly who sat across from him, an anxious look on her beautiful face. His brain was still reeling, along with his other senses. She was too close. Too beautiful. Too damned sexy. "You want to *date* me?"

"I don't want to *date* date you. I just want the single men of this town to see me hanging out with you. Here. The local honky tonk. The Dairy Freeze. The rodeo arena. Cherry Blossom Junction, the local honky tonk, is even gearing up for their annual indoor rodeo next Saturday night. It would be the perfect place for us to hang out and have a few drinks."

"That sounds like a date."

"Not if you factor in that I don't want a relationship and I have absolutely no intention of falling for you."

Been there.

Done that.

No, thank you.

He read the thoughts loud and clear and his chest tightened.

Not that he wanted a relationship with Holly. Hell, no. It was the principle of the thing. All women wanted him and Holly Simms should have been no exception.

She was, and damned if it didn't bug the living hell out of him.

"See, here's the thing," she continued. "You're not the type of guy a serious, marriage-minded girl would go for."

"Is that so?"

She nodded. "You're the type of guy who goes out with lots of different women and likes to have a good time, like what happened between us earlier tonight. On top of that, you're only in town for a little while, which means you won't be sticking around. That makes you all the more perfect for this."

When he didn't say anything, she added, "No marriage-minded woman would go after a guy like you. You're temporary. And a temporary man only hooks up with a temporary woman, which I most definitely am. Unfortunately, I also coordinate happily-ever-afters and so I might as well have *Marry Me* tattooed on my forehead." Determination charged her gaze. "I want to kill that image once and for all and let everyone in this town know that Holly Simms is single and ready for action."

"As in sex?"

"Non-committal sex. Being seen with a guy like you will send a loud and clear message that I don't want to open a joint checking account. I just want to have a good time."

"And what do I get in return?"

"What do you want?"

To finish what they'd started.

The thought conjured a vivid image of Holly's soft throat tilted toward him, her fragrant skin drawing him closer, her lush curves pressed flush against him, her sweet blood flowing into his mouth.

Christ, he wanted it so bad that it was all he could do not to bolt out of the seat, back her up against the nearest wall, and taste her right here and now in front of the entire crowd packed into the tiny bar. He'd never been much for an audience, but it seemed like a damned fine idea right about now.

"Well?" She arched an eyebrow at him. "A big screen TV? An Amazon gift card? Cash?"

"Sex," he murmured.

As much as he wanted to bite Holly, that wasn't an option. She didn't fall under his spell the way other women did and so he had to consider the possibility that she might remember every detail of the time they spent together. He couldn't bite her and risk all hell breaking loose should she discover his true identity.

But he could drink in enough of her sexual energy over the next five days to curb his appetite enough so that he wouldn't crave her blood. Rather, he'd be full and sated and primed for a confrontation when Cody returned and revealed Rose's whereabouts. Then he could go after his sister-in-law at full speed and deal out the punishment that she so desperately deserved.

"I don't think that would be such a good idea," Holly said after a long moment. "But I'd be more than happy to pay you for your time. Maybe an hourly rate."

"I don't need your money." But he did need sustenance, so it seemed like the perfect way to the pass the time. To him, that is.

Holly, on the other hand, didn't look the least bit happy about the situation and damned if that didn't make him all the more determined to get her to agree to his terms.

"You could always find someone else to help you out."

But that was the thing. She couldn't.

He saw the truth in her gaze and watched the push-pull of emotion. A full-fledged throw-down between excitement and *uh-oh* that had him wondering which one would actually win.

As much as she wanted him, she'd sworn off seconds, and as he'd already discovered, Holly wasn't a woman easily swayed once she'd made up her mind.

After what seemed like forever, she finally nodded. "Okay then. Let's do it."

7

TRAVIS STOOD IN the shadows and watched Holly unlock the door of the two-story Colonial house that sat in the heart of Skull Creek, directly across from the small city park. A white picket fence outlined a picture-perfect yard lined with flowers and shrubs. A swing hung from the porch rafters and a large Welcome Mat sat in front of the door.

The place had *family* written all over it, despite Holly's claim that she intended to stay single for a really, *really* long time.

Lights flicked on inside and spilled through the windows. He watched as she set her stuff on the dining room table and headed back outside.

The front door opened. A steady *click-clack* echoed as she crossed the hardwood porch and headed down the steps. She punched a button on her key fob. The trunk made a soft *popppp* and opened wide.

She slid her keys into her pocket and leaned into

the opening to gather up a cardboard box overflowing with wedding leftovers. Her skirt stretched tight over her sweet ass and hunger hit him hard and fast and sharp.

His mouth watered and his fangs tingled and he wondered how in the hell he was going to hold off until tomorrow night.

That's when the charade would start. Nine o'clock sharp at Cherry Blossom Dance Hall, in front of a packed house. The honky tonk was holding the preliminaries for their weeklong indoor rodeo and practically every available cowboy in the county would be there. It was the perfect opportunity to debut the new and improved and totally non-committal Holly, or so she thought.

His chest tightened and tension zipped up his spine. The urge to push her up against the edge of the car, sink his fangs deep and give her the best orgasm of her life nearly overwhelmed him. A few seconds and she would be screaming in ecstasy, totally ruined for any other man. She would give up her stupid quest for mindless sex and spend the next twenty years dreaming about him every night.

If she'd been any other woman.

But this was Holly. They'd already had earth-shattering sex, yet she wasn't the least bit anxious for seconds. Instead, she was scared. And determined.

While she'd agreed to their arrangement, she wasn't the least bit happy about it. Not because she didn't *want* to have sex with him again. She did. But she didn't want to want to have sex with him, and damned if that didn't bother the hell out of him.

Which explained why he'd followed her home. He hadn't been able to help himself. She puzzled the hell out of him and damned if that didn't make him want her all the more.

She pulled the box free and set it at her feet. As she bent down, her luscious breasts heaved against her silky blouse. The top button strained, threatening to pop open. A second later, she straightened and the material relaxed.

Disappointment ricocheted through his body, bulls-eyeing him straight in the crotch. The scent of her—so warm and moist and rich—crossed the distance to him and shattered his already tumultuous control. His blood rushed and his cock throbbed.

He focused, zeroing in on the button and just like that, it slid free of its own accord.

Startled, she glanced down and made quick work fastening it back up. She was about to lean back into the car after the next box when the button popped open again, setting off a chain reaction that didn't stop until the edges of her blouse parted.

He pursed his lips and blew into the still night air. The material fluttered open as if brushed by a faint breeze. He glimpsed the dark shadow of her nipple beneath the lacey cup of her bra and his stomach hollowed out. Another whisper of air and the hem of her skirt lifted, sliding up to reveal one round ass cheek barely concealed by a pair of skimpy bikini panties. A surprised gasp bubbled in the air and a split-second later, a desperate hand smoothed the skirt back down. Trembling fingers caught the edges of her blouse and tugged them closed, killing his view altogether.

Aw, hell.

Just as the thought struck, her head jerked up and he had the crazy notion that she'd actually heard him.

Crazy because he knew good and goddamned well that such a thing just wasn't possible. Vampires forged connections with blood. She would have to drink from him and he would have to drink from her for them to be that closely linked.

No, she hadn't heard him and she never would. The last thing Travis intended was to drink from Holly Simms or have her drink from him.

This wasn't about blood. It was about sex. Sweet, succulent, satisfying sex.

Starting tomorrow night.

In the meantime...

He gave himself a great big mental kick in the ass, turned and headed for the nearest motel. And straight into an ice cold shower.

HOLLY PULLED HER blouse closed and peered into the surrounding darkness. Awareness skittered up her spine and goose bumps danced the length of her arms. The hair on the back of her neck prickled and she had the distinct feeling that someone was watching her.

It was a feeling she knew all too well.

Every day, as a matter of fact, since this past Christmas when her neighbors, the Dunbars, had bought a bird-watching set for their fourteen-year-old son.

Mitchie Dunbar was a video game addict whose parents were desperate to get him off the couch and outside. Instead of the new Xbox 360 he'd been begging for, Santa had brought him a bird-watching set, complete with binoculars, a book on the various species and an online membership to Bird Watchers International where wannabe ornithologists the world over could post about their latest sightings.

Thanks to his adolescent hormones and the desperate need to impress his equally horny friends, the only thing Mitchie had been posting was how many times Holly bent over while watering the grass.

She summoned her most intimidating glare and turned toward his window to scare the bejeesus out of him. She would tell him off, report him to his mother, and then he'd be the one watering her lawn for the next two weeks.

"I see you, Mitchie—" she started to yell, the words stalling as soon as her gaze fixed on the closed window.

The glass was down, the drapes pulled tight, the

house dark. She kept staring, looking for the slightest movement that would give him away.

Nothing. Not even the glow of a computer monitor.

His covert skills were definitely improving.

That, or someone else had joined the party.

She turned back around, her gaze sweeping the lawn before pinpointing a huge tree that sat at the far edge of her property. A strange tingling awareness worked its way through her body before settling in the pit of her stomach. It was the same feeling she'd had back at the bar when she'd made eye contact with Travis Braddock.

Moonlight spilled down through the trees, illuminating the empty spot and proving beyond a doubt that her own imagination was running away with her thanks to the deal they'd made just a half hour before.

Sex.

She still couldn't believe she'd agreed to it. She'd vowed off seconds when she'd taken her Love Busters pledge and gotten her free t-shirt. Not that she didn't *want* to have sex with him again. She did. More than anything. That was the reason she'd sworn not to. Seconds led to thirds and thirds led to fourths and fourths to a bona fide relationship that would inevitably end in major heartache. She didn't want to get hooked on Travis Braddock and end up binge eating another wedding cake.

Not this time.

She'd changed over the past two years. She was stronger now. Wiser. She'd learned her lesson the hard way and it wasn't one she intended to repeat. She had different expectations when it came to the opposite sex—namely, she wasn't looking for love with any one man. She was looking for lust. Hot, raw, uncomplicated lust.

She ignored the *yeah, right* that niggled at her and turned back to the trunk.

"Little perv," she muttered as she re-fastened her blouse and tried to ignore the sudden realization that there wasn't even the slightest breeze in the air. That, and she didn't feel the same aggravation she normally felt when she caught Mitchie playing Peeping Tom.

Because it wasn't Mitchie, a voice whispered.

It was *him*. His tall, powerful body standing in the shadows. His attention fixated on her. His eyes devouring her from head to toe.

The notion didn't disturb her half as much as it made her anxious.

Excited.

"It's about damned time, sugar."

Tootie's voice replayed in her head and she remembered the gleam in her aunt's eyes when Holly had waltzed out of the bar and announced that she and Travis were going to get together the following night.

It *was* about damned time.

Holly had wasted enough of her life falling in love with the wrong men. It was time to have a little fun with the right man.

Right as in perfect for her specific situation, that is. Not *right* as in Mr. Right. Travis was wild and uncomplicated and sexy and temporary.

Mr. Right Now.

Or he would be, once tomorrow evening rolled around and their little arrangement officially began.

She swallowed against her suddenly dry throat. Her tummy quivered and her knees trembled and anticipation rippled through her. Her nipples pressed against the lace of her bra and heat spiraled through her. Drawing a deep, steadying breath, she slammed the trunk and picked up her boxes.

And then she started for the house, and what she knew was going to be *the* longest night of her life.

8

HOLLY HAD LEARNED a long time ago that there were only two certainties in the life of a wedding planner. The first? Despite the pessimistic divorce rate, people still believed in marriage. Regardless of the season, there was never a shortage of couples ready to dish out an incredible amount of cash for a groom's cake shaped like a monster truck or an ice sculpture that looked like Elvis. The second? Out of all those marriage-minded individuals, there was at least one bridezilla at any given moment.

And at this moment, the monster in question was a petite redhead sitting on the pink settee directly across from Holly.

"I've been thinking about the whole floral motif." Darla Lancaster flicked an invisible piece of lint from the lapel of her cherry-colored blouse. "I think we need to forget the tea roses and go with something else. Maybe lilies or peonies."

"I love lilies," Evan offered from the far corner where he sat at his desk, a book of material swatches open in front of him. "They're so romantic."

Holly ignored his vote and focused on the woman sitting across from her. "But the roses are being flown in from Italy as we speak." She'd tracked the order just that morning. "They're in Chicago about to wing their way here for a Monday delivery."

"The roses are fine," chimed in the woman sitting next to Darla. Shelley was the sister-of-the-bride and the first female in the history of nearby Travis County to serve as deputy sheriff. She wore a beige uniform and had her dark brown hair pulled back and pinned at the nape of her neck. "Flowers are flowers." She shrugged. "What difference does it make?"

Darla shook her head. "I just don't think tea roses represent the real me. I want everything at this wedding to scream *Darla.*"

"But the cost of changing at such short notice would be astronomical," Holly informed her bride.

"You can't put a price on love." She glared at Shelly before shifting her attention back to Holly. "Tea roses don't scream. They whisper. Lilies, on the other hand, definitely make a louder statement." Blue eyes stared pointedly at Holly. "Don't you think?"

What?

Holly tamped down on her frustration and tried to keep a calm demeanor in front of her biggest client.

Not only was Darla the most high maintenance

of all Holly's brides, she was also the most high pro-
file. In exactly one week, she was marrying Sam
McGregor, the son of a Texas congressman and one
of the most powerful lawyers in the state. Sam was
wealthy. Educated. Successful. On top of that, he
looked like a Ken doll with his blond hair, great tan
and Crest-worthy smile. Once upon a time, his dad
had been the mayor of Skull Creek. He'd grown up
just two streets over on the most affluent block in
town.

Darla herself had grown up in the Happy Trails
trailer park just on the other side of the railroad
tracks that circled the town. She'd never been to the
governor's mansion or hobnobbed with Dallas' rich-
est oil men. She was Cinderella and Sam was her
Prince Charming, and it only made sense that she
would be a little freaked.

At least that's what Holly told herself every time
she got a visit or phone call changing yet another
detail of the over-the-top event.

First the food. Then the champagne. The band.
Even the dress. They'd gone back and forth between
princess and mermaid styles before Darla had finally
decided to buy one of each. One for the ceremony
and the other for the reception. Now if she could only
decide which one to wear to which event.

Holly forced herself to take a deep, calming breath.
"I really do think the tea roses are perfect for a
formal daytime event, which is what we've planned."

"About that…" Darla frowned. "I was thinking that we might actually bump up the time a little. Make it later, after sunset, so that I can have candles. Lots of candles."

"I love candles," Evan offered again. "They make everything look so dreamy."

Holly cut him a warning glance before smiling at Darla. "I thought you wanted sunlight streaming through the stained glass windows of the church?"

"She doesn't know what she wants," Shelly chimed in.

"I most certainly do." Darla shot a glare at her sister before shifting her attention back to Holly. "Sunlight and stained glass were fine when I was going for a more sedate, classy look." Darla waved a hand and her three carat diamond engagement ring flashed in the early morning sunlight. "But Sam and I really want this to reflect our personalities. I think I'm a little more dramatic than afternoon chic. I'd rather go for something that suits my sophisticated side. Maybe a black tie event with lots of ball gowns. Sort of like *Phantom of the Opera*." She smiled. "I totally loved that movie."

"I loved it, too—" Evan started, only to clamp his mouth shut when Holly shot him another sideways glance. He shrugged. "I mean, it's okay if you buy into the whole dark, dangerous, wounded hero thing, which I don't. Although I absolutely *loved* the costumes. And that mask… Girl, that's definitely the stuff of fantasies."

"That's what I was thinking, too," Darla exclaimed before launching into a quick discussion about possibly handing out masks as party favors at the reception.

"Shoot me," Shelley whispered to Holly.

"I was thinking the exact same thing."

"So it's settled then," Darla smiled. "*Phantom of the Opera* it is."

"But the wedding is in seven days. The classy, afternoon, sunlight-streaming-through-the-windows wedding, complete with a cage full of rare butterflies to release immediately following the nuptials."

Darla waved a hand. "Plenty of time for you to do away with all that nonsense and give me what I really want."

"But the invitations have already gone out specifying the time and the details."

"I'm sure we can send new invitations via overnight mail. Or a text message." Brilliance seemed to strike and she beamed. "Or an email. I'll forward you my contact list as soon as I get home."

"But most of your guests have already made travel arrangements based on the information in the original invitation?" She knew she sounded like a broken record with the *buts, but* months of planning were spiraling down the drain and she couldn't help herself.

Darla stiffened and her gaze narrowed. "It's my wedding and I want *Phantom of the Opera*. If that doesn't work for you, then I'm sure I can find another planner who shares my vision and understands what it's like to marry someone like Sam. You haven't actually been married yourself, have you?"

"No," Evan offered. "She came really close—and I mean *really* close—but didn't quite hit the bullseye."

Not that Darla didn't already know that. Skull Creek was a map dot where everybody knew everybody and gossip traveled faster than the speed of light.

Darla shook her head. "No wonder you can't understand."

Holly's chest tightened. Not that she wanted to be a bride. She'd given up on that fantasy a long time ago. It was the thought of losing an entire shipment of tea roses. She loved tea roses. And it seemed such a shame for them to go to waste.

"I love *Phantom of the Opera*," Holly finally declared. "I'll call the florist first thing and make the changes."

"Okay, now you've both gone off the deep end," Shelley added. "I knew it was just a matter of time."

Darla ignored her sister. "Make sure to tell the florist I don't want small lilies. I want large ones, and have them done up in some really elaborate arrangements. Something that says bold. Aggressive. Something that screams *Darla*."

Or royal bitch.

Holly tamped down the unkind thought and reminded herself that the young woman was just under a lot of stress. She was out of her element and so it made sense that she would be a little on edge. And bitchy. Holly would have done the same had she been in Darla's shoes.

She summoned her most reassuring smile. "I'll take care of everything."

True to her word, she spent the next two hours on the phone tracking down shipments and negotiating prices before she finally managed to pull off Darla's latest request. After that, she tackled the multitude of changes that had to be made.

"You're fired," she told Evan when she finally hung up after an exhausting phone call to the caterer. She'd barely made a dent in all the work that needed to be done, which meant she would have to come in on Sunday.

"For what? Helping you plan the wedding of the century?"

"Killing my one day off. Do you know how much work this is going to be? Or how much it's going to cost?" She stared at the endless list of figures that the various vendors were going to charge for the last minute changes.

"First off, I'm happy to help with the extra work.

Bob plays tackle football with his straight buddies on Sunday and I'm not invited because I busted out crying the last time he got tackled. As for the extra cost, what do you care? It's not your money. If the girl wants lilies, give her lilies."

"She doesn't know what she wants. That's the problem. Tomorrow it could be daisies."

"I love daisies," Evan offered, only to clamp his mouth shut when Holly shot him a withering glare.

"You love everything."

He shrugged. "Love makes the world go 'round."

Amen.

She squelched the thought and spent the rest of the day making changes and going through the list of email contacts Darla had sent her. She had to notify as many guests as possible, as fast as possible.

Forgive me, Martha Stewart.

She sent up the silent plea as she typed in the last address and hit send.

"Closing time," Evan's voice drew her attention and Holly glanced at the clock for the first time since Darla had dropped the bomb on her.

Five o'clock? Seriously?

"I'm meeting Bob for drinks." Evan packed up his desk. "Want to come with?"

"I'm busy tonight."

"Oh, honey, your toes can wait until tomorrow."

"I'm not giving myself a pedicure." She finished making the last of her notes in Darla's file and reached for her purse.

"Manicure?"

"No."

"Facial?"

She gave him a pointed stare. "I'm going out."

Evan arched an eyebrow. "I thought you swore off dating."

"It's not a date. We're just going to hang out."

"Since when do you just hang out?"

She leveled a stare at her assistant. "Since now." And then she headed out the door. It was time to show the entire world that Holly Simms wasn't the woman everyone thought she was.

9

Travis dropped to his knees, shoved his hands into the icy stream and splashed the cool liquid onto his face. Water ran in rivulets down his neck, drenching the collar of his shirt and cleansing the grime of the past few days on the trail. But it wasn't enough to wash away the tickle in his gut. It stayed with him, following him back to the other men sleeping by the fire.

He stretched out on his bedroll and closed his eyes. The seconds ticked off in his head. The uneasiness rolled through his gut. It was stronger tonight than it had been before. Stronger, but not strong enough.

The enemy wasn't close enough yet to alarm the others. The best thing to do would be to keep quiet and push on southward, the way they'd planned, heading straight for the Union supply train on its way to Vicksburg. If they stopped now and waited *for the group of men following them, they would miss the rendezvous point and months of work would go to hell in a hand basket. They had to reach Vicksburg first, and that meant no slowing down.*

His gaze shifted to his oldest brother on the bedroll a few feet away. If Colton knew the damned feelings niggling at Travis, he would vote to stay and take care of the most immediate threat. To play it safe. Colton wanted to get home in one piece.

Hell, they all did. Brent had a steady girl he'd left behind. For Cody, it was a damned saloon full of them. And for Colton? A wife and a son.

Travis was the only one who didn't have anything to go back to. It would suit him just fine if they never made it back to Texas.

Laura Mae Sooner had dumped him the minute he'd told her they were riding out after Cody. She'd forced him to choose and he'd chosen his brothers. They'd always stuck together. They'd had to when their pa had taken off chasing yet another woman. He hadn't come back that last time and Travis and his brothers had been looking out for one another ever since.

When Cody had left for the war, they'd all gone after him. And they'd been busting their asses for the Confederacy ever since.

They'd raided more gun and supply shipments than Travis could count and there had been plenty of times when they'd had somebody tailing them.

But this felt different.

He tamped down on the crazy thought and rolled onto his side. Wadding up the blanket, he shoved it tighter under his head and watched the flames lick at the surrounding darkness.

He was antsy. That was all. Colton had gotten captured a few weeks ago and they'd had a helluva time getting him back.

But they had, he reminded himself. They'd snatched him out of those carpetbaggers' hands just in the nick of time and everything had turned out okay. They'd even had a decent meal that night, thanks to the extra supplies his kidnappers had been stashing. The entire situation had been a close call, but the Braddock Boys had come out on top.

It was all about moving and staying one step ahead.

Travis held tight to the thought and forced his eyes closed. He concentrated on the sounds around him. The crackle of the fire. The buzz of insects. The crunch of footsteps just behind—

The thought slammed to a halt as a bullet cracked open the night sky. A burning sensation ripped through his right shoulder. And then all hell broke loose.

TRAVIS BOLTED UPRIGHT, his body shaking, his shoulder tingling. He could still feel the cold steel of the bullet followed by the hot rush of blood. The smell of gunpowder burned his nostrils. The shouts echoed in his ears.

He touched the jagged scar and fought the nagging voice.

You knew it. You felt it.

Bullshit.

He'd been on edge like everyone else. They'd been ambushed before and so when they'd caught wind that someone was tailing them, he'd feared the worst. Expected it.

He sure as hell hadn't *known*.

But that's not what his granny had told him. She'd died of a heart attack when he was seven, but before then she'd lived with them at the ranch. He and Colton were the only ones old enough to really remember her.

"You've got the sight, boy."

She'd said it all the time when he was a child. Like when he'd shown up for supper before his mother rang the dinner bell. Or when he'd taken off fishing just when his ma was about to make him shovel the barn. Or when he'd side-stepped a rattler that no one else had seen coming at a church picnic.

But Travis had never listened to her. She'd been old and barely playing with a full deck. His mother had said she'd gone a little crazy when his grandfather had died. And while he'd always respected his grandmother, he'd never really paid much attention to anything she said. No one had.

But she'd been right.

He drop-kicked the thought and threw his legs over the side of the bed. The sun had already set and the light from the bare bulb hanging outside his door pushed around the blinds, fighting to get inside the small room. He eyeballed the clock. He'd meant to sleep an extra hour or so, but he knew that wasn't going to happen. A few seconds later, he stepped into a hot shower. The water flowed over him, washing away the memories and the pain.

For a little while anyway.

Without enough rejuvenating sleep, his muscles still ached. Emptiness gnawed at the pit of his stomach and his gut tightened. He desperately needed another round with Holly. Another sweet, succulent orgasm to satisfy the craving deep inside.

But there was something else, as well. An anticipation that had nothing to do with feeding and everything to do with the desperate need to see her. Touch her. Talk to her.

And his granny had been the crazy one?

He gave himself a great big mental kick in the ass. This was all about sex. Sustenance. He needed to kill some time and regain his strength and she needed to sully her glowing reputation. End of story.

With his mind set, he stepped out of the shower, grabbed a towel and went about getting ready for his first official sex date with luscious Holly Simms.

"HOW DOES THIS look?" Holly asked as she walked into the living room where Tootie had planted herself on the couch a half hour ago after marching in and handing Holly her coveted bag of tricks—a tube of red lipstick, some blue eye shadow, a box of safety pins, a pack of pasties, a tube of denture cream and a five dollar bill. "Too skimpy?"

"Way too skimpy," Aunt Tootie said, giving Holly the once over, from the red button down shirt tied just under her breasts, to the cut off blue jean shorts that barely covered her butt cheeks, to a pair of three inch come-and-get-me red stiletto heels. Tootie smiled and her face erupted in a mass of wrinkles that a hundred dollar a month moisturizer habit hadn't been able to touch. "It's perfect." She patted her snow white beehive. "'Course, you could have saved your money and borrowed a few things from me. I've got a pair of shorts just like that, you know."

Holly ignored the sudden image of "Tootie the sexpot" that popped into her head and smiled. "I'll be sure to remember that next time." *Not.*

"Where'd you find that get-up anyhow? One of them adult specialty shops over in Austin?"

"Not exactly."

Her eyes sparkled. "A sex party?"

"Uh-uh."

"The internet?"

"The Piggly Wiggly."

Tootie's excitement turned to bewilderment. "Are you pulling my leg?"

"I got tied up at work today and it was the only place that was still open by the time I got off."

"Since when does the Piggly Wiggly have a clothing section?"

"They were clearing out last year's Halloween costumes. It was either Daisy Duke from the *Dukes of Hazzard* or Tinkerbell from *Peter Pan*. Since I doubt I could pull off a pair of fairy wings, I thought this would be the most realistic." A wave of insecurity rolled through her. "Then again, maybe it's too much of a stretch—"

"It'll do just fine," Tootie interrupted. "Just don't you worry about it."

"I borrowed the shoes from Evan," Holly added. "He and Bob like to play dress up."

"I knew there was something I liked about that boy." Tootie gave her another once over and winked. "Why, they'll be talking nonstop about you at church tomorrow. I just know it."

A girl could only hope.

Holly tamped down the butterflies in her stomach and summoned a smile. There was no way the men in town would fail to take her seriously now. Not when she two-stepped across the floor in this get-up with Mr. Tall, Dark and Delicious himself.

Not that she could actually two-step.

She'd spent so many years dreaming of happily-ever-afters, having fun had sort of fallen by the way-side. Sure, she could waltz. That was a couples thing. She'd taken a few lessons when she and Chad had gotten engaged so their first dance as man and wife would be magical. But waltzing didn't really up the sex appeal value like the salsa or the rumba or the lambada.

You're not cut out for this, a voice whispered.

It was that same familiar little voice that had kept her waiting on Mr. Right all through high school and college instead of sowing her wild oats. But no, she'd listened. And held out for The One. First Allen. And then Ben. And then Chad.

She was breaking the cycle once and for all.

Besides, it's not like they *had* to dance. The point was to naughty up her image by being seen with *the* naughtiest man in town. Not land a spot on *So You Think You Can Dance.*

Drawing a deep breath, she reached for her purse. "Do you want me to drop you off at Bingo on my way?"

Tootie shook her head. "You just run along and have fun. I'll pull out my little black book and have someone here in no time. Maybe Ronald Dupree. He's a handsome one. With his new dental implants, I swear the man doesn't look a day over forty."

"Didn't he have cataract surgery and have to give up his driver's license?"

She stopped to think. "You might be right. Then I'll just call Wade Harlington. He was a Texas Ranger once upon a time and can still fit into the same pair of jeans he wore on his first case. Or maybe I'll give Jim Miles a ring. Or Bob Callahan." She shook her head. "It makes no never mind. I'll find somebody." Her mouth pulled into a thin line. "And I can guaran-damn-tee that I won't be calling Buck Gentry. That man is as old as dirt and just as irritating."

"You went to high school with him, didn't you?"

Tootie stiffened. "I most certainly did not. He was a good two years older than me. Maybe even three. 'Course, he always wanted me, but I never gave him the time of day. He's a great big horse's ass."

He was also the only man in town who hadn't been wowed by Tootie's pink hot pants and massive cleavage. She'd carried a grudge ever since.

"Why, I saw him at the diner last week and he had the nerve to tell me I should stop wearing such bright colors. Said I needed to dress my age. You know what I told him? You're only as old as you feel and I feel twenty-five. So he can just mind his own damned business. I had to take an extra blood pressure pill after that little encounter." When Holly gave her a concerned look, she waved a hot-pink manicured hand. "Stop worrying about me and get on out of here."

Holly forced aside her nerves and gave Tootie a

kiss on the cheek. She swiped on an extra layer of Wild & Wicked Red lipstick, and headed for the door.

If she was going through with this—and she was—it was now or never.

10

THIS WAS *NOT* a date.

Holly reminded herself of that all-important fact when she pulled into the parking lot of the honky tonk and spotted Travis waiting outside for her.

He looked as sinfully sexy as ever in jeans and a plain black T-shirt. The soft cotton molded to his broad shoulders, the sleeves falling just shy of a pair of intricate slave band tattoos that wound around each bulging bicep. A woven leather strap clung to his strong neck and a Stetson sat low on his forehead. He leaned on an old hitching post, arms crossed, booted feet hooked at the ankles.

When she climbed from the car, he straightened and tipped his hat back. The shadow lifted from his handsome face and her stomach hollowed out. Green eyes gleamed with an intensity that kicked her pulse into high gear. His sensuous mouth hitched in a wicked grin.

"You look…different," he said when she walked up to him. His gaze slid down her body and back up, lingering at her breasts for several seconds.

If she hadn't known better, she would have sworn she felt a distinct pressure on her nipple. Like the soft flick of a finger against the ripe tip, teasing, taunting. *Crazy.*

She drew a shaky breath and tried to ignore the frantic pounding of her heart. "That's the idea. I want people to see me differently."

"They'll definitely see you. A lot of you." A thread of jealousy filtered through the words and his brows drew together into a frown. "Don't you think you're going a little overboard?"

Hearing him voice the doubts that had haunted her since she'd first pulled on the skimpy outfit made them seem that much more real. She blurted, "Do I look that bad?" before she could remind herself that it didn't matter what he thought. *He* didn't matter.

But at that moment, he did.

Her gaze searched his and oddly enough, his expression softened.

The frown eased. "Sugar, you look incredible. It's just that I signed up to keep you company, not fight off every man in the place."

The words whispered through her head and sent a rush of warmth through her. The scent of him, so raw and masculine, teased her senses. For an insane moment, she had the urge to lean closer and simply breathe. Fully. Deeply. To draw him in and lose herself.

The way she'd done with every other man in her past.

The realization hit and she stiffened. "I should be so lucky." She reached for the door before he had a chance to open it for her and hurried inside.

Neon beer signs plastered the walls and cigarette smoke fogged the air. A sea of Stetsons bobbed across the massive dance floor, keeping time to the Billy Currington song that vibrated through the building. The smell of beer and sawdust tickled her nose.

"Where to?" Travis's deep voice rumbled in her ear as he came up behind her and awareness skittered through her.

She tried to ignore the sensations and swept a gaze around the room. Small round tables edged the dance floor and a large bar ran the full length of one wall. A crowd filled the far corner, surrounding the pile of mattresses that flanked a mechanical bull that was in high swing. She contemplated crawling onto the monster right here and now, but she was busting at the seams in her outfit as it was. Sharp turns and serious bouncing she didn't need. She was shedding her good girl image, not her clothes.

Then again—

"Don't even think it," Travis murmured in her ear. Before she could give a second thought to the fact that he'd just read her mind, he added, "The bar is more visible." He pressed the hand into the small of her back and steered her forward.

"What now?" she asked when they reached their destination.

"Now, we order a drink." He signaled the bartender and a few seconds later, two shot glasses full of sparkling gold liquid sat in front of them.

She took a huge gulp of the Jack Daniels and nearly spewed the stuff back out. She'd never been a big drinker and when she did indulge, she stuck to the occasional glass of wine. "It's good." *Not.*

A sinful grin tugged at the corner of his mouth. "You can order something a little softer if you want."

She glanced down the length of the bar, her gaze zeroing in on Susie Cantrell, Skull Creek's reigning bad girl. Susie was tall and sexy and always the life of the party, not to mention the sole subject of at least half the prayer meetings over at the church. Forget the daiquiris and the cosmos. She stood amid a group of cowboys, laughing and tossing down tequila shots.

"I'm fine with this." Holly stole another glance at Susie. "It just comes so naturally for her. My Aunt Tootie is the same way. She just gives off this vibe that says *Hey, I'm a party and a half.*"

"And what's your vibe?"

"Run for your single life?"

He grinned. "That's not such a bad thing."

"Not if you want to settle down. But if you don't, it's the kiss of death."

"So you've sworn off settling down completely?"

"It's not that I wouldn't like to. Someday. I just don't think it's in the cards for me." She watched as Susie cast her a surprised glance and then whispered to one of the males next to her. The man looked at Holly, a startled expression on his face that quickly turned to *wow*. "Aunt Tootie says I should revel in being single but I've never really liked it that much."

"Maybe you've never taken the time to enjoy it."

"Have you ever been married?"

He shook his head. "Never have, never will. It's definitely not in the cards for me either."

"Family curse like me?"

His mouth hinted at a grin. "Something like that."

"Looks like Cody broke it."

"For now."

"You don't think it will last?"

"I don't see how it can."

"And I thought I was cynical."

"It's not about being cynical. It's called being practical. Some men aren't cut out for marriage."

"That's what my Aunt Tootie says. Except she says it about women. About us."

"But you don't actually believe her." It was more of a statement than a question, as if he knew she'd yet to toss out the stack of Bridal magazines collecting dust in the back of her closet.

"I'm here, aren't I?" She downed the last of her drink and signaled the bartender, suddenly eager to shift her attention to a different subject. "Hit me again." She was just about to take another gulp when Travis plucked the glass from her hand.

"We'd better do this now while you can still stand up."

"Do what?" she asked as he pulled her from her seat.

"Dance."

"I don't know if that's such a good idea." She dug in her heels as he tried to tug her onto the large sawdust covered dance floor.

"Too drunk?"

"Too clueless." When his gaze caught and held hers, she added, "I don't really do this kind of dancing."

"What kind do you do?"

"The boring kind." Her gaze slid to a man currently spinning his partner and her stomach lurched. "I'm liable to fall on my face."

"I'll catch you first," he promised. As much as she wanted to turn and walk the other way, she knew she couldn't back down now. Everyone in the place was watching her, including Suzie Cantrell and her group of admirers.

She fought down her fear and let him lead her out onto the dance floor.

"Now what?" she asked as he turned to face her.

"Now you relax." He slid an arm around her waist and took her hand. "Dancing is all about letting loose and having fun. If you're worried about what you're doing, you'll screw it up for sure."

"Let loose," she murmured to herself, rolling her head from side to side and shaking out her shoulders. "I can do that."

"And have fun."

"I don't know if I can do that." And that was her problem in a nutshell. She'd been so busy searching for Mr. Right, she'd never taken the time to slow down. Relax. *Enjoy.* And she wasn't sure she even knew how.

A knowing gleam lit his eyes as he stared down at her. "Just follow my lead."

He started slow at first, his foot sliding forward, pushing against her leg and urging her backward. And then the move started all over again with the opposite foot.

They moved around the dance floor slowly, tentatively at first. But soon she fell into step with him and she didn't have to think so much. Her body followed his, leaning this way, sliding that way until she stopped worrying about looking like a hussy. Instead, she started to feel like one with each sultry sway and twist.

"You might be right after all." His deep voice slid into her ears and drew her from the hypnotic rhythm of their movements.

"About what?"

He winked. "You might have a little hussy in you."

His words startled her and she stiffened. "How did you know—? Whoa!"

Before Holly knew what was happening, he twirled her in the opposite direction. She was dead certain she was about to eat some hardwood, but then his fingers tightened around hers. Just as she teetered to the side, he pulled her back to him, turned her under his arm and the roller-coaster ride started all over again.

By the time the song faded to a close, Holly could hardly breathe. Her heart hammered and her pulse raced and she experienced a rush of excitement unlike anything she'd ever felt before.

Okay, so she'd felt it before. The burst of light headedness. The surge of *wow*. The *I can't believe this is happening*.

She'd felt it last night in the closet with Travis. When he'd felt her up and kissed her senseless and plunged so deep that she'd forgotten everything except the lust pulsing through her body.

A slow, sweet George Strait song poured from the speakers and Travis pulled her close. He felt so strong and smelled so good. She actually stopped thinking about what she should do—namely strut her stuff back to the bar now that she'd gotten everyone's attention and toss down a few more drinks to give them something to really talk about.

At the same time, the two drinks she'd already had had obviously gone to her head because instead of *should,* she did what she wanted to do. What felt right.

She moved closer to Travis.

He was so strong and powerful and suddenly she couldn't help herself. She leaned into him, molding herself to his hard frame and closing her eyes.

And for the next few moments, the world slipped away.

TRAVIS HAD NEVER been much for dancing. Sure, it provided a nice little warm up for getting up close and personal, but he'd stopped with the pretenses the night he'd lost his humanity. He much preferred ditching the formalities and getting right to the good stuff.

But when Holly slid her arms around his neck and leaned into him, he had the crazy thought that there might be something to this. It had been a helluva long time since he'd just held a woman.

Since he'd wanted to hold one.

He cursed the crazy notion just as soon as it moseyed into his brain. He didn't *want* to hold Holly Simms. He wanted to push her up against the wall and sink his cock into her lush body and his fangs into her sweet neck.

Sustenance.

That's all he wanted from her.

He tried to focus on the way her pelvis cradled his crotch. He moved against her, setting the pace with a subtle side-to-side motion that made his hard-on pulse and his fangs tingle. He needed to forget about her soft, warm breaths against his neck and the feel of her silky hair tickling the underside of his jaw. He wanted to forget, but then her warmth seeped inside him, chasing away the cold that gripped his bones. His nerves started to buzz.

He held her so easily, as if he'd been doing it his entire life.

He hadn't. He knew that. But there was just something about the steady *thump thump thump* of her heart against his chest.

It felt right.

She felt right.

And Travis held her tighter.

HOLLY FELT HIS arms tighten and a burst of happiness went through her, followed by a whisper of contentment that scared the bejeesus out of her. Because this wasn't about happiness or contentment or happily-ever-after.

Reality bolted through her and every muscle in her body went tight. "I think I need some air." She pulled away, suddenly desperate for a deep breath that didn't smell like Travis Braddock.

A few seconds later, she pushed through the rear door of the honky tonk and out into the back parking lot. A few cars dotted the area and two Dumpsters sat to her right. Laughter and music filtered from inside, mingling with the buzz of crickets. She drank in a huge lungful of oxygen and tried to calm the explosive pounding in her chest.

Happy? Content? *Seriously?*

What kind of Love Buster was she? She could *not* fall for this guy. No matter how strong his arms had felt sliding around her. Or how his eyes glittered so hot and bright. Or how he smelled like leather and fresh air and something so incredibly alluring that she couldn't seem to think straight when he was close.

It was only physical, she reminded herself. Those things were only the result of the intense chemistry that sizzled between them. The lust. It wasn't like they had an actual emotional connection. She hardly knew this guy and he hardly knew her. No way was he meant to hold her like that again and again, 'til death do us part.

"Holly?" His deep voice rumbled in her ears and she became acutely aware of the man standing behind her.

She hadn't even heard the door open and close. No footsteps. Nothing. Yet here he was.

The facts whirled in her head, hinting at something that she didn't have time to think about because *here he was.*

Get it together, girl. Remember your objective.

This is a business arrangement. He gives you some-thing. You give him something.

And that was the problem itself.

She knew the deal she'd made with him, what she'd promised, and what waited at the end of the night—the best sex of her life. And it was that all-important fact that played with her sanity. Sex had always been part of a relationship, the culmination of time spent together and feelings shared. So it only made sense that she would think crazy thoughts her first time out of the gate. Like how no man had ever held her quite so firmly, so purposefully, so perfectly. How no man ever would.

She shook away the ridiculous sentiment. This had nothing to do with a relationship and everything to do with a business deal. Sex was just sex. It was all a matter of keeping her perspective.

She knew she didn't have a chance in hell of doing that inside. It felt too much like a date at this point, the anticipation building with each smolder-ing glance, each lingering touch.

She needed to get out of here, head for the nearest motel, chuck all the niceties and just get to it. Down and dirty. Cheap and tawdry. No strings.

She drew another deep breath and forced her feet to turn. "Okay." She nodded and did her best to control the sudden fluttering in her stomach. "I'm ready."

A frown creased his brow. "Ready for what?"

"You know." She braced herself. "The rest of our deal." She rolled her shoulders as if about to climb into a wrestling ring. "Let's do it."

The words were like a direct bolt of heat to Travis's already throbbing erection. His undead heart pounded. Adrenaline surged through his body and his nerves came alive.

But while it was exactly the invitation he'd been waiting to hear from her luscious mouth, there was just something about the way she said the words— as if she were agreeing to take a spoonful of Castor oil—that jabbed at his ego and tightened his already tight muscles.

"You want to leave now?"

She nodded. "I got what I wanted—everyone saw us. So it's only fair that you get what you want."

And the sooner we get this over with, the better.

Her desperate thought punctuated the statement and kept Travis from throwing her across his shoulder and heading back to his room to collect payment for services rendered.

But suddenly, he didn't want her to have sex with him half as much as he wanted her to *want* to have sex with him.

Plain and simple, he wanted her to want him, the way he wanted her. The need was so fierce and raw that it compelled him to reach out when every ounce of common sense told him to run the other way.

Though she was turned on and anxious, pulling

her into his bed wouldn't be enough. She was still thinking. Still worrying. Still fortifying her guard.

He wanted her to stop. To feel. To *want*. So much that *she* reached for *him*.

"If that's the way you want it." He stepped toward her. "Then let's do it. Right now."

She arched an eyebrow. "Here?"

"Why not?"

11

"I DON'T KNOW if this is such a good idea—" Holly started to say. But then he kissed her, his lips wet and hungry, his tongue greedy.

The humid night air closed around them, upping her body temperature and making it hard to breathe. Or maybe that was him. He surrounded her. His scent filled her head.

"Shouldn't we go somewhere," she breathed when he finally pulled away. "Somebody might see us."

"Isn't that the point, darlin'?"

It was. At the same time, there was just something about the way he held her—so firm and possessive—that sent a wave of *uh-oh* through her.

"You want to convince the entire town that you're a bad girl?" His gaze smoldered. "Then play the part and give them something to talk about."

Amen.

That's what her brain said. She'd waited for this

moment forever. The chance to prove to everyone that she was through being good.

At the same time, she and Travis were in a back parking lot. Their only audience was a crate of old liquor boxes, a Ford Prius that belonged to one of the waitresses and a beat-up GTO.

At least that's what she told herself.

She certainly didn't hesitate because this felt like something more. Her heart pounded at the thought of kissing him, touching him, regardless of their surroundings. There was just something about the way he stared so deeply into her eyes that made her want to slide her arms around his neck and never let go.

She balled her fingers, determined to resist as he dipped his head and caught her lips in another scorching kiss.

His tongue plunged deep, stroking and stirring the inside of her mouth and her heart pounded faster. He tasted of whiskey and dark desire and her knees trembled. Before she knew it, her fingers flexed and tangled in the soft cotton of his sleeves and she held tight. The kiss was thorough, consuming, mind-blowing.

And then it was over.

Thankfully.

That's what she told herself, but there was no mistaking the disappointment that spiraled through her as he pulled away, quickly followed by a rush of anticipation when he reached for the button on her shorts. Strong fingers worked at the opening. The zipper slid and the denim sagged. The frayed ends tickled her legs as he urged the shorts down over her thighs, her knees, until they pooled around her ankles.

He slid his hands around her bottom. His fingertips burned through the lace of her panties as he drew her legs up on either side of his hips and lifted her. A few seconds later, he set her down onto the hood of the old GTO.

He wedged himself between her parted thighs and urged her backward until her back met the cool metal hood. He unbuttoned her shirt and unhooked the front clasp of her bra. The cool night air washed over her bare skin and pebbled her nipples.

"These look good enough to eat," he murmured, touching one ripe tip. He circled the sensitive bud, tracing the areola until it throbbed and her skin flushed hot.

His gaze drilled into hers for a heart-stopping moment before he lowered his dark head. The first leisurely rasp of his tongue against her throbbing nipple wrung a cry from her throat.

Her fingers threaded through his hair as he drew the quivering tip deep into his hot, hungry mouth. He suckled her long and hard and she barely caught the moan that rippled up her throat. Her skin grew itchy and tight. Pressure started between her legs, heightened by the way he leaned into her, the hard ridge of his erection prominent beneath his jeans.

She spread her legs wider and he settled more deeply between them. Grasping her hips, he rocked her. Rubbed her. Up and down and side to side and—

"Where did you say you parked the truck?"

The question barely penetrated the haze of pleasure that gripped her senses. Her eyes snapped open and her ears tuned in to the footsteps in the far distance.

"It's right over here," a man's voice said. "Just relax."

The reality of what she was doing right here, right now, sent a burst of panic through her.

"Wait." She grasped his muscled biceps, but Travis didn't miss a beat. "Someone's coming." She tried to stare past him, but the Dumpster blocked her view.

"Easy," he murmured against her skin. He sucked her long and deep for a heart-stopping moment before leaning back. "If we can't see them, then they can't see us." His fingertip traced the edge of her panties where elastic met the tender inside of her thigh. "Stop worrying," he whispered, dipping a finger inside and testing her moist heat.

One rasping touch of his callused fingertip against her swollen flesh caused her to arch off the hood. She caught her bottom lip and stifled a cry.

With a growl, he spread her wide with his thumb

and forefinger and touched and rubbed as he dipped his head and drew on her nipple.

It was too much. And yet not enough. She clamped her lips shut and forced her eyes open. But he was there, filling her line of vision, his fierce gaze drilling into hers. Searching and stirring and begging her to fall…no!

Her hands trembled and she fought against the pleasure beating at her senses. She stiffened, her hands diving between them to stop the delicious stroke of his fingers.

As if he sensed her sudden resistance, his movements stilled. His chest heaved and his hair tickled her palms. Damp fingertips trailed over her cheek in a tender gesture that warmed her heart almost as much as her body.

"You're going the wrong way. This is the back of the building." The voice pushed through the haze of pleasure beating at her senses. "Let's head around the side." Gravel crunched and the footsteps faded into the pounding of her own heart.

"Do you want more?" His gaze was hot and bright and feverish as he stared down at her, into her. But there was something else, as well. A desperation that reached down deep and touched something inside of her.

She eased back down onto the hood. She spread her legs wider and he slid down her body. At the first rasp of his tongue, she almost jumped out of her skin.

He licked her up and down, side to side and…*there.* Right…*there!*

Her lips parted and she screamed at the blinding force of the climax. Her voice echoed, blending into the sound of music coming from inside. Travis gripped her and held her firmly to his mouth, tasting and laving as she exploded into a million pieces.

Once she could breathe again, she reached down and tugged at the button of his jeans, hungry for more, pulling his zipper down, she freed his hard length. She squeezed him, stroking him from root to tip once, twice, and then she let go, determined to let him take the lead.

To take what he wanted.

He growled, the sound so low and deep that it sent a tremble up her spine. The head of his penis pushed just a fraction of an inch inside her. He swore under his breath, the sound sizzling across her nerve endings and set them ablaze. A split-second later, however, the fire died as a cool wind whispered over her.

"Next time," he murmured.

Her eyes snapped and—

He was gone!

She struggled upright, her gaze searching for him, but the parking lot was empty.

"Next time."

His words echoed in her head and disappointment rushed through her. She'd wanted it tonight. Now.

Just to keep her on track, of course. Sex was a reality check. A reminder that this wasn't a real date.

But damned if she didn't feel as if he'd walked her to the front door and left her with a chaste kiss on the forehead.

TRAVIS LEANED ON the fencepost of Brent's new spread and stared at the cluster of horses grazing just up on the ridge. To the average eye, they looked calm and peaceful. But Travis didn't miss the flare of nostrils or the way one of them—a jet black female with white spots—danced just a little too much when the other horses got too close.

The animal was as wild as the day was long. It was a damned shame. She had the makings of a good cutting horse. A quick gait. An alert eye.

Easy, girl.

The thought whispered through Travis's mind and the animal's head snapped up. Her gaze cut through the distance separating them and her ears perked.

I'm not going to hurt you.

The animal obviously wasn't so sure and she danced backwards after a few moments. Travis debated hopping the fence and seeing how close he could get, but he wasn't here to train horses. Even if Brent had asked for his help.

He'd just driven out to take a look because it seemed like the easiest way to forget Holly and her screaming orgasm.

His fingertips still tingled where he'd drank in her delicious energy for those few precious moments. But it hadn't been nearly enough. He'd wanted to sink inside of her and stir another climax. And another. Until she finally admitted that she really and truly wanted him. To him. And herself.

It would take a while. He already knew that. He'd had no illusions that she would give in tonight. Sure, he'd hoped. But then that was part of what attracted him so strongly to her. Because she was strong. Different. Stubborn.

And he was too damned worked up to head back to his motel room.

He hopped the fence and the herd of horses scattered. All except for the black. She eyeballed Travis, sizing him up as if he was the enemy and they were standing on opposite sides of a battlefield.

As far as she was concerned, they were.

Travis took another step. Slow. Steady. Then another. The animal reared and he stopped.

They stared each other down for several minutes before the black finally turned and bolted after the others.

"She likes you. Otherwise she would have been long gone before you got so close." Brent's deep voice sounded behind him and Travis turned to see his brother standing on the other side of the fencepost.

"How long have you been here?" Travis asked as

he hopped back over the fence to stand beside his brother.

"I heard your truck from the house." Travis arched an eyebrow and Brent added, "and saw you, thanks to the surveillance camera posted at the road."

"A vampire's got to look out for himself, right?"

"You can't be too careful. It's pretty safe here, but we have had some crazy vampire hunters before. I rigged up the system myself. I've got two wireless cams posted at the turn-off. They communicate directly to my laptop. If anyone heads for my place, I know it. So what are you doing out here?"

"Just killing time. You've got a nice spread here." He glanced around at the rich, green pastureland.

"Thanks. I'm pretty proud of it."

Travis nodded toward the herd barely visible in the far distance. "She's good stock."

Brent shrugged. "She's not worth much if I can't get close to her."

Travis drank in a huge draft of air, desperate to kill the scent of Holly that lingered in his head. If he intended to make it through more nights like tonight without giving in to his own hunger, he needed a distraction.

"I'll see what I can do."

12

"YOU'RE LATE," EVAN declared when Holly walked into her office at noon the next day.

"We're not open on Sundays. So I'm early for Monday." She sat her purse on a nearby table and sank into her desk chair. "How long have you been here?"

"Long enough to have your coffee ready and waiting." He handed her a steaming cup. "Two sugars. No cream. Just the way you like it."

"Thanks."

"Oh, and I picked these up on the way." He handed her a plate with a fresh cinnamon bagel slathered with cream cheese. "Your favorite." And then he dropped into the chair opposite her. He watched her take a bite, an expectant look on his face. "So?"

"It's good," she said around a mouthful.

"Not the bagel." His eyes twinkled. "The date. Did you wear the shoes?"

Holly took a sip of coffee. "Yes and I already told you, it wasn't a date. We just hung out."

"Bob's best friend's sister said you were dancing." She nodded and he added, "Bob's best friend's sister also said it was one of those slow, sexy numbers where you wrap your arms around each other and hold on for dear life." He wiggled his eyebrows. "Did your cowboy whisper sweet nothings in your ear?"

"It wasn't like that."

"Did he kiss you good-night?"

He kissed me all over.

The words were there, but for some reason she couldn't quite push them past her lips. Crazy, right? The whole point for her to build a reputation as a good time girl. Lewd and lascivious behavior definitely qualified as a good time. At the same time, this was Evan. Her employee. Her friend. And *the* most die-hard romantic she'd ever met.

He stared so intently at her, a dreamy look in his eyes, that she suddenly didn't have the heart to bust his romantic bubble by going into the tawdry details.

"We had a nice time," she heard herself say.

Evan jumped from his seat and gave a loud squeal. A split-second later, he threw his arms around her neck. "I'm so happy for you. I knew you would find someone."

"He's only in town for a few days."

"Love will find a way. It always does. Just don't

give up hope. And promise me I'll get to be the mister of honor when you tie the knot."

"It's not that serious." *Yet.* The traitorous thought punctuated her words and she shook it away. "I'm just helping him out while he's in town." When Evan looked at her as if she'd just kicked his brand new puppy, she added, "But if the time ever comes, I promise the title will be yours." Not that it ever would. And certainly not with Travis Braddock.

He wasn't the marrying kind any more than she was, which made them perfect for each other.

Right now, that is.

"I knew it." Evan continued. "I don't care what Bob's best friend's sister said. You *do* like this guy."

"I don't *like* him. He's only in town for a little while and I'm showing him around. That's all. Sort of like a good Samaritan. So," She eyed her assistant. "What exactly did Bob's best friend's sister say? Besides the play-by-play action?"

"She said you've climbed aboard the crazy train and you're headed straight to Harlotsville. But don't you worry, I know better." Excitement crept into his expression. "Are you going out with him again?"

"Not tonight. I've got too much going." She stared at the pile of work sitting on her desk. A stack of swatches sat to one side. She had to pick new linens for Darla Lancaster's reception, new place settings, new cardstock for the place cards, new color schemes for the new venue. And, of course, she needed a new venue itself. But it was Sunday, which meant these details would have to wait until tomorrow morning when everyone opened up and she could do a few walk-throughs. In the meantime, she was making decisions and getting as much ordered online as possible. "Plus it's all-you-can-eat wing night at the Iron Horseshoe. Aunt Tootie and I never miss it," she reminded Evan. She'd even gone so far as to leave a message at Travis's motel telling him as much. Tonight was definitely out of the question.

As for tomorrow…

She tried to force the thought from her head. While she was completely committed to changing her image, she wasn't eager for a change of profession. She'd worry about tomorrow night when that came. In the meantime…

She reached for a book of swatches.

"WHAT DO YOU mean you can't make it tonight? It's two-for-one on the fry-the-hair-off-your-ass habanera wings. I've been overdosing on Maalox all day to get ready," Tootie whined.

"I'm sorry," Holly said. "But I'm neck-deep in satin birdseed roses. I tried to get Darla to go for bubbles with the late notice, but she wanted the satin roses. The ones we initially ordered were pink, but Evan found a few hundred red ones leftover from the Valentine's dance we catered at the senior center last year. We filled those with conversation hearts, but they'll hold birdseed, too. Since my week is going to be hellacious as it is, I have to knock out as much as possible, as quickly as possible."

"If I ever get married, I'm having bubbles. Everything else is just too damned much trouble. Not that I am," Tootie added as if she'd just realized what had come out of her mouth. "Marriage is too damned much trouble."

"Do you want me to give you a ride to the bar?"

"You just finish up your work. I can manage. I've got men standing in line, you know."

"I know. See you later."

Instead of sitting at her desk, Holly boxed up her supplies and headed next door to her house.

She changed into a spaghetti-strap tank top and shorts and grabbed a diet soda. Flipping on the TV, she settled cross-legged on the floor—a Jersey Shore marathon blazing on one of the cable channels—and went to work.

The next few hours passed painfully slow as she filled rosebud after rosebud with birdseed. By the time she reached the halfway mark (two hundred and fifty down, two-fifty to go), her neck was stiff, her arms felt *this* close to falling off, and she'd more than earned the carton of Cookies & Cream ice cream sitting in her freezer.

She'd just collapsed onto her couch, fixed her gaze on yet another fight between Ronnie and Sam (the Jersey Shore couple most likely to strangle each other), and shoveled a spoonful into her mouth when the doorbell rang.

A few heartbeats later, she found Travis Braddock standing on her doorstep in faded jeans and a red T-shirt that read *Save a Horse, Ride a Cowboy,* his black Resistol sitting on top of his head. The porch light outlined his broad frame and made him seem big and intimidating. Or maybe it was his frown doing that.

"I went by the Horseshoe and you weren't there." His gaze swept the length of her, from her bare toes covered with pale pink nail polish, up over bare legs, her shorts and tank, to her face. "I thought it was wing night."

"It is. But I was too busy to make it."

"Doing what?"

"Difficult bride." She stepped back and opened the door so he could see the living room and the pile of satin roses stacked high. "She changed her colors and her theme, and everything else, which means the pink roses that were already done won't work. I need red ones." She drew a deep breath and tried to ignore the delicious aroma of hot, sexy male that filled her nostrils.

Some un-nameable emotion flashed in his eyes. Pleasure? Relief? As if he'd been worried she was out with some other guy. As if he cared.

As if.

He rubbed his hands together. "Then I guess we'd better get to work."

"I really don't think that's a good idea." She didn't need Travis sitting in her living room, distracting her, no matter how appealing the idea of a helping hand was.

"Afraid you won't be able to resist my charm?"

"I know I still owe you for last night, but I don't have time for sex. I really need to finish this."

"I'm not here to collect on last night. I was worried about you."

He looked so sincere that she almost believed him. Almost.

But that would mean that he actually liked her. And *that* would really throw a crimp into her plan because she was having a hard enough time not liking him. If he liked her, then she would start liking him, and that would make it impossible to spend time with him and not feel like she was on a date.

At the same time, she was only halfway done. Her hands hurt and she could really use some help. "Okay, but you have to swear to be careful. The satin pulls away from the stem very easily."

"Careful's my middle name," he said. She stepped back, but he didn't make a move forward.

"What?"

"Are you going to invite me in?"

"Didn't I just do that?"

"You said I could help. You didn't say I was welcome inside."

His words struck something inside of her, tugging and pulling at a few memories, but she shook the strange thoughts away. "Please come in and help me."

A grin creased his handsome face. "I thought you'd never ask." He moved past her, his arm brushing the tip of her breast through the soft cotton of her shirt. Heat bubbled inside her and she caught a gasp just before it slid past her lips.

Not tonight. Tonight she had to finish the mountain of roses.

And after they finished?

The question rattled her nerves as she closed the door and turned to follow Travis Braddock into her living room.

13

TRAVIS SURVEYED THE mountain of roses. "Show me how to do this."

"First you take one of these empty ones and open the top…" Her words trailed off and he knew she felt his gaze, stroking up her bare legs.

Heat sizzled along her nerve endings and he read the startling truth in her gaze. The sensation had nothing to do with the way he was looking at her and everything to do with the fact that he was standing in her living room, offering to help her fill birdseed roses, of all things. And she liked the situation far more than any freedom-loving, no-strings-attached good time girl should have.

"You're looking at me."

"So?"

"So don't look at me."

"It's just looking. I'm not doing anything."

"You want sex," she said, accusing.

"Every man wants sex, sugar." His grin stopped her heart for a long moment. "It's genetic." His gaze collided with hers. "But if you want to know the real truth, I think it's you who wants sex. You're the one interpreting my looks. Which means it's *you* who's got sex on the brain. I'm just appreciating the view."

And what a view.

Where she'd looked drop-dead gorgeous last night, it was nothing compared to the woman he saw standing before him now.

She was barefoot, her legs smooth and tanned, with hardly a hint of makeup on her face. A tiny spaghetti strap inched down the curve of her shoulder and his fingers itched to reach forward and push the strap back up again.

But he wasn't here to give in to his own impulses. This was about stirring hers. About turning her on and making her want him until she let go of her inhibitions and reached for him the way she desperately wanted to.

And that meant he wasn't touching her. No pushing the strap back up or pulling it all the way down. Or stripping her bare and laying her down on the living room rug and spreading her long, tanned legs and—

"Travis?"

"Yeah?" He shook away the lustful images and ignored the tightening in his gut.

"Did you hear what I said?"

"Open rose, pour birdseed inside. Gotcha." Just to resist his own damned lust and bolster his defenses, he sat down on the opposite side of the pile. With a few feet between them, he was sure to keep his head and resist the beast growling inside of him.

He tried to tell himself that for the next few hours, but it was damned hard to believe it with her sweet scent filling his head and her soft breaths echoing in his ears. Despite the distance, he'd never felt quite so close to a woman. Or so at home.

The thought struck and he gave himself a mental shake. He'd lost his home. Rose was responsible and he was going to make her pay just as soon as Cody came back and spilled the beans on her whereabouts.

Until then, he was stuck here.

Stuck, he reminded himself.

If only he wasn't starting to feel as if this was the one place he was always meant to be. Here. With her.

"Why not just fill up a bucket and have everybody grab a handful?" he blurted, eager to distract himself from the dangerous thoughts. "It would save a helluva lot of time."

"It's not about convenience. It's about creating a moment that's memorable."

"How is this memorable?"

"It's one of the small touches that come together to make one big memorable event. It's not always birdseed roses, either. Some people like bubbles. Some shoot off fireworks while the bride and groom run for the car. I even had one couple that wanted the guests to blow whistles." At his questioning look, she added, "They were the girls and boys basketball coaches from the local high school. When they tied the knot, they wanted to feel like they were about to start the championship game. Hence the whistles."

"Sounds ridiculous."

"Maybe to you, because you're not a basketball coach. Speaking of which, what do you do?"

"I train horses."

"More of a hay tossing guy."

"I don't want people tossing hay at my wedding."

"You say that now, but once the wedding bug bites, you'd be surprised what you start asking for. First it's a little hay at the reception, maybe a rawhide neck tie to go with the tuxedo. The next thing you know, you want an ice sculpture that looks like Mr. Ed."

"You're a regular comedian."

She grinned and worked on a few more roses. "So how did you get into working with horses?" she asked after a long, silent moment.

"My family used to own a ranch in West Texas. I trained all of our cutting horses." He paused. "We lost it all in a fire. So now I go from ranch to ranch, working other people's horses."

"I hope no one was hurt."

"My brothers and I were the only ones to make

it out. My mother and my nephew both died. Not to mention our foreman and some of the workers."

"I'm really sorry."

He'd heard the same sentiment time and time again. From all of the people in town. From everyone who'd ever known about his past. But the words had never really eased the ache in his chest. Until now.

"I like fireworks."

"Excuse me?"

"Bubbles seem kind of lame and birdseed isn't very exciting. I think fireworks would be cool."

She smiled. "Me, too." Excitement leapt into her eyes. "The fourth of July has always been one of my favorite holidays. Aunt Tootie used to take me to the park and we'd stretch out on a blanket and watch the fireworks."

He had a quick vision of a small, blond-haired girl in pigtails, lying flat on her back on a gingham blanket, her eyes reflecting the spray of fireworks. His chest hitched.

"It sounds nice." So much that the vision quickly shifted and he saw the two of them, hands intertwined, staring up at the brilliantly lit sky.

They fell into a comfortable silence for the next few moments until he asked, "Is that what you had planned when you were engaged? A spray of fireworks?"

Her head snapped up as if he'd tapped some deep,

dark secret, but then her expression eased. "I guess it was just a matter of time until you heard the gossip. Hazards of a small town, right?" She shrugged. "Don't I wish. But Chad—my fiancé at the time— hated fireworks. He had a roman candle backfire when he was a kid and he never got over it."

"So what did he want?"

"I don't really know." She shook her head. "He didn't help in any part of the wedding planning. He said it was a girl thing and to just do what I wanted— with the exception of the fireworks, of course. But it was his wedding, too. I wanted to do what he wanted." She laughed, but there was a sadness in the sound that made his chest tighten. "Turns out, he wanted not to be married." She shrugged. "At least I figured it out before we actually said 'I Do.'"

"Did you love him?"

"He was a great guy. Nice-looking. Good job. Liked animals."

"But did you love him?" Travis persisted.

"I agreed to marry him, didn't I?"

"That still doesn't answer my question."

"It's a dumb question. If you agree to marry some-one, of course you love them."

"That or you love the idea of being in love."

The minute he said the words, she wanted to refute them but nothing came to her lips.

Because he was right.

The realization hit her as she sat there stuffing

birdseed roses, Travis sitting so close, his gaze so intent that she felt as if he could see all the things inside of her that even she couldn't see.

But Travis could. He saw inside her thoughts, to her deepest darkest feelings. How she'd wanted so badly to be the one in her family to break the cycle. To fall in love and live happily ever after like the proverbial fairy tale.

It was a silly notion. Travis didn't believe in fairy tales and he sure as hell didn't believe in the whole one man/one woman. Particularly since he was only a shell of a man now. But sitting there, staring into her soft eyes, feeling the contentment seeping through him, damned if he wasn't starting to think that maybe, just *maybe,* Cody and Brent were a damned sight smarter than he was giving them credit for.

"So where's this guy now?" he asked, eager to kill the sudden silence. His brothers were playing with fire by thinking for even a second that they could be happy. It was just a matter of time until the whole thing went down in a smoldering mess.

"Married to someone else." She laughed, but there was a sadness in the sound that made his chest tighten. "It turns out he didn't have an aversion to getting married. Just an aversion to getting married to me." She stiffened. "But all's well that ends well. I've got a great career and now all I have to do is move my personal life in the right direction. So what about you? Have you ever been engaged?"

"Once. A long, *long* time ago. But it didn't work out. We were too different."

"At least you both realized it before it was too late."

"I did, but she wasn't so lucky."

"What's that supposed to mean?"

"After the breakup, she committed suicide." Travis wasn't sure why he told her. He shouldn't have, but the softness in her gaze compelled him and damned if he could help himself. "She killed herself because of me." He'd thought those words many times, but he'd never said them out loud to anyone. He'd never wanted to. Until now.

Until Holly.

He waited for her to turn horrified eyes on him, to order him out of her house because he was such a despicable person. Instead, she shook her head and stared at him, her gaze sympathetic. "People don't commit suicide because of someone else. They commit suicide because they're weak. I should know. I've spent enough time watching my mother destroy herself, quote—over someone else—end quote, when it's really not their fault, but hers. While my Aunt Tootie refuses to ever get married, my mom refuses to give up on it. She thinks if she finds someone who loves her, it will make her love herself. But it doesn't work, because at the end of the day, she's still the same person. Needy. Dependent. Insecure. She gets so wrapped up in a man, so determined to ignore all her shortcomings, that the breakup is a devastating eye-opener and she can't deal with it. After number one, she started drinking. Number two sent her into a bottle of Prozac and lots of therapy. Three and four pushed her into prescription pain meds and five sent her on a six month sabbatical with a religious zealot who worships a ceramic turtle. She's about to marry a guy she met at one of the revivals. She'll probably end up on an episode of *Cult Intervention* after this one."

"Or the sixth time could be a charm and actually work out."

Her tense expression eased into a grin. "If I didn't know better, I'd say there was a romantic streak buried deep down inside of all that sex appeal."

"It's called practical. She's already been through the worst. The odds are in her favor for a good outcome." His gaze met hers. "And there you go, making a pass at me when I'm on my best behavior."

"I'm not making a pass at you."

"You said I had sex appeal."

"That's not a pass." She shrugged. "It's a fact." They fell into silence for a few moments and he knew she struggled with the push-pull of emotion rising inside her. Right versus wrong. Crazy versus common sense. Lust versus love. "A pass would be if I touched you or kissed you. I haven't done either one of those things." *And I won't.*

Determination gleamed hot and bright in her

gaze and he knew the emotional battle was over. Common sense had won and disappointment ricocheted through him. Still, Travis wasn't about to be put off.

"But you want to," he persisted.

"All I want is for you to pretend to be my boy toy when we're out in public. You're the one who wants sex."

"And you don't want it at all? Not even a little bit?"

He watched her struggle a bit more before she found her courage.

"What I really want is to finish these birdseed roses before midnight." She shifted her attention to the task at hand, as if she weren't this close to launching herself at him and kissing him senseless.

She was.

He saw the truth in the trembling of her hands and the quivering of her bottom lip. Felt it in the heat radiating from her luscious body.

She wanted it, but she didn't *want* to want it.

It wasn't enough. Not yet.

"What are you doing?" she blurted when he reached across and stroked the smooth inside of her leg.

"Making a pass." He caught her lips in a desperate kiss, his tongue plunging deep, stroking and tasting until she moaned into his mouth. His gut twisted and the beast stirred and it was all he could do to tear his mouth from hers.

And then he got the hell out of there before he gave in to the hunger that urged him to forget his pride and simply feed.

That day was coming, he knew. He could only hope that Holly made her move first and ended the deprivation. Otherwise, Travis was going to find himself well past the breaking point. And he feared that once he reached for her, he wouldn't be able to stop until he'd tasted her completely.

Her body and her blood.

14

IT WAS ALMOST nine o'clock when Holly finally opened her eyes the next morning. She took one look at the clock and panic bolted through her. She raced for the bathroom and had just stepped into a hot shower when she heard Aunt Tootie's voice over the answering machine.

"Rise and shine. It's a beautiful morning."

Wait a second.

She wiped at the soap dripping into her eyes and peeked past the shower curtains at the clock hanging on the wall.

Eight fifty-two. In the *morning*.

At the best of times, Aunt Tootie didn't roll out of bed until noon. Especially after tying one on with a platter of hot wings and several beers to wash them down. Even when she wasn't out the night before, she liked to sleep in.

"You don't stay looking as hot as me all these years without getting plenty of shut-eye."

Holly snatched up a towel, her hair still dripping with soap, and rushed for the phone.

"What's wrong? Are you okay? You're not hurt, are you?"

"Good morning to you, too," Tootie said. "And I'm as right as rain."

"You do know what time it is, don't you?"

"'Course I do. I been up since seven. Listen, I need a lift to Bingo tonight."

"Isn't Bingo for blue-haired ladies who have nothing better to do?"

"Bingo is a game for all ages. Besides, if you win three pots in a row, you go into a drawing for a singles cruise. That's what Buck said."

"Buck? *The* Buck Gentry? I thought you hated his guts."

"I do, but it's not like I could throw a wing in his face just for telling me about bingo. Besides, he was there alone and I was there alone and it seemed pretty damned silly for us to eat at separate tables. Do you know he likes the chile lime wings, too? Not without a Maalox chaser, of course. He's as old as dirt, after all. Did you know they have discos on those cruise ships?" Tootie went on a few more minutes about the dancing and the fun night life before Holly finally managed to hang up and head back to the shower to rinse the soap out of her hair.

Ten minutes later, she grabbed her birdseed roses and headed to the office.

"No way," Evan declared when she walked in, her arms overflowing. "You must have been up all night."

"A wedding planner's gotta do what a wedding planner's gotta do." Holly sat the roses aside and collapsed at her desk while Evan went on and on about how dedicated she was. She stifled a pang of guilt and kept her mouth shut about the extra pair of hands she'd had on the task. She knew what would happen. Evan would blow the whole thing out of proportion and before Holly knew it, she'd be picking out a china pattern and changing her relationship status on Facebook.

And really, they hadn't even fooled around.

They'd talked. Gotten to know each other. Shared. *Like a date.*

She shook away the notion and reached for the steaming cup of coffee sitting on her desk. She'd been honest about the sleepless night, but not because she'd been working on the roses. Thanks to Travis, she'd been almost done when he'd cut and run, and so she'd finished up before midnight.

No, she'd stayed up all night tossing and turning. Thinking. Wanting.

Sex.

Her sleepless night certainly had nothing to do with the fact that she liked Travis and that she couldn't forget the strange camaraderie she'd felt as

they'd worked side by side. Or the connection between them when he'd told her about his past and
she'd shared hers.

It didn't mean anything. He was only here until
the end of the week. And she'd sworn off relationships. So nothing could come of it.

To drive the point further home, she powered on
her computer. The familiar Love Buster logo blazed
across her screen. The chorus of Love Stinks by the
J. Giles Band blared from the computer speakers.

"Here," Evan said, handing her an energy drink.

"I've got coffee. I'm fine."

"I think you should drink it."

"Why?"

"Because you've got a long day ahead."

"Actually, it isn't so long because I made a dent
in things last night with the roses. I do need to look
at venues. I was thinking we might actually go with
the old theater downtown. With the right décor, it
could hold the number of people attending and it
would really suit the new theme."

"I've already booked it. We've got bigger fish to fry."

"Meaning?"

"Darla called a few minutes ago. She wants another dress."

"She's already got two."

"She's thinking a ball gown might be nice to
change into for the reception. She also wants to look
at bridesmaids dresses."

"We already have bridesmaids dresses."

"Tea-length dresses. She wants floor-length."

"For twenty-two bridesmaids?"

"Twenty-three. She added her cousin's wife."

"By Saturday?"

"Exactly."

"*This* Saturday?"

"That's the one."

"That's impossible," Holly blurted, panic bolting through her. "Did you tell her that's impossible?"

"Of course." He averted his gaze and Holly knew in an instant that something was up. "What else would I say?"

"Maybe that the idea of a floor-length ball gown and elbow gloves sounds positively dreamy?"

"Actually, I used the word stunning, but it's practically the same thing." Excitement leapt into his eyes. "Doesn't it sound totally awesome? And she's going to have all the girls carry these super fab little opera glasses I found online." He shoved a printout in front of her. "Aren't they divine? If we order today, we can get them over-nighted for only an extra hundred dollars."

Holly shook her head. "I think I feel sick."

"I promise to hold your hair if you start puking. Now drink up." He indicated the energy drink. "We're meeting Darla and her girls at the dress shop."

"When?"

"In five minutes."

"THE SLEEVES ARE just too puffy," Darla declared later that afternoon, vetoing dress number twenty the moment the salesperson held it up.

Holly resisted the urge to pop another Tylenol and settled for downing the rest of her Diet Coke. "Hit me again," she told Meg Sweeney, the owner of It's About You, the one and only exclusive dress boutique in Skull Creek.

Meg and Holly had grown up together. She'd married her high school sweetheart, once-upon-a-time-geek Dillon Cash, and they were now living happily-ever-after at a nearby ranch. Meg specialized in special occasion wear, from wedding to prom dresses to evening wear. She'd pulled out her entire stock the minute Darla had walked in, but after eight hours of Darla trying to make up her mind on not only her own dress, but the one for her bridesmaids, the choices were dwindling. They'd narrowed things down, but Darla still hadn't quite made up her mind.

Holly took the soda Meg handed her and glanced at the short black cocktail dress that hung on a nearby peg. Meg had brought it out a few hours ago out of desperation when Darla had quickly done a thumbs down on nearly every dress Meg put in front of her. The dress had looked great on, but Darla still wasn't sure it was what she wanted. Nor was she sure the silver number hanging nearby, floor-length and full, was what she wanted either.

And so they were all still here after five o'clock on a Monday afternoon.

"Don't you even want to try it on?" Darla's sister Shelly sprawled in a nearby chair, an anxious look on her face. She was decked out in her deputy sheriff attire, complete with a walkie talkie on her hip that buzzed every few minutes with an update on what was happening at the local sheriff's office.

"I can see how puffy the sleeves are without trying it on," Darla told her sister.

"Maybe your arms will fill up enough space to eliminate the puffiness," Shelly offered before pressing the button pinned to her lapel and informing the dispatcher that she still wasn't done. "Just try it and let's get this over with."

"I need to think," Darla declared. "Why don't you try on a few more dresses?"

"Because I already tried on twenty-three and you said we could go with number sixteen. Which means it's done. I'm finished. End of story." Shelly pushed to her feet. "I've got to get back. They're transferring a prisoner this afternoon from Austin and I have to be there to process him."

"You can't go now," Darla insisted. "I still haven't picked anything."

"If you don't like number sixteen, pick something else. Go long." She indicated the rack of floor-length gowns that they'd spent the whole day looking at.

"Go short." She indicated the one short black cocktail dress that Meg had scrounged up out of desperation when Darla had vetoed her entire stock. "They're all fine. I don't care."

"Me neither," offered another of the bridesmaids. "I've got a dinner I can't miss."

"Me, too," another bridesmaid offered.

"I've got a yoga class."

"Zumba," another added.

In a matter of seconds, the dressing room had cleared out with the exception of Darla, Meg and Holly. Even Evan had made a run for it, claiming a dinner date with Bob's parents who already hated his guts and would totally despise him if he showed up late.

Holly gathered her courage, preparing herself for the fit Darla was about to throw. But instead of frowning, a sad expression touched her face. Her eyes widened and grew bright. "I guess I'm doing this by myself," Darla's words faded into a sniffle and her chest caught.

So much for bridezilla.

Holly felt her own eyes burn and she blinked. "Meg, why don't you clear some of these dresses out of here while I talk to Darla for just a second?" Meg nodded and left the room, the curtains swishing closed behind her.

"I'm sorry," Darla blurted. "I know I shouldn't get

upset over something so small. Sam keeps telling me that. But it's just that he's so perfect and I want this wedding to be perfect."

"It will be. As long as the two of you are there, that's all that really matters. You just need to re-member why you're doing all of this in the first place. Because you love him." A strange expres-sion crept over Darla's face, as if Holly had struck a nerve. She knew then and there that something wasn't right with her bride-to-be. "You do love him, don't you?"

"Of course, I do." Darla forced a laugh, as if Hol-ly's question was the most ridiculous thing she'd ever heard. "Are you kidding? I'd be crazy not to love him. He's everything I've ever wanted in a man." She wiped at her eyes and gathered her com-posure.

Just like that, her cool, confident, everything-better-be-my-way-or-else mask slid back into place. "I'll go with the silver gown." She pointed to number six that hung nearby. "And the girls can wear that one." She pointed to a floor length taffeta number with red and silver trim. "I really need to get going. Sam and I are having dinner with his parents. Make sure they put a rush on the dresses," she added when Meg walked into the dressing room. And then she was gone.

"You think you can pull this off?" Holly asked the boutique owner.

"I've got a store in Austin that I work with. They've got more of the bridesmaids dresses. We'll have to have them altered, but we can pull it off. The bride's dress is custom, but she's close to the sample size so we can alter that one. All in all, I think we can make it happen." She let out a long breath, then turned to Holly. "What about you? You've been eyeing that little black number all day. Are you going to try it on or what?"

"I can't imagine where I would wear something like that," Holly said, before she caught herself. If she wanted people to start seeing her differently, she needed to start acting differently. "Okay, I'll try it."

Meg smiled, grabbed a handful of dresses to return to stock and disappeared from the dressing room. The curtain swished closed behind her.

Holly glanced outside—it was starting to get dark. Still, she had time. She unbuttoned her white blouse and shimmied out of her black pencil skirt. She reached for the little black number and was about to step into it when she heard the deep, familiar voice.

"I like it."

Her head snapped up and she found Travis Braddock lounging in the doorway behind her, a sinful grin on his face and a wicked light in his eyes.

And where he'd been dead set on helping her out with the roses last night and keeping his hands to himself, she knew the moment their gazes locked that he had something much different on his mind tonight.

Sex.

A girl could only hope.

15

I LIKE YOU.

The words whispered through her head and sent a prickle of heat to every erogenous zone—from her earlobes to her nipples, the backs of her knees to the arch of each foot and a zillion spots in between.

Her hands stalled and she became keenly aware of a few all-important facts. Number one, she was almost naked. Number two, she was almost naked in front of Travis Braddock who lounged in the dressing room doorway. Number three, she was almost naked in front of Travis Braddock, and it made her very nervous because she couldn't help but wonder what he was thinking.

Crazy.

It didn't matter what he thought. Or what she thought. Their relationship was strictly physical. There were no games. No guessing. No wondering when the other would call or show up or what food they liked to eat or what they liked to drink.

Never again.

She concentrated on the buttons rather than the handsome picture he made standing there wearing jeans and a button down black shirt, the sleeves rolled up to the elbows, his hat tipped low on his handsome face.

"That's definitely my favorite outfit in the store."

"I'm still wearing my underwear." She indicated the dress in her hands. "I haven't actually put anything on yet."

A fierce green gaze swept the length of her in a leisurely motion that made her nipples pebble and press against the cups of her favorite lace bra. "That's the point, sugar." He grinned and stepped inside the room. The curtain swished shut behind him.

She put her back to him, as if that could shut him out. The room, set up like a giant octagon, had mirrors on all sides and she couldn't escape his reflection. "What are you doing here? We're not supposed to meet for another couple of hours."

His gaze captured hers in one of the mirrors. "I thought we could get started early. You need all the help you can get." He grinned and an echoing shiver went through her body.

She tried to undo the buttons on the dress, but before she could take her next breath, his arms came around her and his hands closed over hers. "Let me help," he murmured as his long, lean fingers helped her work the buttons through the openings.

She tried for a calm voice. "I think I can manage on my own."

"Two's a charm."

"I thought three was the charm."

"Not in this case." His deep, compelling voice vibrated against the shell of her ear.

"This isn't part of our deal," she heard herself protest.

His hands fell away and he let her slide the last button free, but he didn't step back. He simply stood there, behind her, close but not touching. "What are you talking about?"

"The flirting. You're flirting with me and I didn't agree to flirting."

"Darlin', flirting implies playing and I'm doing no such thing. I'm serious." His fingertip prowled along the slope of her bare shoulder and goose bumps danced down her arms. Her fingers went limp and the dress slithered to the carpeted floor.

She managed to swallow. "Then let's do it."

"To get it over with?"

"Something like that."

"Something like that or that?" He stared at her. "You either want to or you don't."

"I want to." Her voice softened as the sleepless night spent thinking about him finally overwhelmed her. "I really want to."

He closed the heartbeat of space between them, his denim-covered thighs pressing against the backs of her legs, his groin nestled against her bottom so she could feel just how serious he truly was. His cotton shirt cushioned her shoulder blades. The material brushed against the sensitive backs of her arms as he slid his hands around her waist. Strong, work-roughened fingertips skimmed her rib cage, stopping just shy of her lace-covered breasts.

It was highly erotic watching him in the mirror, his dark hands on her skin, his powerful body framing hers. It was like tuning in to one of those HBO after hour shows, but even better. Because it was real and she could actually see what he was doing to her, as well as feel it.

The heated flush creeping up her neck, the goose bumps chasing up and down her arms, the part to her lips, the catch of her breath.

"So pretty," he murmured huskily as his large hands cupped her breasts.

"It's Belgian lace."

"Not the bra, sugar. I was talking about this." He fingered the tip of one dark nipple peeking through the scalloped pattern. "And this." He touched the other throbbing crest, rolled it between his thumb and forefinger. "Definitely the prettiest thing I've seen in a long time."

Lightning zapped her and she barely caught the moan that slid up her throat.

His hand moved down, stroking over her abdomen until he reached her panties. He caught the edges, tugging them down her hips, her thighs, until they pooled on top of the dress at her feet.

He slid his fingers between her legs and touched her. He slicked his thumb over her clitoris in a delicious touch that made her close her eyes and clamp down on her bottom lip.

She wanted to melt, but he was there to keep her from sliding to the floor, his strong arms anchoring her to the hard length of his body.

"Open up, sugar. I want to see you when you go wild." He rubbed her a few more breathless moments before sliding a finger deep inside. She trembled and he drew her closer, holding her with one hand while he drove her crazy with the other. He moved his fingers, plunging and stroking. The pleasure was intense, but it was nothing compared to the brightness of his gaze as he held hers in the mirror. The green of his eyes was so intense that it seemed to shift, brighten, glow into an amazing purple

She blinked and the color faded. He moved his fingers again and sensation bolted through her. A delicious orgasm gripped her body. She caught her lip, fighting back the cry that worked its way up her throat, the same way she fought back the sudden fear coiling inside of her, a feeling intensified by the way he stared so deeply into her eyes.

As if there was something much more intense going on here than a little quickie.

His shoulders shuddered and she had the incredible thought that he was feeling the same sweet orgasm that crested inside of her. His muscles tightened and the tendons in his neck stood out in stark relief. Ecstasy glittered in his gaze and a growl rumbled up his throat.

At the same time, there was no mistaking the hardness throbbing against her buttocks. Proof that he hadn't come close to a climax.

She somehow knew that he didn't need to. This was more than just sex between them. The connection was deeper. Stronger. *No!*

"I—I need to get out of here," she said, grappling for her panties.

For a split-second, she didn't think he would let her go, but then they heard the swish of drapes.

Holly grabbed the dress pooled at her feet and yanked it up a heartbeat before Meg's familiar voice echoed around them.

"I found a couple more dresses you might like to try—" The words stumbled to a halt as the boutique owner came up short in the doorway. Her gaze darted between Travis and Holly, and a knowing gleam lit her eyes. "I'm sorry, I didn't mean to interrupt. I didn't know anyone was back here—"

"I'll take this one," Holly blurted, yanking up the

straps on the dress at the speed of light. "Can I wear it out?"

"Certainly." Meg cast a glance between the two of them and a grin tugged at her lips. "I'll ring it up."

"Great." Holly grabbed her purse and bolted past Travis as fast as her high-heeled sandals could carry her. "I've got to go. I'll meet you later." But first she needed to clear her head and forget the crazy thoughts pounding at her sanity.

Like how there was more to Travis Braddock than met the eye and how she liked it.

How she liked *him*.

Crazy.

At least that's what Holly tried to tell herself. If only she actually believed it.

16

TRAVIS BARELY RESISTED the urge to haul ass after Holly.

He wouldn't.

He'd pushed her a little too far tonight and now it was time to back off. He'd shown up at the dress shop, determined to tease her until she gave in to the need bubbling inside of her. She had. For a few precious moments. But then Meg had interrupted them. Reality had hit, and Holly had run hell for leather.

"I'll meet you later."

Fat chance. He came to that conclusion as he sat parked in front of the honky tonk later that night, waiting for Holly to show up.

Hours ticked by, but Holly didn't show.

He tried to tell himself that maybe she'd had a flat tire, maybe something had gone wrong. But deep in his gut he knew better. He didn't feel the unease.

The panic. The fear. Rather, he felt an overwhelming sense of disappointment.

Because oddly enough, he wanted to see her. To hear her voice, the steady beat of her heart and the deep, soft whisper of her breaths. He liked being with her, and she liked being with him. She just didn't want to admit it.

That, in itself, should have been enough to send him inside, in search of another female to bide his time with until Cody came home. He didn't do *liking* any more than he did monogamy. It was the nature of the beast. He was compelled to seek out women.

Oddly enough though, he didn't feel compelled at all as he watched a group of single women walk into the bar for girls night out. Any one of them would have wanted him.

The thing was, he didn't want any of them.

He wanted Holly. Her arms wrapped around him, her lush body open and inviting beneath his, her sweet blood flowing into his mouth.

He slammed the door on that last thought and headed back to the motel, and straight into a cold shower. He stood under the icy spray for several long seconds, trying to clear his head and cool the fire blazing inside of him.

No such luck.

He toweled off and stretched out on the bed. His muscles felt stiff. His body ached. The ceiling fan whirled overhead and the air whispered down the length of his body, over his bare chest, his abs, his stiff cock.

Desire knifed through him, cutting him to the quick and he growled. He was hard to the point that his teeth literally hurt. Frustration welled inside of him and he barely resisted the urge to go over to her house. To pound down her door, throw her onto the nearest horizontal surface and sate the hunger raging inside of him.

She wouldn't have stopped him.

No, she would have given herself to him because, hey, she owed him. He was helping her and so she intended to pay up. But while she would be willing, she would also convince herself she was doing it to keep her word. Not because she wanted to.

Because she wanted him.

He'd vowed to hold back until she gave herself to him, free and clear. And he meant it.

Just because he'd backed off, however, didn't mean he had any intention of letting her stand him up. She was acting on an *out of sight, out of mind* policy, and so she was keeping her distance. It was a strategy that would have worked with the average guy.

But Travis was far from average.

They'd had sex—*great* sex—and forged a connection. Not as strong as that forged with blood, but still, it was viable. If he chose to use it.

He never had before. In fact, he'd always run the

other way, moving on, fortifying the distance until the link between vampire and human weakened and ultimately disappeared. That's what would happen with Holly, as well.

But until then, Travis meant to use it to his full advantage.

He closed his eyes and thought about the way she'd felt in his arms tonight. How warm and soft and trembling. He could still smell the lush scent of her arousal. Hear the frantic thud of her heart in his head. Feel the silkiness of her skin against his...

The feelings shifted, until he wasn't just hearing her heartbeat. He heard the rush of water and the sound of a radio playing softly in the background. The sweet aroma of strawberries and cream filled his senses and soap bubbles tickled his skin.

He saw her then, standing in the shower, her hair streaming wet down her back, her body slick and naked.

And then he touched himself.

WATER PELTED HOLLY, running in rivulets over her heated flesh. She turned her face toward the hot spray and tried to clear her head. She needed to stop thinking about what had happened in the dressing room. About the way Travis had looked at her. As if he'd never seen a woman he wanted more.

As if.

Women were his thing and Holly was just another

in a long, endless line. She didn't mean anything to him. She never would because he wasn't sticking around. And even if he had been, she wasn't about to make the same mistake she'd made three times already.

She wasn't falling for him.

She turned the temperature up a few notches and steam fogged the air around her. She put her back to the spray and let the water soothe her exhausted muscles. She needed to relax. To sleep.

She had a full day tomorrow with Darla and the myriad of changes they were still trying to execute in time for Saturday's event. They were changing the menu from a buffet to a sit-down dinner, not to mention they needed new table linens and china and place cards and...

The list went on and on and the only way she was going to keep her sanity would be if she got some much needed sleep. That meant no tossing and turning and thinking about Travis Braddock.

His name stuck in her head and conjured all sorts of lustful thoughts. She saw herself naked and panting on her back, Travis between her legs, plunging into her over and over until she cried out. Travis below her, grasping her hips, helping her ride him fast and furious. Travis standing in the shower right in front of her, reaching for her...

She shook away the image and grappled for the soap. Steam thickened the air and water burned her eyes. Her fingers wrapped around the bar and she concentrated on lathering her hands. The feel of wet, slick soap made her palms tingle as bubbles squeezed between her fingers. Sliding the bar back into the tray, she ran her soapy hands up and down her throat, over her shoulders. But she didn't feel her own fingertips, she felt his. Trailing over her skin, circling her nipples, grasping the ripe nubs and twisting until she felt the pull of desire between her legs.

Her hands stilled and she drew a deep, steadying breath.

She wasn't doing this. She wasn't fantasizing about a man she'd made up her mind not to fantasize about. No fantasizing, no dreaming, no planning.

No getting her hopes up.

That's where she'd gone wrong in the past. She'd looked to each and every man in her life, thinking 'this is it.' The one. The future.

She'd been wrong. Just as she was wrong now.

Travis wasn't her future. She hardly knew him. Sure, they'd talked and she felt more connected to him than she had any man in a long time. *Ever.* But that didn't mean anything.

Even more, it didn't change anything.

Travis Braddock was temporary.

So give it a rest, will ya?

She focused her attention on reaching for the shampoo bottle. The sooner she finished, the sooner she could pile into bed and forget everything. She popped the push-up lid and was about to squirt the creamy liquid into her palm when the hard, smooth plastic brushed the ripe crest of her nipple. Lightning zapped her and her nerves buzzed.

She wasn't going to do it.

That's what she told herself, but her hands seemed to have a mind of their own. Her fingertips slid around the bottle, circling and grasping as she rasped the edge against her nipple. Once. Twice. *Yum.*

The cool hardness was a stark contrast to her soft, heated skin, and sensation saturated her senses. She moved the bottle again, slowly at first in a soft, seductive motion. Pleasure rippled through her body and her heart pounded. She played with the ripe nub a few more seconds before touching the edge to her other nipple. It sprang to life immediately, greedy for attention.

She meant to stop. Really she did. But it felt so good and she'd been so on edge and so damned needy after the encounter with Travis in the dress shop. And maybe, just maybe, if she did this now, she might be able to satisfy the lust burning inside of her and forget him long enough to sleep.

The edge of the bottle slid down, following the underside of her breasts, the sensitive skin of her belly. The hard coolness trailed over her belly button and lower until she reached the vee between her legs.

Hunger spurted through her when she felt the edge

of the bottle ruffle the damp curls that covered her mound. The sensation moved lower still. The hard, cool edge teased the slick folds and rasped her clit. Her lips parted on a gasp and her knees trembled. The air seemed to thicken even more, the steam fogging the shower glass and cocooning her in a thick blanket.

She blinked and just like that, Travis was there with her, right in front of her, steam edging his tall, powerful form. He was completely naked, his broad, powerful chest covered with a sprinkling of dark hair. His penis was hard and thick, the base surrounded by a swirl of dark hair. The same hair sprinkled his hard, muscular legs.

The water sluiced over him, running in rivulets down his tanned skin and she couldn't help herself. She reached out, touching the slick muscle.

She blinked, thinking he would disappear, *hoping*.

He didn't. He was still there. Right in front of her. Wet and naked and real.

"I missed you tonight." The words whispered through her head, so clear and distinct that a ripple of anxiety went up her spine.

Followed by a rush of excitement as he took the shampoo bottle from her hands and touched the edge to her nipple. He rasped the edge back and forth, teasing, taunting. She caught her lip between her teeth as pleasure spurted through her and the pressure tightened between her legs. The sensation grew, wringing a frantic whimper from her. She was so close to the edge. Another glide of the bottle and she would plunge straight over.

But then the bottle disappeared and she felt his hands. Cupping her breasts. Teasing her nipples. Swirling down her abdomen. Slipping between her legs. He rubbed her, teasing and taunting before sliding a finger deep inside.

Sensation bolted through her and a delicious orgasm gripped her body. She caught her lip, fighting back the cry that worked its way up her throat, the same way she fought back the strange sensation coiling inside her.

A feeling that something wasn't right.

That he wasn't right.

Real.

She reached for him then, sliding her hands around his hard, pulsing shaft. She moved, slicking her palms up and down, tracing the ripe purple head until he growled so low and deep that she felt the sound pulling between her legs.

He caught her lips in a fierce kiss, plunging his tongue deep, devouring her with his mouth as he thrust his erection into her grasp, over and over, letting her work him into a frenzy.

A growl vibrated the air around them and he pulled back. She opened her eyes to see him through the thick steam. He stared down at her, his gaze pulsing a hot, vibrant purple as he plunged deep into her hands one more time. His lips parted and she caught a flash of white as he bared his teeth—

She blinked and just like that, the image disappeared, fading into the steamy mist that filled the shower and leaving her with an odd sense of emptiness.

As if he'd left her.

As if he'd ever been there in the first place.

She stared down at her empty hands clutching the shampoo bottle and gave herself a mental shake.

Shoving open the shower door, she stepped out into the bathroom and reached for a towel. She rubbed at her body, eager to dispel the memory of his hands.

Her own hands, she reminded herself. This had been a one-man show, no matter how it had felt otherwise.

It was as if Travis wasn't just in her memories, but he'd crawled deep down inside of her head. Her heart.

She hadn't just felt him surrounding her in the shower. She'd felt him inside of her. His passion blazing through her body. His need mingling with her own.

Wait a second.

What was she doing? Losing it, that's what. That explained the purple eyes and the fangs. Seriously? *Fangs?* There were fantasies and then there were fantasies. She'd definitely crossed the line into the land of the looney.

On top of that, the old Holly was rearing her ugly head, making more out of the situation than what was actually there. Imagining a connection when really, it was just her own wishful thinking.

That's what was happening.

She was sliding right back into her old ways.

Sliding, but she hadn't gone completely down the drain. She could climb back up. She just had to remember how miserable she'd been after Chad. And the others before him. If she could focus on those disastrous relationships, she'd be okay.

Burying herself under the covers, she closed her eyes and tried to conjure an image of Chad's lying, cheating face. Nothing came. It was the same for Ben. And Allen.

She saw only Travis staring down at her in the shower. Travis's reflection in the dressing room. Travis sitting in her living room. *Travis.*

Holly blew out an exasperated breath, climbed out of bed and headed downstairs to the living room. A few minutes later, she flipped on the TV and cranked up the volume, determined to distract herself and ignore the truth niggling in her head.

That like it or not, she was falling for Travis Braddock.

17

HOLLY SPENT THE next few days neck-deep in making the changes for Darla's wedding. All of her other brides got put on hold until she could breathe the following Monday. Until then… It was all about Darla.

Thankfully.

With her week so swamped, Holly barely had time to think about Travis, much less see him.

Except in her dreams.

He came to her every night in the most erotic fantasies.

Erotic and vivid.

Dreams that had her waking up in a feverish sweat, her body damp and pulsing, her lips swollen and bruised.

Dreams.

She held tight to the thought and tried to concentrate on Darla who stood in the local catering kitchen of Millicent Dupree, Skull Creek's equivalent of Rachel Ray and the culinary genius responsible for Saturday's formal sit-down dinner.

"But it's Thursday," Millicent was saying. "You can't make anymore changes at this point. The wedding is the day after tomorrow."

"I know, but I want filet mignon."

"I already have prime rib au jus in the works for five hundred people." Millicent stared at Darla as if the bride-to-be just asked her to sacrifice her first-born. "What am I supposed to do with all that meat? And there's only three days before the event. It's impossible to get enough filet delivered here in time."

"We're smack dab in the middle of ranch country," Darla countered. "We've got beef coming out of our ears."

"Fine then. Why don't you head on down to the Circle B and see how many you can round up, butcher and package for me? And of course, you know that the filet has to be aged a certain amount of time before I will even consider cooking and serving it."

"Holly," Darla said, turning to her. "Do something."

"She can't do anything," Millicent said. "Because this is not going to happen."

Darla cast imploring eyes on Holly, but all she could do was shrug. "Millicent's right. This is one detail you're going to have to bend on. It's impossible to get that quantity of meat delivered here in time."

"Meat is meat," Shelly chimed in, fingering the handcuffs hanging from her belt as if she were seriously considering using them on her sister. "Why are you making such a big deal about this? Can we go now? I really have to get back to the station. Matt's given me so much time off for this wedding that I want him to take the afternoon off before the craziness really gets started." Sheriff Matt Keller was fairly new in town. He was married to the local salon owner and ex-beauty queen. They'd both caused quite a stir a year or so back when Sheriff Keller had been caught in some racy photographs, or so everyone had thought. But since then, he'd proven that the pictures were bunk and he'd won his first election with a landslide.

"But my bachelorette party is tonight?"

"I'll be there. I might be a few minutes late—"

"But you're in charge of it."

"There are plenty of people to cover for me for a few minutes."

"But Sam's sister will be there."

"And?"

"And what will she think?"

"That I have a life. She can serve cake until I get there. Don't sweat it." She motioned with her hand. "Let's move this along. We'll take the prime rib."

"No, we won't," Darla argued.

"Perfect." Millicent waved them out. "Now get out of my kitchen. I'm doing cannollis for the Bachman Birthday party tonight and I need to get into my pastry zone." She turned her back, effectively dismissing Darla who looked ready to explode, and left the room.

"But—"

"Darla, why don't we go see what the baker came up with for the cake?" Holly offered.

"I don't want to see the cake," Darla insisted. "I want to settle this."

"It's settled," Shelly said. She murmured a few words into her walkie talkie. "I've got to go. I'll see you later." And then she disappeared in a blur of beige.

"We can't have prime rib," Darla whined once her sister had left. "We just can't."

"I happen to like prime rib. So do a lot of people I know."

Darla shook her head. "The entire wedding is going to be ruined because the reception is going to be ruined because the food is all wrong."

"It's a small detail in the big picture of things. I'm sure you'll see that once it's all said and done. Millicent makes an excellent prime rib. I know you don't like it, but—"

"I do like it. But Tom's favorite is filet mignon."

"But this wedding isn't just about Tom, is it? I'm sure he'll understand—"

"I *have* to have the filet." She turned desperate eyes on Holly. "It has to be right." *I have to be right.*

The truth gleamed in her gaze and Holly couldn't help herself. She had to ask again.

"Darla, are you sure you're in love with Tom?"

Anxiety stretched across her expression as she seemed to search for words. "He's a great guy," she finally said. "The perfect man."

"Yes, but do you love him?"

"I love everything about him."

"But do you love him?"

A strange light flickered in Darla's gaze and Holly knew the truth in an instant—that the young woman didn't love Tom so much as she loved the idea of marrying someone like him. She wanted a Prince Charming. A Mr. Perfect.

"I can't get married without filet mignon." Darla's voice drew her from her thoughts. "I just can't."

No problem. That's what Holly should have told her. She would call every supplier from here to Dallas if she had to in order to find enough and get it here in time for the wedding.

That's what Darla's wedding planner would have said. Particularly a wedding planner who didn't receive the last half of her fee until after the event.

But at that moment, Holly didn't care about money. She knew what Darla was going through. She'd felt it. She just hadn't had the courage to step up and stop it. Instead, she'd been so obsessive that she'd pushed Chad away until he'd called it quits.

Holly knew because she'd felt the exact same way.

The truth crystallized as she stood staring at her distraught bridezilla. Travis had been right about her. She *had* been more in love with the idea of being in love than with the man himself.

The moment when Chad had broken off the engagement, she'd actually felt relief. A quick feeling that had lasted only a few heartbeats until she'd had to face the world with her failure and mourn the carefully planned happily-ever-after she'd mapped out for herself. But she hadn't been miserable because she'd loved Chad. She hadn't.

Not like she loved Travis.

The thought struck and she pushed it back out and slammed the door. She barely knew him. Several days was not long enough to fall for someone. Even for a woman with her record.

She didn't love him. Not yet.

And she was keeping it that way.

"So don't get married," she heard herself say. "Postpone the wedding for a few months. Just until you can get everything right," she added when Darla looked shocked. "Take your time," she continued. "That way, you can get everything just perfect." *Or realize what a big mistake you're about to make.*

"Extra time would be nice," Darla said as indecision danced across her expression. But then her cell phone beeped with a text, drawing her from her thoughts and she shook her head. "The prime rib is fine," she muttered, staring at the screen on her phone. "We'll just go with that. I've really got to run. The party is in a few hours and I still have to meet Tom to sign the pre-nup." She left the caterer and Holly headed next door to the baker to check on the changes to the wedding cake.

By the time she got back to the office, it was almost six o'clock.

"Quitting time," Evan announced, powering off his laptop. "Our last evening off before the craziness starts. Bob's treating me to dinner." He arched an eyebrow as Holly closed several files and straightened up her desk. "What about you?" His gaze twinkled. "Are you seeing Mr. Tall, Dark and Luscious?"

She'd been avoiding any mention of Travis, but she knew it was truth time. She averted her gaze and busied herself packing up. "We're not seeing each other any more."

"Oh, no," Evan squealed. He reached her in a heartbeat and threw his arms around her shoulders. "You must be a wreck!"

"I'm fine." She hugged him back for a second before pulling free. "Really. It's no big deal. I told you it was nothing serious. He's only going to be in town for a few more days." She shrugged. "But it was fun while it lasted."

Evan eyeballed her a split-second before reaching for the phone.

"What are you doing?"

"Cancelling with Bob. You need someone to talk you off the ledge."

"I'm not on the ledge. I'm not even close. Seriously."

"That's what they all say. But the next thing you know, they're drowning in a gallon of Ben & Jerry's Chunky Monkey." He shook his head. "I won't let you do this to your hips."

"My hips aren't exactly small."

"That's what I'm saying. You can't afford even an ounce." He started to dial. "I'll just call Bob and then you and I can pick up some sushi and have a girl's night—"

Holly punched the button and broke the connection. "Thanks, but no thanks. I'm fine. Really."

"You can't go home alone."

"I'm not going home," Holly added. She wanted to forget Travis. With Evan playing twenty questions all night and trying to console her, that would be impossible. "I'm going out."

"Bingo with Aunt Tootie is not going to cheer you up."

"I'm not going to Bingo. Besides, Aunt Tootie doesn't play Bingo on Thursday nights." She hardly played Bingo at all. When Holly had talked to her yesterday, Tootie had said she'd had an alright time on Sunday night but that it wasn't something she wanted to do again. She needed excitement. "They're having their pool tournament at the honky tonk tonight. It's part of the in-door rodeo. No way would she miss it."

"Tonight's the weekly pot. Tootie's in contention for the grand prize. That's what Bob's friend's cousin said. She said Tootie is the reigning Bingo champion. She played twenty cards last night and won three pots."

"*My* Aunt Tootie?"

"You know another eighty-one-year-old in blue eye shadow and zebra print pants?" Evan wiggled his eyebrows. "He also said she was sitting next to Buck Gentry the entire time."

"She hates Buck Gentry."

"Just like she hates Bingo?" Evan shook his head and gave her another concerned look. "I'm calling Bob—"

"I'm going out," Holly blurted, "on a date." *What?*

"Yeah, a date. Tonight."

Evan's hands stilled. "With who?"

Good question. "Just a friend of a friend of a friend. We're going to dinner. And dancing. So, you see, there's no need to worry."

He eyed her for a long moment, as if searching for some sign that she was about to go on an ice cream binge.

"Well, all right," he finally said. "But I'm doing a drive-by later tonight and you'd better not be home."

Not a problem because the last thing Holly wanted was to fall into her own bed. She knew what waited for her in her dreams. As exciting as that was, she was too mixed up inside to deal with it tonight. She needed to get out. Live it up. Forget.

Besides, it was time to test out the new Holly.

Her one outing with Travis at the honky tonk had actually done some good. Tommy Peterson had tipped his hat to her at the diner yesterday. And Jim Mitchell had given her a wink when she'd gone into the pharmacy. Both men were die-hard cowboys known for their escapades with women.

Holly had never been on their radar except when Jim had asked her to plan his parents' fiftieth wedding anniversary last year. He hadn't winked at her then. Instead, he'd called her ma'am and barely looked her in the eye. No long, leisurely treks up her body with his hooded gaze. No wicked thoughts. Nothing.

Until now.

He'd been with Susie that night at the bar and he'd seen the new improved Holly with his own two eyes. And obviously he'd liked what he'd seen.

There was only one way to find out.

Her mind made up, she packed up her things and headed home to change.

18

SHE WAS WEARING the dress.

His gaze zeroed in on the woman currently boot-scootin' her way across the dance floor.

She wore the short, black spaghetti strap sequined number she'd been trying on that night at the dress shop. Add a pair of black stilettos that emphasized her long legs, and Holly Simms looked like the hottest ticket in Skull Creek.

But it wasn't just the skimpy clothes that made her so sexy. Her hair, slightly mussed from all the dancing, flowed down past her shoulders. Her skin was flushed and glowing. Her eyes sparkled with excitement and wonder, as if she couldn't quite believe she was here and this was happening.

Every man in town was falling all over her. She was on her fifth dance partner in as many songs and Travis could see at least two more guys sizing her up, wanting a turn.

Initially, when she'd first presented her cockama-mie idea, Travis had had his doubts that a little face time with him could dirty up her image. But damned if she hadn't been right. The men in this town had eaten it up.

Including the cowboy she was currently dancing with. He looked ready to take a great big bite out of her and damned if she didn't seem to like it.

Travis took a deep swig of Coors, but the liquid didn't ease the tightening in his gut or sate the thirst that clawed at his throat. He needed to feed in the worst way.

While he'd been communicating telepathically with Holly and they'd had some of the hottest sex ever, he hadn't actually satisfied his hunger. Sure, he felt every moment and he'd enjoyed the experience. But to actually soak up her energy, he had to touch her with more than just his mind.

Hunger gnawed at him and he forced his gaze away from her, to the multitude of women milling around him. There were plenty. All his for the taking. One glance and he could be in the nearest bathroom, getting it on with anyone who caught his fancy.

He would.

Just as soon as he finished his drink.

He took another swig and watched as the cowboy holding Holly bent her backwards in a dip before pulling her back up and into his arms. He twirled her, then pulled her back against him.

Travis downed another gulp and barely resisted the urge to cross the room and throw her over his shoulder. Hell, he'd taught her that last move, for Christ's sake. And here she was, doing it with someone else. Where was the gratitude?

That's all he wanted—for her to be a little bit appreciative and remember how she got here. She ought to be throwing her arms around *him* and thanking him for all he'd done.

Her arms looped around the guy's neck instead. A smile curved her full lips and she stared up at the cowboy with smoldering eyes, as if he were the answer to her most erotic dreams.

As if he'd been going to her every night, touching and stirring and tasting her, instead of Travis himself.

Not that he cared.

Hell, he didn't give a rat's ass. It was time to call it quits and move on. He knew that. This was too hard. Besides, he was leaving in a few days. What the hell difference did it make anyway? He could have any other woman in the world, so why worry over this one?

Sure, she had a great smile and a nice laugh. And he actually liked talking to her. But so friggin' what?

Any woman would do.

He forced his attention to a tall, leggy brunette and smiled. She smiled back and he knew in an instant that she would gladly abandon the schmuck sitting next to her. She turned, said a few words and excused herself. A split-second later, she slid onto the bar stool next to him.

"My name's Nicole."

He nodded. "Travis."

"So where are you from, Travis?" she asked, starting with small talk, licking her lips suggestively every now and then, her gaze hooded. She leaned into him with a comment or two and stayed there, her arm against his, her hand resting on his thigh. It was too easy.

And everything with Holly was too damned hard.

He was too hard.

His groin twitched and his muscles tightened when he glanced at Holly again. Their gazes collided for a brief moment and excitement jerked through him. Followed by a rush of *what the hell?* when she didn't so much as smile.

There was no wave or nod of acknowledgment. Nothing. It was as if she wanted to forget him as much as he wanted to forget her.

Fat chance.

He could feel the steady thud of her heart, taste the excitement in her mouth, hear her breathless "Yes," when the cowboy asked if she wanted to leave.

The song ended and they headed for the nearest exit.

Travis clamped his hand around his beer and tried to resist the urge to go after her. He damned well would NOT. She was a grown woman. If she wanted to sleep with every damned cowboy in the place, it was her business.

What did he care?

He didn't.

That's what he tried to tell himself. At the same time, he stayed tuned into her. The crunch of gravel echoed in his ears as she followed the guy out to his truck. He felt the rush of *uh-oh* as the man reached for her and hauled her close.

Wait a second.

Uh-oh.

That wasn't the thought of a woman ready to jump into the sack.

He focused and sure enough, she wasn't half as anxious to get up close and personal with this guy as she should have been. Rather, she dodged his kiss and twisted away. He caught her arm and then—

The connection shattered as a bolt of pain zapped Travis and shook his entire body. His gut tightened as fear rushed up his spine.

And for the first time in his life, he didn't try to tell himself that he was overreacting or that it was nothing or that he was certifiable because he suddenly knew—*he knew*—that something was wrong.

He pushed to his feet and went after her. And he could only hope that this time he wasn't too late.

HOLLY CAUGHT HER breath against the incredible pain gripping her ankle. Her eyes watered and she blinked frantically. She wasn't going to cry over a sprained ankle. Even if it was two days before the biggest event of her career.

"Get your hands off of her." The deep, familiar voice sounded a split second before she heard Cal's surprised "What the *fuck?*" and a fierce thud as he landed on the ground beside her.

"It's okay," she said. "He didn't do anything. He tried, but I gave him a knee to the groin. When I went to turn, my heel broke and I twisted my ankle—" The words trailed off as her head snapped up and she saw Travis towering over Cal.

His eyes blazed bright and intense and bloodred. A growl vibrated in her ears and his sensuous lips drew back, revealing a pair of lethal-looking fangs.

Her heart pounded, echoing in her head, drowning out the music drifting from inside and the *crrrunch* of gravel as a car pulled into the parking lot. She blinked once, twice, but it didn't erase what was right in front of her.

What she'd known all along.

Travis was a vampire.

Her brain fought against the truth despite the memories that rifled through her head. The way his eyes had seemed to change colors and how he'd touched her without really touching her. *And the dreams.*

"No," she murmured, fighting against the truth.

The one word seemed to yank him from the angry rage he'd been caught in and he turned toward her.

Immediately, his eyes cooled into a dark, vibrant green and his fangs retracted. He was on his knees in that next instant, reaching for her, his touch gentle, possessive.

"You're mine."

His voice whispered through her head and she knew it wasn't her imagination this time. The words were clear. Distinct. Undeniable.

Shock jolted through her, followed by a wave of panic that crashed over her, tugged her under and tried to suck the oxygen from her lungs. She scrambled to her feet and tried to move. To get away as fast as she could. Not from him, but from the crazy feelings whirling through her. Because despite the truth, she wanted him.

As much as he wanted her.

Mine.

It was her own voice she heard this time. In her head. Her heart. She turned and tried to move. White hot pain ripped up her leg. Suddenly, it was all too much to take in. Her vision blurred and she stumbled. The ground seemed to shake and she pitched forward.

And then she fell head first into a pit of nothingness.

19

ANOTHER DREAM.

That's what Holly told herself when she opened her eyes to find that she was snuggled deep in her own bed, her favorite T-shirt tangled at her waist. She tried to move, her ankle throbbed. And she knew in an instant that it had all been real.

As real as the vampire stretched out in the chair beside her bed.

He sat, his legs stretched out in front of him, his arms folded, his eyes closed. He looked like any other handsome, sexy man keeping watch over his woman. More so with the tiny crease in his brow, as if he wasn't sleeping quite as good as he should have because she was hurt.

A man, she told herself, trying to ignore the sudden rush of memories.

She saw him that first night in the back parking lot of the honky tonk, his eyes gleaming a hot, bright purple as he'd loomed over her.

The image faded into yet another and she saw him standing on her doorstep, insisting that she invite him in properly. The way he'd stood in the shower with her, touching and stirring. There one minute. Gone the next. *Impossible.*

It would be if he was just a man.

But he wasn't.

She closed her eyes, desperate to deny the truth niggling at her. There were no such things as vampires. Such creatures only existed in movies and books and the fantasies of millions of young, *Twilight*-loving teens. It was hype. Not reality.

Still, the memories kept nagging at her. The eyes. The way he seemed to read her thoughts—

"It's part of what I am." His deep voice jarred her from the mental examination and she opened her eyes to find him staring at her. "When I look into a person's eyes, I can tell what they're thinking. I can also levitate and move faster than the average human. I can even lift an SUV if I feel like it. I can see myself in a mirror just like anyone else. But I am allergic to sunlight. Stakes are bad, too, if they're through the heart. Otherwise, I'm pretty invincible. Garlic and crosses don't bother me. Holy water, either."

"But you work with horses. Aren't animals afraid of vampires?"

"I had a knack for horses before I turned. Once I became a vampire, those characteristics became magnified. Horses spook a little at first, but they sense more friend in me than foe. My brother Brent was good with a gun before and now he's unbeatable. Likewise for Cody. He always could hang on for the full eight seconds. And his balance and endurance only magnified once he turned." He stared at her and she knew he saw the multitude of questions swimming in her brain. "I sleep during the day," he added, "which means I work horses at night."

"Isn't that hard to explain to a rancher?"

"Not really. Really good horse trainers have almost a mystical connection to the animals. Ranchers just think it's a quirk in my personality."

She tried to focus on his words, letting everything he said sink in. But every answer drew another question. "Do you really drink blood?"

He nodded. "But vampires don't just feed off of blood. We also crave energy. Sexual energy. The more lusty the woman, the better."

"That's why you followed me into that closet at the wedding?"

He nodded and a grin hinted at his lips, easing the frantic beating of her heart. "That and I liked the way you filled out that black skirt."

A warmth stole through her and she stiffened. So what if he liked the way she looked? She didn't care. She shouldn't care.

His grin faded as he regarded her. "I usually

like sex and blood at the same time. You're the first woman I haven't bitten."

"Lucky me." It was a sarcastic remark, but she couldn't help but think that maybe, just maybe, it did make her lucky. Like maybe there was something different about her. Special. "Why didn't you bite me?"

"I meant to, but then you rushed out of the closet so fast that I lost the chance. I still can't believe you walked away from me. Usually I'm the one walking away and it's the women who are begging me to stay." He ran a hand through his hair and stared at her as if he'd yet to figure her out.

Crazy, she knew. He could read her thoughts. She was practically an open book.

At the same time, she had the distinct feeling that she wasn't nearly as transparent as she should have been, and that he didn't like it one bit.

"When I look into a woman's eyes, she's powerless," Travis continued. "She'll do whatever I say, whenever I say it. But not you. You've got a stubborn streak that I can't touch."

"So no reading my thoughts?"

"Oh, I can read your thoughts. Right now you're not half as afraid of me as you are of yourself. You're afraid because you're not afraid. You're still madly attracted to me."

She wanted to deny it, but then he looked at her, into her, and lust stirred, fierce and quick and far more powerful than the throb of fear keeping time with her frantic heartbeat.

"Stop doing that."

"Doing what?"

"Influencing me."

"That's the trouble, sugar. I can't influence you. I've been trying for days and damned if I can do it."

She shouldn't believe him. It would be so easy to write off her aching body as a reaction to his vamp charm. Yet, there was just something about the frustrated look in his eyes that hinted he was telling the truth. He couldn't influence her at will and it bothered the hell out of him.

Ah, but he could influence her other ways.

His scent—raw and male and oh, so intoxicating—filled her nostrils and created the most damning thoughts of two bodies tangled together, touching and twisting and kissing. Sex at its most primitive level, but even more savage.

An image of him, fangs bared, popped into her head. And where she should have been afraid, she found herself wondering what they would feel like.

"It doesn't hurt," he said, reading her thoughts. "In fact, it's a pretty incredible sensation. Better than sex. It'll definitely make you forget your sprained ankle."

But other than a dull throb, she'd already forgotten about it. She was too focused on him. Her body trembled, urging her to turn, to reach out, to touch him and see for herself.

She wanted to.

She'd been denying herself for so long and suddenly playing it safe and keeping her distance didn't seem nearly as important as reaching out and seizing this one moment.

This one memory to add to all the others.

Because vampire or not, Travis Braddock was still temporary with a great big capital *T*. Their time together was running out. It was already after midnight, which meant Friday had officially arrived. He was leaving tomorrow. He'd said it himself.

Which meant she could either make the most of their time together or run the other way and live with the regret.

She shoved back the covers and struggled to the side of the bed, ignoring her throbbing ankle.

"What are you doing?"

"What I should have done a long time ago." She pushed to her feet and then she reached for the hem of her T-shirt.

TRAVIS WATCHED AS the soft cotton slid over her head. She wasn't wearing a bra and the first whisper of air against her nipples brought them to throbbing awareness. She hooked her fingers in the waistband of her panties and shimmied them down her legs. She stood there, naked and beautiful, offering herself to him. But it wasn't enough. He wanted to be sure. He needed it.

"I want you," she murmured as if reading *his* thoughts.

A sense of urgency rushed through him and he was on his feet in a split-second. He grasped the hem of his shirt and pulled it up and over his head before he reached for her.

He lifted her, taking the pressure off her ankle as he held her close, dipped his head and drew one sensitive nipple into his mouth. She tasted every bit as good as he remembered and he couldn't seem to get enough. He suckled her, holding her tight against his growing erection, cradling her, loving her.

The thought struck and damned if he could push it away. Even though he knew the feelings he had for her wouldn't last. They never did.

Still, he couldn't help himself. He held tight to the emotion rushing inside of him, pressed her down into the mattress and then proceeded to make love to a woman for the first time since he'd turned vampire.

His woman.

For now anyhow.

20

HOLLY CLOSED HER eyes to the wonderful pull of Travis's mouth on her breast. He sucked her so hard and so thoroughly that she moaned. Wetness flooded the sensitive flesh between her legs and she trembled. He drew on her harder, his jaw creating a powerful tug that she felt clear to her womb. An echoing throb started deep inside, more intense with every rasp of his tongue, every nibble of his teeth…

His *fangs*.

There was no mistaking the razor-like sharpness against her hyper-sensitive flesh. She stiffened.

His muscles tightened and he stopped his delicious assault on her breast.

She opened her eyes and found him staring back at her, his face only inches away. He looked at her, into her, his eyes hot and vivid, his fangs fully visible. He looked as if he'd like nothing more than to throw her down and sink himself and his fangs into her body, but he didn't move.

Instead, he waited, his hold on her firm and secure, his muscles stretched taut.

Are you sure?

His thought echoed through her head, sending a rush of amazement through her. The connection was so fierce between them. So intimate. So special.

She cupped his face, felt the rasp of his stubble against her palms and smiled. And then she leaned forward and touched her lips to his.

She kissed him slowly, deeply, tangling her tongue with his, drinking in his taste as if he were a tall glass of water and she desperately needed a drink.

He let her lead for a few tantalizing seconds before taking control as if he couldn't hold back. The kiss grew more intense, his lips nibbling at hers, his fangs grazing the fullness of her bottom lip. She grasped his shoulders and held on for dear life as he tore his lips from hers and licked a tantalizing path down the side of her neck, nibbling at the spot where her pulse beat frantically.

But he didn't bite her.

No matter how much she suddenly wanted him to.

His mouth moved lower as he dipped his head, licking a path over her collarbone, down between her breasts before catching one nipple between his teeth. He bit down just a little and pleasure bolted through her, pulsing along her nerve endings, heating her body until she felt like she would explode.

He didn't touch her with his hands. Just his mouth. He worked her until she moaned long and low and deep in her throat and her nipple practically screamed in ecstasy. Her legs trembled. Her tummy quivered. Goose bumps chased up and down her arms.

"Now," she murmured, but he didn't give in to her demand.

He seized the other nipple and delivered the same delicious torture. She grew wetter, hotter, her body shivering with each movement of his mouth. Heat clawed at her and lust beat at her senses.

And then his mouth was on hers again, his hot fingers rolling and plucking her damp nipples. She felt the sharpness of his fangs against her lips, and the sensation sent a shiver of excitement through her. He clamped down on her bottom lip just a little and she tasted the salty sweetness.

The growl that vibrated up his throat sent an echoing shiver through her body and she knew he was feeling the same pleasure she felt.

He urged her legs up on either side of him, pulling her flush against his crotch, his hands trailing down her bare back, stirring every nerve ending along the way. He rubbed her against the massive erection straining beneath his zipper and the friction sent delicious waves of heat through her.

Suddenly she couldn't get close enough. She grasped his shoulders and clawed at his shoulders. His erection rubbed against her slit and she moaned. She couldn't get enough of him, kissing him with all of the passion that she'd held back for so long.

She needed more. Now. *Please.*

His hand slid between them and played the slick flesh. His thumb grazed her clitoris, rasping back and forth, over and over. She bucked and arched as delicious tremors racked her body and she exploded in his arms.

She was so lost in the throes of her orgasm that she didn't even notice that he'd laid her down until she felt the soft mattress at her back.

She glanced up in time to see him unfasten his jeans. He shoved the denim down in one smooth motion, his erection springing forward, huge and hot. A white drop of pearly liquid glistened on the tip and she leaned forward, catching the drop with her tongue before sucking him in, greedy for more.

He groaned, long and low and deep, his fingers catching her hair and holding her to him as she sucked and licked and tasted.

"Not yet," he finally murmured. "I want to feel you all around me when I come." He pushed her back onto the mattress and followed her down. Urging her legs apart, he settled his erection flush against her sex.

He kissed her then, licking her lips and sucking

at her tongue before he caught her legs and bent her knees just enough to open her wider. He slid his hands beneath her bottom to tilt her just so and with one powerful thrust, he slid deep inside her.

She closed her eyes to the rush of pleasure.

"Look at me, Holly," he murmured and her eyelids fluttered open. "I need you to look at me." *To want me.*

He didn't say the words, but she heard them anyway because they were connected on a level that went much deeper than anything she'd ever experienced.

This was what she'd dreamt of. This meeting of the minds. Of the souls.

Hunger blazed hot and intense in his gaze and while she knew he'd looked at every other woman in his past the exact same way, for some reason it felt different. She felt different.

"You *are* different." His fangs glittered in the moonlight as he poised above her.

He didn't move a muscle for a long moment and she knew he was waiting on her. Giving her one last chance to refuse him. She was the one woman who could. Because as much as he wanted her, he couldn't make her want him back.

He'd admitted as much and the knowledge sent a rush of empowerment through her. She'd spent her entire life looking for that special someone, wanting to be that special someone.

And at that moment, she was.

She tilted her head, baring her neck, offering it to him. Not because it was what he wanted, but because *she* wanted it. She wanted to connect to him, fully and completely. She wanted to take all that he offered and give everything she had in return, not because it gave her some payoff in the future, but because she wanted him now. Right here. Right now.

Regardless of what happened later.

He dipped his head. His mouth closed over the side of her neck where her pulse beat a frantic rhythm. He laved the spot with his tongue, stroking and tantalizing before he sank his fangs deep. So deliciously deep.

True to his word, it didn't hurt. Rather, she felt only a slight prickle, followed by a rush of intense pleasure that made her gasp.

He thrust into her, pushing deep with his body, all the while sucking with his mouth. He drove her mindless, pushing and sucking, giving and taking, in a frantic rhythm that pulled the air from her lungs.

The pressure inside of her built, climbing higher until she couldn't take anymore. This was it. He was it. *Now!*

She cried out, bursting into a thousand pieces.

He quickly followed her over the edge, his entire body tensing, vibrating. He trembled, drinking in her blood the same way he drank in the sexual energy that rushed from her body.

His mouth eased and he leaned back. A fierce groan rumbled from his lips as he thrust one final time and she felt the spurt of warmth deep inside.

His body shook with the force of his climax, then he slumped on top of her, his face buried in the crook of her neck.

A few frantic heartbeats later, he rolled onto his back and fit her firmly against the side of his body. He held her close, as if he feared she might slip away from him.

He didn't have to worry. She could barely move. She felt weightless, floating, as if she didn't have a care in the world. And while she knew that wasn't true and she would have to open her eyes soon, right now the only thing she wanted to do was stay right here in his arms.

She rested her head on his shoulder and drank in several deep breaths of air. A tiny trickle of warmth slid down her collarbone and she reached up. Her fingertips brushed the two tiny pinpoints where he'd bitten her and a sharp burst of heat sizzled through her. She jumped.

She was surprised. Startled. And turned on.

"Easy, sugar." His hand came up to soothe the area. Not that it worked. It only served to stir her up even more. Her nipples pebbled and her thighs clenched. She closed her eyes as warmth bubbled between her legs and sizzled through her. She felt his smile even before she saw it. "I told you it would make you forget about the ankle."

"What ankle?"

His warm chuckle vibrated along her nerve endings as he slid his hand down the length of her body, stroking, soothing, lulling.

She snuggled deeper into his embrace, rested her head in the crook of his neck and went to sleep.

TRAVIS LISTENED TO her deep, steady breaths, relishing the sound until the shadows outside the window seemed to shift and the veil of blackness lifted just enough to tell him that it was close to dawn.

He pulled her arms from around his neck and slipped from the bed, careful not to disturb her. He pulled on his jeans and T-shirt and then reached for his boots. Snatching up his hat, he plopped it onto his head and turned back to survey the woman stretched out on the bed. He tucked the blanket up around her, his hands lingering at her hair for a long moment, relishing the silkiness.

She was so damned beautiful. And stubborn, he reminded himself. He hated that about her. And loved it.

Love?

Hell, no. He didn't love her. Sure, he liked her a lot. A helluva lot. Unlike most women he came into contact with, he'd taken the time to get to know her. He knew that she had two left feet, that she liked pink and that she loved her job. He knew she liked fireworks, that she ate ice cream when she got stressed, she used strawberries and cream shampoo and that she loved her aunt more than anything in the world. She was determined and loyal and strong, and he liked it. He liked all of it.

Still, the foundation of their attraction was still based on lust. That's what had pulled him to her in the first place, what had made him agree to her plan. He'd wanted her body *and* her blood. And now he'd had both.

That meant it was time to walk away for good this time.

He gave her one last lingering glance and then he turned and left.

21

"I REALLY THINK you should wear your hair down."
Wanda Lancaster added yet another swipe of red
lipstick to her lips as she eyed her daughter in the
mirror. "It looks lots better, sweetie."

"That's *much* better, Momma," Darla corrected,
"and I already told you, I like it up. It looks more
sophisticated. All the major brides are wearing their
hair like this." She indicated the bridal magazine
sitting open on the table not far away, the model on
the cover showcasing an expertly coiffed updo. She
cast another glance at her mother. "Do you have to
wear so much red lipstick? That went out ages ago.
Try some lipgloss."

"I like red lipstick and I'm wearing red lipstick,"
Wanda insisted. "That's what you need." She held out
the tube to Shelly who stood in a floor-length silver
and black dress, white gloves to her elbows. Her hair
was pulled up just like Darla's and she looked as if

she was nursing a major migraine. "You need some color. You're pale."

Darla touched her own updo. "That's because these bobby pins feel like they're piercing my brain." She waved away the tube. "That stuff gives me the hives."

The hustle and bustle went on for several more minutes as Darla checked over everyone's dresses, flowers, hair and make-up while Holly went over her checklist with Evan.

"I think we're just about ready," she told her bride.

"That's right, pigskin. Ten minutes and you're getting married."

"Mom, please don't call me that. I hate that name."

"But I thought you liked pork rinds."

"About a hundred years ago. And while I liked to eat them, I don't appreciate you calling me that name."

Wanda shrugged. "I think it's sorta cute."

"That's sort of, Momma. There's no such word as sorta." The door opened then and an older woman in her fifties waltzed in wearing a floor-length blue sapphire suit with rhinestone buttons. Her expertly colored blond hair was done up in the latest style, her make-up immaculate.

"There she is," she declared, a wide smile on her face. "My soon-to-be daughter-in-law."

Darla smiled, but Holly didn't miss the flicker of apprehension in her eyes.

"Well come here and let me look at you."

Darla stepped forward and the woman took her hands. "Why, you look lovely. My son is a lucky young man. You've got such beautiful skin. And that hair…" Her smile faltered just a little as she took in the hairstyle.

"What is it?" Darla blurted. "What's wrong?"

"I just didn't realize that you were going to wear your hair up."

"I thought it would be more flattering to the veil."

"She always did like wearing ponytails," Wanda offered. "Why, we would have called her ponytail if it wasn't for the fact that she was always munching on all those pork rinds."

"Not now, Momma," Darla whispered. "You really don't like it?"

"It's fine, dear. I just think it would be more flattering down. That's all. It's your choice." She waved it off and turned. "I'd better get out there. I've got a handsome young usher waiting to walk me down the aisle."

"Me, too," Wanda said, heading for the door. "See you out there, sugar."

"I'm sending the maid of honor out," Holly said into her headset. "Get the rest of the bridesmaids ready."

"10-4," Evan said.

Holly motioned to Shelly and sent her out the door and then she turned to Darla. "Are you ready?"

"What do you think about my hair?" the bride asked her pointedly.

Holly saw the indecision, the uncertainty, the fear and her heart went out to Darla, regardless of what a bee-yotch she'd been lately. She knew what it was like to want something so badly that she would do anything to get it. Even convince herself she was marrying the right man.

She also knew what it was like to want something so badly that she would convince herself she was turning her back on the wrong man.

But Travis wasn't wrong for her. He was so right that it made her teeth ache. Not that it mattered. He obviously didn't feel the same way. He'd left before dawn on Friday morning and she hadn't seen him since. She'd spent the entire day listening to Tootie talk about Buck Gentry and how he wasn't such a bad fellow after all, on account of he'd turned her on to Bingo. Heck, she might even like him a little. Not that it was any reason to get excited. It wasn't like she was going to marry him.

At least that's what she'd said, but Holly had seen too many brides over the past few years to believe her aunt. She had the same anxious light in her eyes. And while she would never have thought it in a million years, she was starting to think that even Aunt Tootie might take the leap and head to the altar.

It was now Saturday evening and Travis would be leaving in a matter of hours. She'd heard from one of the hairdressers that Cody and Miranda were arriving at seven tonight. Travis would get his chance to talk to his brother, and then he would leave.

"So?" Darla pressed.

"I think it doesn't matter what I think. It matters what you think." As she said the words, realization dawned. Travis might be all wrong, but when she was with him, he made her feel right. He was right.

Not that she was telling him. She'd rather spare herself the embarrassment.

Darla turned and stared in the mirror. For a split-second, Holly thought she would actually leave her hair as is. But then she started yanking bobby pins until her hair hung around her shoulders. She shook out the curls, worked at the veil for a split-second and then she turned. "Let's get this show on the road."

"Bride walking," Holly murmured as Darla hauled open the door and headed down the hallway.

Darla refused to listen to her heart and Holly didn't blame her. She would be giving up so much. Comfort. Safety. Her future.

It wasn't about embarrassment for Holly. She was scared. Scared of the way Travis made her feel. Scared of what might happen tomorrow. Scared that it wouldn't be the comfortable little future she'd mapped out for herself.

That's why she refused to take the initiative and call him. Take a chance.

"I can't do this," Darla's voice pushed into her

thoughts and she saw her bride standing in the entryway outside the main ceremony area. "I don't want to
do this. I like Tom, but I don't love him." The minute
she said the words, a weight seemed to lift from her
expression. Panic quickly followed.

"What do I do?"

"Go find him. I'll take care of everything else."
Holly sent Darla off to the holding area for the
groomsmen and then she told Evan what was happening. "Explain it to the parents and then let everyone else know," she told him as she pulled off her
headset and handed it to him.

"Where are you going?"

"I need to talk to someone." And then she went
to find Travis.

It was time she took her own chance, no matter
what the future held.

"WE'RE ALL HERE," Travis said, motioning around the
dining room table where all the Braddock brothers
gathered for the first time since that fateful night.
While they were all called back to the place of their
turning every year on the anniversary, it was different. They'd been spread out at the ranch, one on one
side, another over here, another over there. Together,
yet alone. But they were all here now.

Colton, the oldest, sat next to Travis looking as
somber and as quiet as ever. He'd walked in a half
hour ago just before Cody arrived home. He hadn't

said much. He didn't have to. His eyes said it all. They glittered with an anger that Travis had never seen before. Colton was hurt. Betrayed. And even God wouldn't be able to help the woman responsible once he caught up with her.

Brent and Cody sat on the other side of the table. Miranda sat next to Cody, her hand in his while Brent sat with his arm around Abby. And despite the subject matter, they didn't look half as tense as Travis felt. Rather, they seemed relaxed. Happy. Loved.

A pang of envy shot through Travis and he couldn't stifle the thought that maybe he was wrong. Maybe he could have the same happiness with Holly if he just gave it a chance.

He'd been so damned convinced that the lust would drive him straight into the arms of another woman, but he wasn't so sure anymore. It had been twenty-four hours and he still couldn't stop thinking about her. He'd spent all night working with the wild black mare and he'd managed to break her. But all the work hadn't been enough to distract him from thoughts of Holly. She was under his skin. In his head. In his heart.

He hadn't wanted to believe it, but seeing his brothers, seeing how happy they were, suddenly he wanted it. He wanted it more than anything.

Even more than the revenge he'd been so deadset on for so many years.

No⁴ that Holly wanted him. She hadn't made a

move to contact him any more than he'd tried to contact her. She wouldn't. She'd taken her Love Buster vow. And while she'd fallen off the wagon, she would climb right back on. She was a stubborn thing. Too stubborn for her own good.

"So where is she?" Colton demanded. "Just give me a location and I'm on my way."

"Sit back down."

"Why?"

"Because she's right here, or she soon will be. We have something she wants. There was a prisoner transferred to the jail a few days ago. A young man about twenty-two."

"And what does this have to do with Rose?"

"He's her last living relative. I had a private investigator do some checking once we found her. It seems she's been helping this guy out, keeping an eye on him. I'd be willing to bet she's on her way to Skull Creek right now—"

The ring of a doorbell drowned out his words.

A minute later, Holly appeared in the doorway. She took one look around the room and Travis saw the flash of recognition. Even so, she wasn't the least bit intimidated by a roomful of bloodsuckers. She headed straight for him.

"I love you," she blurted out. "I know you might not love me, but I love you anyway. There it is." She put her hands on her hips and stared him down. Waiting. Worrying. "I know you're a vampire and, well, it presents a few problems. But I'm willing to deal with them. That is, if you want to try. I know it won't be perfect. No daytime wedding or anything like that. That is, if we even get that far. But I'm willing to give it a shot and see where it goes." When he just kept looking at her, she added, "Well? Aren't you going to say something?"

"It's about damned time." Travis was on his feet in that next instant, pulling her into his arms.

"Is that all you're going to say?"

He stared down into her eyes and saw the emotion he felt deep inside mirrored in her gaze. There was so much they would have to work through. At the same time, with her in his arms, it seemed like there was nothing he couldn't do. *Nothing.* "I love you, too, but only if I get fireworks instead of birdseed."

She grinned and then she kissed him.

* * * * *

THE PLEASURE PRINCIPLE

1

As owner and operator of the only bar in Cadillac, Texas, Eden Hallsey came into contact with more than her fair share of men. Males of all shapes and sizes—rich and poor, young and old, annoying and nice, homely and handsome. But never had she seen one as handsome, as sexy, as *hot* as the man standing on the side of the road, next to a steaming black Porsche.

Handsome, as in short, dark hair that framed a *GQ* face, complete with a straight nose and strong jaw and sensual lips.

Sexy, as in the sensual way his white dress shirt outlined his muscular shoulders and broad chest, while soft, black trousers accented a trim waist and molded to his hips.

Hot as in the beads of perspiration that clung to his forehead, slid down his cheeks, the tanned column of his throat. He wiped his brow as he lifted a hand to flag her down.

Before she even realized what she was doing, her foot shifted to the brake and she started to slow. A few seconds later, she pulled up in front of the sleek sports car and rolled down her window.

"Need some help?" she asked as he walked up. She reached beneath the seat for the Triple A kit her waitress and friend Kasey had given her last Christmas. A click and she started rummaging in the tackle-size box. "Let's see. I've got jumper cables. A jack. Spare can of oil." A girl had to be prepared, as Kasey always said. Of course, in this situation her friend would have been referring to the tube of Passionate Pink lipstick she'd taped inside the top of the tackle box.

Eden barely ignored the urge to grab the tube and rub some of the color on her lips. Eden Hallsey primped for no man, even one as handsome as this one.

"Pick your poison," she told him after she'd licked her lips and ticked off the remaining contents of the box.

"A gun would be nice."

Her head snapped up and her gaze collided with his. She realized he looked vaguely familiar as her breath caught and her mouth actually went dry at the sight of the most intense, vivid blue eyes she'd ever seen.

A crazy reaction, because Eden's mouth never

went dry over a man. Sure, she appreciated the opposite sex. She even enjoyed them on occasion—though the last being so long ago she could hardly remember. She liked men, all right, as everyone well knew. But she never, *ever* let any one man get to her.

Until this man.

She ignored the crazy thought and concentrated on finding her voice. "Pardon?"

His grin was slow and easy and as breath-stealing as the record-breaking hundred degree heat baking the surrounding stretch of pasture. "To put her out of her misery." He motioned behind him. "The engine block is cracked and nothing short of a miracle is likely to revive her."

She couldn't help but return his smile. "Sorry, but I'm fresh out of miracles today."

His grin faltered and something passed in his gaze. "Me, too. Thankfully."

His last comment, coupled with the flash of relief in his blue eyes, made her think that Mr. Handsome, Sexy and Hot wasn't all that disappointed to see his fifty-thousand-dollar car steaming in the midday heat.

The thought passed as he turned his attention back to her. A hungry light fired his gaze and her breath caught. It was a look she was all too familiar with since she'd given her virginity to Jake Marlboro back in high school. He'd violated her trust and turned what should have been something beautiful into a tawdry good time to brag about to his friends. Thus, her reputation had been born and she'd endured it ever since. The bold pick-up lines, the raunchy comments, the hungry looks.

But this was different. Her response was different. She didn't just want to slap his face. She wanted to throw her arms around him and see if his lips felt as soft and mesmerizing as they looked.

"If you don't mind, I could really use a ride."

The last word lingered in her head and stirred a vivid image of him stretched out on her flower print sheets, his body dark and masculine and hard beneath her.

"But if it makes you uncomfortable, I could just walk."

But that was the kicker. The notion of giving him a ride, in or out of bed, didn't make her uncomfortable in the least.

Just hot.

"I'd be happy to help." The words were out before she could consider that the man was a stranger, no matter how familiar he looked. He could be a serial killer for all she knew. A Porsche-driving, Gucci-wearing madman.

Then again, she'd been on blind dates that looked far more scary and intimidating. This guy was neither, and her gut told her he wasn't dangerous either—except to her hormones. But she could maintain control of herself for the five minutes it would take to drive him to Merle's Service Station.

Eden Hallsey *always* kept her control. She was notorious for it. She was notorious for a *lot* of things.

"I really wouldn't want to put you out," he went on, mistaking her silence for hesitation.

"You're not. You're the one who'll be inconvenienced. I'm afraid the closest gas station is about two miles straight into town."

"It's no inconvenience. That's where I was headed."

His words surprised her. She'd figured he'd pulled off the interstate near the town's only exit out of pure necessity, not by choice. They didn't see many of his type in a desperately small town like Cadillac. Not that the place didn't have its share of wealth. Cadillac was home to two of the largest ranches in Texas, not to mention Weston Boots, the oldest and largest western boot manufacturer in the country. But the wealthy were still just locals. Country folk. Men like old Zachariah Weston and rancher Silver Dollar Sam—so named because of the silver dollars he handed out to the kiddies when he played Santa Claus at the yearly winter festival. While they might drive fancy utility vehicles and wear solid gold belt buckles, they still spent their Saturday nights having ice cream at the Dairy Freeze right alongside everybody else.

Her gaze shifted to the man standing outside her

truck window, with his expensive Italian suit and his elite sports car. Again, a strange sense of familiarity hit her, as if she'd seen him in this exact pose before.

She shook away the crazy thought and reached over to unlock the opposite door. If she had come into contact with him before, she couldn't imagine ever forgetting. He was too handsome, too sexy, too stirring.

Then again, maybe she was remembering. A memory from long ago. A man who'd been just a boy…

She searched her mind as he climbed in beside her. But then the door closed and his scent surrounded her, and her thoughts scattered. Her heart pounded and her stomach jumped and it was all she could do to concentrate on pulling away from the shoulder of the road, out onto the main strip leading into town.

"So," she licked her lips and tried to calm her thundering heart, "are you visiting friends in town? Family?"

"Both." He didn't spare her a glance as he drank in the passing scenery, as if he were seeing pasture-land and farmhouses for the very first time. "At least I hope so."

"Have you ever been to Cadillac before?" she asked, eager to satisfy the curiosity bubbling inside her.

"Yes." He didn't offer any more information, telling Eden as plain as day, that he wasn't as interested in getting to know her as she was in getting to know him, despite the openly hungry look he'd directed at her earlier.

It seemed that not only had her response to this man strayed from her usual indifference, *he* was acting different from most men. Any other man would have taken the opportunity to flirt and tease and even openly proposition her should they have found themselves alone with her in the close confines of her truck.

Not that Eden was some irresistible beauty queen. Far from it. It wasn't her average looks that made her attractive to men. It was the rumors. She'd learned over the years that a woman with a reputation was like a plate of free cookies. Even if a person wasn't hungry, they reached for a sweet just because it was there and it was free and everybody else was taking some.

It was a fact of life. Men flirted with her. All men. Her gaze snagged on the man seated next to her. The guy didn't so much as spare her a glance. Okay, so make that most men.

Then again, if he wasn't from around these parts he didn't know her or her reputation. As far as he was concerned, she was just another woman.

Eden bit her bottom lip to keep from asking him more questions. He didn't want to talk and she wasn't going to make a pest of herself no matter how much she suddenly wanted to know everything about him, from his name to his likes and dislikes. Instead, she fixed her attention on trying to place him in her memory. He'd admitted that he'd been to Cadillac before. Maybe she had seen him. Eden was still searching her memory when they pulled into Merle's Gas-n-Go.

"Thanks," he said as he started to climb out, that same preoccupied look in his gaze that made Eden wonder yet again if she'd only imagined that initial hungry look he'd given her.

"Wait," she said as he moved to close the door. "Don't forget your duffel bag...." The words faded as she leaned over to grab his bag and her gaze snagged on the worn boots he was wearing—*worn* when the rest of him was polished to the max. The heel had the familiar trademark *W* branded into its side.

An image rushed at her of a blue-jean-clad senior with long legs and an easy smile. He'd worn a similar pair of boots as he'd stood on the side of the road next to his granddaddy's pickup, one of the rear tires as flat as Jamie McGee's hair after a good ironing.

Eden's head snapped up and her eyes collided with his. "Brady Weston. You're *Brady Weston.*" *The* Brady Weston. The boy who'd been every girl's dream, Eden's included.

His grin was as slow and as warm as she remembered on that hot July day when she'd given him her tire jack and a long swallow of her ice-cold Coke.

"The last time I looked."

"It *is* you." Her heart pumped ninety-to-nothing at the realization. "Y-you probably don't recognize me. I'm—"

"Eden Hallsey," he finished for her. "I'd know your smile anywhere. Thanks for saving me. Again." Then, with a wink, he closed the door and Eden was left with the startling knowledge that after a bitter fight with his grandaddy and an eleven-year absence, Brady Weston—the captain of the hockey team, the heir to the Weston Boot fortune and the star of Eden's wildest adolescent fantasies—had finally come home.

HE WAS HOME.

Reality hit Brady as he stood before Merle's gas station and stared at the fading red sign that hung in front. The same painted oval that had always teetered back and forth from two small chains. The edges were a little more worn than he remembered, the paint chipped in several spots, but otherwise it was exactly the same. The same name with the same familiar twenty-four hour service guarantee printed just below. A red-and-white T-ball banner flapped in the wind depicting one of the local teams in the peewee league. The same team—the Kansas City Royals—that Merle's station sponsored each and every year.

Thankfully.

Brady had seen too many new barns, new fences,

even a few new houses dotting the horizon on the drive into town and the scenery had made him worry that maybe things had changed too much for him to simply waltz back home after all these years and pick up where he'd left off.

And he wanted to. Christ, he wanted it more than his next breath of air.

He glanced behind him at the familiar span of buildings lining main street, from Turtle Jim's Diner, where he'd eaten chili cheese fries after school every Friday afternoon, to Sullivan's Pharmacy, where he'd purchased his very first condom. The breath he'd been holding eased from his lungs and he drank in another lungful of Texas heat.

Home.

He'd dreamt about this moment so many times over the past eleven years, when the stress of a fast-paced advertising career and a less than perfect home life had overwhelmed him and he'd longed for the peace he'd known while growing up. The freedom. The control.

He'd been the one in control back then. But for the past eleven years, life and circumstance and his ex-wife had called the shots, dictating the how, when and where.

Only because he'd allowed it, he reminded himself. It wasn't as if he'd been forced away from Cadillac. He'd fallen in love, or so he'd thought at the time, and walked away by choice—to do the right thing. In the end, however, everything he'd done that fateful day and every moment since had been wrong. So wrong.

Not now. Not ever again.

The past was just that—the past. Over. Finished. Bye, bye. It was the future that mattered now, and Brady wasn't making any more mistakes. Rather, he was finally going to set things right.

He ran a hand through his sweat-dampened hair and spared a glance around him. A handful of kids were gathered around a nearby candy machine at the far corner of the building. Brady turned, letting his gaze sweep the other side. The gleam of an old-fashioned Coke machine caught his eye and he smiled. Yep, Cadillac was still good old Cadillac.

Sliding a coin into the slot, he pushed the same button he'd pushed every day after school since the moment he'd been tall enough to swipe quarters from the top of his older sister's dresser once she'd left for school in the morning.

The machine grumbled, then stalled the way it always had for several long moments before finally spitting out a can of Orange Crush. He popped the tab and lifted the opening to his lips. Anticipation rolled through him, thirst coiled in his stomach— familiar feelings that he'd felt every time he'd stood in this very same spot with his favorite drink.

Yet, at the same time, he felt different. Hotter. More anxious. Downright *needy*.

Thanks to Eden Hallsey.

He took a long swig of soda, but it did little to ease his body temperature which had soared the moment she'd pulled up in her beat-up Chevy to rescue him from his own stupidity.

At first, he'd been convinced she was a mirage. He'd been stranded on the highway just miles from his hometown. It only made sense that he would conjure the sexiest girl from his past.

But then she'd touched him, just a soft gesture on his hand, and every nerve in his body had jumped to awareness. In a matter of seconds, he'd been as hard as an iron spike.

He'd reacted the same way on their one and only date. That had been before Sally, or rather, before his head had lost the battle with his hormones, he'd fancied himself in love and had forgotten to wear a condom on one of their dates. She'd gotten pregnant and they'd gotten married, and his dating days had been over. She'd lost the baby shortly after, but it was too late. He'd taken sacred vows, and he *had* loved her, or so he'd thought at the time, and she'd claimed to love him. He'd believed her, up until six months ago when she'd run off with one of his business associates.

So much for love.

But before…

There'd been Eden Hallsey. From tenth grade on, she'd been the prettiest and sexiest girl around and the fantasy of every boy at Cadillac, Brady included. He'd heard every rumor about her, and while he didn't believe them all—he'd known her before tenth grade—when she'd been shy and naive and a nice girl—he knew there was at least a kernel of truth. She *was* sexy.

And he'd wanted her.

The date had been nothing more than tradition. He'd been the star prize in the yearly football lottery, where girls bought tickets for a chance to win a date with their favorite jock. He'd been surprised to see her raise her hand when the number had been called. After all, Eden hadn't needed to buy a ticket to get a date. She could have any guy. But she'd bought a ticket for him. For a few seconds, he'd been excited until a friend had alerted him to the fact that she was making her way through the football team and he was the last on her list. Just another conquest.

Oddly enough, he hadn't wanted to be another in a long line. He'd wanted to be different. To stand out, and so he'd done what no other guy had ever been able to do—he'd kept his distance. Barely.

That had been a long time ago. His hormones had never been more out of control than at this time, or so he'd thought until he'd climbed into the cab beside her today. He might as well have been sixteen again, with raging needs and a permanent hard-on. The reaction was the same. Fierce. Immediate.

Thankfully, that reaction had jolted some common

sense into him. He'd let his passion get him into trouble before. He'd lost everything because of one night and it wasn't happening again just because Eden was every bit as luscious as he remembered. He wouldn't screw things up again before he'd even had the chance to set them right.

A chance. That's why Brady was back in Cadillac. He wanted a chance to reclaim his old life. A chance to make amends for mistaking lust for love and beg his grandfather's forgiveness for forsaking his family for a girl who'd never really loved him.

Not that love had been the sole deciding factor that had figured into his decision to forfeit an all expense paid education at Texas A & M for two jobs and community college in Dallas. Duty had been a part of his decision as well. And responsibility. And commitment. They were the reasons Brady had left.

The reasons he'd finally come back.

"Say there, son. Can I help…" The words trailed off as astonishment lit the old man's face as he walked around the corner of the building. He wore faded jean overalls and a worn Kansas City Royals T-shirt beneath it. Salt-and-pepper hair framed a wrinkled face, and a matching mustache twitched on his upper lip. "Why, I declare. Brady Zachariah Weston! Is that you, you ole sonofagun?"

"It's me, all right." He took the older man's hand for a hearty shake. "It's good to see you, Unc."

Merle Weston was Brady's great uncle, his grandfather's little brother, and the classic black sheep of the Weston clan. For as long as Brady could remember, Merle had been the outsider. He'd declined any part of the Weston boot business and opened up his own gas station some thirty-odd years ago, despite his older brother's fierce objections. After all, Weston Boots was a family affair and Zachariah Weston didn't take too kindly to his kin going against family tradition.

Brady knew that firsthand.

Merle had never seemed to care, however. If anything, he'd gone out of his way just to stay at odds with his older brother. He'd traded the family business and fortune for his own service station that barely made ends meet.

He'd married the wrong woman, at least according to his older brother whose definition of right involved money—lots of money. And he'd moved clear across town, away from the family ranch that still housed three generations of Westons.

The older man scratched the side of his head with a faded, rolled-up issue of *Popular Mechanics*. "Why, I was wonderin' when you'd finally make it back—hey, there!" His attention shifted to the kids poking around the candy machine. "You young'uns either put some change in or skeedadle, otherwise I'll take a hickory switch to every single one of you!" He turned back to Brady and his face split into a grin. "You're lookin' awful good, son. A little slick," he said, his gaze sweeping Brady from head to toe as he let out a low whistle. "Awful fancy threads you got there."

"One of the hazards of working in Dallas. I see you're still too cheap to spring for a current edition of *Popular Mechanics*." He indicated the rolled-up magazine.

"The back issues I get from the beauty parlor every six months when Eula cleans off her coffee table are plenty good enough for me." He winked. "What can I say? The price is right."

"There is no price."

"That's why it's so right. I ain't made of money like some folks around here." He winked. "Speaking of which, I heard you're headin' up one of them highfalutin ad agencies out there."

"*Was*. I'm through doing the corporate thing. I want to slow down. Speaking of which, my car quit on me out on the highway. You think you could dig up a wrecker and give me a tow?"

"Sure thing. What kind of car?"

"Black."

"I'm talking make and model."

Brady drew in a deep breath. "A Porsche 366."

Merle let loose another whistle. "Slick car to go with the duds."

"Not for long. These clothes are a mite too hot for me. I'm thinking of changing before I head over to Granddaddy's place."

"You sure as hell better. He's still a little attached to his Wranglers, and anybody who ain't wearin' them amounts to an outsider."

"I've got a pair in my suitcase." Several pairs to be more exact. While Brady had left straight from his office and hadn't taken the time to change, he had come as prepared as possible to face his grandfather after all these years.

"Since my car's out of commission, you have any loaners you can spare?"

"All's I got is ole Bessie out back."

"You mean she actually still runs?" Brady remembered the old Chevy pickup being on its last legs back when he was in high school.

"On occasion. She's pretty reliable, so long as you stroke the console 'afore you start her."

"Will do."

"I don't think your grandfather will take too kindly to you driving up in Bessie."

True enough, but Zachariah would like it even less seeing his only grandson drive up in a fancy car the likes of which no salt-of-the-earth cowboy would be caught dead in.

"A truck's a truck. So," Brady went on, eager to change the subject, "you're looking really good. Still sponsoring the same T-ball team and wearing the same shirt."

"It ain't the same. They give me a new one every year. One of the perks. As a matter of fact, I made 'em give me two shirts this past year 'cause I hit my twenty-year mark."

Brady grinned. "Still spittin' vinegar, I see."

Merle winked before casting a glance at the kids and giving them a look that sent them running. "And pissin' fire," he added, turning back to Brady. "Thanks to Maria's cookin'."

"She still make the best tamales this side of the Rio Grande?"

"And the best dadburned enchiladas. I keep tellin' her she ought to put all that good cookin' to use and open up a restaurant. Then I could retire and let Marlboro have this old place."

"Jake Marlboro?"

He nodded. "He's been itchin' to buy me out all year. Already talked Cecil over at McIntyre Hardware into selling his place."

"Why would he want the old hardware store?"

"He's fixing on putting in a Mega Mart. It's got everything from hardware to groceries. Opened one up over in Inspiration and it's a big hit. Folks like the convenience, I guess. Me, I'm just a little attached to this place. Not to mention, I ain't sold Maria on the restaurant idea. She says she's too busy with all the young'uns."

"How many are you up to?"

"Out of seven grandkids, we've got nineteen great-grandbabies, and number twenty's due any day now." A smile creased his old face. "Your gramps is pickle green with envy."

"And you're loving every minute of it."

Merle's grin widened. "I never had too many chances to one-up your old grandpa when we were growing up, and I ain't ashamed to admit that it's a mite satisfying to know there's something the old coot wants that he cain't have." At Brady's smile, Merle shrugged. "What can I say? Things ain't changed much in the past eleven years."

Brady sent up a silent prayer. "That's what I'm counting on."

2

"Brady's home!" The shout preceded the frantic embrace of Brady's youngest sister. Before he could so much as get in a hello, she opened the front door, threw herself into his arms and held on for dear life.

For the next few moments, Brady forgot his doubts and simply relished the feeling. It had been a long time since he'd been hugged so fiercely…since he'd wanted to hug so fiercely.

"You're here," his sister murmured into his shoulder. "You're really here." Another quick squeeze and she pulled back enough to give him a scolding look. "It's about damned time."

"Ellie Jane Weston." The admonishment came from a tall, slender, sixtyish woman with silvery hair and stern blue eyes who appeared in the entryway behind Ellie. "You watch your language."

"Sorry, Ma. Brady's home," Ellie announced to the woman.

"I heard. Why, I wouldn't be surprised if every one of the surrounding counties heard." Claire Weston eyed her only son for a long moment, before her gaze softened. "It's about damned time," she finally declared, moving past her daughter to pull her son into her arms. "It's been much too long."

"I wanted to come home sooner, but I didn't—"

"It doesn't matter." She shook her head. "You're here now. That's all that matters." Another hug and she pulled away.

Surprisingly, her eyes glistened with tears and something shifted inside of Brady. While growing up, he'd seen his mother cry only once and that had been at his father's funeral. Claire Weston, as strong as the 150-year-old oak tree growing in the backyard, had buried relatives, seen her family through many trials, and not once had she lost control of her emotions, a character trait that no doubt pleased her father-in-law. Tears were for the weak, and there wasn't anything weak about the Westons.

One hundred years ago, Miles Weston had started Weston Boots all by himself. He'd handtooled leather from sunup to sundown, using little more than a make-shift tin shack out behind his barn as a workshop. He'd started something that generations after had continued. The Westons were hard workers, diligent, persistent, *strong*.

"It's good to see you," Brady said, giving his mother a warm smile.

"I hope this means what I think it means," she told him.

"That depends."

"I don't care what the old man says, you're staying."

"We'll see." He smiled and wiped at a stray tear gliding down her cheek. "You're looking as sexy as ever."

She sniffled and gathered her composure. "I see you've still got a fresh mouth."

"And you're still the prettiest woman in Cadillac." A loud cough and he turned toward his sister. "One of the prettiest women." Ellie rewarded him with a smile. "And speaking of pretty women, where are Brenda and Marsha?" Brenda was his oldest sister and Marsha the next to the oldest.

"Brenda's in Arizona for the next few weeks learning all about her uterus," Ellie said.

"What?"

"She and Marc are finally going to give in to Granddaddy's nagging and do the baby thing. But you know Brenda. She's a perpetual planner. Before she even thinks of going off the pill, she wants to know everything there is to know about conception and babies. She's at a convention given by Dr. Something or Other who wrote that book *My Uterus, My Friend.* Marc's going to the workshops with her."

"And Marsha?"

"She's at a sales meeting in Chicago. She wants to

expand the business, but Granddaddy isn't so sure. She's testing the waters with a few samples of next year's line of snakeskin boots. You should see the new rattlesnake—"

"I really don't want to talk business on an empty stomach," their mother cut in. "You," she said turning to Brady, "are just in time for lunch. I'll get Dorothy to set another plate and we'll catch up on old times. And then you two can talk about whatever you like."

"Yes, ma'am. I see she's still a slave driver," he told his sister.

"What do you expect? It runs in the family."

"Yes, but she married into the family."

"That's even worse. It's a double whammy. We're cursed."

"Lunch," Claire said as if keeping with her image. "Now."

Brady managed two steps before he heard his grandfather's voice drifting from the dining room.

"...need is a damned sheriff who knows the difference between a bull and a heifer. Why, John Macintosh is as citified as they come and only on the lookout for his own interests and those old cronies over at city hall. Damned politicians..."

The voice, so rich and deep and familiar, sent a wave of doubt through Brady and he hesitated.

He'd envisioned this moment the entire trip from Dallas. He was about to face his past, his present, his future. *If* Zachariah Weston could find it in his heart to forget and forgive. Or at least forgive.

"He's still as salty as ever, but I can promise he won't bite."

"That's a matter of opinion," Ellie piped in behind them. "When I had my hair colored last month, he'd liked to have chewed me a new butthole."

"Ellie Mae Weston. I'll not have that kind of talk in this household."

"Sorry, Ma, but I can't help it if it's true."

"You colored your hair green. It's understandable he had issues with it. You represent Weston Boots. I wasn't too thrilled myself."

"I'm stuck behind a stack of accounting ledgers and a computer screen. No one even sees me. Besides, green hair was no cause to go and write me out of your will."

"I did no such thing and you know it." She pinned her youngest daughter with a stern glare. "But I wouldn't go counting your chickens yet, young lady. There's still time, especially if you keep pushing me."

Ellie touched the now purple tufts of hair sticking up on her head. "It's just fashion, Ma."

"It's *purple,* for pity's sake." Another shake of her head and Claire Weston sighed. "I swear you're trying to send me into an early grave."

"Hey, I'm not stupid." Ellie winked at Brady.

"Can't give her a chance to change the will, now, can I?"

"Ellie Mae Weston!"

"Sorry, Ma."

Claire shook her head and turned back to Brady. "Pay her no nevermind. Your grandfather is as ornery as ever, that's true. But he's missed you. We all have."

"I've missed you all, too."

"Now." She hooked her arm through his. "Let's go in and say hello." Before he could protest, she ushered him forward, steering him down the hall and into the dining room. "Look who's joining us for lunch," she announced as they walked into the room.

"If it's that freeloading Slim Cadbury from the VFW, just tell him to go find his own apple pie. I don't care how nice he is, he isn't getting so much as a whiff. Why, the man's only interested in you for your food, Claire. Don't I keep telling you that—" The old man's words stumbled to a halt as his gaze lit on Brady.

Time seemed to stand still for Zachariah Brady Weston for the next several moments as he stared at his only grandson, his gaze as black, as unreadable, as Brady remembered.

His first instinct was to turn and run. He'd always felt that way whenever he'd been under his grandfather's inspection. Every Sunday morning before church. Every afternoon at the boot factory. Every Friday night after one of his high school hockey games.

And he'd always reacted the same. He'd simply stood his ground and waited for the criticism to come, praying for the approval. More often than not he'd received the first, but on occasion, the old man had smiled and congratulated him on a job well done.

This didn't seem to be one of those occasions.

Rather than dwell on the doubts raging inside him, Brady took the time to notice the changes eleven years had wrought.

His grandfather's hair had gone from a salt-and-pepper shade to snow-white. The lines around his eyes seemed deeper, the wrinkles etching his forehead more pronounced and plentiful. He looked older, yet his eyes were as blue and as bright as they'd always been. Brady knew then that eleven years might have aged the elder Weston on the surface but, deep down, he was the same man he'd been way back when.

Unease rolled through Brady and he had the urge to turn and walk away again. Now. Before he put his pride on the line and subjected himself to his grandfather's rejection—again.

Brady forced a deep breath and met the older man's penetrating stare. He wasn't going anywhere. He'd waited for this moment for much too long. Dreamt of it when his life had been less than perfect and he'd regretted leaving in the first place. He couldn't turn back now. He wasn't going to, no matter the outcome.

Brady's gaze clashed with blue eyes so much like his own and if he hadn't known better, he would have sworn he actually saw joy in the old man's eyes. The same joy he'd seen time and time again when he'd been younger, following his grandfather around the boot plant or the pasture or the barn.

Brady had always followed, at least when it came to his family. Among the rest of Cadillac, he'd been a leader, but at home he'd let others lead, content in knowing that one day he would have his chance to step up to the plate and bat.

He'd been a good, obedient grandson until he'd thrown it all away that one fateful day and gone against his family's wishes. All in the name of love. A no-no as far as Zachariah Weston had been concerned.

"There ain't room in a man's life for both work and family. Take your daddy for instance. He tried to have it all and worked himself into an early grave. You've got plenty of time to have a wife and family. Now's the time for work. For focus," he'd said.

"Aren't you going to say something, Zach?" Claire prodded, disrupting Brady's thoughts. "Brady's come all this way to see us."

The man reached for his napkin and tucked it in

at his neck. "When are we going to eat?" he asked Claire.

She planted her hands on her hips the way Brady remembered from his childhood. While she held the same values as her father-in-law, she'd never been quite as obedient as he'd wanted when it came to standing up for what she thought was right. And, of course, she'd distracted Brady's father at a time when he should have been focused on the company.

"Is that all you have to say?" Claire asked.

"What are we eating?"

Claire growled. "You're stubborn, you know that?"

"I'm hungry, that's what I am. Call it what you like."

She eyed him a few moments more. Then, as if she'd decided on a new approach, her expression softened and she smiled. "Doesn't Brady look good? Thanks to those Weston genes, of course."

Brady stood stock-still beneath his grandfather's disapproving gaze as the man swept him from head to toe. He knew what the elder Weston thought of his attire—the silk dress shirt. The expensive slacks. Yuppie, that's what Zachariah Weston was thinking. His only grandson had turned into a yuppie.

The sad truth was, he was right. Eleven years had taken their toll.

But no more, Brady vowed for the umpteenth time. He was shedding his image and getting back to his roots. His past. His *family*.

The old man's gaze dropped to the dusty cowboy boots Brady had unearthed the day before he'd left Dallas.

"Those are Weston boots," he told Claire, obviously intent on giving Brady the silent treatment.

"They're *my* boots." While Brady had inherited his sense of duty from his grandfather, he'd also inherited his mother's spunk. "You gave them to me, remember?"

"Tell this young man that, of course, I remember. I ain't that old." He eyed the boots again. "They're still Weston boots."

"And I'm a Weston."

Zachariah didn't say anything for a long moment. He simply stared and thought. Brady could practically see the wheels spinning as the old man decided his grandson's fate in those next few tense moments.

"Well, don't just stand there," the man finally barked at Claire. "Get the boy a seat. He's here. He might as well eat."

Brady let out the breath he hadn't even realized he'd been holding, and the tension eased. Zachariah Weston didn't eat with strangers. He only broke bread with friends, loved ones, *family.*

A warmth filled Brady as he slid into a nearby seat, followed by a swell of regret. Regret for all the lunches he'd missed. For the family he'd missed.

But he was home, and he was going to make up for lost time starting right now.

"DOROTHY REALLY OUTDID herself." Zachariah leaned back in his chair and puffed on his pipe. "Never had apples that tender."

"They were good," Brady commented, but his grandfather didn't so much as spare him a glance. He kept his gaze trained on his daughter-in-law.

"Ask him why he left Dallas."

"Why don't you ask him? He's sitting right in front of you."

"I don't belong there," Brady spoke up before his mother could give the old man a piece of her mind. And she would. Claire Weston had never had trouble standing up to her husband when he'd been alive and the same went for his ornery father. "I never did."

His gramps didn't say anything for a long moment. He simply puffed on his pipe and stared at Brady.

"Ask him what his plans are," he told his daughter-in-law.

"Listen, old man, I'm not your puppet—"

"I was thinking I might like to try my hands at making boots again," Brady cut in.

"Did you hear that?" Claire leveled a frown at Zachariah. "Or do you need to turn your hearing aid up?"

"I don't wear a hearing aid, little lady, and you'd do well to remember who you're talking to." He waved his pipe at her. "I can't imagine he still knows anything about making boots or that he's ready to give it his all."

"Just like riding a horse," Brady said. "Once you've climbed into the saddle and taken a good ride, you never forget and I wouldn't give anything less."

"Horse riding," Claire paraphrased, obviously tiring of arguing with the old man. "You never forget and he's dedicated."

The old man nodded and puffed a few more times before a thoughtful look crept over his expression. "I could use an extra pair of hands down at the factory. Not for some frou-frou position, mind you." He motioned to Brady's silk shirt. "I've got Ellie running the office and she doesn't need a bit of help. She's a whiz with numbers and loves every minute."

"I'm not an accountant," Brady told his grandfather, who didn't so much as spare him a glance. "I'm an ad man." *Was* an ad man.

"Tell him I ain't got room for one of those either."

"Good." Brady spoke up before his mother could open her mouth. "Because that's not the type of position I'm interested in."

"It takes focus, not to mention he's liable to get his hands dirty," Granddaddy warned.

"Just the way I like them."

"We'll see," Zachariah said as he puffed on his pipe and gave his only grandson one long, slow look. "We surely will."

"THIS IS BULLSHIT," Ellie declared later that afternoon as she pulled her Jeep Wrangler into the parking lot and braked to a halt. "You should be in charge of operations instead of hammering soles onto a bunch of cowboy boots. *Hammering,* of all things. I can't believe he's starting you out at the bottom. You might as well be just another—"

"—guy off the street," he finished for her. "Right now, I am. He doesn't trust me and I can't say as I blame him."

"What?"

"I betrayed him."

"You stood up to him. There's a big difference."

"Not to him, and until I prove myself again, then this is the way it's going to be. Lots of hammering and lots of silence."

"And that's another thing. Have you ever seen anything so juvenile as him talking to you through other people? He's crazy. That's all I have to say. And mean. And I have every intention of telling him so. Not that he'll listen to me either, but I'm going to do it anyway."

"Let it go, Ellie. If putting me through my paces and giving me the silent treatment will make him feel better, then that's what I'll let him do."

"You've got a college degree, for Pete's sake."

"And he's got a lot of resentment towards me. He needs to vent."

"So you're going to be his whipping boy until he comes to his senses, is that it?"

"I'll do what I have to do. I knew what I was facing when I left Dallas." And he'd been eager to get back anyway. To escape the daily grind and put the past eleven years behind him.

"But it's still not right," she persisted. "You shouldn't be doing something you hate. No one should." A faraway look crossed her eyes and Brady had the distinct impression that she'd died her hair green, then purple, not to make a fashion statement, but to make a personal one. Namely that she wasn't as happy hiding behind those ledger books as his grandfather apparently thought.

"Maybe not." But it felt right. Brady had worked in the hammering department as a teenager and he knew the work. What's more, he liked it. The heavy weight of the hammer in his hands and the scent of leather in his nostrils. "Trust me, I'm looking forward to every minute. You don't know how much I missed this place." He stared through the windshield at the large brown building that sat on the far edge of the Weston Ranch.

Once a barn, the structure had been expanded throughout the years and bricked over to accommodate the growing boot company. A small gravel parking lot sat to the right of the building. Brady trained his eyes on the patch of trees just beyond and glimpsed a large corral in the distance. He didn't need a closer look to know that the place stood empty. Gone were the animals that had once put muscle behind the large machinery used in the leather process when Brady had been a small boy. He'd been barely four when his grandfather had converted to the much cheaper and more convenient electricity. The massive tanning machines operated at the flick of a switch. Ovens that had once been fired up every morning by hand now had temperature knobs.

His grandfather had been determined to keep Weston Boots competitive in the ever-changing market place. Factories pumped out more and more and so the man had been hellbent on doing what he could to compete. And he'd succeeded. Somewhat.

The company was holding its own, but it wasn't moving. Ellie's books had indicated a steady profit over the past six years and while the numbers weren't dropping, they weren't increasing to represent the changing economy. The company needed a boost. He pushed the thought aside, however appealing. He wasn't an ad man. He made cowboy boots. End of story.

"Don't get me wrong." Ellie's voice pushed past his thoughts and drew his full attention. "I'm glad you're home. Damned glad. But after living in Dallas all these years, I wouldn't be surprised to see you go stir crazy over the next few days. This place is hardly the Exxon Towers."

"No," he agreed, "it's not even close." Which was the point exactly. The fading structure was completely opposite from the sixteen stories of steel and concrete he'd grown accustomed to. "Accustomed," as in tolerant. But he'd never developed a true liking for the skyscraper, much less the surrounding big city.

This he liked. The smell of grass. The sight of trees. The feel of the sun beating down on him, making sweat run in trickles from beneath the brim of his faded Resistol.

A smile tilted his lips as he climbed from the passenger seat and followed his sister toward the building. Familiarity rushed through him as he touched the rusted wagon wheel that hung on the front door of the building—the same wheel that had been hanging on the door since Weston Boots first opened back in the late 1800s.

"I keep telling Granddaddy to get rid of that," Ellie said as she came up behind him. "But you know better than anyone how stubborn he can be." She drew in a deep breath. "We're running with a skeleton crew since it's Saturday—Granddaddy's only day off—so you're not likely to get the real feel until the place is packed and all departments are up and operational. That'll be first thing Monday."

"That's okay. It'll give me a chance to get the feel of things again without worrying about slowing down production." He pushed open the door for his sister, then followed her inside.

"No problem, but do it fast because I've got a surprise planned for later."

"What surprise?"

"If I told you, then it wouldn't be a surprise, now, would it?" She smiled as if she held a big secret. "Let's just say, it's not every day the prodigal brother comes home. The occasion definitely calls for a celebration."

"As in a party?"

Excitement lit her eyes as she nodded. "As in an intimate party with the old gang."

He returned his sister's smile. "You never could keep a secret."

"How could I when you practically stuffed haystack needles under my fingernails to get me to talk?"

He grinned and let the door rock shut. Nostalgia rushed through him, along with a sense of peace and he simply stood there in the doorway, absorbing the sight and sound and smell of the place.

"What's wrong?" Ellie asked, her brow wrinkling as she studied him.

"Nothing," he said, sliding his arm around her as he guided her inside. "Everything's right. For the first time in a long time, everything's right."

"I'M AFRAID I'VE got bad news and good news," Merle, still clad in overalls and T-shirt, told him after

Ellie dropped him off at the service station to check on his car later that afternoon.

"Give me the bad news first."

"I cain't exactly do that. It really is bad news *and* good news all rolled into one. See, Janie Gingrich— she's the lady that used to rent the room above the garage before she married Trent Mulberry—had this nasty crow that got loose and took up residence in the tree just in back of the shop."

"Is this the good news or the bad news?"

"Both, I told you. Bad news because the critter's been living in the tree behind the shop. Only comes out when he hears my wrecker pull up. Came squawking by when I pulled in with your sports car and pooped all over the hood. I shooed her away." He waved his rolled-up issue of *Popular Mechanics*. "But it was too late. She scratched the paint before I knew what had happened."

"And that's good news, too?"

"Sure enough. I'll have to wait until Monday to get the paint from Austin, but good because I'd have to have the car until then anyway so's I can take a look at that cracked engine block and look for any permanent damage. I know, I know," Merle said when Brady started to talk, "it's not in keeping with my twenty-four-hour guarantee, but this being Saturday and all and Sunday not counting, it's technically only twenty-four work hours." He eyed his nephew. "You're not mad about the poop, are you?"

"Not if you've still got that room above the garage."

Merle grinned and fished in his pocket. "It's yours," he declared as he handed over a slightly bent key. "It ain't much, just a one-room with a kitchen, but it's clean. Maria sees to that."

"That's good enough for me." Brady took the key and retrieved his bag from the backseat of his Porsche.

"Mighty pretty car," Merle said as he trailed his hand along the door. "Minus the poop, of course."

"Yeah, it is nice." Nice was an understatement. It was the best, like everything else in his life. Sally never would have settled for less. Even when they'd been dead broke, she would spend the last dollar to buy one gourmet cookie that lasted all of a few bites, rather than a loaf of bread to last them all week.

The dollar days had passed and he'd gone on to bring home more money, which she'd promptly spent. Always buying the best, from clothes to cars to fifty-dollar decorative handsoaps that he hadn't been allowed to use. They'd been for show like everything else in her life. Status had meant everything, and so she'd moved on when someone with more status had come along.

Thankfully, she'd finally done what he couldn't because of his damned conscience. She'd ended their marriage. Cut him loose. Sent him on his way so she could climb higher on the social ladder.

Or was that why she'd left?

I need a real man who can satisfy me.

He pushed aside the words as he headed up the stairs to the one-room efficiency. He wasn't dwelling on the past. He was living for the moment. For right now. And right now involved taking a shower so he could meet his younger sister and the rest of his old buddies for a much-needed drink.

"Look out, Cadillac. Here I come."

3

"I NEED A screaming orgasm in the worst way."

"You and me both," Eden told the woman who plopped down at the bar later that evening, a near empty glass in hand.

Dottie Abernathy was a regular Saturday-afternoon customer and one of the few who didn't give a fig about Eden's reputation.

Then again, Dottie had had her own reputation to contend with before she'd married the local fire chief and made a respectable woman of herself. Bib boobs—and Dottie had been blessed with two Double D's—equaled an even bigger reputation, and so the woman understood what Eden had had to endure. She was in her late forties with graying red hair and a die-hard makeup habit that made the town's only Avon lady the number-one-ranked salesperson in Texas. Dottie had a few too many gray hairs and her crow's feet were deepening, but in her prime she'd stirred her fair share of gossip.

"I know why I need one," Dottie said, taking the very last sip of her drink. The woman was referring to the outrageously named beverage, while Eden had an entirely different orgasm on her mind. "James is at home planted in front of the TV and I'm here alone. But what's your excuse?"

Withdrawal. That's what had stirred Eden's hormones into a frenzy the moment she'd spotted Brady Weston. Sure, he was handsome and sexy, but he was still just a man. A walking Y chromosome. Nothing to get all excited about, unless the woman getting excited had been so busy the past six months working and worrying over the future and Jake Marlboro and what new stunt the slimeball was going to come up with to screw up her business that she'd completely neglected her personal life.

No wonder she'd been hot and bothered since walking into the Pink Cadillac after dropping Brady off at Merle's. She was deprived. Desperate. Due.

Yep, she was *definitely* due for a good, quality orgasm.

Not that she'd ever had anything close to a *screaming* one. Sure, she'd whimpered. She'd sighed. She'd even moaned a time or two. But no man had ever made her scream. Despite the rumors circulating around the small town.

Rumors. That summed up Eden's life to a T, at

least from the tenth grade up. She was one great big rumor. Her past. Her present. Her future.

Rumor had it that she'd slept with the entire football team her sophomore year, and that she was presently sleeping with every elk over at the ledge, including Homer Jackson who, everyone in their right mind knew, preferred bulls to heifers any old day. As for the future? She would probably sleep her way through the city council, or maybe boff every police officer on the ten-man force.

Rumor. That's all it was, with the exception of one really cute elk Eden had met last New Year's Eve at the annual holiday party. They'd dated a few times and slept together once, and that had been the end of it. He'd been a horse trainer for one of the nearby ranches, and once breaking season had ended, he'd left for New Mexico and another ranch.

She'd moaned with him. Not so much because the sex had been great. Looking back, she could objectively qualify it as so-so. But she'd been coming off a long dry spell after her last fling nearly four years ago at a bartending convention in Austin, and even so-so had been an occasion for moaning.

But a bonafide *scream?* Not this girl. Not with any of the handful of men she'd actually slept with, much less the hundreds that filled her make-believe résumé since Jake Marlboro had lied about her and made her the scarlet woman of Cadillac, Texas.

"Eden?" Dottie waved her empty glass. "Are you still with me?"

"Uh, yeah. Sorry. I guess I zoned out for a little while. It's been so hot out." She turned and twisted the air-conditioning knob a few notches cooler.

"You're telling me. Hit me again."

Eden had nothing against a woman quenching her thirst, but she wasn't in the habit of contributing to the delinquency of friends. Particularly when she sensed an underlying motivation propelling Dottie toward a second drink.

"Haven't you reached your one orgasm limit?"

Dottie Abernathy let out a pitiful sigh. "Usually, but I'm feeling *very* neglected today." She stared down at her empty glass. "Not that I really need the calories. Jerry's sure to run the other way if I pack on a beer belly."

Eden winked. "That's a screaming orgasm belly, and I can't imagine Jerry doing such a thing. He loves you."

"He loves me from February through July. It's August." At Eden's blank look, she added, "Preseason. I've dropped to number two on his priority list." She sighed. "At least it's not number three. I don't drop that far until October when deer season opens. Right now, I'm going head-to-head with the Dallas Cowboys." She eyed the bowl of honey-roasted cashews sitting on the counter behind Eden.

"What about those? Those are healthier than an orgasm, right?"

"Definitely the good kind of fat," Eden told her as she grabbed the bowl and placed it in front of Dottie. "And I won't have to drive you home."

"Men," Dottie said around a mouthful of nuts. "I'll never understand them."

"Amen." Eden popped a cashew into her own mouth. She'd tried understanding them. When Jake Marlboro had taken the treasured gift of her virginity and turned it into a sleazy strip show, she'd tried to see the entire event through his eyes. Had she done something to make him think she was sleezy? Had she come on too strong? Too soon? Had she been deserving of his nasty rumors?

Hell, no. That's what she'd finally decided, after a lot of soul searching and years of heartache. The fine, upstanding citizens of Cadillac could see what they wanted to see—namely that Jake was a wealthy, enterprising member of the community and she was little better than a cow pattie stuck to the bottom of his boot.

As if she cared.

She'd stopped caring a long time ago about other people's perceptions—make that *mis*perceptions— when she'd finally come to terms with the fact that her first true love was nothing more than a lying, conceited, egotistical jerk.

Then and now.

Her gaze swept the nearly empty bar. *Empty* when she'd always been packed at this time of afternoon. Even Mitchell Wineberg who gathered with his cronies for Saturday-afternoon dominoes wasn't in his usual corner. He was over at the VFW, thanks to Jake who'd donated a twenty-seven-inch color TV to the rec room that put her small nineteen-inch black-and-white to shame. Who wanted to watch Pat Sajak and Vanna White in black and white when they could see that wheel spin in vivid technicolor? Not a one of them would give the Pink Cadillac a second glance thanks to Jake's latest contribution. If Eden wouldn't sell out, Jake would force her out by making the Pink Cadillac obsolete when it came to fun and entertainment.

Or so he thought.

She wasn't going down without a fight. She didn't know what she was going to do, but it would be something foolproof. She wasn't selling the Pink Cadillac, no matter how much money he offered her.

Eden told herself that for the umpteenth time and turned her attention to Dottie and the bowl of cashews.

"...the Cowboys, of all teams," the woman was saying. "I could understand if he had me going head-to-head with the Packers. Now there's a decent football team. And cute. Why, they drafted a wide receiver with muscles out to here and a butt that begs to be pinched."

Dottie's comments stirred a vision of another very pinchable butt and Eden's attention shifted back to Brady and the picture he'd made standing on the side of the road, looking so hot and sweaty and sexy and...*hot.*

A twinge of longing shot through Eden and she reached for a handful of cashews.

Wait a second. Longing?

No way. Not when it came to a man. If she'd learned anything in her lifetime it was that men were a dime a dozen. Sure, there were those few good ones. Her father and Reverend Talbot and old Mr. Murphy over at the grocery store who climbed his apple tree out back every afternoon so his ailing wife could have fresh fruit with her lunch. Eden wasn't so jaded that she'd stopped believing in Mr. Right. He just wasn't lurking anywhere in Cadillac or the surrounding six counties.

But someday...

She dismissed the thought. Eden wasn't the type to sit around dreaming about the future. She made the best of the present and the matter at hand— which, right now, was her business—and the only thing she longed for was a rush of customers. That would show Jake Marlboro that he couldn't win at everything. While he'd certainly gotten the best of her once, it wasn't going to happen again.

"These days, the Cowboys ain't worth the price

of a hot dog at Texas stadium. But way back when they could make me sit up and take notice. Why, I remember when Jimmy Johnson was running the team..." Dottie droned on about the good old days and the nostalgia of the past as Eden poured herself a soda.

Nostalgia. That explained her reaction to Brady Weston. It wasn't so much that she was attracted to him now. No, she was remembering her attraction to him then.

The daydreams... All those times she'd sat in the bleachers and watched Brady throw a winning pass and fancied herself the head cheerleader and the object of his sexy all-star smile.

The fantasies... When she'd lounged on the bank of McKinney's Lake and watched Brady swing out over the lake in his best Tarzan imitation with the rest of his buddies. The rich kids. The haves. While Eden had sat on the opposite side with the have-nots, and pretended she was his Jane.

The reality... That one hot summer day when he'd had a flat and she'd given him a lift. In the close confines of her dad's beat-up pickup truck, with Brady so close and the heat so overwhelming, she'd come so close to living up to her reputation, sliding across the seat and kissing the devil out of Brady.

She'd wanted to, more than she'd ever wanted anything in her life. The feeling had been just as strong when they'd been on their "date." Throughout the night, Eden had wished he would ask her out for real. And she'd also wished he wouldn't be such a gentleman.

But that was in the past. Fond memories. A young girl's crazy infatuation with the sexiest boy in high school. Those days were over and she was all grown up now, and she didn't salivate over any man, no matter how handsome.

Besides, he wasn't *that* good-looking. Gone was the clean-cut, freshly shaven golden boy who'd taken the Cadillac Texans to the state football championship not once, but twice. The years had added a hardness to his once soft brown eyes. He was older now, with tiny lines rimming his eyes and a roughness about him that came with years of hard living.

Not her type at all. Eden preferred pretty-boy Ricky Martin to the Marlboro man any day. Brady Weston was a little too different from the All-American who'd dominated her adolescent fantasies. He was too masculine, too sexy, and he was here—

Her thoughts slammed to a halt as she straightened and focused on him standing in the doorway. His gaze collided with hers and he smiled, and for five full seconds Eden actually forgot to breathe.

"Hey, Eden!" The greeting came from Brady's sister Ellie, who came up next to him. The woman waved and steered her brother into a nearby booth.

Eden had barely forced a calm breath, much less responded when the door swung open again. A group of men and women walked in and made a bee-line for Brady and his sister.

The past pulled her back as she remembered all the lunches spent staring across the school cafeteria. She'd sat with her friends while Brady had held court amid the A-crowd in the center of the lunchroom.

There were several beer bellies now and a few pairs of fake breasts, but otherwise the group could have been plucked from the yearbook pages as they smiled and laughed and piled into several booths surrounding Brady and his sister.

"Looks like tonight's going to be busy," Dottie said, drawing Eden away from her musings and back to the fact of the matter—she had customers.

Her gaze shifted to Brady, to his sexy smile and the handsome picture he made sitting there in a straw Resistol, faded jeans and a white T-shirt. Gone were the designer clothes and the preoccupied look from this afternoon. He'd transformed back into the good-natured, relaxed cowboy who'd smiled at her from the side of the road that day so long ago. The same cowboy she'd stared at day after day in her English class.

Only he hadn't stared back at her then, not the way he stared at her now.

The look he fixed on her was different. Older. Wiser. *Hungrier.* What's more, that looked called her forward. Beckoned to her. Along with a deep, sexy male voice.

"We'd like to order."

The prospect of getting close, of feeling his body heat the way she had the other afternoon had an immediate effect on her. Heat rushed through her, making her nipples throb and her thighs ache, and for several long moments it was all she could do to simply breathe.

"I think they want to order." Dottie's voice finally drew her away from the sound of her own thundering heart, back to the present and the fact that her feet were still glued to the same spot, despite the fact that she had a booth full of much-needed customers.

Her first instinct was to call Kasey. Eden hadn't taken a break in several hours and the young woman could easily leave whatever chores she was doing out back to fill in for Eden out front. To *save* her.

The minute the thought hit, she forced it aside. What was *wrong* with her? She was bold and daring Eden Hallsey. She was the one who made men nervous, not the other way around. She made them sweat and want and *need.* Drawing in a deep breath, she gathered her courage and reached for her order pad.

Eden barely managed a few steps before Ellie called out, "Bring us some of your best champagne. We're celebrating. Brady's home!"

Saved by the little sister.

Relief swamped her and she turned before she could dwell on the feeling and the fact that she was actually nervous about approaching Brady Weston.

She headed through the double doors that led past the restrooms to the back room where she kept her stock.

She was *not* nervous.

She was pleased. Thrilled. Ecstatic. She had a dozen new customers and it was shaping up to be the most promising Saturday evening she'd seen in a very long time. All she had to do was ignore her ridiculous schoolgirl fantasies and concentrate on her business.

Sexy or not, Brady Weston was just a man. And men she could handle. She knew what they thought when they looked at her, what they wanted, what they expected, and the knowledge gave her an advantage.

That's what she told herself as she retrieved the champagne and pushed through the storage-room doorway. She'd barely taken two steps before she ran smack-dab into a wall of solid warmth.

One of the half dozen bottles she cradled in her arms slipped and hit the floor with a thunk and a roll.

"I'm sorry. I didn't see—" she started, the words dying in her throat when her gaze shifted and collided with bright blue eyes.

"No harm done. I'm just glad nothing broke." Brady dropped to his knees and retrieved the wayward bottle.

"Wh-what are you doing back here?"

"Call of the wild."

The answer stirred several images. Of tangled

sheets and sweaty bodies and *them*. Touching and kissing and...

She shook the thought and gathered her control. He was presumptuous, all right. But she hadn't expected anything different. He was a man. "You'll have to answer the call someplace else, buddy."

He arched an eyebrow and stared past her at the men's-room door. "You mean that isn't the men's room?"

Reality dawned and heat rushed to her cheeks. "You mean wild as in nature wild," she blurted. "I'm sorry. I thought you meant...I mean..."

"Thanks again for the ride this afternoon," he said, saving her from her own embarrassment.

"Glad to do it." She accepted the bottle from him, fighting back the heat that burned her cheeks. She'd misjudged him.

Maybe. Sure, she'd misread his comment, but that didn't mean that Brady Weston was different from the other men she ran into. She'd still caught him staring at her with that smoldering look in his eyes.

Like now.

"You haven't changed a bit," he told her.

"Really? And how would you know? You never even noticed me back in high school."

"Oh, I noticed you, all right. I couldn't help but notice."

"And what exactly did you notice?"

Here it comes. The cheesy comments about how

pretty she was and how much he'd wanted to talk to her and go out with her and—

"You always smelled like peanuts."

Eden had heard enough pick-up lines to fill an entire volume, *Cheesy Comments that Desperate Men Make,* but this one actually surprised her. Still, original or not, it was just a line. A prelude to the kiss that was sure to come.

And he *was* going to kiss her. She could see it in his eyes, feel it in the tightness of his body as he leaned toward her.

Eden's heart pounded and she licked her lips in anticipation. *Here it comes...*

His mouth opened and his head dipped and he sniffed her.

Wait a second. Sniffed?

"Pistachios?" he murmured, his warm breath fanning her temple.

"Honey roasted cashews," she managed, doing her best to stifle the disappointment that rushed through her.

He leaned back and grinned. "That was my next guess. The champagne's getting warm," he said as he moved past her toward the restroom. "Thanks again."

Before Eden could take her next breath, he disappeared into the men's room and she was left staring at the closed door, her heart pounding and her lips tingling and her mind racing.

He'd sniffed her, of all things. No kiss. No attempt at a kiss. Not even a touch. Just a sniff. A *sniff.*

"Mitch," she called out, turning to walk back into the back storage room where her employee was stocking cases of Lonestar. "Take over the bar." She handed over the bottles, pulled off her apron and retreated into the kitchen.

Brady had just proven beyond a shadow of a doubt that he wasn't like the other men she came into contact with. He was different, one of a kind, and Eden wanted him.

For the first time in her life, she actually wanted a man. She wanted to kiss him and touch him and talk to him, and the realization scared her.

Almost as much as it excited her.

He was stupid.

Stupid, stupid, *stupid.*

Eden had been practically begging for his kiss and he'd *sniffed* her, of all the crazy things.

What the hell was wrong with him?

The question echoed through his head for the entire evening as he talked and laughed and got reacquainted with his old crowd. But it was the answer that followed him down the street toward his room above the Gas-n-Go and crawled into bed with him much, much later.

"I need a man who can really satisfy me."

Satisfy. That's what it all came down to and, after

eleven years of a not-so-satisfying marriage, Brady didn't know if he was up to the task. He wasn't, according to his ex-wife.

Then again, she couldn't see him right now. A quick glance down at the bulge in his jeans and he smiled.

And then he frowned. After all, having the equipment roaring and ready to go was different from actually doing the job. There were lots of guys out there who could get it up. It's what a man did with what he had that separated the stallions from the plow horses.

Satisfaction.

Did he have that something extra—be it know-how, an inbred sexuality, whatever—that would enable him to truly satisfy a woman? That special something that would make her call out his name in the middle of the night?

Forget call. He wanted a woman to scream for him.

But did he have it? Did he know what really turned a woman on?

Brady wasn't sure if it was the four beers coupled with the glass of champagne he'd chugged down at the Pink Cadillac, or the fact that he was half-exhausted and not thinking too clearly, or just a textbook case of insanity that made the answer suddenly obvious. Hell, it could have been all three. He didn't know. He just knew there was a solution to his problem.

He'd find a woman and satisfy her fifty ways 'til Sunday.

Then he would *know,* deep down in his soul, that his ex had been a gold digger like his family had claimed, and that he was still the same man he'd been when he'd walked away from Cadillac. Still a Weston. Still in control of his life and his destiny and his identity.

But it couldn't be just any woman. It had to be *the* woman that had haunted him so many nights when he'd been a naive high school kid.

Eden Hallsey.

The name stirred a vision of her as she'd been tonight, staring up at him in the hallway, her lips plump and parted, desire gleaming in her eyes.

She was all woman. Hot. Sexy. Temporary.

His groin tightened and he shifted in the bed to make himself more comfortable. Yes, he was going to sleep with Eden Hallsey. And prove to himself, once and for all, that he was every bit a man.

4

"WAIT UNTIL YOU hear the hot news," Kasey Montgomery announced as she waltzed into the stockroom at the Pink Cadillac for Sunday-morning inventory.

Eden glanced at her watch. Make that Sunday-afternoon inventory. "You're late."

"I think my Timex stopped." She slapped her oversized tote down on the floor and sat down on a crate of Lonestar.

"You don't wear a Timex," Eden pointed out. "Or any watch for that matter."

The blonde glanced at her bare wrist as if seeing it for the first time. "Wow. No wonder I'm late." Kasey popped the tab on her Diet Coke and cast an excited gaze on Eden. "So there I was coming out of the TG&Y—they just got a special order of the Vampin' Red lipstick I've been lusting over ever since I saw it in last month's issue of Cosmo—and who do you think I saw?"

"Laurie Mitchell with her very own tube of Vampin' Red." Laurie was the town's reigning beauty queen and Kasey's arch enemy since she'd taken her Miss Cadillac crown and her reputation as the local beauty authority. The comment drew the expected frown and Eden smiled. Since she couldn't bring herself to dock Kasey's pay for her notorious tardiness—she and Kasey had been friends since sixth grade when they'd shared a pack of Bubblicious gum during gym, followed by a stint in detention for getting caught—the least she could do was yank the girl's chain every once in a while. "Can you pass me that jar of swizzle sticks?"

"For your information, Laurie wouldn't know her Vampin' Red from her Seductive Scarlett if her poor, pathetic, bleached blond life depended on it." Kasey handed over the container of multicolored sticks and her frown disappeared as excitement crept back into her expression. "I saw Anita Kingsbury," she announced. "That's who."

"Anita practically lives at the TG&Y. She does needlepoint and it's the only store that stocks the thread. That's not hot news."

"Of course it's not. Anita was carrying the news. She'd just been to the Piggly Wiggly where she'd just run into Janie Tremaine who'd just been to Mabel's for a permanent."

"Janie traded in her straight hair for a permanent?"

"And a haircut, but that's not the point. See, while

Janie was having the extra small rollers done on her crown, she overheard Sarah Waltman who'd just come in for a bilevel trim with shagged bangs."

"Sarah's going with shagged bangs?"

"Wild, isn't it? But that's not the point either."

"Then what *is* the point?"

"Guess who Sarah ran into before she arrived at Mabel's?" Before Eden could answer, Kasey rushed on, "*Him,* that's who."

"That tells me a lot. Do you know how many *hims* there are in this town?"

"Approximately .75 for every female," Kasey replied. "And you're not listening. I didn't say him. I said *him.*"

"Now that clears up the mystery. Can you turn around and give me a pretzel count?"

"I can't believe you've forgotten." Kasey reached for a jar of pretzels instead and popped the lid. "Fifth period," she said around a mouthful. "Mrs. Jasmine's sophomore English class."

Eden penciled in the pretzel figures. "You're eating up all my profit."

"It's just a handful." She put the lid back on. "Just add them to my bill. So guess who's back in town?"

"Mrs. Jasmine."

"No, silly." Kasey grabbed the clipboard and reached around Eden for a bag of popcorn. "It's Brady Weston. You know Brady with-the-cutest-butt-at-Cadillac-High Weston? Don't tell me you've forgotten the highlight of our pathetic sophomore lives?"

If only.

The trouble was, she remembered all too well. How cute he'd looked walking down the hall in his tight jeans and letterman's jacket. How sexy he'd seemed every time his full lips had curled into a grin. How irresistible he'd been standing on the side of the road that unbearably hot summer day.

Eden pushed the thought aside. Okay, so she was attracted to him. She was also a grown-up rather than a hormone-driven teenage girl. She'd perfected her control over the past ten years.

"You *do* remember him?" Kasey persisted, opening the bag and dishing a handful of the butter-flavored snack into her mouth.

"Vaguely."

"And Laurie and I are the best of buddies."

"Okay, so I remember him. That goes on your tab," she told Kasey as the girl reached for another handful of popcorn.

"Him and his butt."

"Remembering someone usually entails all parts of them."

"Man, that was an ultra-fine butt. Go on," Kasey prodded. "I know you remember. Just admit it. Confession is good for the soul."

"Okay, so he has an ultra-fine butt."

"*Has,* as in present tense?" Kasey folded up the

half-eaten bag of popcorn and studied her. "You're holding out on me."

"Maybe I've seen his butt for myself." When Kasey looked ready to burst with curiosity, Eden added, "Yesterday I picked him up on the road outside of town and gave him a lift."

"And you didn't tell me?"

"This is the first time I've seen you since yesterday."

"That's worthy of a phone call. So?" she prodded after a long moment when Eden didn't say anything.

"So what?"

"So what does he look like now?"

"Would you believe a receding hairline and a pot belly?"

"Brady Weston? Not on your life. C'mon and spill it."

"The same." At Kasey's doubtful look, she gave in to the smile playing at her lips. "Better."

"I knew it!" Excitement flashed in the girl's eyes as she wiggled her eyebrows. "Does he still sound the same? All deep and sexy?"

I know who you are. Brady's words echoed in Eden's ears and heat shimmered along her nerve endings. "Deeper and sexier."

Kasey let out a whoop. "I knew it. And his smell?" A dreamy look crept over her expression. "Does he still smell as good as he did back in English?"

Eden's nostrils flared at the memory of Brady

sitting next to her and stirring her senses with his clean, musky scent. "Better."

"I knew it. It's the age thing. Brady is like a classic '69 Mustang. Granted, way back when it was still a hot car. But now...it's mega-hot. A classic. Maturity makes all the difference. The added years make Brady look better. Sound better. Even smell better."

"And here I thought my cologne was responsible for that last one." The deep voice slid into Eden's ears and shimmered over her nerve endings. The hair on her arms stood straight up and heat rushed to her cheeks as she turned to find Brady standing in the storage-room doorway.

"My, my, if it isn't Mr. Brady Weston." Kasey slid off the crate and stood, tugging at her blouse as if she were fourteen again, back in Miss Jasmine's class. "Why, it's been ages since I've seen you."

"Much too long," Brady agreed, but his gaze wasn't on Kasey. His attention rested solely on Eden.

She wanted to look away, to break the connection between them and regain her composure. The trouble was, she knew it was a useless effort. She'd never had it together where Brady was concerned. He was different. He'd always been different. From the moment he'd pushed all rumor aside and planted that soft, sweet kiss on her cheek after their first and last date.

Brady was the sort of man dreams were made of.

The gallant white knight. And time seemed to have changed little.

Unfortunately.

"So how long have you been standing there?"

"Long enough to be thankful that I don't have a receding hairline and a pot belly."

"That long, huh?" She shook her head and tried to ignore the strange sense of self-consciousness he stirred.

If only.

"I guess you heard us carrying on about you, then," Kasey said. "Man, you were something."

"Were, meaning past tense." He grinned. "Thanks a lot."

"Oh, it's not just the past. The present is pretty fine, as well."

"Kasey has no shame," Eden said when Brady chuckled.

"Shame'll get you nowhere on a Friday night. A girl has to go after what she wants. Speaking of which," she grabbed another bag of popcorn and headed for the doorway, "I need lunch."

"That makes ten bucks," Eden told her as the girl scooted by.

"You should be the one paying me," Kasey whispered. "Most women would kill for a chance to be alone with such a cute hunk."

But Eden wasn't most women and Brady Weston wasn't just any hunk. He was the *only* hunk she'd ever really been attracted to. She'd gone out with guys and kissed more than her fair share, but none that she'd really *wanted* to kiss. She'd kissed and petted because it had been expected of her, but with Brady she'd felt the need clear to her bones.

The winning ticket had been a godsend, or so she'd thought. One date. The chance to finally, *finally* satisfy her curiosity and kiss him. There'd been no doubt in her mind that it would happen. Brady was just a guy, after all, and all guys reacted to her— or rather, her *reputation*—in exactly the same way. They expected to score and wasted little time with preliminaries. She'd had no doubt that things would be the same with Brady, but the notion hadn't upset her. She'd wanted him too badly and so she'd been ready. Excited. A first for Eden Hallsey where boys were concerned.

She'd had another first that night, however. She'd learned that all men were not hormone-driven, ego-tistical low-lifes. There were a few white knights out there, namely, one handsome, luscious football team captain who'd treated her like a lady the entire eve-ning and given her a chaste good-night kiss on her forehead.

She'd been disappointed and thrilled at the same time. A deadly mix that had her daydreaming the rest of her high school career about things Eden Hallsey had never dared to dream before.

Or since.

Things like marriage and babies and happily-ever-afters.

But Brady had been too much one of a kind. While he'd renewed her faith in men, she'd yet to meet another man like him.

"I never knew there was a Brady cheering section," he told her once they were alone.

She shrugged and did her best to look nonchalant. "Maybe there wasn't. Maybe I knew you were there all along and Kasey and I were just carrying on for your benefit."

Something passed over his expression the moment she voiced the possibility. A strange look of insecurity, but then it was gone and his grin slid back into place. "So you remember my butt, do you?"

She tried to sound nonchalant. "Vaguely."

He grinned. "I remember your butt, too. And," he added, his gaze sweeping her from head to toe, "all the rest."

Her heart pounded at the prospect. "Really? And here I thought you never gave me a second glance."

"Oh, I gave you a second look. And a third. I just couldn't do any more back then."

Because he'd had a girlfriend. A beautiful, popular, possessive girlfriend, and while Eden had heard many rumors that things weren't so great in paradise, Brady had never let on otherwise. He'd been loyal, and Eden had liked him all the more because of it.

She still liked him, if the thunder of her heart was any indication.

"I…" She licked her lips and tried for a calm voice. "I—I think something's wrong with the air conditioner. It's really hot in here."

"Amen to that," he said. His eyes fired a brighter blue and she knew he wasn't referring to the air surrounding them, but the heat flowing between them. "But it's not your air unit, darlin'. I think it's you. And me."

"I don't know what you mean." The statement was so unlike her. With any other man she would have flirted rather than played the coy virgin. She wasn't a virgin, and she certainly wasn't coy. Not since that day when she'd offered herself to Jake the Butthead Marlboro.

But this was different. He was different.

"There's chemistry between us," Brady pointed out. "There's always been chemistry, but it's stronger now. Too strong to ignore." He leaned closer and ran his fingertip along her jawline. "You feel it, don't you?"

She nodded.

"We should do something about it."

She nodded, her heart pounding faster. This was it. The moment she'd dreamt of all through high school. Brady Weston was actually going to ask her out on a real date.

"Sleep with me."

The request sent a burst of disappointment through her, followed by a rush of excitement unlike anything she'd ever felt before. All those years of holding him up on a pedestal suddenly seemed so useless. He was no different from the other men she'd met. His request proved as much.

Now she knew the truth. Her head did, that is. But her body, with its fluttering heart and sweaty palms and shaky knees, had yet to get the message.

"The attraction between us is too powerful to ignore, darlin'. What do you say? Just for one week?" he continued, a sexy grin on his lips.

Eden pondered the problem. She still wanted this man despite the fact that he'd clearly proven himself to be just as much of a jerk as every other man. She could see only one solution.

Once she slept with him and turned Brady from a dream man into a plain, ordinary, flesh-and-blood male, she would stop responding like some silly, naive teenager. His image would be totally shot and he would be out of her system, her curiosity satisfied once and for all.

"Yes."

Yes?

Was she totally nuts?

Hell, no. You're Eden Hallsey. Cadillac's most notorious bad girl, and you're going to do what any bad girl would do with such a hot, sexy man. You're going to have sex with him.

That's what Eden told herself. The trouble was, this was Brady Weston. The one man Eden had lusted after since puberty. The only man who hadn't lusted back.

Until now.

It seemed as if Brady had turned out to be just another one of the guys wowed by her bad girl image. Far from the gentleman she'd initially thought.

The realization left a bitter taste in her mouth but, at the same time, she couldn't suppress the excitement that pounded through her at the prospect of next Saturday night—the first in a week of nights to remember.

They'd made all the arrangements of a traditional date—Saturday night, the Pink Cadillac, eight o'clock—but the evening to follow would be anything but.

Cheap, tawdry and degrading.

Those were the adjectives that should have come to mind. They'd eliminated even the tiniest bit of romance by planning a night of sex as if it were a trip to the dentist.

But over the next few days as the weekend approached, it was *sexy, exciting and empowering* that kept her heart beating fast and her blood racing.

With his wicked smiles and brilliant blue eyes, Brady was the epitome of *sexy*.

For a woman whose sex life had been practically nonexistent, the prospect of being with such a man was *exciting*. Like a child about to open a present she'd been eyeing under the Christmas tree, she was finally going to know what it felt like to really kiss the man of her dreams. But it was also *empowering* because, despite the intense disappointment she felt at discovering Brady wasn't the white knight she'd always envisioned, there was still something oddly liberating about doing away with all the silly cat-and-mouse games that most men and women played. They both knew what they wanted and they were adult enough to cut right to the chase. No flowers and candy. No empty promises. Just a night of hot, wild sex to sate the lust burning between them.

Yes!

5

"YOU'RE UP AWFUL early this morning." The comment came from Zeke Masters, an old high school hockey buddy and the newest addition, besides Brady, to the Weston Boots hammering department. "I'm only here this early because once 7:00 a.m. rolls around, we run out of hot water over at Mrs. McGuire's," Zeke continued.

Mrs. McGuire ran the only boarding house in town, which was where Zeke had been living since a very public breakup with his wife of ten years. She'd taken the house over on Main and his job at her parents' horse ranch, while Zeke had ended up with the clothes on his back and a pop-up tent he'd been using prior to the hellacious rain that had blown the canvas away six weeks ago. He'd had to resort to renting a room, which meant he needed money, which explained his presence at Weston Boots. "Cain't stand the cold on my bare back, so I'm up and out 'afore the crack of dawn. What about you?"

"Thought I'd get a head start on things." That, and catch his grandfather who was notorious for beating the workers to their spots. The man lived for sunup and Brady was determined that whatever Zachariah Weston liked, he was going to give him.

He eyed the white pastry bag and steaming foam cup sitting on his work bench.

"Is that what I think it is?" Zeke asked, his nostrils flaring.

"White crème-filled donuts with chocolate sprinkles fresh from Gentry's Bakery." His grandfather's all-time favorite.

"Sure does smell good."

"That's what I'm counting on."

But the crème-filled donuts didn't live up to his expectations ten minutes later when his grandfather walked into the building.

"Good morning," Brady said as the old man walked by. Other than the slight flare of the man's nostrils, he gave no indication that he was even aware of Brady's presence, much less interested in pastries.

So much for an edge.

Brady grabbed the bag of donuts and handed them to Zeke. "Knock yourself out."

"Thanks," the man said a moment later around a mouthful of donut.

"It's nothing." Unfortunately. But Brady wasn't

giving up. He'd known that winning his grandfather's favor back wouldn't be easy, but he was determined to try. Today was just the beginning.

"I HATE MONDAYS," Ellie groused later that morning as she walked into the Weston Boots office, a cup of cappuccino in one hand and a donut in the other.

Brady pulled off one of his gloves and wiped the sweat from his brow. "Think of it this way. Monday is the beginning of the week. A fresh start."

She frowned. "I should have known it."

"What?"

"With all that smiling you've been doing. All the grins and the winks, and all without benefit of caffeine." She eyed him and nodded. "Yep, it's a sure thing."

"What?"

"Dallas turned you into one of those bright-eyed and bubbly morning-a-holics."

Actually, that transformation had come about just a few short days ago when Brady Weston had rolled back into Cadillac to reclaim his former life. Before that he'd been like every other big city suit—consumed by his work. He'd spent his evenings, his weekends and most holidays at the office. And all to maintain the lifestyle that Sally had grown accustomed to. He'd worked his ass off to please her. To live up to his responsibilities. To honor the commitment he'd made when he'd said "I do."

She's not your kind. His grandfather's words echoed in his head the way they had so many times over the past ten years, but Brady forced it aside. He wasn't dwelling on the past. He'd made his mistakes and learned from them. Today was a new beginning. The first day of the rest of his life right here in Cadillac.

He grinned and raised the blind. Sunlight streamed into the office and Ellie shielded her eyes. "You're trying to kill me, aren't you?"

"Now why would I do that to my favorite sister?"

"You're still mad because I told Katy Milner that you wanted to give her a hickey."

"Actually, little sis, I'm glad you told Katy. She stopped playing hard to get and came after me." He grabbed her donut, took a bite and winked. "Don't work too hard."

Ellie snatched back what was left of her breakfast and growled. "I'd say the same to you, but I know you're not going to listen. You're determined to make the rest of us look bad."

"I'm just glad to be back. To be doing something I actually like."

"I wish I could say the same." Ellie's words followed Brady out the door and down the hall to the staircase that led to the second-floor administrative offices. He'd started to wonder if his presence was to blame for his little sister's perpetual foul mood. After all, she'd had their grandfather all to herself for the past ten years and now she had to share him. But there was something else going on, something deeper, and Brady once again speculated that, perhaps, Ellie wasn't happy with her life.

"Hey there, son." His grandfather's voice sounded behind him and killed any more exploration of the subject. "Ready to tackle a full day's production?"

The question drew a full grin. The old man had actually asked him a direct question.

At least, that's what Brady thought until he found his grandfather staring past him at Zeke, who still had a speck of white crème at the corner of his mouth.

"Why, yes, sir. I'm always ready."

"Hear you were here early today. I like that."

"I like to get a jump on my work."

"Or a jump into the shower," Brady grumbled. Not that he was being a bad sport. He'd known winning his grandfather's favor back wouldn't be easy, but he was determined to try.

So determined that he showed up the next morning with his grandfather's favorite pancakes and sausages from the Turtle Diner over on North Street.

The old bull at least did more than sniff. He actually glanced at the foam box before ignoring Brady's good-morning, congratulating Zeke on his punctuality and heading for his office.

"Man, are you sure you don't want some of this?" Zeke asked when Brady handed him the breakfast.

"I've lost my appetite."

For food, that is. But he was still hungry for something else. For someone else. For, although his days were filled with thoughts of winning over his grandfather, his nights were overflowed with fantasies of Eden.

The thought drew a vision of her, her lips slick and pouty from his kiss. They'd just shared one kiss. But come Saturday night there would be more. More touches. More kisses. *More.*

His heart pounded at the thought. But as the week progressed, the nights long and sleepless and the days filled with work, his excitement turned to anxiety. After all, he was going to sleep with the woman. Time to find out the truth.

I need a real man.

"Damn, boy. What's wrong with you?"

"Nothing," Brady replied before he realized that his grandfather's question wasn't directed at him. As if he could expect anything different.

"Zeke," he said to the young man fighting with the branding iron, "you got to get a better grip than that if you want the brand to be deep enough to last, and everybody knows a real pair of Western boots has a brand that lasts."

"Sorry, sir, but I used to break horses, not brand them. I'm afraid this is new to me."

"Now, Granddaddy, stop grousing at Zeke. Everybody who's ever picked up a brand knows it takes time to get it right," Ellie said as she waltzed past, box in hand, and handed out paychecks, the late Friday-afternoon ritual.

"New? Why, he's been here a full two weeks. I was branding on my first day."

"Which is why you're the boss," Ellie told him as she handed over the box of checks and walked over to Zeke. "It's really not that hard," she told the young man. "Just think of it as branding a heifer, but a lot less trouble. After all, the boot's not going to whine or put up a fight. There's zero chance you'll get kicked. See—" She took the branding iron in one hand and a brand-new boot fresh from the tanner in her other. "Hold it just like this for about five seconds and, presto, you've got a custom-designed, one-of-a-kind Weston boot."

"Thanks, Miss Ellie," Zeke said after she demonstrated a second and then a third time before handing him the branding iron.

"Anytime." She winked before turning and retrieving the paycheck box.

"I need those account reports by this afternoon," their grandfather told her.

"I'm on it."

"And last month's invoices."

"Why didn't you tell me that earlier? I've still got to finish up the balance sheets for the previous month and it's already noon."

He slid his arm around her shoulder and gave her

an affectionate squeeze. "Guess you'll have to order in for the three of us. Zeke and I are going to take a look at that old tanning machine that keeps cooking the leather. I like to show all my new guys all the equipment, even the malfunctioning kind."

New, as in Brady. Only Zachariah Weston wasn't treating him like the other newbies. He was ignoring him. Punishing him.

Brady clamped his lips together and turned back to the hammer and leather at his fingertips.

"I checked the timer on that old machine last week," he told Zeke as he ushered him down the hall, "and it seems to me—"

"It ain't the timer," Ellie said as she followed.

"Sure it is."

"But I tested it myself and—"

"Give Murray over at the Pig-n-Pit a call, would ya, darlin'? And order us up a couple of double rib burgers with onion rings. It'll be my treat since Zeke, here, has been so punctual every morning. Got to reward good work habits."

"But I…" She caught her bottom lip and chewed for a long second before shaking her head. "No problem."

"That's my girl." He patted her shoulder and a smile spread across her face. But the expression didn't quite touch her eyes and Brady got the feeling that she wasn't nearly as pleased with their grandfather's comment as she wanted him to think. "And you'll have the reports by this afternoon."

"Never a doubt in my mind, honey. Now you run along and let us get to work."

Work. The one and only thing that helped Brady get through the rest of his day. He could focus his attention on something constructive rather than fret over his grandfather's coldness, not to mention the coming weekend.

And he was fretting.

What had started out as excitement had quickly morphed into full-blown anxiety as the moment of truth approached.

I need a real man who can satisfy me.

His ex-wife's parting words haunted him for the next few days, feeding his anxiety until Friday night arrived and Brady found himself questioning his decision.

Did he really think he could satisfy a woman like Eden Hallsey?

He knew her reputation. She wasn't some wet-behind-the-ears virgin who would cling to him. She was a real woman. A sexy-as-all-get-out woman who wouldn't be content with clumsy kisses or a mediocre performance in bed. For Eden he would have to go the extra mile.

The trouble was, after eleven years in an unhappy marriage, Brady wasn't sure if he knew what that *extra mile* entailed.

But he intended to find out.

With that vow in mind, he pulled out of the parking lot of Weston Boots late that Friday evening and headed into town for some reinforcements.

BRADY STARED THROUGH his windshield at the red tin building located one street over from the main strip through town. White trim accented the door and window shutters and gave the place a barn look. Of course, it *had* been a barn way back when Cecil Montgomery had used it to house his milk cows before selling out to Lulu Kenner—the oldest, meanest math teacher to ever smack a hand while working out an algebraic equation. Thanks to a double order of chili fries that had sent her husband Jeb to his death and a nice, fat insurance check, Lulu had given up her ruler, taken an early retirement and gone into business for herself.

Brady glanced up at the red neon sign glittering in the window. Miss Lulu's Video World.

Hey, it wasn't Lookin' for Love, the adult store located a few blocks over from his office back in Dallas, but it would have to do. He'd seen the blazing red neon sign on more than one occasion, but he'd never had a mind to pay a personal visit. He'd been too busy working himself from dusk 'til dawn, living up to his responsibilities to worry about his carnal knowledge.

Or lack of.

He closed his mind to the negative thought and climbed out of his pick-up. Coming home wasn't about regret. It was about living. Today. Tomorrow.

Tomorrow night.

Boots crunched gravel, the sound mingling with the buzz of crickets as he walked to the entrance. A bell tinkled, announcing his arrival, and Brady soon found himself in the new release section of Miss Lulu's.

"Can I help you?" The voice drew him around and Brady found himself staring at a young teen, a Cadillac High football jersey pulled tight across his young chest. A straw cowboy hat sat perched atop his head while a toothpick wiggled at one corner of his mouth. "If you want *Coyote Ugly,* there's only one copy and we're fresh out. We're always fresh out since I finally talked Granny into ordering the danged thing in the first place." He grinned. "Said there wasn't much of a story line, but then I convinced her it weren't the story line that was going to sell the blasted thing and we were in business. Now I do all the ordering. And the clerking when I finish practice. So what can I do you for? You looking for a particular title?"

"Not really."

"Something featuring a certain actor. Me, I watch everything with Demi Moore. She's hot."

"I'm not too particular. I just need something that a woman would like."

"You mean a chick flick? One of those tear-jerker movies? I got just the thing. *Steel Magnolias*. It's got all this female bonding stuff and—"

"Not that kind of a chick flick. Something more... romantic."

"Sure thing. *Ghost*. It's an older movie, but the chicks really go for it. It's like a psychological, undying love sort of thing and—"

"I mean *romantic* romantic."

"Sure thing. Right over there is *Gone with the Wind*. You can't get more—"

"Sexy. I need sexy."

"Well, there's always *American Gigolo*. I can't see it myself, but my girl says Richard Gere's about as sexy as they—"

"Sex," Brady blurted. "I need sex." He drew in a deep breath. "Do you have anything that's romantic and physical with a female slant?"

A light bulb seemed to go off in the young man's head and he smiled. "Sure, man. I've got just the thing."

Several minutes later, Brady found himself walking out of Miss Lulu's with a bagful of videos, including *9 1/2 Weeks,* an erotic thriller guaranteed to give him some pointers on really satisfying a woman.

After eleven years in a not-so-satisfying marriage, Brady needed all the help he could get.

"So I TOLD him, it's either me or Rudy T."

"I thought Jim was into football," Eden told the twenty-something blonde sitting at the bar, nursing a beer late Saturday afternoon. Trina McWilliams had married her college sweetheart, Big Jim, a little over six months ago. The entire town figured them for the perfect couple. Whenever Big Jim was out plowing his field, Trina would be perched up on the tractor right next to him.

"Jim *is* into football."

"Well, I hate to tell you, but Rudy T is the head coach for the Houston Rockets." At Trina's blank look, Eden added, "They're a basketball team."

Reality seemed to dawn and Trina shook her head. "No wonder he looked at me as if I'd grown a third eye. I'm not really into sports." She shook her head. "Maybe marrying Jim was a big mistake. After all, what do we really have in common?"

"It's only been a few months. Give it some time."

"And it'll only get worse," Dottie Abernathy said as she slid into her usual seat at the bar and requested her screaming orgasm. "Now it's football," she told Trina as she reached for a nearby bowl of popcorn. "Next year he'll be into baseball. Then there's basketball. And hockey. And just wait until hunting season." Dottie rolled her eyes. "When it's us or a big buck, darlin', guess who's plumb out of luck?"

Trina's face seemed to brighten. "Big Jim doesn't like to hunt. He's more into fishing."

"A buck or a bass, it makes no nevermind. The end result is the same. Zero time together."

"Don't listen to her," Eden said as she replaced Trina's empty beer bottle with an ice-cold Coke. "She's married to one of the nicest men in the county."

"Nice has nothing to do with it." Dottie turned to Trina. "I want attentive."

"Me, too. I mean, Big Jim is as sweet as a moon pie, but when the TV is on, I might as well not even exist."

Eden filled a bowl with honey-roasted cashews and slid it across the countertop toward Dottie. With the way she was already going on about her husband, she deserved to indulge tonight. "It's not full of testosterone, but maybe this will make you feel better." Eden turned her attention to her third and last customer. "Hey there, Grace. You okay with that soda?"

"Sure thing, sugar. But I sure could use some more of this popcorn." Her gaze never wavered from the television set perched in the far corner of the bar. Gracie McVie was one of the oldest residents of Cadillac and a die-hard court TV fan. Since the old folks' home out on the highway had hired a new social director who was also a fanatical dieter, the TV room had turned into a workout gym filled with back-to-back *Sweatin' with the Oldies* videos.

Gracie was too old to sweat, or so she'd told Eden the first day she'd walked through the front door and asked if Eden had a television. She hadn't had one back then, but she'd pulled her own from her apartment above the bar and hooked it up on a shelf in the far corner. Gracie had been forever grateful and had come in every Saturday since.

"Judge Jackie's about to give the heave-ho to that there seamstress for goofing on the plaintiff's wedding dress the day of the wedding. Imagine that. The day *of.* Why, if someone had goofed on my dress the day I married my dear, sweet Bernie—God rest his soul—I would've let loose a couple of rounds of buckshot and asked questions later. Of course, that was before my arthritis set in." She flexed her fingers. "It's hell getting old."

"You're not old," Eden started, but Gracie had already waved her into silence.

"The judge is about to deliver his verdict."

Eden was about to turn and head back to Trina and Dottie when she heard the voice behind her.

"Kind of slow for a Saturday night, isn't it?"

She tried to calm the sudden pounding of her heart. "Actually, this is the usual. The Pink Cadillac isn't the hot spot it used to be."

"Since when?" Brady asked as he reached the bar.

"Since Jake Marlboro decided he wanted to buy me out," she told him, noting how potently masculine he looked in his soft cotton shirt and Wranglers.

"I never would've had Jake figured for the bar owner type."

"He isn't. He wants the Pink Cadillac and every other business on this block so that he can put up a MegaMart."

He nodded. "My uncle mentioned that. I never pictured him owning a department store."

"He doesn't own them. He just builds them. Mega hired him to site out the best location and construct store number two hundred twenty-seven."

"And you got lucky."

"It's not luck. This bar has been in my family for years and it's staying in the family as long as I have anything to say about it." The trouble was, with business declining, Eden wasn't sure how much longer she would have something to say about it. Her savings would only last so long. After that, suppliers would stop supplying if the bills weren't being paid and then...

She forced the thought aside and turned her attention to Brady. Her nostrils flared and the hair on her arms stood straight up. "Did you come here to talk about my business?"

"I didn't come here to talk at all. Are you ready?"

This was it. Her chance to back out. To give in to the doubts racing through her mind and preserve the dream she'd nursed for so many years.

The trouble was, Brady had already killed that dream when he'd propositioned her. So there was no turning back.

Insecurity rushed through her, feeding her anger.

Brady shouldn't make her feel so…self-conscious. He *wouldn't*. Not after tonight. Not after her body finally understood what her brain had known since the beginning of the week—that Brady Weston was just like any other man. Nothing special. Certainly not the shining white knight she remembered from high school. His propositioning her had colored the picture. Following through with it would shatter the entire thing and Eden could go back to thinking about her bar and forget all about the man who'd rolled back into town and turned her thoughts upside down.

"Let's go."

6

"WHAT ARE WE doing here?"

Brady glanced from Eden to the grocery store where they'd pulled up. "I thought you might be hungry."

"I'm not," she stated, stiffly holding the flowers he'd handed to her when they'd reached the car.

"Well, I am." He started to climb out.

"But I thought we'd just cut right to the chase. I mean, you didn't say anything about us eating together."

"I didn't say anything about us not eating together. I just need to pick up a few things. Why so jumpy?"

"I'm not jumpy." She was clingy. The truth hit her as she glanced down to see her white-knuckled grip on the flowers. Taking a deep breath, she forced her fingers to relax. "I'm just not one for wasting time."

"It won't be a waste. I can promise you that much," he said before disappearing inside the store.

Eden spent the next ten minutes doing her best to relax. Not an easy task with his scent swimming around her, teasing her nostrils, stealing inside her head. Why did he have to smell so good? Or look so good? Or be even nicer than she remembered?

Good-looking and arrogant, she could have handled. While confident, Brady wasn't the least bit full of himself. If she hadn't known better, she would have sworn she'd sensed a moment's hesitation when he'd climbed out of the car. As if he, too, was nervous.

Crazy. *He'd* propositioned *her,* after all. A woman was the last thing that would cause Brady Weston to be nervous, particularly Eden herself. Men had been many things around her—arrogant, insincere, flirty—but none had ever been nervous. Except Mikey over at the diner. But he was fifteen, with a face full of acne and a body full of raging hormones.

Brady Weston was a grown man. A handsome, sexy, grown man and she was just plain, old Eden Hallsey who'd sat behind him in English and lusted after him along with the entire adolescent female population.

"You must be really hungry," Eden commented when he deposited a bag full of groceries on the seat between them.

"You can bet on it, sugar." His eyes glittered as they locked with hers and she knew he was talking about more than dinner. The crazy notion that he might actually be nervous about their interlude faded in the smoldering depths of his eyes.

The line begged for a comeback, but the only thing she managed was a weak, "That's nice," as they pulled out of the parking lot and headed down the main strip through town.

Thankfully, the drive to his garage apartment was blessedly quick. Otherwise, Eden felt certain she would have died of lack of oxygen. As she climbed from the cab, still clutching the flowers, she drew in a deep, lifesaving breath and tried to slow her pounding heart.

It wasn't the close confines, she decided as he ushered her up the stairs. They were out in the open and she still couldn't get enough air. It was the quiet. The unnerving quiet filled with nothing except the buzz of crickets and the thunder of her own heart.

"So this is where you live?" she asked once he'd kicked the door of the apartment shut behind them.

"For now." He deposited the sack of groceries on the sink and started to unpack.

Eden glanced around and noticed the squares of white cardboard littering the nearby sofa. She didn't mean to be nosy, but she desperately needed to be distracted from listening to her heart hammer in her chest.

"What are these things?" she asked, picking one up and studying the drawing of an old cowboy boot.

"Nothing. I've just been playing with a few ideas to beef up business."

"Your granddaddy has you working on advertising?"

Brady shook his head and Eden could have sworn she saw a look of pure longing on his face. "I'm working production. I *like* working production. This is just something I'm playing around with." He pulled a carton of ice cream from the bag. "But I'd rather play with you." His eyes gleamed. "What do you like? Chocolate or vanilla ice cream?"

"Chocolate, but I'm really not hungry." Her gaze swept the one-room efficiency, from the small kitchen to the leather sofa to the bed visible just beyond an open doorway. The place was small, but expensively decorated despite its location. Then again, she expected nothing less from the Westons. Even when they roughed it, they had style.

"Nice clock," she said as her gaze lit on a glittering chrome hubcap hanging on a nearby wall.

"Merle made it." He held up two jars. "You like chocolate or caramel syrup?"

"Caramel." her gaze went to the row of framed photos lining the wall. Each image depicted a group of children sporting the same uniforms. "These are the T-ball teams Merle has sponsored?"

"Yep."

"They're nice. I sponsor a team, too," she added.

Now, why had she said that? Because they were about to do the deed and she suddenly had the strange urge to get to know him. To share something about herself.

"Yeah, the Houston Astros, pint-sized edition," she continued. "I've sponsored them for the past eight years."

"I didn't see the team banner at the bar. Don't all sponsors have banners?"

"The league president, Conrad Phillips, doesn't like the fact the kids are sponsored by a bar. And I agree. I do sell alcohol, after all."

"And so does the Longhorn Steakhouse, but they have a banner."

"It's okay. Conrad's never really liked me, not since I turned him down for a date several years back."

"But he's been married ten years."

"I know." Eden studied the pictures again. "These are really nice. So…have you settled things with your grandfather?"

"Nut preferences. It's cashews, right? And just what do you know about the situation with my grandfather?"

"Yes to the cashews, and I know what everyone else knows. That you left and he got mad."

He took the flowers from her hands and placed them in some water. "He got more than mad. He disowned me."

"I know. I'm sorry."

"So am I, but I don't blame him. He had every right."

"You were only eighteen. Just a kid, and kids make mistakes."

"True, but a man's gotta do what a man's gotta do."

The comment hung between them for a few moments as he unloaded the rest of the groceries and Eden glanced around the near empty apartment.

"So this is your sofa? It's nice."

"Thanks."

"And your TV. It's nice, too."

"Thanks again."

"And I really like this lamp." Even as she stared at the base, also made from a giant hubcap, she couldn't believe the words that were coming out of her mouth. She'd never been into small talk. Neither had she ever nursed a pounding heart or tried to calm a racing pulse or fought for every breath.

Then again, this was Brady Weston. *The* Brady Weston.

"Look, can we just get to it? We agreed to sex, so there's no reason for all this small talk. I know you, you know me. We know what we want."

"Almost." He held up two small crates. "Strawberries or blueberries?"

"For the last time, I'm not hungry."

A slow grin spread across his face and a smoldering light lit his eyes. "Then let's see what we can do about that."

"WHAT ARE YOU doing?" Eden blurted as Brady stepped across his kitchen, a satin blindfold in hand.

"It's called foreplay." He circled and came up behind her. The hard wall of his chest kissed her shoulder blades. "You do want to play, don't you, darlin'?"

"Yes, but I was thinking more along the lines of a little kissing, some heavy petting. I don't see—" She stopped abruptly when his arms came up from behind and his palm brushed her cheek. Electricity skimmed through her body as two strong fingertips pressed against her lips.

"You don't need to see," he murmured. "You just need to feel." Before she could protest, his hand fell away and she felt the cool glide of silk against her skin. "As for the kissing and petting…I plan to pet you until you purr like a kitten. Make no mistake about that."

"I've never done anything like this," she blurted, a zing of panic rushing through her as the silk blocked out the light. With her sight gone, her other senses took control and became sharper in those next few seconds. Her nostrils flared with the aroma of warm, husky male. Her skin prickled from the heat of his body. Her ears seemed to tingle as they tuned in to the deep, husky murmur of his voice.

"Then this is a first for both of us."

Her heart thundered at the thought before common sense intruded. She fought for a calming breath. "I mean, I have," she rushed on, determined to take back her previous naive statement. Granted, it was true, but he didn't know that. No one did, and Eden intended to keep things that way. She had a reputation to uphold, after all. "Done this, that is. It's just, I didn't expect it. You said sex. Just sex. So I assumed this would be pretty straightforward. No frills. Just the basics." She knew she was rattling, but damned if she could help herself. Not when he smelled so good and felt so warm. "The bare bones. The nuts and bolts—" The words died on her tongue as something cool pressed to her lips. The scent of chocolate filled her nostrils and she realized it was one of the fudge truffles she'd seen him pull from the grocery sack.

"Let's see if you can do something else with that beautiful mouth of yours besides talk." His voice, so rich and deep, stirred her even more than the decadent aroma wafting through her nose. "If I didn't know better, I'd say you were nervous."

But he knew better. The whole town did. She was Eden Hallsey, bad girl extraordinaire. A woman who'd been around the block and then some, or so most people thought. What she wanted the entire town to think.

Everyone except Brady Weston.

The minute the thought pushed its way in, she pushed it right back out. Brady was no different. He was every man she'd ever slept with—the few and far between—and every man who'd ever wanted to sleep with her. Nothing special.

And so Eden gathered her precious control and did what she did best. She put on her I-know-all-the-ropes persona and stuffed that small insecure part of herself down deep where it belonged. "I can do plenty with this mouth," she murmured in her most sultry voice. Her lips parted and she sank her teeth into the sweet confection, focusing on the burst of flavor rather than the strange fluttering of her heart.

This had nothing to do with her heart. It was all about satisfying her body and proving to herself once and for all that Brady Weston was just a man. Tonight would be exactly what they'd agreed upon....

"Just sex," she murmured to herself as she took another bite.

Just sex?

The thought stuck in his head as he watched her mouth work at the truffle. Was she crazy? Tonight was about more than a little no-frills mattress dancing. Much more. It was about great sex. Stupendous sex. The best of her life. So Brady spent the next few hours recreating his favorite scene from last night's erotic movie.

He'd picked what he'd dubbed the cherry scene, in which Mickey Rourke and Kim Basinger had sat in front of an open refrigerator and engaged in a uniquely delicious form of foreplay. With her eyes closed, Kim had sat dutifully in front of Mickey while he'd fed her everything from cherries to honey. The scene hadn't featured the sex act itself, but rather the buildup. Mickey had been intent on stirring all of Kim's senses, on truly turning her on.

Exactly what Brady wanted to do for Eden.

He succeeded over the next hour. She'd smiled quizzically when he'd told her about renting the video, but he'd also seen her hands tremble as she reached blindly for another spoonful of chocolate mousse. Her ripe nipples pressed against her T-shirt as he trailed ice down her chin and the slope of her neck. Her bottom lip quivered as she opened her mouth for a trickle of honey.

She had great lips, so full and pouty and kissable. It had taken all his willpower back in high school not to kiss her that night she'd won the date with him. But he hadn't wanted to be just every other guy in her eyes.

He'd wanted her to see him differently, as more than just a conquest, though the notion hadn't sounded so distasteful. Particularly when she'd stared at him with all that young hunger in her eyes as he'd walked her to her door.

"You'll never know how much I wanted to kiss you that night. I wanted it so bad."

"Right." The incredulous look on her face almost made him smile. Almost, but he was too aroused, too intent, too eager to see if her nipples tasted as ripe as they looked beneath her thin tank top. The incredulity faded into curiosity. "You *really* wanted to kiss me?"

"Darlin', every guy in school wanted to kiss you. I was no exception."

She frowned and, for a split second, Brady had the distinct feeling that he'd said the wrong thing. But then her mouth tilted and she smiled, and the notion faded in the sudden burst of heat that shot through his body.

He moved to feed her another cherry, but she caught his hand. A few swift tugs behind her head and the blindfold fell away.

"May be if you're nice to me," she told him as she tossed the slip of silk to the side, "I'll give you that kiss now."

"That's not going to work."

"You're not going to be nice to me?"

"I've already been nice, and I'm not going to settle for a kiss after all this effort." He popped a cherry into his mouth and swallowed. "I want more, darlin'. I want you." And then he did what he'd been wanting to do since the moment he'd rolled back into town and Eden Hallsey had offered him a ride.

He picked her up and took her to bed.

WHILE THE PAST hour had passed with excruciating slowness, the next few moments were a dizzying blur. One moment Eden was sitting on Brady's kitchen floor and the next she was sinking down on the edge of his bed.

She watched, her lips parted, her breathing shallow, as Brady stripped in front of her. When he pulled off his shirt, her mouth grew dry at the sight of hard, smooth planes of his wide chest. When his hands went to his fly, her breath stopped completely. She had the barest glimpse of white cotton before he drew her to her feet and grasped the edge of her T-shirt. He held her gaze for one charged moment before pulling it over her head, swiftly and expertly. She wanted to step back, to take a good long look at his body, but she burned too fiercely for him. When his hands reached for the waistband of her jeans, a small voice in her head urged him faster, faster. He slid her button free and urged her zipper down. Cool air swept over her legs as he pushed down her jeans, leaving her in only bra and panties. He urged her down onto the bed and followed, his hard body covering the length of hers. The sudden sensation of heated skin against skin made her gasp.

Before she could draw in her next, ragged breath,

he captured her lips with his own in a kiss that was even better than she'd anticipated. Hotter. Wetter. A moan worked its way up her throat and her lips parted for him. His tongue slid against hers, coaxing and hot, a fierce contrast to the coolness of the cherries she'd eaten just moments before. Sensation overwhelmed her and Eden closed her eyes, reveling in the flood of heat.

His fingertips slid toward the clasp of her bra and sanity zapped her. She caught his hand an inch shy and shook her head. "I like it on. It's sexy."

"It's in the way."

"Not really," she mumbled, glancing down at the dark tip of one nipple peeking up between the lace.

"I can see your point." He dipped his head, catching the ripe peak between his lips. His tongue lapped at the sensitive bud and her panic faded in a rush of heat.

He trailed his hand down her side, hooked his thumb in the edge of her panties and dragged the lace down until it pulled free and she lay naked beneath him. Almost. She still had on her bra and Eden intended to keep it that way.

Brady obliged her. He was too focused on other things, particularly the triangle of curls at the base of her thighs. His fingers ruffled the hair and slid along the dampness between her legs.

Her entire body seemed more alive than ever before in those next few moments. She felt *every-*

thing. The rasp of his chest hair against her lace-covered nipples. The glide of his big toe down the inside of her calf as he shifted his position and nudged her legs apart. The pulse of his now condom-covered erection as it settled in the damp heat between her legs.

The past hour had, indeed, stirred her hunger and brought her body to throbbing awareness. She was on fire and each touch made her burn hotter, brighter.

Dipping his head, he kissed her again, rubbing his erection against her sensitive slick folds. Back and forth. Again and again.

She arched against him, every muscle in her body taut. Her breath caught on a sob as he pushed the head of his penis just a fraction inside her. Just enough to tease, to tantalize, to send a burst of feeling through her and push her close. So very close…

Through the haze of pleasure, she found him staring down at her, his eyes dark and smoldering as he watched. Meeting his gaze, she felt an intense jolt of awareness at the intimacy of this moment, this act, with a man she'd only ever fantasized about before. In that overwhelming moment, Eden did what any desperate woman would have done. She tilted her hips just so, drawing him deeper despite his obvious efforts at restraint.

He muttered a curse before giving in to her demanding body and plunging deep. His eyes closed and relief flooded her, followed by a burst of heat as he again plunged deep. So deliciously deep...

She wrapped her legs around his waist, holding on as he shoved his hands beneath her bottom and tilted her, driving deeper, stronger, pushing her closer to the brink until she could take no more.

Her orgasm crashed over her like a tidal wave, consuming her, turning her inside out and upside down. It was fierce. Intense. Mind-blowing. She barely managed to catch the cry that rolled up her throat.

But she did.

Old habits died hard and Eden had been holding herself back, hiding behind a cool, seductive wall for much too long to stop now, even in the face of such delicious heat.

Because of the heat. It was too fierce. Too intense. Too...unexpected.

The realization stayed with her for the next few heart-pounding moments, as Brady drove deep one final time. That was the only time he broke the eye contact between them. As if he couldn't help himself, his lids shut and his back arched. Every tendon in his neck went taut as he groaned, long and low and deep.

Eden fought back the urge to touch his face, to trace the curve of his cheekbone, to feel the heat of his skin against her palm. Instead, she concentrated on her own body, on slowing the spasms that still rocked her.

He collapsed on top of her, his head resting against the curve of her shoulder, his lips pressed to the furious beat of her pulse, and it was over.

Over.

So why did she feel the need to do it all again? To feel the delicious pleasure? To give him the same pleasure again?

Eden closed her eyes as the truth crystalized in her brain. She'd anticipated a good orgasm. After all, he was so sexy and hot and so…Brady. She couldn't imagine anything less with the boy-turned-man who'd haunted her thoughts for so many years. But this…*this* went beyond a great release.

She wanted to jump. Shout. Laugh. Cry.

Worse, she wanted to throw her arms around him and beg him for another. And another.

The notion sent a burst of panic through her, and she did what any self-respecting bad girl would have done at that moment. She scrambled across the bed and reached for her clothes.

"Where are you going?"

"It's late," she managed in her calmest, coolest voice. She *was* calm and cool. And in control. And now was no different from any of the other sexual experiences she'd had in her past. They were finished, and so she was leaving.

"It's only midnight."

"Sorry, but I'm always in bed by midnight." Just as the words left her mouth, she felt his fingers encircle her wrist. A strong but gentle tug, and she found herself tumbling backward onto the bed.

"Then you're right on schedule, darlin'." His grin was slow and easy and heart-stopping. Heat rushed to her cheeks.

Great. Now she was blushing. First she'd stammered. Then she'd trembled. Now she was blushing, of all things.

She definitely needed to get out of here.

"*My* bed," she clarified.

"Lead the way, darlin'. I'm game again if you are."

"About that..." She crawled from beneath him and reached for her clothes. Blushing? She was *not* blushing, and she wasn't crawling back beneath the covers as she desperately wanted to. This was no different from any other sexual liaison. *He* was no different, even if he did touch her just so and kiss her until her toes curled and her hands trembled and... "I really have to get out of here."

"What about our date?"

"Tonight was hardly a date. It was an agreement. We agreed to sleep together. Mission accomplished."

"I thought we could get a bite to eat. I don't know about you, but I'm starving."

"I had dinner earlier."

"Then we'll have dessert." He quirked an eyebrow at her and grinned. "You don't have to run off. I won't bite. Unless you want me to, that is."

His words stirred a vision of him over her, kissing his way down the curve of her neck, nibbling the slope of her breast, licking the tip of her nipple…

The urge to jump back into the bed nearly overwhelmed her and panic rushed through her, sending her scrambling for her shoes. "Look," she said as she pulled on her boots, "it's nothing personal, but let's not make more out of this than it really was."

"And what exactly was it?"

Earth-shattering. Mind-blowing. *Romantic.* "Nice," she finally murmured, determined to get a grip on the small voice inside her that kept insisting otherwise.

Any man.

His grin died and his eyes narrowed. "Nice, huh?"

"Very nice. But now it's back to the real world. We've done the lust thing and now I really need to get over to the bar and help Kasey. She's probably swamped. Saturday's our busiest night, after all."

Dream on, sister.

"I thought you were going home to bed."

"I am. I mean, I was. I mean…" Great. She was stammering again. It's just, he smelled so good and looked so good, so dark and tanned sprawled there against the pale yellow sheets. Heat rushed through her body and her thighs tingled. She wanted another touch. And another kiss. And—

It's over.

"I am going home to bed," she managed as she snatched up her purse and made a bee-line for the door. "After I go to the bar." She reached for the doorknob. "I'll see you around."

"You can sure-as-shootin' bet on that, darlin'."

"I THOUGHT YOU had a date tonight," Kasey said when Eden walked into the bar ten minutes later.

"It wasn't a date. We just got together to talk over old times."

"Is that what they're calling it now?"

Eden shot Kasey a frown. "What's that supposed to mean?"

"Nothing. It was a joke. Since when did you get so touchy?"

Since Brady Weston had rolled back into her life and made her feel so nervous and anxious and…just *feel*. Something Eden hadn't allowed herself since she'd run from Jake's house crying the night she'd lost her virginity. She'd buried her feelings from then on, hiding behind her cool persona. But Brady shook the image and drew her feelings to the surface. He stirred her so fiercely that she couldn't bury the feelings anymore.

At least until tonight. But now that they'd done the deed, she'd gotten him out of her system. Her infatuation with him was over and done with. No more thinking and dreaming and seeing himself as anything other than the flesh-and-blood man that he was. No way was she going to keep trembling or hoping or dreaming. And no way did she want to do *it* again. Even if he had talked about a whole week.

"We might as well go ahead and close up," Kasey said, her gaze sweeping the empty bar. A familiar sight since Jake had set about using his strong-arm tactics to persuade the town that the Pink Cadillac was best left alone.

Strong-arm as in monetary incentives. Jake wasn't man enough to put any muscle into his threats. He simply bought his way around Cadillac, providing the bingo hall with a new speaker system in exchange for extended hours that cut into Eden's business and kept the Senior Singles playing double and triple cards rather than playing darts and nursing sodas in Eden's back room.

"You go on ahead. I think I'll get a headstart on tomorrow's inventory." Because the last thing Eden wanted to do was go home and climb into an empty bed. Heck, she didn't even want to *see* a bed. Not with her body still on fire. Still alive and wanting and—

You're doing it again.

Yep, inventory was what she needed, all right.

She locked up behind Kasey and headed toward the stockroom. Picking up her clipboard, she made her way toward the pantry and the twenty-odd jars of maraschino cherries.

A very vivid of image of Brady popped into her mind. His gaze dark and intense as he fed her a piece of the ripe succulent fruit. Her nipples pebbled at the remembrance and her blood rushed and the need to turn and bolt for his apartment nearly overwhelmed her.

She flicked the light switch off and plopped the clipboard onto the counter.

On second thought, inventory could wait until to-morrow.

7

NICE?

What kind of word was *nice?*

Brady pulled on his jeans and walked into the kitchen a good half hour after Eden left, a half hour he'd spent thinking and remembering and doing his damnedest to figure out what had happened.

Where was the screaming? The begging? The noise that follows supreme, earth-shattering sex? Hell, he would have settled for a smile of satisfaction, *anything* other than the passive look on her face as she'd donned her clothing and left him to question his manhood.

He sank down onto the sofa, a beer in hand. He popped the tab and downed a long swallow. *Nice* described a sunny Saturday afternoon or the pitter-patter of rain on a barn roof. The term didn't come close to touching the past two hours spent with Eden.

He'd had sex before, but never had it been so hot, so intense, so damned terrific.

Then again, that was his opinion. Not hers.

Nice.

Had he failed to push her hot buttons?

The question bothered him all of five seconds, until he remembered the flush that had crept across her silky skin, the desire that had flashed in her eyes. Her body had milked his in a mesmerizing rhythm that had made him come harder and heavier than ever before, and his gut told him it had been the same for her.

She'd been turned on, all right. Hell, she'd been on fire. But, for whatever reason, she'd been dead set on controlling the flames. She'd concealed her pleasure on purpose, pushed it away just the way she'd pushed his hands away when he'd tried to remove the last stitch of her clothing—that lacy wisp of a black bra that had revealed a helluva lot more than it had covered.

I like it. It's sexy.

No doubt it was sexy, but Brady couldn't help but think there was more to it than that. She'd been too nervous when her fingers had grasped his. Too desperate when he'd toyed with the clasp of her bra. Too *scared.*

Eden Hallsey, bonafide bad girl and the sexiest woman he'd ever had the pleasure of touching, had actually been frightened of him.

Or herself.

The notion reminded him of the bashful, bright-eyed girl he'd known back in tenth grade, the girl she'd been before that Monday morning that changed everything. Eden had looked stricken and distant. And during the lunch hour, Brady had discovered why. According to Jake Marlboro, Eden had stripped for him *and* his entire baseball team. *Hardly.* Brady hadn't believed it then and he didn't believe it now. Yep, Eden was scared, but she needed to face her fear. And he was just the one to help her.

He got to his feet and walked over to the bag he'd brought home from the video store. While Eden might be of a mind that they were finished, he wasn't nearly done.

He pulled out another video and popped it into the VCR. Tonight had just been the warm-up. Brady was armed and ready for more, and he wasn't about to stop until she was back in his bed, completely naked, out of control and conscious of nothing—her insecurity, her anxiety, her fear—*nothing* save the heat that burned between them.

"COME AND SHARE your misery." Kasey's eyes lifted from the neon pink flyer. "I don't know much about advertising, but this doesn't exactly make the Pink Cadillac sound like the happening place to be on a Saturday night."

"The book I'm reading says to play off emotion

and that's what I'm doing. I'm thinking, if Dottie and Trina—both football widows—like to come in to eat snacks, toss down a few brews and share war stories, some of the other women in town might want to join in also. See, these ladies aren't out to have a good time. They're interested in a sympathetic ear. A little friendly advice. Some understanding. That's what this flyer is all about. It calls to those lonely hearts in need of kinship, and that's what the Pink Cadillac is all about."

"Please don't tell me you're going to sing the theme from *Cheers* right now. After the night I had—" Kasey touched her head "—I don't think I could take it."

Eden couldn't stifle her grin. "Actually, I thought we could do a few verses of 'Kumbaya.'"

"You're trying to torture me, aren't you?"

"The hangover is doing that. I'm just trying to make you see that you don't have to compete with Laura Winchell on *everything*. Who cares if she can drink six hurricanes and still recite her ABC's? You don't have to follow suit."

"It wasn't as if I had anything better to do. *I* didn't have a date with the hottest cowboy in Cadillac."

"For the last time, it wasn't a date, and Brady Weston isn't a cowboy." Once upon a time he'd been the classic hero wearing the white Stetson and riding the white horse, but no more. He'd changed, despite the fact that he'd given her flowers and gone to all the trouble of renting a sexy video just to turn her on.

It had all been part of the game. The seduction.

The thing of it was, no man had ever gone to so much trouble to seduce Eden. Because of her reputation, men assumed she was like a light switch. One flick of a button and she was blazing hot. No muss. No fuss. No foreplay.

Certainly not three hours of it.

So? The end result had been the same. Sex. Granted, it had been outstanding sex, but the big S nonetheless. And now it was over and done with.

"Are you okay?" Kasey's voice pushed into her thoughts. "You look flushed."

"It's hot in here."

"We're in the refrigerator."

"It's still hot in here."

"It's sixty degrees."

"It's hot. Would you stop changing the subject. When are you going to learn that you don't have to drink seven hurricanes to prove your superiority?"

"It was seven and a quarter, and it's the principle of the thing. Laura thinks she's so much better than me. She always has."

"That's just her opinion."

"Her and her dozen or so friends down at the Cut-n-Curl."

"It shouldn't matter what those old biddies think."

Kasey's eyebrows lifted. "Excuse me. This from the woman who puts her slinkiest dress on to go to church just so she can set those very same biddies tongues to wagging?"

"That's different. It's not that I care what anyone thinks. I don't care, which is why I dress the way I want to." At Kasey's skeptical gaze, Eden rushed on. "But we're not talking about me. I'm not nursing a throbbing head and a queasy stomach."

"The queasiness passed. I'm in full-blown nausea as we speak."

"Go home and get some sleep."

"But I can't leave you here all by yourself," Kasey protested, even as she abandoned her clipboard and reached for her purse.

"I think I can make it."

"You're sure? Because all you have to do is say the word."

"Go."

A smile split Kasey's face. "That's the word I was hoping you'd say." Then she turned serious. "But just so you know, I would be the first to stay if you absolutely, positively, unequivocally needed me."

Eden arched an eyebrow. "Unequivocally? Are you and Laura taking an expanded language course?"

"Three nights a week at the community college." She started for the door. "Speaking of which, I'll need off early tomorrow night."

"How early?"

"Early enough for a full manicure. Laura practically lives in a French set."

Eden wondered briefly what it would be like to worry so much over something so superficial.

She'd never had the luxury. Her problems had always been real—not enough money, enough food, enough class.

That had been a contributing factor to Jake's rejection and betrayal. She'd been the wrong girl for him and so he hadn't taken her feelings seriously.

But she'd been serious. For those heart-pounding five minutes when she'd bared all, she'd been deadly serious. And scared. And hopeful.

No more. She was a grown woman and she knew the score. Namely, the haves didn't belong with the have-nots. Sure, it happened in movies. She was still a die-hard *Pretty Woman* fan. But real life? Eden had spent too many years with a reputation she hadn't earned, and all because she'd been from the wrong side of town. Jake would never had spread rumors about Mitzi Carmichael, the only child of city councilman Buford Carmichael and heir to the Double C—one of the largest purebred horse ranches in the country—even if Mitzi had done it with the Cadillac Wolverines' entire defensive line, and all in the same night. An incident that wasn't hearsay, but the God's honest truth. Eden had seen for herself when she'd walked into the back bedroom in search of an extra bathroom at one of Myra Jackson's infamous after-game parties.

Eden had seen it, all right, and the guys involved

had even bragged about it, but no one had truly believed it because Mitzi was the product of good breeding and old money. Not the sort of girl to do something so outlandish.

But Eden? She was just the sort. Her parents were gone now—both killed in a car accident years ago—but before that—her mother had served beers for a living while her father had poured them. Neither had ever set foot in church except on special occasions. They'd incited a fair share of gossip themselves when they'd been young, particularly since they'd lived together for several years before ever tying the knot.

They'd been the talk of the town way back when, and their daughter had inherited the title.

But while her parents hadn't been Ozzie and Harriet, they had loved one another, and they'd loved Eden. She hadn't had the best of everything, but she'd had all the basics. Food. Clothes. A warm bed in a clean house. Unfortunately that house had been located on the wrong side of Kendall Creek, and so Eden was an easy target for gossip, the sort that drew a man's attention. She was the outcast not even worthy of sponsor recognition for a local T-ball team.

And when it came to Brady Weston, she'd best keep that in mind. A pang of regret went through her—a feeling she quickly squashed. The last thing she wanted to feel was regret. Relief. Now there was an appropriate emotion. They'd done the deed, her curiosity had been satisfied, her drought ended, and now she could concentrate on her business.

Unfortunately, she'd felt anything but relieved when she'd climbed into her bed late last night after closing up the bar. She'd tossed and she'd turned and she'd remembered.

The way he'd touched her, kissed her, cried out her name when he'd reached his climax. The way he'd stared at her when she'd reached hers.

As if he'd been waiting. Expecting.

She forced the thought aside. It didn't matter what Brady Weston had thought at that moment because *he* didn't matter.

One night.

And that night was now over.

She grasped that thought and turned her attention to the jars of salted peanuts lining one of the shelves. There was inventory to be taken and a bar to be cleaned. Eden spent the rest of the afternoon taking care of both.

It was well past sundown before she finally set her clipboard aside and removed her apron. Exhaustion tugged at her muscles and she smiled. The more exhaustion she felt, the better her chances of getting a solid, good night's sleep—

The thought crashed to a halt as the lights flicked off and darkness swallowed her up.

"Stupid lights," she muttered as she felt her way down the aisle, past several large shelves. Another step and she stubbed her toe. Pain rushed up her leg and pierced her brain and she sucked in a breath. A few more steps and she reached the cabinets at the far end of the room. She reached blindly inside the cabinet and felt for the flashlight. Her fingers closed around the familiar shape and a few seconds later a single beam sliced through the darkness. Eden was about to search for a spare bulb when the flashlight beam hit the light switch and she realized it was in the off position.

She closed the cabinet door and moved to the switch. A flick of her finger and brightness cracked open the darkness. Her heart pounded faster as she realized that it wasn't a bad bulb at all. *Off.*

As the truth crystallized in her brain, the hair on the back of her neck prickled. She glanced up just in time to catch a glimpse of a tanned hand before the lights flicked off and darkness settled in again.

Panic bolted through her, followed by a rush of fear. There was someone in the room with her. Someone standing directly behind her.

The thought registered a split second before she felt the hard strength press against her back and the warm rush of breath against her ear.

"Definitely strawberry."

The deep, familiar voice rang in her head and relief swamped her for the space of two heartbeats before anger set in.

"What are you doing?"

"Smelling you." His nose grazed the sensitive shell of her ear and he inhaled. "Last night, I wasn't so sure because of all the food. The cherries. The chocolate." With each word, a vision pushed into her head. Heat licked across her nerve endings and her nipples pebbled. "But you definitely use a strawberry shampoo."

"No, I mean what are you *doing?* You scared the daylights out of me." She reached for the light switch and flooded the room in blessed brightness. While she wasn't as frightened as she had been a few moments before, there was something highly unnerving about standing in the dark with Brady Weston, listening to his voice, feeling his warmth, knowing he was directly behind her, so close that all she had to do was lean back just so...

It's over, she reminded herself.

If only her body didn't keep forgetting that all-important fact.

"And for your information," she said as she turned to face him. "It's not shampoo. It's a conditioner. And I only use it once a week." She wasn't sure why it mattered so much, but the fact that he was so in tune to her that he could smell a conditioner she hadn't used in days was almost as unsettling as his presence.

This wasn't about being in sync. It was purely physical. And it wasn't even that. Not anymore.

"You sound hostile. I even brought you the flowers you forgot last night." He grinned and nodded toward the end of the bar where they stood in a vase. "How can you be mad, darlin'?"

"I'm annoyed."

His gaze dropped and his hand touched her chest before she had a chance to pull back. As if she had any place to go. With the wall at her back and Brady blocking her front, she was trapped.

"Your heart is pounding." His grin widened. "That's good."

"You're making about as much sense as Jeanine Mitchell after three margaritas."

"I want your heart pounding."

"That's why you turned the lights off. To scare me into a pounding heart?"

"Actually, I was trying to piss you off, not scare you."

"Mission accomplished." She flicked the switch back on. "Now get out."

"The point is to get in, darlin'." He flicked the lights off and caught her fingers when she tried to turn them back on.

"When did you turn into such a jerk?"

"At about half past midnight, after watching *Sea of Love*. Have you ever seen that movie, darlin'?"

"I can't say that I have."

"Well, there's this scene where Al Pacino and Ellen Barkin have a disagreement and she tells him to leave. But she doesn't really want him to leave."

She wasn't going to ask. "What does she really want?"

"This." He whirled her around so fast that she barely had time to draw in a breath before she felt the hard wall of his chest against her back. His hips shifted and she realized he was fully aroused. A thrill of awareness shot through her, immediately followed by a rush of guilt.

Over.

Her head knew that, but her body... Her damned body wanted more of his touches, his kisses...everything.

"Your heart is still pounding," he said as his hand came up and settled over her chest, an inch shy of one throbbing nipple.

"That's because I'm mad and getting madder by the minute."

"You know what I think? I think you're excited. And getting more excited by the minute."

"You're wrong." *If only.* While she was angry, all right, it didn't make her want to resist his touch. It fed the anticipation heating her blood.

"I told you we weren't finished yet," he murmured.

"You're wrong about that, too. We're done. It's—"

Over stalled on the tip of her tongue as his teeth sank into the curve of her neck. He nipped her there, not painfully, but with enough strength to remind her that he was in control. The realization sent an alarm through her, but then his hands slid down her arms and he palmed her breasts.

"Spread your legs," he whispered. "I want to touch you."

She resisted at first, determined to keep her body in check, to ignore the delicious heat teasing her senses. But then his fingertips trailed down her belly and lower, and he touched the apex of her thighs. Heat spiraled through her and for a split second, she actually went weak in the knees. Forget holding herself rigid or pulling away or fighting his touch. Resistance fled and it took her total concentration to keep from sinking to the floor.

She sucked in a breath as his touch moved under her skirt and between her legs. He drew lazy circles against the crotch of her undies, right over ground zero. Round and round. Over and over. Until she could hardly breathe, much less stand. Had it not been for his strong arms anchored on either side of her, she would have sunk to the floor.

"Your panties are soaked, darlin'." He trailed a fingertip over the drenched area, back and forth in a maddening rhythm before he paused, protected both of them, then pushed just a fraction into the moist heat. "Am I making you wet, Eden?"

Sensations whirled inside her and she could barely nod as a burst of heat rushed from his fingertip to every other erogenous zone in her body. Her nipples hardened. The backs of her knees tingled. Her breasts quivered. Her toes curled.

"Tell me, darlin'." His voice, so rich and deep, stirred her almost as much as his touch. A thread of warning went through her, quickly lost in the delicious sensation that burst as he pushed a fraction deeper. "I want you to talk to me. To scream for me. I want to know how much you want me. How good I make you feel. Do I make you feel good, baby?"

Yes. The word rushed to the tip of her tongue and her lips parted. The only sound that escaped was a breathless moan.

"I can't hear you."

"Yes." The word trembled from her lips.

"Louder, darlin'. I can't hear you. I need to hear you."

"Yes. You make me feel good."

"Good." He flicked her earlobe with his tongue before tracing the sensitive shell. Goose bumps chased up and down her arms. "Talk to me, Eden. Tell me what I'm doing to you. Tell me what you want me to do. Do you want this?" His finger dipped beneath the elastic band of her panties. His touch rasped against the sensitive tissue of her clitoris and she trembled before his finger slid lower and plunged deep.

A gasp caught in her throat and every muscle in her body went tense at the fierce invasion.

"I…" She searched for the words, but she couldn't

seem to think of them. Her entire universe centered on the finger embedded inside her, stroking and moving.

"Tell me." He withdrew and plunged into her again and her body throbbed in response. Her hips shifted and sensation burst through her. She moved again, searching for him, pulling him deeper, wanting him so badly she could barely think. Wanting *it,* she reminded herself. An orgasm. A physical release that had nothing to do with him and the way he held her against his body—so close and fierce, as if he never meant to let her go—and everything to do with lust burning her up from the inside out.

"I can't hear you," he murmured, pushing deeper, wringing a shudder from her body.

"Just do it," she breathed, giving in to her body's needs and the hunger that burned inside her for Brady Weston. "Stop talking and let's get to it."

While he might be every other man in her past, he was also different. More sexy. More handsome. More determined. He wanted her again, and while she didn't want to want him again, she did. The chemistry between them was too fierce to burn up in just one night. But two. Or even three…

The notion sent a burst of excitement through her, but then Brady withdrew his hand to tug at the band of her panties. The lace slid down and cool air swept her bare bottom. The sensation yanked her back to reality, to the fact that she was now half naked.

Half. But not all the way, and not with the lights on.

"We need to set some ground rules," she managed in the I'm-a-woman-who-knows-what-she-wants voice she'd perfected over the years.

"I thought you wanted to stop talking."

"I do. Once I'm sure we're on the same page." A gasp punctuated her statement as his jeans rubbed her sensitive buttocks.

He stroked her bottom before working at the waistband of his jeans. "There are no rules for this, darlin'. Anything goes."

"When it comes to lust. Just so long as you remember that this—" she caught her bottom lip as one fingertip trailed down her buttock and tickled the back of one thigh "—*this* doesn't mean we're seeing each other."

He licked the curve of her ear. "I can't see a damned thing." He reached for the light switch, but she followed, her hand flicking it off a split second after he'd turned it on. "I mean, *seeing* each other. As in dating. We are not dating. This is just sex."

A deep chuckle vibrated the air near her ear. "I'm afraid you're wrong about that, darlin'. This isn't sex, darlin'. This," he said as he bent his knees and plunged deep with one thrust, "now this," he groaned once he was buried deep, deep inside, "*this* is sex.

"And just so you know," he whispered after several delicious moments, the words so soft and low she marveled that she could hear them over her pounding heart. "That light's coming on sooner or later."

Not if she could help it, she vowed as she closed her eyes and gave in to the desire beating at her senses.

Not now.

Not ever, *ever* again.

8

"HOLD IT RIGHT there." Merle's voice sounded behind Brady just as his foot hit the first step leading up to the garage apartment. He turned into the beam of light shining from Merle's flashlight.

"It's just me," Brady declared. "Don't shoot."

"As if Maria lets me keep any ammo in my shotgun. At least not anytime from February through October. Now duck season is a different story altogether."

"One I'd love to hear, Unc, but it's late."

"You're telling me. It's hours past my bedtime, but I been waiting up for you." He dangled a set of car keys up in front of him. "She's gassed up and ready to go."

"You waited up 'til midnight to tell me that? Couldn't it have waited until morning?"

"You're up earlier than Jesus himself, so no, it can't wait. Besides, that would make it twenty-eight hours instead of twenty-four and that ain't good." He glanced at his watch. "I told you I'd have her fixed before the day was up. Twenty-two hours and thirty-two minutes and she's as ready as Emma Beacher on singles night over at the bingo hall."

"You replace the brake pads?"

"Done."

"And checked the fan belt?"

"You know it."

"And went over the radiator pump?"

"Ancient history."

"How about the spark plugs? Did you change those?"

Merle frowned. "You didn't say anything about spark plugs." He glanced over his shoulder at the gleaming Porsche sitting several feet away in the garage drive. "I can't imagine she needs new spark plugs."

"Are you kidding? Porsches, particularly this model, are notorious for faulty plugs."

"Since when? I ain't never heard of such a thing."

"*Popular Mechanics* just last month. An entire issue dedicated to quality plugs." When Merle looked skeptical, Brady rushed on. "They even did a cover shot of several new Chevy plugs. Real beauts, I'll tell you that."

"Maybe I ought to get a subscription. After all, it don't hurt to be well-informed. It's just that the danged mailman always comes during *Wheel of*

Fortune and by the time I'm done, I'm usually too pumped to sit still. That's when I take out the garbage. Then after that, I'm too tired to do anything but sit still. Forget turning pages or trying to concentrate." He looked thoughtful. "Faulty plugs, you say?"

"You really should check them out."

"That shouldn't take long."

"Then there's the distributor cap. I have a feeling it's on its last legs."

"Looked fine to me."

"That's just it. Looks can be deceiving, and the last thing I need is to find myself stranded on the road again. I swear I nearly died of heat stroke the last time. If it hadn't been for Eden, I'd have been as cooked as beef jerky. I'd really appreciate it if you could—"

"Say no more. But this is gonna cost you. You still get a discount, of course, bein' you're family and all, but I'll have to charge you for parts and half the labor costs. This is taking up my time and I've got Mrs. Pinkerton's Buick that come in right in back of yours. She needs a good tune-up and new shocks."

"Take care of Mrs. Pinkerton first. I'm in no hurry for the Porsche."

"No can do. I've got my reputation to think of. Twenty-four-hour turnaround time. 'Course, that refers to each new problem, not the original."

"Your reputation's safe with me." Brady turned and started up the stairs. "See you tomorrow."

"You know," Merle's voice followed him up the stairs, "if I didn't know better, I'd say you like driving old Bessie."

Brady paused on the upstairs landing and stared down at the older man. "Now why would I do something so crazy? We're smack-dab in the middle of a major Texas heat wave. Why would I sweat it out day after day when I could be sitting pretty with a powerhouse air conditioner keeping me cool? I'd have to be plum loco."

Merle nodded. "Certifiable."

"Which I'm not."

No, Brady wasn't crazy. He was desperate. He wanted, *needed,* to reclaim his old life and get back to his roots, to the small-town existence he'd loved with all his heart, and he wasn't about to do that cruising around town in a car that cost more than most people's houses.

He wanted to fit in again. To feel at home the way he had so long ago when he'd had a bright and happy future awaiting him. He'd not only had his family, but friends, as well. He'd been well liked by all. Respected by the men. Sought after by the women.

Every woman, that is, except for Eden Hallsey.

His thoughts shifted to the storeroom, to his latest movie reenactment and the woman who'd come apart in his arms.

And she *had* come. He'd felt it in the tensing of her muscles, heard it in her sharp intake of breath and the low moan that had slipped past her luscious lips despite her best efforts.

For whatever reason, she still seemed determined to hide her pleasure from him. Or to deny it to herself.

For the next few heartbeats, Brady couldn't help but wonder which. More importantly, he wondered why? What was there in Eden's past that kept her holding on so tightly to her self control when it was obvious she wanted to let go?

Had some man broken her heart?

The thought sent a surge of anger through him, a feeling he quickly stifled. He didn't want to feel anger on Eden's behalf, or concern or any of the other dozen emotions that stirred when they were together. Useless feelings, because Brady had no future with Eden. They were too different even if they were compatible in bed. Brady had let his hormones do his thinking for him in the past, but not this time. A little fun was fine, but anything more would be useless.

Not that Eden wanted more. She'd made their relationship, or lack of, very clear. Hell, she wouldn't even have dinner with him.

So be it. He didn't need dinner or dating or any of the other rituals that came into play when a man and woman hooked up. All he needed was Eden, panting in his arms, her voice trembling in his ears. He needed to know that she felt the same intensity that he did. The same desire. The same consuming pleasure.

He felt pretty sure she did but, with his track record, he wasn't positive.

Not yet anyhow.

"WE NEED MORE popcorn."

"Here. Take extra peanuts."

"But they want popcorn."

"We're out of popcorn. I forgot to order it yesterday."

"You forgot? But you never forget anything. I can't remember the last time we ran out of anything. Are you feeling well?"

Well didn't begin to describe Eden's present state. She was great. Fantastic. More alive than ever before.

And stupid, she thought as her gaze went to the empty space behind the bar where she kept the popcorn. How could she have forgotten a major staple? Especially one loved by all of her female customers.

"I'll give you one word—riot. Peanuts are not going to cut it for this crowd."

"Give everyone a free drink."

"The purpose of the promotion is to make money."

"The purpose of the promotion is to bring in customers. And if we want repeat customers then we need to get their mind off the snacks—"

"Or lack of."

"—and on to the beverages. Those I haven't exhausted."

"I need two beers, an iced tea and a fuzzy navel, and don't forget the cherry in the iced tea. Doris Williams loves cherries."

"Coming right up." Eden ducked down and reached for the jar of maraschinos. The empty jar.

"Don't tell me."

"I'll send James over to the Piggly Wiggly right now. You stall for time."

"Stall? These women are thirsty and angry. Do you know that Floyd Piedmont hasn't kissed his wife since the Cowboys lost their first practice game over six weeks ago? And John Henry hasn't so much as glanced at Maggie since the Packers signed that new quarterback last season. She's this close to painting herself green just to get him to look at her."

"Stall," Eden said again.

"I could tell war stories. I once went out with this guy who was more interested in his Chevy than me. Granted, it wasn't exactly a football team, but the principle was the same."

Fifteen minutes later, Eden slid a fresh jar of maraschino cherries beneath the bar, along with several canisters of Butter Pecan Toffee and breathed a sigh of relief. A temporary sigh.

First thing tomorrow, she was getting on the horn with her suppliers. She'd been distracted during last night's inventory, but it wasn't going to happen again—no matter how good Brady Weston looked wearing a pair of Wranglers and a tight white T-shirt.

Her heart kicked up a beat when she realized he was standing in the bar doorway looking so handsome and sexy and determined. The fierce light in his eyes sent a ripple of heat through her, along with anticipation of what was to come.

"Great idea," he said as he tossed a flyer onto the bar top. "I don't think I've seen this many people here since I got back into town."

"You haven't. This is definitely a record this year." She couldn't help the grin that tugged at her lips. "Jake will have a heart attack when word gets back to him."

"I hear he's hot to buy up this entire block, Merle's place included, for that megastore."

"I don't know about everybody else, but he's not getting this place. The Pink Cadillac is a legacy. *My* legacy. I grew up here." At his raised eyebrows, she added, "I know it's not exactly the ideal atmosphere for a child, but it was the best my parents could do. They had to work and watch me, and so I spent my afternoons after school behind this very bar helping my dad." A smile touched her lips as she remembered all those long afternoons spent eating peanuts and arranging glasses. It hadn't been the ideal childhood, but she'd liked it. The Pink Cadillac had been her home away from home. No way was she going to let Jake Marlboro get his slimy hands on it.

"Jake's offering an awful lot of money from what Merle tells me."

"Not enough. Not nearly enough for what he has in mind."

"I don't know about that." Brady fingered a deep knick in the bar where old Monty McGuire had carved his initials one Saturday night when he'd been too drunk to know what he was doing and her father had been too busy to care. "Seems like you could open up a brand-new place out on the highway, right in the line of traffic. From an economic standpoint, it makes a lot of sense."

"I'm not thinking about economics. This is my home. This is me." She shook her head. "I guess that's hard for you to understand."

"Not too hard. I didn't come back here for the scenery, that's for damn sure."

"Why did you come back?" There is was. The question that had haunted her since she'd seen him standing by the side of the road, looking so hot and sweaty and sexy. "Why did you leave Dallas?"

"There wasn't anything there for me."

"Then the rumors weren't true."

"And what rumors would those be?"

"The ones about you finding fame and fortune."

"The fortune part might have a little truth to it. I had a good job. Good from an economic standpoint."

She grinned. "But you weren't interested in economics."

"I was. In the beginning." He shrugged and wiped a trickle of condensation from the side of his beer mug. "I had to be if I intended to make Sally happy, but it wasn't enough. I busted my ass from sunrise until well past sunset, and in the end it just wasn't good enough."

In his gaze she saw that it was more like he thought *he* wasn't good enough. She saw the doubt and insecurity. The betrayal. Feelings she knew all too well.

"You must have loved her."

"Love never figured in. It was all about doing the right thing. She was pregnant and so I married her and spent the next eleven years paying for my mistake."

"Why did you stay when she lost the baby?"

"Because Westons don't run away from their mistakes. That's what my grandfather always said. They stay and face the music. I didn't do that then, but I am now. I'll face anything to set things right and make it up to him. I really disappointed him."

"We all make mistakes. The key is to learn from them."

"That's the truth. I should have listened to my grandfather. He told me Sally was just after a free ride, but I didn't listen. Never again. Sally wasn't the right sort of woman for me. I just didn't see it at the time."

The words sent a surge of disappointment through her, crazy as that was. He was only telling the truth. He and Sally had been worlds apart. Brady had lived in a fine ranch house while Sally had lived two houses down from Eden clear on the opposite side of town. Clearly a have-not while Brady epitomized the haves.

"From what I heard," Eden found herself saying, "all you saw was a good time where Sally was concerned."

"True enough. Not that there's anything wrong with that as long as both parties involved have the same idea."

"Like us."

"Exactly. We both know what we want from each other."

"One week of sex," she said, reminded herself, eager to shake the strange sense of camaraderie she felt. So what if they had a few things in common other than lust? Who cared if she understood his reasons for coming home the way he understood her reasons for refusing to sell? Seeing eye to eye on a few things didn't make them compatible, and it certainly didn't change the fact that she was Eden Hallsey, bar owner and bad girl, while Brady was the town's golden boy—wealthy and handsome and heir to the Weston fortune.

"Which brings me to the reason for my visit. We have a date."

"We do not have a date."

"We have a nondate."

"We don't have anything."

"Not here. Not with all these people watching." His gaze darkened. "Unless you want someone to watch. Is that it, Eden?" He leaned across the bar, his fingertips playing over hers as she held a sweaty beer bottle. "Is that one of your fantasies?"

You're my fantasy.

The answer echoed through her head and poised on the tip of her tongue. She couldn't, wouldn't, admit such a thing to him. To any man. Eden Hallsey was the object of men's fantasies. Not the other way around. Even if the man in question happened to be Brady Weston who reduced her to sophomore status with one slow, sexy grin.

She fought for her most nonchalant voice. "It could be. Then again, I do like my privacy."

"What else do you like?"

You. She shrugged, ignoring the answer that whispered through her head. "I'd like to get back to work. It's not every day the place has this many customers."

"That's not what I meant."

She couldn't help but smile. "I know."

"So Jake's really making things tough, huh?"

"He's trying, but obviously he's not succeeding.

Not anymore. I was hoping this idea would pan out, but I wasn't sure if the women would actually come out to congregate while their hubbies watched the game over at the VFW hall."

"Why the VFW?"

"Free pizza and beer during half-time. With the way those guys eat, serving up freebies would defeat the purpose of advertising to bring them in. I'd have to up the offer, which would mean more pizza and beer."

"Unless you offered something else."

"I don't think they'd go for yogurt-covered pretzels."

"They might go for a bigger TV, as in a big screen."

"Those are expensive." She chewed her bottom lip, her mind doing the math and she calculated the added expense. "But it might be a good investment. If it worked."

"You'll never know unless you try. Besides, it might be worth a try just to piss off Jake."

She grinned at the prospect. "He already hates me. This would really get in his craw."

"Hell hath no vengeance like a woman scorned, eh?"

"Amen to that."

"You must have loved him a lot."

"Once. A long, long time ago. But he killed any feelings right away when he betrayed my trust." At his raised eyebrows, she had the insane urge to blurt out the truth to him, that Jake had lied about her. That she hadn't done half the things he'd said. That she wasn't the bad girl everyone had been led to believe.

Maybe not then, but now...

Now she was every bit the loose woman the world thought her to be. Her affair with Brady was proof of that.

"What happened between you two?"

"I made a mistake. One I never intend to make again." She retrieved two more bottles of beer and added them to Kasey's tray. "I really have to get back to work. Now's not a good time to hash over all this." Particularly when she was feeling so vulnerable after talking to him, looking into his eyes, wanting so much to trust him.

She killed the last thought. *Never* again.

"Fifteen minutes." He motioned toward the door and the limousine visible just beyond the window. "Me and my ride will be waiting."

"That's yours?"

"For tonight. For you and me."

"But I can't just leave—"

"Kasey can fill in." He indicated the waitress dishing out bowls of peanuts in the far corner before he reached for the small white box he'd sat on the bartop next to him. He pushed the container toward her.

"What's this orchid for?" she asked as she opened

the box to find the delicate flower nestled in tissue paper.

"It's a wild orchid, darlin', and it's for tonight."

She pulled the flower from the box and turned it around, searching for a wrist band or a lapel pin. "I don't get it. You want me to wear it tonight?"

His grin was slow and heartstopping, the expression not quite touching his eyes which remained dark and intense and hungry. So very hungry. "No, darlin'. I want you to experience it."

The minute the words left his mouth, the truth hit her.

Wild Orchid. He was referring to the movie she'd seen ages ago with Mickey Rourke. Suddenly, her mind conjured a specific scene of a man and a woman in the backseat of a limousine. But she didn't see the man and woman from the movie. She saw Brady and herself, and heat rippled through her.

"Fifteen minutes," he said as he paused in the doorway, his deep voice barely carrying above the croon of Kenny Chesney drifting from the jukebox. "I'll be waiting."

9

SHE'D DONE IT in a limousine.

Eden stared out the window and watched as the sleek black car eased away from the curb.

Not only had she done it in the back seat of the limo, but the driver had been just a few feet away, his gaze trained on the road ahead.

At least that's what she'd thought at the time. When she'd actually thought. But thinking had been the farthest thing from her mind when Brady Weston had pulled her into the car, and into his arms.

At least her rendezvous hadn't been as blatantly obvious as that in the movie. The stars had not only done it in the backseat of a limousine, but they'd gotten down and dirty with other people sitting in the opposite seat. Watching.

The only other person in the car with them had been the driver, and there had been no indication that he'd had any clue as to what they were doing.

Still the possibility that he knew, that he'd heard, had been just as much a turn-on as an actual audience.

And just as embarrassing.

Eden pushed away the strange feeling. Embarrassment was an emotion better reserved for the shy, demure types who didn't have a reputation to uphold.

Eden, on the other hand, was a bonafide bad girl. A worldly woman. One who wouldn't so much as blink an eye at the prospect of hot sex in a limo, much less blush over it...

The thought trailed off as she lifted a hand to her hot cheek. Oh, God, she *was* blushing, despite her determination to stay calm and cool and aloof.

She was far from calm with her heart beating ninety to nothing and cool was a distant memory thanks to the flush making her skin burn and tingle. As for aloof?

She remembered the way her chest had tightened when she'd opened the florist box containing the wild orchid. No man had ever given her flowers before Brady.

And in this case, it was only one flower. One measly little flower that hadn't set him back more than five bucks at the most.

It didn't matter. He might well have shown up with a dozen roses that had cost him an entire paycheck. She remembered the giant ranch house that sat on the outskirts of town. The expensive Expedition his grandaddy drove around town. The enormous amount of money his sister had tipped just a week ago when she'd given Brady his welcome home party. Okay, so Brady could very well buy the entire flower shop with one paycheck.

Instead, this time he'd shown up with a single, inexpensive flower, and she'd loved it. It wasn't the quantity or the money involved. It was the thought he'd put into the action that touched something deep inside her. The fact that he'd taken time out of his busy day to visit the flower shop and pick out something so beautiful and so fitting for the occasion. No man had ever taken the time to discover her true desire. To make it come true.

Just admit it. You like him. You really like him.

That's what her heart said, but this wasn't about her heart, despite the fact that she looked forward to seeing his smile even more than she anticipated his touch. This was purely physical and she intended to keep it that way.

It was all about control, and the only reason she was having such soft feelings for him—the fluttering heart and racing pulse and sheer warmth she felt whenever she saw him—was because Brady had taken that control from her. He was the one dictating the how, when and where—something she'd allowed only one man in her past to do. And that man had broken her heart with his betrayal.

Not this time.

They weren't friends, no matter how much it seemed otherwise.

Eden retrieved her purse and slipped out the back door. Climbing into her pickup, she gunned the engine and headed toward the local video store.

It was all a matter of control, and from here on out, Eden was the one calling the shots.

"I CAME AS quick as I could. What's wrong—" The words stalled in his throat when Brady caught sight of Eden's reflection in the hall mirror.

"I'll be out in a minute," she called out.

She stood in front of her closet, almost completely nude and oblivious to his presence.

He should look away. That would be the polite thing to do, but there was nothing polite about his relationship with Eden. It was wild and wicked and lusty and so he looked. Not so much because he wanted to, however. He had to. She was far too beautiful and he was far too worked up, his heart still pounding from her recent phone call.

You have to come over right now. I need you.

That's all she'd said, and so he'd been left to wonder what it was she needed. Need in a sexual sense. Or need in a handyman, can-you-unstop-my-toilet sense?

He'd played with the various possibilities on his way over before his mind had conjured a third alternative. Could she be in trouble? Just that thought had sent him tearing down Main Street, his truck tearing up pavement at an alarming rate. The notion of her sick and helpless had filled him with a surge of protectiveness the likes of which Brady Weston had never felt before.

The feeling had morphed into full-blown panic when he'd knocked and knocked, and no one had answered. He'd tried the door, found it unlocked and braced himself for what he would find inside.

A half-naked woman.

But not just any half-naked woman. This was Eden Hallsey.

Sultry. Sexy. *Waiting for him?*

His gaze started at the bottom and traveled up, over trim ankles and shapely calves, smooth thighs and rounded hips. His attention snagged on the triangle of fine blonde hair peeking past the white lace of her bikini panties and his mouth went dry. His heart pounded and for a long, breathless moment, Brady thought he might actually have a heart attack.

Crazy.

He drew in a ragged breath and forced his gaze higher, over the soft roundness of her abdomen, the dark shadow of her belly button, to her bare breasts. Soft and round and full, they trembled as she pulled a dress from the closet. Rose-colored nipples pebbled beneath his study and for a few frantic heartbeats, he got the impression that she was more aware of his presence than she wanted him to think.

But then she leaned over, her breasts swaying as she stepped into the dress, and his thoughts scattered.

Everything about her screamed *sin*. The way she moved, her breasts bobbing and her bottom swiveling as she shimmied the material up her thighs, over her hips. The way she looked, with her full, sensuous lips partially open, her hair long and tousled, as if she'd just rolled from beneath the covers.

A man didn't have to be a genius to understand how she'd gotten her reputation. He'd lay money that there weren't too many men who could look at her, clothed or otherwise, and not think about sex. She was the original Eve. Lush and tempting and irresistible. Poor Adam. It was no wonder he'd taken a bite of that damned apple. As hard and as desperate as Brady felt, he would have gobbled down an entire bushel, cores and all.

He was just a man, after all, and Eden Hallsey would tempt even the most devout.

Although the thought of her tempting anyone else sent a surge of anger through him.

Crazy.

He'd deliberately picked her because she was so tempting. The perfect woman to validate his manhood.

His and no other.

He shook the notion away. Eden Hallsey was everything his grandaddy had warned him about where women were concerned. A vamp. That's what the old man would have called her. That and a few other choice words. Zachariah Weston's idea of the ideal woman had nothing to do with lust and libido and looks, and everything to do with background and breeding and money.

We marry our own kind.

He hadn't. He'd married his complete and total opposite. A mistake he didn't intend to repeat ever again.

When, if he ever made that walk down the aisle, it would be with his family's blessing, with someone they found suitable. Someone with the same values, the same hopes and dreams. Marriage was hard enough without adding conflicting interests which was exactly what he'd had with his first marriage. Sally had valued money above family.

But money didn't solve problems or bring happiness or keep people together. Love did that.

The only thing Brady and Eden had in common was their lust.

His gaze made another long, slow trek up her body and back down again, his heart thundering, his breathing coming in short gasps. She was dressed now, yet he was still rock hard. And growing harder by the minute. Particularly when she reached beneath the dress and pulled down her panties. She stepped free of the lace and his erection jumped.

The clothing should have helped calm his libido. *Out of sight, out of mind,* or so the saying went.

It didn't matter.

It wasn't just seeing what lay beneath the clingy white sundress that turned him on. It was the knowing.

That she'd shed her panties. She wore nothing but the dress. A very short, sleeveless little white number that clung to every curve.

No slip. No bra. No panties. *Nothing.*

The thought replayed in his head as he watched her lift her arms and pull her hair back into a simple ponytail. Her fingers worked at the rubberband and he found himself mesmerized by the soft ripple of muscle in her biceps as she pushed and pulled and—

"There," she announced, her voice jarring him from his speculation.

Letting her arms fall to her sides, she turned fully toward him and smiled. As their gazes met, he knew in an instant that she'd been fully aware of his watching her.

That she'd liked it.

"Sorry if I kept you waiting."

"Uh, no. I mean, yes. I mean…" What the hell did he mean? "Yes, you kept me waiting."

"I didn't mean to."

"Careful. Your nose is liable to grow."

"Along with another certain particular body part, I see." Her attention dropped to his waist before she met his gaze again. Her smile widened, but it didn't quite touch her eyes. They were dark and smoky and filled with desire and he knew the playfulness was just a show.

"I'd rather you touch, darlin'."

"Not yet." She moved back before he could slide his arm around her and for a split second, he glimpsed the hesitation he'd seen earlier. A self-consciousness that told him she wasn't nearly as in control as she was pretending to be.

"Then why did you call me over here. I could have come by on my way home from work. That's what I was planning."

"Maybe I have different plans."

He quirked an eyebrow at her. "Judging by the way your bottom lip is trembling, the way it always trembles when you're turned on, your plans can't be that different from mine."

"I thought we could go out to dinner first."

"I thought we weren't dating."

"This isn't a date date. It's eating. We just happen to be doing it at the same time. Together."

"So this is what you meant by *needing* me?" he asked as he ushered her out the door and down the stairs to his truck.

"Exactly."

He glanced around and noted that her truck was missing. "You need transportation."

"I loaned Kasey my truck." She climbed into the

passenger side of his vehicle. He moved to shut the door, but then she pulled the hem of her dress up and moved to cross her legs.

His heart stalled as he caught sight of the tiny blond hairs between her legs and the swollen pink slit. Then one knee hooked over the other and the vision disappeared.

He drew in a deep breath and lifted his gaze to find her smiling at him.

"So why does Kasey have your truck?" he asked a few seconds later as he climbed behind the wheel and tried to ignore the fact that she was completely naked beneath her dress.

"She's picking up supplies for tomorrow night's football widows' party."

"A big screen is the way to go," he told her.

"If you've got money to burn, which I don't. Then again, maybe my lottery numbers will come in tonight."

"Now that's burning money."

"Haven't you ever gambled on anything before?"

"I prefer a sure thing."

"So do I."

There was just something about the way she said the words that drew his attention. He turned to see her lick her lips before they dropped to his lap.

"You're up to something."

"Actually," she said as she leaned toward him and stroked his thigh an inch shy of the erection already throbbing in his pants. "The plan is to get *you* up, and I think we're right on schedule."

"ARE YOU SURE you want to go here?" Brady's voice drew her attention and Eden turned to see him sitting behind the wheel, staring through the windshield at the building that sat in the distance. "The place looks awful crowded. Chances are we're not going to get a table."

"I made reservations," she said as she climbed out and rounded the front of the truck.

He met her halfway. "I thought it was pure chance that we happened to be hungry at the same time."

"Pure chance resulting from a carefully laid out plan." She grinned and reached for his hand. "Come on."

A few minutes later they were seated in a quaint corner of the steak house. The inside consisted of dark paneled walls covered with all sorts of ranch paraphernalia, from rusted horseshoes to branding irons. Checkered tablecloths covered the tables. Mason jars held flickering red candles. It was Texas chic, if there was such a thing, and Eden's favorite place to eat since she'd first walked in on the night of her high school graduation.

Her parents had splurged and taken her to the expensive restaurant to celebrate. Many of the other parents had had the same idea and the restaurant had been filled with high school kids and their families. She'd sat in the restaurant and talked and laughed like all the other kids she went to school with, and for the first time, she'd felt as if she belonged.

It had been a short-lived feeling. Her reputation had already been established by then and on the way to the car, Jeremy Michaels had slapped her butt as she'd walked by.

But for those few precious hours before then...

She'd had one of the most normal experiences of her life. Growing up, she'd spent most of her free time in the bar. Her parents had worked hellacious hours to afford the mortgage on the place, her mom waiting tables and her father tending bar, and they'd had very little time for traditional family outings.

She'd loved the Longhorn ever since, even though she rarely had a chance to dine there. The prices were high and her income low and so she settled for her memories most of the time.

But not tonight. Tonight was about control and the Longhorn was her place.

Unfortunately, it felt more like Brady's place as customer after customer walked by and greeted him. Then again, she should have expected it. He was the town's golden boy. Zachariah Weston's only grandson. Heir to the Weston fortune.

Different.

She forced the notion aside and concentrated on

dinner, on leaning over just enough to give him a glimpse of her cleavage. Under the cover of the long table cloth, she slid off her shoes and trailed her bare toes along the inside of his jean-clad thigh.

She'd just worked her way under his napkin when she heard the familiar voice.

"Well if it isn't Eden Hallsey."

"Jake," she growled as she retracted her foot and slid her sandal back on. She put on her most fake, pretentious, I-think-you're-an-asshole-and-you-know-it smile. "You're looking as good as ever."

He flexed. "Owe it all to the Tummy Tightener. They're on sale this week at the Killeen MegaMart. You need it, we got it."

She eyed him. "I guess you're not into pharmaceuticals."

"Sure we are. We've got a full line of vitamins, cold remedies—we cure what ails you."

"No Rogaine?" She shrugged. "I swear your hairline's receded a good three inches since I last saw you."

"I was just in your place last week."

"I know. That much must be some kind of record, don't you think? I bet Guiness is beating down your door."

"You can insult me all you want. You're not going to make me retract my offer. I still want to buy your place."

"And I'm still saying no. There's plenty of land down by the Interstate. Buy there."

"I'll buy where I want. You've got a prime location."

"And you're doing a prime job of running everyone out of business. But you're not doing it to me."

"Why don't you stop being so stubborn and take what I'm offering you?"

"I don't think you heard the lady. She's not interested."

"Stay out of this, Weston. This is between old friends. Ain't that right, Eden? We go way back, don't we?"

"And from the looks of things," Brady said as he patted Jake's middle. "You lied just as much then as you do now."

"What's that supposed to mean?"

"I'm just saying that you probably don't even own a Tummy Toner. In fact, I hear tell you owe those abs to a plastic surgeon over in Austin."

"Who told you that?"

"Hazards of a small town. People talk. You know that better than anyone."

"Well it's not true. It's a lie."

Brady winked at Eden. "You'd know that better than anyone too."

"That was a long time ago. Eden's not still mad about it, are you, sugar?"

"Maybe she's not, but I am." Brady leaned back and folded his arms. "And she's not your sugar."

"YOU'RE MAD," Eden said an hour later as they walked into her apartment. After Jake had stomped away, they'd eaten the rest of their dinner in silence. She'd tried the footsie move once more, but Brady wasn't receptive. "You are mad."

"I am not."

"You didn't have to interfere. I could have handled him myself. I *was* handling him."

He dropped down on the sofa and stared up at her. "And you were doing a damned good job. Most women would have climbed up on their high horse and put on airs."

"I don't put on airs. I call it like I see it and Jake was, is and always will be, short of some major life-changing miracle, a bonafide jerk."

"I agree."

"Is that why you butted in? Because he's a jerk?"

"Because he was being a jerk to you." Brady shook his head. "I didn't like it. And I didn't like the way Hershell Marks was staring at you from the next table. And the way the waiter kept staring at you. And the way every man in the whole damned place, short of Reverend Skelly, was staring at you." He frowned. "You should put on some clothes."

Her first instinct should have been to tell him to go to hell. Wasn't that just like a man to blame a woman for attracting attention? She'd butted heads with her fair share of jealous men. Men who wanted her.

Men who wanted to own her.

But this was different.

He was different. The way he looked—so angry and offended and *protective*—sent a burst of warmth through her.

And so Eden did what she'd been wanting to do since the moment she'd felt his gaze on her while she'd been dressing earlier that evening.

She walked up to him, took his face between her hands, and kissed him.

10

HIS MOUTH FIT hers perfectly. She didn't have to think about kissing him. It happened as effortlessly as breathing. His mouth opened and hers opened, as if they'd shared this very same moment time and time again. A familiarity forged over years rather than a few nights.

The realization startled her, but then his hands covered hers and he deepened the kiss and she forgot everything save the deep probe of his tongue and the warmth of his fingers against hers.

Their tongues tangled and the world seemed to fall away. She forgot all about the rest of her plan— to lure him into the bedroom, tie his wrists to her bedposts with the satin sash from her favorite robe and seduce him until he begged for mercy.

They made it to the sofa. He fell into a sitting position and she followed him. Her dress rode up past her hips, leaving her exposed and naked as she straddled him.

"You drove me crazy all night," he murmured in between kisses. "I kept thinking of you like this."

"That was the idea." She reached for the snap on his jeans and felt the hard, thick length of him. His breath caught on a hiss as she took her time unzipping, exploring and stroking until he could take no more.

"Stop." The word, so raw and deep and pleading, sent a burst of power through her. He might not be tied up, but he was at her mercy.

As much as she'd been at his the past few days.

"Stop right now."

"If that's what the man wants." She started to unstraddle him, but he caught her hips, jerking her back down and rubbing her along the length of him. His jeans created a delicious friction against the slick heat between her legs.

"*This* is what I want," he said, slipping his fingers between her legs, tracing the moist slit before touching her clit with one callused fingertip. She trembled as sensation, white-hot and consuming, speared her. The cry jumped to the tip of her tongue, but she managed to hold it back. Barely.

The realization that he had such fierce power over her, that he could make her want to break free, to cry out, sent a wave of fear rolling through her, followed by determination. This was her show. Her chance to slide back into the driver's seat, and she did just that.

She forced a deep breath, leaned over and sucked his bottom lip into her mouth, nipping as she moved her hips, rubbing herself up and down his bulging crotch until he groaned. He donned a condom, then caught her bare bottom in his hands and held her still. "Wait."

"No," she murmured, lifting herself. She clenched her teeth as she guided herself down on him.

Even as he grasped her hips, he didn't try to force her into his rhythm, but let her find her own. She raised and lowered herself, rubbing the tips of her breasts against the soft hair of his chest and returning his deep, devouring kisses. She felt strong and sure as she met his passion.

A woman in control.

Sensation built and the pressure increased as she rode him. The steady rise and fall of her pelvis pulled him deeper and pushed her higher. The pleasure was sharp and intense and sweet. So very, very sweet.

"Damn, you're beautiful."

She barely heard his voice above the thunder of her own heart, but when she did, her eyes opened and she found him staring up at her, his gaze full of blazing heat. He was watching the way he always did, but this time it didn't send her into a panic. She was the one in control. The one setting the pace for their pleasure.

The knowledge fed the fire burning inside her and she moved faster, drawing him in and out in a frantic rhythm that matched the pounding of her heart.

Her climax hit her hard and fast, rolling over her like a giant wave, sucking her under. Her entire body trembled and her legs tightened, holding him deep, milking him as spasm after spasm gripped her.

Somewhere in the far distance she heard her own voice. The sound, high-pitched and frenzied, vibrated from her lips and split open the breath-laden silence.

"Brady!"

Fire flashed in his gaze, as if the sound of her voice excited him even more than being buried deep inside her. But then his eyes closed, his teeth clenched and he arched his neck. He gripped her hips, holding her to him as he plunged deep one last time and gave in to his own orgasm.

Eden collapsed on top of him and buried her face in his neck. He gathered her in his arms and held her.

Their hearts thundered together, one pressed against the other. She touched a soft kiss to his salty skin, loving the taste and the texture of him.

Loving him.

The thought jarred her, then filled her with dismay. She didn't love him and he didn't love her. This was purely physical. A temporary tryst. A hot affair.

So what if she'd cried out his name?

It wasn't as if she'd stripped naked and bared all. She was still wearing her sundress. It was just a silly little cry.

The memory of her own voice echoed and a wave of embarrassment washed through her. Okay, so it had been more like a scream. So what? No doubt women screamed for him all the time. It was no big deal.

She'd regained her control tonight and she wasn't going to lose sight of that fact because of a minor slip up.

Chances were he hadn't even noticed.

"Basic Instinct," he finally murmured, confirming her thoughts. He hadn't noticed at all. Instead, he'd been trying to figure out which movie she'd used as inspiration for tonight's seduction.

She wasn't sure why the notion should bother her, but it did. She didn't want him so totally and completely focused on her that he noticed nothing else, especially the breaking of her vow of orgasmic silence.

Yet, at the same time, the fact that he hadn't noticed something so monumental sent a wave of annoyance through her.

"I knew the thing with the dress seemed familiar, but I couldn't figure out why."

"Really?" She tried to pull away but he held her still.

"Wait a second." He stared up at her, a grin tilting the corner of his mouth. "We're not done yet."

"Yes, we are. You had an orgasm. I had an orgasm." Boy, had she ever. "We're done."

He grimaced. "I don't know who came up with this one orgasm per encounter rule, but I'm getting damned tired of it. We're changing it."

"Too bad because I happen to like it."

"You know what I think?" Without waiting for a reply, he rolled her over onto her back and pressed her into the sofa. His weight urged her legs even further and he sank a fraction deeper. The grin faded as his gaze fired bright. "I think you like me."

"Liking someone complicates things."

The comment wiped the grin from his face. "And we don't want complications, do we?"

He'd directed the question at her, but she had the distinct feeling he was asking it more of himself. As if he were weighing the merits of complicating their relationship.

As if.

His grin was quick and sure when it slid back into place and she was left to wonder if she'd just imagined his sudden change of mood. "You like me, all right."

"I do not like you." She didn't like him. It wasn't about like. It was about lust. *I'll take lust over love any old day.*

That's what she told herself, but the sound of her own voice still echoed in her ears. Loud. Intense.

She'd shared orgasms before and none of them had made her scream.

But then none of the men she'd been with had been Brady.

As if he read her thoughts, he grinned again. "Your mouth says no, darlin', but your body says yes." He shifted ever so slightly and she tightened around him, her muscles acting on their own accord. "Yes," he told her.

"No."

He withdrew ever so slightly and slid back inside. Her body accepted him eagerly, grasping him as if it didn't want to let go. "Yes," he said again.

"No." The word was breathless this time, her nerves buzzing from the delicious pressure deep inside her.

"Yes." He plunged again. Harder this time. Deeper.

"No," she managed after a long, heart-pounding moment.

"Yes," he urged as he pulled back and thrust again. "Yes." And again. "Yes." And again.

"Yes!" she cried out before she could stop herself. She wrapped her arms and legs around him and gave herself up to the delicious feel of Brady Weston.

So much for control.

SHE'D SCREAMED. And cried. And even begged.

The knowledge should have sent a wave of satisfaction through Brady. It would have, only despite her intense reaction, he thought she was still holding back.

He eyed the skimpy sundress that she still wore, the thin white material stretched tight across her full breasts. He could see the faint shadow of her nipples beneath, the dimples of her areola. A shadow. That's all she'd allowed him.

She was still hiding, all right.

He knew it had something to do with Jake and the striptease she'd supposedly performed. Despite her erotic performance for him earlier that evening, he couldn't picture Eden taking it all off for a horny group of teen ballplayers.

She'd been too shy and quiet back then. Too trusting. He couldn't forget how open and wide and honest her light blue eyes had been whenever she'd stared at him during English class. How every expression had always showed on her beautiful face. Her embarrassment. Her longing.

Before the rumor.

A rumor he hadn't believed, despite her sudden change. He couldn't quite associate the outrageous antics that had been spread around the locker room to the shy girl who'd looked away every time he'd glanced at her. Even if that shy girl had done an about face and turned into Cadillac High's baddest bad girl.

The rumor had brought about the change rather than any sexual encounter with Jake and the rest of the team. Eden had been hurt and she'd decided to bottle her feelings up and pretend she didn't have any.

He knew what that was like all too well because he was doing it right now with his grandfather. Pretending he liked hammering soles day after day. Pretending he didn't like Eden near as much as he did.

His thoughts went to her, to the way she'd chewed on her full bottom lip and stared back at him with those guarded blue eyes last night, when she'd been on top of him and he'd been deep, deep inside her.

She liked him, all right. She just didn't trust him.

She didn't trust any man.

So? Their relationship wasn't about trust. It was all about proving something to himself and he'd done just that by making her cry out. Crying, begging, pleading. That's what he'd wanted from her. He shouldn't want more.

But he did.

The realization stayed with him all the way back to his apartment, to the empty bed where he tossed and turned until dawn came and with it, a full day's work.

God help him, but he wanted her completely naked and vulnerable and trusting and—*Ouch*.

Pain bolted through him as Brady slammed the hammer down on his thumb. The sensation jarred him back to reality, to the fact that he'd been hammering the same sole for the past fifteen minutes because of Eden.

"I think she's just about done," Zeke said as he glanced over at Brady.

"Um, yeah." He tossed the boot to the side and reached for another sole.

"Seems like something's bothering you." Zeke hammered a few times. "Or maybe someone's bothering you." His gaze met Brady's. "Mitchell Jenkins saw you and Eden Hallsey over at the Longhorn last night."

"And?"

"And you two looked mighty friendly is all." He hammered a few more times. "She is awful pretty."

"What's that supposed to mean?" Brady wasn't sure why the comment bothered him so.

Hell's bells, who was he kidding? He knew why it bothered him. He was jealous. Damned jealous. Of all the ridiculous, stupid, crazy things to be.

"It don't mean nothing."

"It means something all right. A person doesn't just comment on a man's dinner company unless he means something."

"I just think it's strange, is all."

"Because I was out with a pretty woman?"

"Because you were out with that particular pretty woman. She just don't seem your type, is all."

"And what type is she?" Brady had stopped hammering. He stepped closer to Zeke who'd abandoned his work.

The man held out his hands. "Look, let's just forget it."

"Say it," Brady said. He knew he was overreacting, but he'd reached his limit. After seeing so many men ogle his woman, he'd just about had it with all the attention she drew. And now to have Zeke commenting on her... He'd reached his boiling point.

He was itching for a fight.

"Say it," he said again, backing the other man up a step. Zeke tripped in the process and fell backwards onto a freshly nailed boot. His hand snagged on the edge of a nail and he cut himself.

"Let's just forget about this."

"No," Brady said as he grabbed Zeke by his good hand and helped him to his feet.

Zeke examined his bleeding hand. "I really don't think—" The words stalled as Brady grabbed him by the collar.

"Say it."

"She's just a little worn, is all. I mean, that's what I've heard. Not that I know myself. I was totally faithful to Mabel while we were married. Never even looked at another woman. But I used to hear talk out at Mabel's daddy's ranch when I worked out there."

Brady tightened his grip and pulled Zeke nose to nose. "Don't believe everything you hear, and don't go adding to the gossip."

"What's going on here?" The sound of Zachariah Weston's voice cut into the argument and Brady loosened his hold on Zeke.

Surprise rushed through him as he realized that the old man had spoken to him. He'd finally spoken.

Brady turned toward the old man.

"Zeke? Is something wrong?" Zachariah directed a concerned stare at the young man.

"I should have known," Brady muttered. He leaned over and retrieved the bakery bag he'd picked up earlier that morning. "I've got caramel-covered cinnamon rolls." He held up the bag, but the old man wasn't paying any attention. As usual. "Your favorite."

"You get on over to First Aid and let them take a look at that cut," Zachariah said before he turned to walk away.

Brady's frustration peaked and before he could remember his vow to endure the old man's silence, his mouth opened.

"Can't you just say good morning?" he shouted after his grandfather.

The old man stopped dead in his tracks.

"Just once," Brady pleaded, his voice softer, filled with the desperation bubbling inside him. "Can't you just say it?"

For a long moment, he thought the old man would actually turn around. Time seemed to stand still.

Brady's breath lodged in his chest as he waited for the old man's reaction. A word. A nod. Something.

Zachariah Weston stepped toward his office.

"Dammit," Brady muttered.

"Sorry about what I said," Zeke said. "I didn't mean nothing. Just trying to warn you."

But there was no need for a warning where Eden Hallsey was concerned. He wasn't in danger because their affair was over. Last night had been Saturday. One full week since their first encounter, since he'd made up his mind to seduce her until she lost her precious control and cried out his name.

She'd done just that, even if she had been wearing a sundress at the time.

"Here." He tossed the cinnamon rolls at Zeke. "Knock yourself out."

"You're not mad?"

He *was* mad, and frustrated and tired of killing himself to please a man who obviously didn't have an ounce of forgiveness in his heart.

For the first time, Brady actually considered the possibility that he might not be able to win back his grandaddy's favor. And with that thought came a sense of failure that stayed with him throughout the day and sent him searching for an escape later that evening.

THE PIGGLY WIGGLY didn't exactly have the sit-down, drown-your-misery atmosphere Brady needed at the moment, but it would have to do. The Pink Cadillac was the only bar in town and that, like the beautiful owner, was now completely off-limits.

As if his thoughts conjured her up, he rounded the corner to find Eden standing in the snack section, her arms overflowing with bags of cheese curls and pretzels.

She wore her usual attire—a pair of jeans and a tank top. The soft white cotton was a stark contrast against her tanned skin. A ponytail tugged her long blond hair away from her face with the exception of a few wayward tendrils that hung loose at the nape of her neck. Her skin glowed with perspiration and he knew she'd been hard at work all day the way he had.

She looked as tired as he felt, and the urge to rush to her side and hold her nearly overwhelmed him.

But getting close to Eden Hallsey was not part of tonight's plan. He'd been there, done that, and now it was over.

He wasn't even going to talk to her. It was better to slip away quietly and carry on with his plans. That's what he told himself, but then she dropped a bag and he didn't even think. He simply reacted.

She was on her knees, gathering up bags when he dropped down next to her and reached for some wayward Doritos. "Thanks," she said. "I guess I should have hunted for a basket, but they were all take—" Her words died as her gaze collided with his. "Uh, hi."

"Hi, yourself."

She lifted a hand to her face and pushed a wayward strand of hair behind her ear. "What are you doing here?"

He held up a bottle of wine.

"You've got to be kidding."

"What? You have something against Blueberry Delight?"

"Actually, it has something against me." She made a face. "Ninth grade. Tracey Jones's birthday party. I drank four glasses and spent the entire evening hanging over the toilet in her parents' bathroom."

He grinned, remembering the way she'd been. So naive and sheltered and *accepted.* Before the rumors. Before she'd been hurt so badly she'd stopped trusting all men.

Brady barely ignored the strange urge to gather her in his arms and simply hold her right there in the middle of the grocery store in front of the Cheetos display. *Crazy.*

"It wasn't pleasant," she added with a shudder. "One of the worst moments of my life."

"Eighth grade. Fred Tate's Fourth of July barbecue. We raided his parents' liquor cabinet after they'd left to watch fireworks at the park. Only it was eight glasses and his parents' pool hasn't been the same since."

She grimaced as she glanced at the bottle. "I would've thought you'd learned your lesson."

"What can I say? I'm feeling a little nostalgic."

"Why don't you come on over to the bar and I'll pour you a beer? On the house." She grinned. "Sort of a farewell between friends."

"Friends, huh?"

"We are, aren't we?"

He nodded. At that moment, he wanted to be her friend even more than he wanted to kiss her. The notion was crazy, and yet it was true. So true that his chest ached at the prospect.

"Thanks, but I'm really not up to a crowd right now." He wasn't going to say it. Not no, but hell no. "Why don't *you* come with *me?* I thought I'd take a little ride out to Morgan's Creek the way we used to on Saturday nights."

"You *are* feeling nostalgic." She looked as if the idea held more appeal than anything she'd heard in a long, long time. "I'm afraid I can't. The football widows' party is in full swing and we ran out of snacks."

"I thought Kasey borrowed the truck to go after snacks?"

"She did, but then she ran into Laurie over at the Dippity Do. The girl challenged her to a nail polishing race and by the time she'd reached the Top Coat, the wholesaler was closed. I swear," Eden said with a shake of her head. "Those two are going to give me even more gray hair than I already have."

"Gray hair is nice on a woman."

She gave him a what-potato-truck-did-you-fall-off-of look. "Come again."

"Nice." He leaned close enough to finger a strand of her hair. "You'd look nice in any color."

The compliment had the desired effect on her. She blushed and there wasn't a prettier sight.

Silence descended for several long moments as she shifted bags around and tried to adjust her arms. He simply stared at the way her cheeks had flushed such an enticing shade of pink. It was a sight he remembered from English class.

Christ, he *was* feeling nostalgic.

"Where is Kasey now?" he asked, suddenly determined to get her to accompany him to the river. He wanted, no he needed to spend some time with Eden. This Eden. Not the bold, brassy I'll-take-lust-over-love-any-old-day woman he'd come to know intimately, but this soft-spoken, easygoing, blushing woman.

"Waiting tables the last I saw."

"Then she can cover for you. We'll drop the snacks off on the way and you can hand over the keys and let her lock up later."

"I really can't…" He watched the indecision play across her features, along with longing and he felt himself pulled back to English class where he'd glanced behind him so many times and seen the same look. The same open, honest desire.

Feelings she'd had, but had never acted on.

But some of the bold, brassy, headstrong woman she'd become must have figured in now because where she would have shook her head and turned away so long ago, she now smiled. "The party is almost over, and Kasey deserves a little stress for screwing up the supply trip. I guess you've got yourself a date."

THEY WERE NOT on a date.

Eden told herself that as she climbed into the cab of the old pick-up and rode out to Morgan's Lake with Brady. Of course, she'd called it that, but it had been merely a figure of speech. A stupid slip. And this was *not* a date.

As nervous as she felt, the minute Brady stared over at her and smiled, she seemed to relax. She felt his heat seeping across the truck seat to her and the way he stroked the steering wheel hypnotized her. Her reservations faded and the truck ride ended up being much more pleasant than she'd ever imagined.

She felt comfortable. At ease.

And excited. She'd never actually been to the lake with a boy. Another first for her, thanks to Brady Weston. He was showing her all she'd missed out on. All the normal teen girl stuff.

But you're not a teenager. You're a woman. You know the score.

She did, but at that moment, she couldn't help but pretend. And with the fantasy came the rush of feelings she would have felt way back then. The excitement. The anticipation. The happiness.

She held the feelings close and relished them as she watched the sun creep toward the horizon.

The ride was short and sweet and soon they pulled up to the shimmering lake and climbed out. Brady popped the tailgate and they both settled down. The radio filtered from Bessie's cab, filling the growing darkness with a slow country song.

Unscrewing the bottle of wine, Brady filled the two Dixie cups he'd pulled from the Piggly Wiggly bag.

He downed his with one long gulp while Eden sniffed and took a tentative sip. She grimaced and he laughed.

"How'd you ever drink four entire glasses of it?"

"It was a dare."

"Then I dare you."

She eyed him and then eyed the wine. "What do I get if I do it?"

"What did you get back then?"

"Kasey's brand new tube of Viva La Pink lipstick."

Brady rummaged in his pocket. "Would you settle for some Chap Stick?"

She eyed his offering. "What flavor?"

"Cherry."

"You're on." She took a deep breath, held her nose and downed the entire contents in one long, sputtering drink.

"Ugh. That was just as awful as I remember." She held out her hand. "Gimmee."

"Not so fast. You owe me three more glasses. It was four glasses, remember?" He filled her cup to the brim. "Drink up."

"If I didn't know better, I'd say you were trying to get me drunk."

"Actually," he said before filling his own cup and downing it in one gulp. "I'm the one trying to get drunk."

Don't ask, she told herself. *Just drink your wine and keep quiet.*

The last thing she needed to do was sit next to Brady Weston while he poured out his troubles. She had her own to contend with. But at that moment, with the lake shining in the moonlight and Brady suddenly looking so dark and troubled, she couldn't help herself. She felt his worry even more than her own. His fear. She couldn't help herself.

"What's wrong?"

"Nothing." He shrugged. "Hell, everything." He stared out at the still water. "You don't need to hear this."

"No, but I want to. And you probably need to say

it. Haven't you heard that confession's good for the soul."

He shot her a quick grin before turning his attention back to the river. His expression fell. "No matter what I do, it's not good enough. He won't forgive me." Brady took another drink of his wine and shook his head. "Maybe coming home wasn't such a good idea. Christ, who am I kidding? This isn't my home. Things have changed."

The irony of what she was hearing struck her and she couldn't help herself. She laughed.

"What's so funny?"

"I'm sorry. It's just that if anyone belongs here, it's you." She shook her head as the past welled up inside her and where she would have kept her mouth shut with anyone else, she felt a closeness with Brady. An intimacy. Not just in a physical sense, but an emotional one. Because Eden Hallsey knew what it felt like to be an outsider.

She'd spent the past ten years striving to be just that, and succeeding. The fact had always given her comfort before, until now. Now a sense of longing bubbled inside her and floated to the surface. The regret. The desperation to have it all back again and be the way she'd been before. Soft and approachable and likeable.

"I don't think things have changed so much, as you've changed." At his sharp glance, she went on. "That's it, isn't it? You're not afraid that Cadillac is

different. You worried that you are. That you don't
fit in, not because people won't accept you, but because you don't really want to fit in. You don't like
the same things you did ten years before. You're not
the same person you were when you left."

"That's crazy."

"Is it? Who has ad sheets spread out across his
apartment when he's supposed to be working in the
production department? It's not the same person who
used to skip classes so he could hang out over at the
factory. You don't like being in the production department."

"That's bullshit. I like it. I love it. I always did."

"*Did,* as in past tense. But this isn't the past. It's
the present. You've changed, but that's not such a bad
thing, Brady. You're a better person now. Stronger."

"I feel like a failure." The word were soft and quiet
and so full of heartache that Eden couldn't help herself. She covered his hand with her own.

"You left here and made it when all the odds were
against you. Sounds like success to me. And you've
got courage too. When things didn't work out, you
found the strength to come back, to set things right."

"But they aren't right."

"Not yet. Your granddaddy's stubborn. Give him
time."

Brady didn't want to ask the question that had
haunted him ever since he'd rolled back into Cadil-

lac, but he couldn't help himself. "And what if that isn't enough? What if I'm not enough?"

"You're his grandson. His blood. His family.

"And you *do* belong here," she went on, her voice so full of conviction that Brady actually believed her. "This is your home and Weston Boots is your legacy, whether you like hammering soles all day or figuring out ways to beef up business."

"It's just that I never used my brain back then. I was too busy having fun. Too eager to please my grandfather."

"That's something that hasn't changed," she pointed out. "You're still vying for the man's favor."

"And failing."

"Didn't you learn anything working your way through college?"

He gave her a slow, easy grin. "Never give up, even when there's just bologna in the fridge and no bread in the bread box."

"Exactly. If you want him to forgive you, you have to keep trying. Most of all, you have to stop beating yourself up and trying to pretend that you're something you're not."

As she said the words, he turned his hand palm up. Strong fingers twined with hers and Brady drew comfort from the woman sitting next to him. Comfort and warmth and courage, until the future didn't look so dismal.

He *had* changed, and while he wasn't so certain

his grandfather would support his new interests, he wasn't going to give up working for the man's forgiveness.

"And what about you?"

"What about me?"

"Why do you stay in a town that's ripe with rumor about you?"

"Same reason as you. This is my home."

"Your parents are gone. You've got no family here."

"I've got the Pink Cadillac. It's all I have left of my parents now that they're gone. They worked hard to keep it going, and I intend to do the same, no matter who runs their mouth. I don't care what people say about me."

"You know what I think?" He eyed her. "I think you *do* care. I think you want them to say things— outrageous things—on purpose because you want people to think you're a bad girl. But deep down inside, you're not so bad. You miss being accepted. You're desperate to hang one of those T-ball banners in your bar and line your walls with pictures of the team you sponsor."

He saw a flicker of regret in her eyes, before she averted her gaze and fixed it on the bottle in his hands.

"You're also drunk." She picked up the bottle. "I wouldn't rely too much on what you think right now."

"Is that so? For your information, I've only had

two glasses and I'm as sober as ever. Sober enough to walk a straight line with my eyes closed."

She plopped the Chap Stick between them and he knew their conversation was over. "Go for it."

"And sober enough to hop in place on one leg."

Eden pulled a keychain from her pocket and slapped it on the tailgate. "Let's see it."

"And sober enough to kiss you senseless."

The comment hung in the air between them for several long moments and Brady thought for a split second that he'd crossed the line. This wasn't about another rendezvous. It was a walk down memory lane. A heart-to-heart talk between friends.

The thing was, it didn't feel like another tryst. This was different. There was just something about the darkness, the moonlight, the closeness he now felt with Eden that drew them together on a deeper level.

And he could no more resist than he could have jumped up on the tailgate and snagged the moon hanging overhead.

He kissed her. Soft and slow and easy, his tongue gliding along her bottom lip, dipping inside, tasting the blueberry wine she'd just drank. The kiss was slow and thorough and breath stealing, and it stirred him even more than the fierce, hungry kisses they'd shared in the past. Because it wasn't planned or anticipated. It simply happened.

"This isn't ringing a bell," she managed to gasp

when he'd finally pulled away. "What movie is this from?"

He grinned. "Brady and Eden Waltz Down Memory Lane."

She managed a smile despite the trembling of her lips. "I don't think I've seen that."

"I have. It starts like this." He kissed her again. This time the kiss was even deeper, more mesmerizing and when it was over, they were both gasping for air.

"And how does it end?" she asked him.

He leaned over and murmured, "You tell me," and then he claimed her mouth again.

11

EDEN TOOK A deep breath, gathered her courage and reached for the hem of her tank top. She pulled the covering over her head and let it slip from her fingertips. She wished she could see his expression, but the moonlight glittered behind him, casting his face in shadow.

She could only hear his reaction. His sharp intake of breath as she reached for the clasp on her bra.

Her fingers faltered and she damned herself for the rush of insecurity. But old habits were hard to break and while she was determined to do this, she couldn't help but put off the inevitable.

Nervous fingers went to the snap on her jeans. She slid the fastener free. A long, slow *zzzzziiippp* and her jeans parted in a deep V that revealed the lace of her panties.

She slid the material down her legs and stepped free. She still had on her bra and panties, but as she stared deep into Brady's eyes, she might well have been wearing nothing at all. He made her feel open and vulnerable.

His eyes. That was the difference now. Jake Marlboro had been too busy ogling every inch she'd revealed, but Brady stared into her eyes, held her gaze, gave her strength and courage and fed her desire.

She reached behind her and worked at the catch of her bra with trembling fingers. The undergarment came free and the straps sagged on her shoulders. Sliding the lace down her arms, she freed her straining breasts. Then her hands moved to her panties.

He was on her in an instant, his hands catching hers. Warm, strong fingers closed over hers. "You don't have to do this."

"I want to." The words were out before she could even think about them. Not that she needed to. They were true. However frightened, she wanted Brady to be the man to see her completely naked.

She knew that no matter how hard she tried, she would never, ever find another man like Brady Weston. Tonight was their last night together and she wanted it to be special. Memorable.

He'd given her something special tonight. He'd trusted her enough to open up to her, to talk about his feelings. His fears. And Eden wanted to do the same.

"I really want to," she added, sliding her fingers from his to push the panties down over her hips. Lace slid along her flesh and pooled at her ankles. She stepped free and stood before him, open and honest and frightened.

The urge to cover herself was nearly overwhelming, but she fought it back down, determined to stand her ground, to be as honest with him as he'd been with her.

Just this once.

She fixed her attention at a point just beyond his shoulders as his gaze left her face and made a slow trek down her body and back up again.

The air lodged in her chest as she waited for his reaction. Crazy. She shouldn't care what he thought one way or the other. She'd never cared what anyone thought.

But she did. She cared about Brady, his feelings, his thoughts, his hopes, his dreams, his desires.

She cared.

She didn't want to think about why. Instead, she focused on holding her shoulders back, her head up, her arms down by her sides.

"Well?" she finally asked, her nerves pushed to the edge. She needed to know what he was thinking, and he summed it up in one word that sent her heart soaring.

"Beautiful." And then with one swift motion, he pulled her into his arms.

His kiss was fierce and deep and drugging. She wasn't sure when he got rid of his own clothes. She was only aware of his strong touch moving over her, his mouth eating at hers.

His hands slid down her back, cupped her bottom and urged her legs up on either side of him. With a quick lift, he set her on the edge of the tailgate. She would have teetered forward, but he was right there in front of her, between her legs, his arms locked around her.

A few tugs on his zipper and his erection sprang forward, the tip nudging her slick opening. He rubbed the head along her slit, stirring her into a frenzy before pushing just a fraction inside.

Her arms snaked around his shoulders as she tried to cling, but he pulled her away and urged her backward until her back met the bed of the truck.

"I like to watch you, darlin'. I like you to watch me."

He pushed into her, a slow glide that stole her breath and refused to give it back until he was buried deep, deep inside her.

She gasped as he withdrew. Then the delicious pressure started all over again with another long, leisurely stroke that took both their breaths away. One thrust led to another and another, until he was pumping into her, pushing them both higher and higher up the mountain until Eden reached her peak.

She screamed out his name and it was all he needed to send him over the edge. He buried himself one last and final time and she felt the hot spurt of his seed deep in her womb.

The sensation, so sharp and sweet, brought tears to her eyes. Or maybe it was the way he pulled her into his arms and held her close as if he never meant to let her go.

Maybe both.

Either way, her tears were bittersweet because, as Eden lay there nestled in his arms, she finally admitted the truth to herself. She really had found her knight in shining armor, and she'd fallen in love with him.

The trouble was, Brady Weston didn't love her back.

MERLE WESTON RANG the doorbell of the sprawling ranch house and stepped back to wait. He wiped his grease-ridden hands on his overalls and mentally calculated the work still left back at the garage. He had four cars waiting and number five was parked back at his house thanks to Brady's Porsche which had been taking up prime space in his garage.

Nothing was wrong with the blasted thing as far as Merle could tell, and he'd been servicing cars since he'd gotten his first job pumping gas at the age of fifteen while his older brother had been following their dad around the boot factory.

Darkness had settled and the porch light pumped

out bright light. June bugs flittered and bumped at the bulb, crickets buzzed and Merle waited.

At one time, a long, long time ago, he would have walked right in. He'd been born and raised in this house, right alongside his older brother. But things were different now. Zachariah had inherited the house and the company, while Merle had forfeited his share.

He remembered the day that his daddy had delivered the ultimatum.

If you go through with this, you can call yourself something else besides Weston.

Merle couldn't help but smile. He'd gone through with it, all right, and it had been the best decision he'd ever made.

And the hardest.

Even so, he didn't regret his choice. He had something more to show for his life than a wood and brick structure and a factory full of cowboy boots. Merle had the family he'd always dreamed of. The warmth. The acceptance. And neither hinged on his life choices. He could sell his gas station, which his younger boy loved with all his heart, and his son would still love him. Along with the rest of his kids. And his wife. Their family ties involved love not money.

If only the Westons felt the same.

"This is what I get for staying at home while the entire house goes out for a nice dinner—" The words came up short as Zachariah Weston hauled open the front door.

Merle grinned. As much as he hated seeing Zach, he loved it, as well. Because he loved his brother, even though the older man couldn't stand the sight of him. And, of course, Zachariah put on no airs when it came to his feelings.

Merle thought of Brady and what the boy had been putting up with. Thanks to Ellie, who still dropped by for a Coke and a tank of gas every Friday, Merle knew all about Zach's silent treatment and the fact that he had his college-educated grandson hammering soles from dusk 'til dawn.

"What do you want?" Zach grumbled.

"Hello to you, too."

"Hello," Zach grumbled. "Now what the hell do you want?"

Merle indicated the Porsche parked at the curb. "I can't catch Brady, so I thought I'd leave the car out here. I need more room in my garage."

"Business that good?"

"It ain't bad."

"That's not what I hear."

"Well then you ain't listening too good. I'm not rolling in the green, but I'm not starving, either."

"You ought to sell to Jake."

"And you ought to stick to bossing around your employees." Merle dangled the car keys. "Can you give these to Brady and tell him everything checked out fine."

"What do you think I am? Your personal messenger? I don't have time to hunt that boy down."

"Besides, it wouldn't do any good since you're not speaking to him, right?"

"Damn straight."

"Anybody ever tell you you're about as stubborn as a hog-tied mule?"

"Who are you calling stubborn?"

"If the cowboy boot fits…" He glanced down at his older brother's black snakeskin Weston specials. "Those new for the fall?"

"How'd you know that?"

"You might not pay your only brother a visit, but that don't mean the rest of the family agrees."

"Who's been paying you visits? Is it Ellie? I swear that girl—"

"Is about as fed up with your behavior as everyone else. You're a bully."

"I am not."

"Are, too."

"I'm not."

"You always have to have your way."

"No, I don't."

"And you always have to have your say."

"Like hell."

"And you try to make everybody into what you want. Not what they want. Take Ellie for instance.

She's the best production boss you've ever had on your payroll."

"She's not in charge of production. She's doing the books."

"Says you, but that's not what she wants."

"She's good at it."

"She's better in the factory, hands-on."

"But she handles the books," he said stubbornly, "and it's no business of yours."

"Says you. Ellie's my blood and I'll damn well speak up for her if I feel like it. You keep that in mind."

"What's that supposed to mean?"

"That this ain't just a business call. It's a warning. You treat 'em right. Both of 'em, and that means letting them decide things for themselves. Listen to them. And talk to them." Merle tried to hand over the keys, but Zach refused.

"That don't belong here."

"It sure as hell does, just like the boy living in the room over my station. You're just too damned stubborn to admit it."

Zach glared. "You don't belong here, either."

"For your information, that's my daddy's picture hanging in the foyer behind you."

"And wouldn't he be sorry to see how his youngest boy turned out." He glanced at Merle's grease-stained overalls. "A grease monkey, of all things."

"It's honest work, and so long as my wife approves, then it's fine by me."

Zach shook his head. "When are you going to learn that women are a dime a dozen. They'll ruin a man's life if he gives 'em half a chance."

"And they'll make it all the sweeter if he gives 'em the other half."

"Daddy warned you about her. He said she'd drag you down."

"And he was wrong. She keeps me up. She makes me happy. Not that you'd know the meaning of the word. You thrive on misery, Zach. Just like Daddy. He never wanted me to have anyone or anything that might mean more to me than that damned boot company. The thing of it is, that company can't keep you warm at night, or cuddle next to you on the couch, or sit on the porch swing and grow old with you. A good woman can do all of that. But you wouldn't know because you let the one good woman in your sorry life slip away. Hell, you drove her away and you've regretted it ever since."

"I don't know what you're talking about."

"I'm talking about Esther." Esther had been Maria's older sister and the reason for Merle meeting the woman of his dreams in the first place. Esther had followed Zachariah home every Friday with various offerings—a fresh-baked apple pie, a jar of orange marmalade, a bowl of stew. She'd been sweet on Zach since the moment they'd walked into the same freshman math class at Cadillac High, and he'd liked her back. But he'd never acted on that like because he'd been afraid to displease their father. Where Merle had longed for freedom from the family legacy, Zach had striven for acceptance. And in the process, he'd closed the door on his one true love.

After five years of pining away for Zach Weston who had rarely given her the time of day, Esther had moved to California to attend nursing school. She'd met and married and spent the past thirty years having her own family.

"She's widowed, you know."

"I know." At his slip, Zachariah shook his head. "I mean, I think I heard something like that last year."

"She still asks about you every week when she calls Maria."

"She does?"

"You might try giving her a call sometime, if you find the time. I know business keeps you tied up."

"Yeah, well, that's how it is when a man's committed to something."

"I know." He winked at his brother. "It's the same when a man's committed to someone. Only it's a lot warmer at night." And with that, Merle tossed the keys at his brother and walked away.

HE'D FORGOTTEN TO use a condom.

The truth haunted Brady the rest of the night after he dropped Eden off and headed back to Merle's.

He'd tried to sleep, to get his mind on something other than her. He'd crawled into bed and closed his eyes, only to crawl right back out because sleeping was impossible. Not with her still on his mind. Under his skin. He could still smell her—the faint hint of apple cider and cinnamon. He could still feel her— the silk of her hair trailing between his fingertips, her hot, flushed skin pressed against his. He could still see her—completely naked and open and vulnerable....

He'd forgotten the friggin' condom!

He, Brady Zachariah Weston, the poster boy for Trojans, had had unprotected sex.

What was wrong with him? He never forgot a condom. *Never.*

But Eden had looked so hot and sexy and scared, and the only thought in his mind had been to pull her into his arms and comfort her. Love her.

Love?

Forget losing it. He'd already lost it because no way did he love Eden Hallsey. He couldn't love her. There were too many things about her that annoyed the hell out of him. The way she dressed. The way she lifted her chin and glared at him whenever he crossed her. The odd snorting sound she made when she laughed.

Strangely enough, those were the same things about her that he liked. The sexy way she dressed. The way she threw back her head and glared at him when he crossed her. The odd snorting sound she made when she laughed. All three and a whole lot more.

He'd forgotten the condom.

Brady tried to focus his attention on the pile of hot coals in front of him and the branding iron in his hands. He and Zeke had moved from hammering to branding a few days ago thanks to a summer flu that had taken two good workers out for the remainder of the week. Since Brady was the only person with experience in more than one department—albeit eleven-year-old experience—he'd been recruited. He'd taken Zeke along because he felt bad about nearly knocking the guy out the other day, and the more Zeke knew about the other departments, the more valuable he would be to Weston Boots. The more secure his job would be.

Brady grabbed the new boot and touched the tip of the branding iron to the heel.

He needed to think about work, not the fact that he was repeating his past, falling for a woman when he had no business falling for anyone. Least of all Eden Hallsey. She was the classic good time girl. She didn't believe in love and marriage and any of those soft emotions. She was every man's fantasy, and Brady had lived his. Thanks to her, he had confidence in his sexual abilities. Problem solved. Now the future lay right in front of him. A future here in Cadillac, helping his grandfather, living up to the

Weston legend. He didn't have time for love and marriage and babies. Hell, he didn't have the strength.

Not after the past eleven years spent killing himself for a woman who'd been his complete opposite. More interested in his name than his feelings. More concerned with the size of his bank account than his dreams.

So what if Eden was a good listener? Sally had been a great listener too. Of course, Sally had only pretended to listen, while Eden had actually taken his predicament into account and offered advice. And Eden had made him feel better. Stronger. As if he really could win back his grandfather's trust. Meanwhile, Sally, with her parting words *I need a real man* had chipped away at his self-esteem.

"Good mornin', all."

The familiar voice intruded on Brady's speculation and drew his attention from his work to the older man strolling through the production department.

Actually strolling, his boots making a steady slap on the concrete as he moved, a smile on his face.

Wait a second. His grandfather never strolled and— *Good mornin'?*

Brady glanced behind him, expecting to see Zeke over at his station, the object of his grandfather's greeting.

The chair sat empty and Brady remembered that the younger man had excused himself to go to the men's room.

"Uh, um, good morning."

"Nice day today."

"Uh, yeah." He studied the old man. "Are you all right?"

"'Course I am. The weatherman says we're in for sunshine today, but lots of humidity."

"Um, yeah." He tried to think of something to say, to keep the man talking to him. But his brain was still stuck on *good mornin'.*

"I hear there's no humidity in California."

"California?"

"Don't ask," Ellie said as she walked up behind their grandfather.

Brady glanced at his sister and then did a double take, noting her leather apron, a stash of papers protruding from one large pocket, and the work gloves covering her hands. "I'm relieving you."

"What—"

"Don't ask any questions. I'm still trying to absorb the news myself."

"Ellie's in charge of production," his grandfather told him.

"He put you in charge of production?"

Ellie motioned to Zachariah Weston who was busy inspecting a pair of newly branded boots while humming an off-key version of "California Girls" by the Beach Boys. "He came in at eight this morning and handed me this apron and gloves. Said he was having an office temp sent over from Austin to take my place. I know, I know," Ellie said as she noted his incredulous expression. "We're playing out our very own episode of the *X-Files* and Grandaddy is this giant pod person who looks like a Weston but really isn't. Here." Ellie grabbed Brady's hammer and handed him the computer printout she'd had stuffed in her pocket.

"What's this for?"

"It's the cost specs for the new ad campaign you mentioned to me."

"That was just talk."

"Great talk from what I hear," Zachariah Weston said. "Ellie told me all about it last night and I had her do the numbers before I relieved her of her duties."

"What am I supposed to do with these?"

"Get your ass up to the second floor and start setting everything up," Ellie told him. "You're in charge of advertising."

"And Gramps is okay with this?"

"It was his idea," she said. They both shifted their attention to Zachariah who'd retrieved a pair of sunglasses from his shirt pocket. "Yep, I hear California's just right this time of year and it's been much too long since I had a vacation."

"Who's going on vacation?" Zeke asked as he walked down the hallway, stuffing his shirttails in along the way. He lifted the lid on the Styrofoam box sitting on the countertop and retrieved a venison sausage.

"Me," Zachariah said as he snatched the sausage from the younger man's hands and took a hearty bite. "My favorite," he said around a mouthful. He snatched up the container and started down the hall. "Thanks, son."

His grandfather's voice echoed in Brady's head long after the man had disappeared and Brady had traded his branding iron for a desk on the second floor.

He'd actually done it. He'd won the old man's forgiveness. And his trust.

The realization should have made him happy. Ecstatic. Unfortunately, it only screwed things up even more. His grandfather was sure to disown him once more if he found out that Brady was following the same path he'd taken as a wet-behind-the-ears teen. He was falling in love with the wrong woman all over again.

But his grandfather *didn't* know it, and he wouldn't. There was one major difference between Sally and Eden. While Sally had longed for marriage, the last thing, the very *last* thing Eden Hallsey wanted was a happily-ever-after.

12

SHE LOVED HIM.

The knowledge sank in during the following morning as Eden went about her normal routine.

The trouble was, she didn't feel so normal. She felt sad and empty and *in love*.

"What's wrong with you?" Kasey asked her when she arrived for Sunday inventory.

"Don't ask."

"You're not sick, are you? Because if you want to call this quits and save it for another day, or at least later in the day, I'll totally understand."

Eden managed a smile. "Late night?"

"It started over at Shanghai's out on the highway after I left here. Laurie was there, of course, and she was downing Long Island Iced Teas like they were Hawaiian Punch."

"Let me guess. You had to outdo her."

"It started out that way, but then one thing led to

another and we were so drunk, that we both passed out in the ladies' room. We woke up close to 4:00 a.m. when the cleaning lady came inside to straighten up. Then we went out to breakfast together."

"You mean you had a pancake eating contest for the sacred title of Blueberry Hotcake Queen."

"No, we just ate together. She had the pancakes, but I had the breakfast tacos." Kasey must have noticed the stunned look on Eden's face because she added. "Funny how close you can get to someone when you hold their head over a toilet bowl while they spill their guts."

"You did that for her?"

"She did that for me. I've never been able to handle my Long Island Iced Teas."

"So she won."

"We called it a tie. So what about this morning? You're too sick to work, right?" She peered closer. "Why, I think your eyes are bloodshot. Are you suffering with a fever?"

More like a broken heart.

The thought filled Eden with dismay, but she pushed it aside in favor of hard work. She finished inventory in record time, much to Kasey's delight, and decided to tackle the hardwood floors in the bar.

"We're waxing today?"

"No time like the present."

"But it's the holy Sabbath. Even the Lord didn't wax on Sunday."

"The lord didn't have one hundred square feet of scratched up wood. You can go on home if you want to."

"You're sure? Because you know how much I love to wax."

"Go home."

"But—" Kasey started. While Kasey hated extra work, she did have a conscience.

"If you say one more word, I'm keeping you here."

"Adios." Obviously a major hangover could kick guilt's butt any day of the week.

Eden retrieved her mop and bucket from the back storeroom and headed for the main bar area. Four hours and eight bottles of Mop-N-Glow later, she could barely stand up. She was exhausted, and still every bit as miserable.

She missed him.

His warmth. His touch. His smile. She tried to convince herself that the past week had only been about sex, but it had been more.

In between the erotic movie reenactments, they'd talked with each other. She'd gotten to know the man he was now, as opposed to the boy he'd been way back when. He'd opened up to her and the process, he'd drawn out the shy, naive girl inside of her. A part of herself she'd tried desperately to bury all these years.

She'd succeeded. She'd covered up the pain and insecurity. But in the process, she'd buried her other emotions, as well, determined never to really feel anything for anyone in a romantic sense.

Romance had been a myth. Far from reality.

No man's kiss could make a girl's knees go weak or her palms sweat or her head spin. That had been pure fantasy. Fiction.

Then Brady Weston had walked into her life, her reality and proven her completely and totally wrong.

She'd forgotten her dreams of a happily ever after, but with his seductive charm and his handsome grin, he'd reminded her of a bonafide Texas version of Prince Charming. More so, he'd reminded her of how much she longed to find such a man. Her one true love. Her knight in shining armor who would rescue her from her lonely, guarded existence and give her everything—marriage and babies and forever.

She'd found him. The trouble was, she wasn't *his* one true love. She was bad girl Eden Hallsey and Brady was strictly out for a good time. An affair. A very *temporary* affair that was now over.

As she stood there alone in her bar, the jukebox whining a sad country tune about lost love, Eden regretted the woman she'd become. Because that woman wasn't good enough for Brady Weston. No woman was because he put his family first. He wasn't interested in love and marriage, or any of the things that Eden wanted so desperately, and so there was only one solution to her predicament.

She was keeping her distance from Brady Weston.

HE WAS IN love.

Brady admitted the truth to himself after a night of tossing and turning and getting no sleep at all. He couldn't rest, not with his mind consumed with visions of Eden and his heart aching because he wanted to pick up the phone and call her.

He couldn't. He wouldn't. They'd agreed to a temporary affair. Nothing more and he wasn't about to make a fool of himself.

Despite the tender way she'd touched him down by the river, the sympathy in her gaze, he knew she wasn't a sentimental woman. She liked things up front, out in the open, and she never, ever, intended to fall in love.

Love makes people stupid.

That's what she'd said time and time again, and she was right.

Brady had fancied himself in love with Sally and had nearly ruined his life as a result. He knew better than anyone else the amount of brain cells that could be destroyed by falling in love.

Eden would never return his feelings. Not that he wanted her to, mind you. He'd sworn off love himself. He'd just had a major breakthrough with his grandfather. The last thing he needed was to screw things up by walking down the same path as before, which left only one thing to do.

He was keeping his distance from Eden Hallsey.

EDEN'S VOW LASTED a full week, until she ran into Brady at the Piggly Wiggly again.

"How are you doing?" Brady asked as they came face-to-face in the chip aisle.

Run. That's what Eden's instincts screamed. What she'd resolved to do. But her feet wouldn't budge. Besides, she couldn't very well be rude. "Fine. And you?"

"Fine, just fine. Busy," he blurted.

"Me, too."

He held up a bag of gourmet roast coffee. "We were out of French Roast when Ellie came downstairs this morning—I drank the last cup yesterday— and so I figured I'd better hightail it over here before she does anything nasty."

"I take it she's not a morning person."

"Not before about five cups. After that, she's semidecent. If you want to get her all the way to tolerable, she needs at least six." They both laughed and then an awkward silence fell.

"I really have to get back," he murmured, but he didn't budge. And neither did she.

"I heard you were living back with your family," she finally said, eager to kill the awkward silence. "Congratulations. Your granddad finally came around."

"Finally. He's still got a ways to go, but at least we're talking."

"I'm happy for you."

"So what about you?" He eyed the contents of her basket. "What are you up to?"

"Breakfast. Pancakes and sausage."

"Man, I haven't had pigs-'n-a-blanket in a long, long time."

Don't ask. She wasn't going to. The last thing she needed was to see Brady Weston sitting across the breakfast table from her.

Then again, it *was* just breakfast. It wasn't as if she were going to invite him back to her place for some wild, hot sex.

That part of their relationship was over. Now they were nothing more than acquaintances. Buddies. Friends. And friends ate together all the time.

Besides, at the moment, the thought of sitting across from him, talking to him, laughing with him was even more appealing than being in his arms.

"Are you hungry?"

His gaze darkened. "More than you can imagine."

"Just so long as we're clear on what's being offered here."

"Pigs-'n-a-blanket?"

"And maybe a little conversation."

"Sounds good to me."

In fact, it sounded like heaven. Brady had missed her so much, and while he wasn't about to try to pick up where they'd left off—loving her or any woman for that matter was not a part of his plan—he did want to see her again.

In a strictly platonic, nonromantic capacity. *Friends.*

"For the last time, we're just friends."

"That's not what Darlene Vagabond said when she saw you two over at the Pantheon buying tickets to see that new movie with Brad Pitt and Julia Roberts. She said you only bought one bag of popcorn."

"So?"

"So friends buy their own popcorn, which amounts to two. You only bought one, which means you're going to share. And one box of chocolate-covered peanuts."

"Those were hers."

"And one box of gummi bears."

"Those were hers, too."

"So you're saying you didn't even have one tiny bite?"

"Maybe one. Hell, maybe a few. Just because we shared popcorn and some candy doesn't mean we're an item."

"Sure, big brother."

"And just because we went to the movie together doesn't mean we're an item."

"Sure."

"And just because Darlene said we looked mighty friendly doesn't mean we were."

"Sure."

"Darlene needs to mind her own business."

Ellie eyed him. "You like her."

"I don't like her." He loved her. Big difference.

"You like who?" his grandfather asked as he walked into the dining room, a plate of apple pie à la mode in his hands.

"Nobody."

"Eden Hallsey," Ellie piped in. "They went to the movies together."

Brady shot his younger sister a hard glare, before turning to his grandad. "We're just friends."

"Good friends," Ellie added.

"*Just* friends."

She wiggled her eyebrows. "Best friends."

"It's nothing," Brady assured the old man. "Nothing at all."

"So this is where you work?" Eden stared at the dark paneled office where Brady had brought her once the sun set and the factory closed for the evening. "It's nice."

A large oak desk dominated the center of the room. Shelves lined one wall. A row of cowboy boots, starting with the first model ever made by the Weston Boots Company, lined the shelves. There were all colors of boots, all styles. Only the familiar Weston brand tied them all together.

It was the first boot, the oldest that drew her attention. It had the old-fashioned cowboy heel, the pointy toe. The leather was soft and supple and she rubbed the sides between her hands.

"I like this one the best."

He studied her from his place behind the desk. "Why?"

"It's got character."

"That's exactly it," he said. "That's what we've lost. What I'm going to get back for us. Our character. Nobody knows who Weston Boots really is right now. Are we one of the big boys? Or do we still have our heart right here in Cadillac? We can't be both. That's where we've been missing the boat. We've grown and expanded. We're bigger, but we haven't lost our heart. We're not cold and callus. We're not sitting out in California or up in New York churning out a product. We're crafting boots by hand, the old-fashioned way. The cowboy way." He grinned and indicated the glossy ad design spread across his desk. It depicted a rough looking cowboy. A real cowboy, from his worn Wrangler jeans to his work gloves, to the frayed cowboy hat sitting atop his head. The only thing new about the picture was the boots he wore. Weston Boots. "We're going to play up the nostalgia of our company. Its history. Its heart."

She studied the ad layout and a smile spread across her face. "This is wonderful. You're really good at this."

"I ought to be. I slaved from dusk 'til dawn for the past ten years doing just this thing." He grinned. "Look at this." He pulled out a pair of shiny red cowboy boots. The familiar Weston brand gleamed from the side of the heel, but there was something different about it. "It's a new concept we came up with for the women's line. A triple WWW to represent the three Weston women responsible. My sisters. These are the first pair of Triple W's to come off the line."

Eden turned the boots over in her hand, trailed her fingertips over the soft leather. "They're beautiful."

"They're yours."

She shook her head. "I couldn't accept anything like this. These are too expensive. They are, aren't they?"

"They're hand-tooled so we can charge a higher price, but don't think about that. They're yours. My way of saying thank you for that night down by the river. You said all the things I needed to hear. Otherwise I might be back in Dallas right now."

"That's what friends are for." She eyed the boots again and a smile spread across her face. "This is the best surprise I've ever had."

"This isn't the surprise." Brady reached behind the desk and pulled out a box wrapped in shiny silver paper and a matching bow. "This is the surprise. Happy birthday."

"My birthday's not for another two months."

"So I'm early." He grinned. "Go on. Open it."

Eden tore into the package with all of the excitement of a ten-year-old. She didn't think about maintaining her control or appearing far-removed the way she did in the real world. When she was with Brady, she lost her inhibitions. He made her feel comfortable, relaxed, loved.

For the first time, she actually entertained the idea that he might be falling in love with her. They had so much fun when they were together. They talked and laughed and...*maybe.*

"I can't believe you did this." Eden stared at the present she'd just opened and a lump formed in her throat.

"Happy birthday."

"It's not my birthday."

"Then happy anniversary. Four weeks ago today you picked me up on the side of the road and gave me a lift to Merle's."

She couldn't help herself. A tear slid free as she pulled the T-ball shirt from the box, the meaning behind the gift as touching as the actual gift itself. "It's got my team's logo." She lifted misty eyes toward him. "Why did you do this?"

"It's our anniversary."

"I know that. I mean, why did you do *this?* Why this shirt?"

"All the other sponsors have shirts. You should have one, too. It's great what you do for the boys, Eden. You try to act like it's no big deal to you, but I know it is. I see it in your eyes when you talk about them, about all the games you've missed and all the sponsor parties you've forfeited because you don't think you're good enough for the rest of the bunch."

"That's not—"

"You *are* good enough. You're a productive member of this community. You belong here. And you deserve a shirt."

"This is the nicest thing anyone's ever done for me." And before Eden could stop and think about what she was doing, she walked around the desk, leaned down and kissed him.

She'd intended to stop with a soft press to his lips, a show of gratitude. A simple thank-you.

But there was nothing simple about the fierce desire that grabbed hold of her and turned her inside out. Before she could draw her next breath, he pulled her across his lap and then they were kissing, mouths open, tongues dancing.

It was a hot, deep, ferocious kiss that left them both breathless and wanting more.

"We should stop," she said, but she didn't stop. She kissed him again, opening her mouth, and he returned her kiss.

"You're right. We should." He slid his tongue along her bottom lip before sucking it deep into his mouth and nibbling. "But I can't. Hell, I don't want to."

"Brady, are you still here? I'm trying to get everything off my desk before I leave next week." The words preceded the loud creak of a door.

Brady and Eden jumped apart and whirled, coming face-to-face with Brady's grandfather.

The old man's gaze darted between the two of them. "What's going on in here?"

"We were just—" Eden started, her mind racing for a plausible excuse. But Brady killed the need with his next word.

"Nothing," he cut in. "Nothing at all. Eden just stopped by to ask me to help coach the little league team that she sponsors." He held up the shirt. "I told her I didn't have the time, but the company would be glad to pay for a new banner for the team if that's all right."

"Fine, fine. Just talk to accounts payable."

"First thing Monday morning." He turned to Eden. "Say, why don't I walk you down to your car?" Before Eden could reply, Brady grabbed her by the arm with one hand and snatched up the shirt and boots with the other.

"That was close," he said once they were out in the hallway. "He almost saw us."

"Would it have been so terrible if he had?"

He turned a puzzled gaze on her. "What do you mean? You wanted him to see us?"

She shook her head. She didn't know what she wanted. She only knew that it wasn't this. This... *nothing.*

"I need to get going."

"But I thought we could go out to dinner."

She shook her head. "I've got early inventory tomorrow. I need my sleep."

"Are you okay?"

She nodded, but she was far from okay. Her stomach churned and her heart ached and she felt like a complete and utter fool.

Nothing.

That's what she was to him, what they'd shared. She'd known there could never be more. She'd told herself as much, but over the last two weeks, she'd actually started to think that maybe, just maybe Brady was starting to have stronger feelings for her.

That maybe, just maybe he was falling *in* love with her. The way he looked at her, smiled at her, touched her, even though they'd shared nothing more than dinner and an occasional movie.

She'd been so certain…

And she'd been so wrong. The way she'd been wrong with Jake. Eden Hallsey had given up her own "lust only" rule and played the fool yet again.

The thing was, it hurt so much more than it had then because she didn't just have a school girl's crush on Brady.

She loved him.

But he didn't love her.

"Goodnight," he murmured as he touched a kiss to her cheek.

But Eden wasn't just saying goodbye for tonight. When she kissed him and murmured the one word, she meant it for good.

"PRETTY GIRL," Zachariah Weston remarked when Brady walked back into his office to see his grand-father perched on the corner of the desk, cost spec sheets in hand.

"Really?" Brady rounded the desk and sank down into his chair. "I hadn't noticed."

Zachariah quirked an eyebrow at his only grand-son. "You'd have to be dead not to notice, son."

"Well maybe I noticed." He shook his head. "I'm not interested."

"That's a shame. She seems nice, too. Sponsors little league and everything. Eden Hallsey, isn't it? She comes from good stock. Her parents were both hard-working, down-to-earth people, from what I gathered. You could do a lot worse."

"If I didn't know better, I'd say you were actually encouraging me."

"Maybe I am."

Brady forgot all about the cost sheets and eyed his grandfather who seemed absorbed in his own work. "What did you say?"

"A man should have a little fun in his life. Other-wise, he's liable to end up old and dried up and alone." His grandfather lifted his attention from the computer sheets in his hand and met his grandson's gaze. "Like me." A serious expression covered his face. "Work is important. This place is important, but it's not everything."

"Does this about-face have to do with this vacation you're taking next week?"

"This about-face has to do with the fact that I'm tired of being alone and there's a nice little woman out in California who's expecting me. Me and her go way back."

"You've got a girlfriend," Brady stated.

"A lady friend. I'm all grown up now, boy. Old. I could have had a girlfriend a long time ago, but I kept thinking I had all the time in the world for a social life. Work was now. It was demanding. Then one day I woke up, and suddenly, I'm ordering off the seniors' menu over at the Dairy Freeze. I just don't want the same for you."

"But I thought—"

"I know what you thought. It's what I've always preached, but maybe I was wrong. Maybe there's more." A smile covered his face as he reached into his pocket for a folded Polaroid picture. "Merle's latest grandbaby. Born just the day before yesterday at two in the afternoon." He laughed. "A nice, healthy screaming baby boy. Why, you should have seen him in that nursery."

"You were at the hospital? In the middle of a workday?"

He frowned. "I can't work all the time. A man's

got to relax once in a while." His gaze softened. "If you've ever remembered anything this old man has said, remember that, son. Remember and don't hate me too much for pushing you the other way all those years ago. I didn't know better. I didn't know what it felt like to be old and all alone."

Brady didn't want to know what it felt like either. He wasn't going to, not if he could help it. He was going to lay his feelings for Eden on the line.

She'll laugh in your face.

Maybe, but he kept remembering the tenderness in her touch, the concern in her eyes, the smile she gave him whenever he glanced over the dinner table and saw her looking at him. None of that had anything to do with lust. That was something else. Something more.

Hopefully.

And there was only one way to find out.

"I LOVE YOU."

The words echoed through Eden's head as she stared at Brady who'd just walked into the bar with a dozen red roses and blurted out the phrase she'd been longing to hear.

The words she'd dreamed of night after night.

From the man she'd dreamed of night after night.

"I'm really busy."

"Didn't you hear what I said? I love you."

"I heard you."

"And?"

"And what?"

"And the general response when someone says that to you, is to reply in kind. *If* you feel the same. Do you feel the same?"

She nodded and blinked frantically at the tears stinging her eyes. "But it doesn't matter because it's not enough."

"What are you talking about?"

"I don't want to be a three-way split, Brady. I want a man who wants me and only me. I want to be the most important thing in his life. You have too many other things that mean more to you." She nodded. "I'm not going to compete." And then Eden walked away from the one man, the only man, she'd ever loved in her entire life.

EDEN'S ATTENTION SHIFTED to the new big-screen TV sitting in the far corner and the five men clustered in front of it. Last week Willie and his buddies would have been down at the lodge watching their big screen, but since she'd taken Brady's advice and invested in an even bigger model, Willie had found his way to her bar, along with his handful of football buddies.

Adding the round of beer to Willie's ever-growing tab, she walked over and served the drinks, along with two large bowls of snacks.

"Thank you very much, little lady."

"Sure do like what you've done to the place."

"Can't beat a big screen."

"This thing's got digital."

"Glad you like it, boys. Don't forget to tell your friends."

And he did, and they told their friends, and so on until Eden found herself with more than she could handle in a matter of just a few days.

Since she and Merle and a few other brave souls had flat-out refused to sell, Jake Marlboro had finally given up and purchased several acres out near the Interstate. Of course, his surrender had more to do with the historical society, who'd decided to step in and preserve the buildings along Main Street. It seemed that things were looking up for the Pink Cadillac. Eden had even started to advertise for a busboy. She'd had three inquiries and her first interview was scheduled in five minutes.

She was alone, hunkered down behind the bar when she heard the doorbell tinkle and her first prospect walked in.

"There's an application right there on the bar. I'll be finished in a minute."

"Take your time." The familiar voice sent a rush of heat through her and she banged her head on the bar edge as she bolted to her feet to see Brady Weston sitting across from her. He held the Help Wanted sign in one hand.

"You won't be needing this because I aim to get this job."

"You have a job. A job that you love."

He shook his head. "Not anymore. And the job wasn't all that great. Not without the person I love."

As the meaning behind his words sunk in, tears sprang to Eden's eyes. This couldn't be happening to her. She sniffled and wiped at her nose. "I'm sorry, but it doesn't pay much."

"I don't need much. Just you, Eden. Just you."

She looked into his eyes for a long moment, gauging the emotion she saw there. When she recognized the love, the acceptance, in his gaze, she practically crawled across the bar and into his arms. After a fierce, frantic kiss, he pulled away and eyed her.

"Does this mean I get the job?"

She shook her head. "You already have a job."

"You wanted me to give it up."

"I wanted to know that you'd give it up. I don't want you to leave something that makes you so happy. I want you to be happy."

"Then marry me and make me the happiest man in the world."

She nodded and threw herself into his arms for another kiss.

"Is this how it ends?" she asked when the kiss finally ended. "The erotic adventures of Eden and Brady. Is this how the movie ends?"

"No." He stepped over and locked the door, then

pulled her around the bar. "This," he said as he tugged her down onto the floor and started unbuttoning her clothes, "is just the beginning. We've got forever to finish the script, but I have a feeling it will end happily ever after."

And then he proceeded to make slow, sweet love to her because Brady Weston had found Eden Hallsey's ultimate turn-on.

To love and be loved, and they lived happily ever after.

* * * * *

Harlequin® *Blaze*™

COMING NEXT MONTH

Available August 30, 2011

#633 TOO WILD TO HOLD
Legendary Lovers
Julie Leto

#634 NIGHT MANEUVERS
Uniformly Hot!
Jillian Burns

#635 JUST GIVE IN...
Harts of Texas
Kathleen O'Reilly

#636 MAKING A SPLASH
The Wrong Bed: Again and Again
Joanne Rock

#637 WITNESS SEDUCTION
Elle Kennedy

#638 ROYALLY ROMANCED
A Real Prince
Marie Donovan

HBCNM0811

REQUEST YOUR FREE BOOKS!
2 FREE NOVELS PLUS 2 FREE GIFTS!

Harlequin® *Blaze*™

red-hot reads!

YES! Please send me 2 FREE Harlequin® Blaze™ novels and my 2 FREE gifts (gifts are worth about $10). After receiving them, if I don't wish to receive any more books, I can return the shipping statement marked "cancel." If I don't cancel, I will receive 6 brand-new novels every month and be billed just $4.49 per book in the U.S. or $4.96 per book in Canada. That's a saving of at least 14% off the cover price. It's quite a bargain. Shipping and handling is just 50¢ per book In the U.S. and 75¢ per book in Canada.* I understand that accepting the 2 free books and gifts places me under no obligation to buy anything. I can always return a shipment and cancel at any time. Even if I never buy another book, the two free books and gifts are mine to keep forever.

151/351 HDN FEQE

Name	(PLEASE PRINT)

Address	Apt. #

City	State/Prov.	Zip/Postal Code

Signature (if under 18, a parent or guardian must sign)

Mail to the **Reader Service**:
IN U.S.A.: P.O. Box 1867, Buffalo, NY 14240-1867
IN CANADA: P.O. Box 609, Fort Erie, Ontario L2A 5X3

Not valid for current subscribers to Harlequin Blaze books.

Want to try two free books from another line?
Call 1-800-873-8635 or visit www.ReaderService.com.

* Terms and prices subject to change without notice. Prices do not include applicable taxes. Sales tax applicable in N.Y. Canadian residents will be charged applicable taxes. Offer not valid in Quebec. This offer is limited to one order per household. All orders subject to credit approval. Credit or debit balances in a customer's account(s) may be offset by any other outstanding balance owed by or to the customer. Please allow 4 to 6 weeks for delivery. Offer available while quantities last.

Your Privacy—The Reader Service is committed to protecting your privacy. Our Privacy Policy is available online at www.ReaderService.com or upon request from the Reader Service.

We make a portion of our mailing list available to reputable third parties that offer products we believe may interest you. If you prefer that we not exchange your name with third parties, or if you wish to clarify or modify your communication preferences, please visit us at www.ReaderService.com/consumerchoice or write to us at Reader Service Preference Service, P.O. Box 9062, Buffalo, NY 14269. Include your complete name and address.

HB11B

New York Times *and* USA TODAY *bestselling author*
Maya Banks presents a brand-new miniseries

PREGNANCY & PASSION

When four irresistible tycoons face
the consequences of temptation.

Book 1—ENTICED BY HIS FORGOTTEN LOVER

Available September 2011 from Harlequin® Desire®!

Rafael de Luca had been in bad situations before. A crowded ballroom could never make him sweat.

These people would never know that he had no memory of any of them.

He surveyed the party with grim tolerance, searching for the source of his unease.

At first his gaze flickered past her, but he yanked his attention back to a woman across the room. Her stare bored holes through him. Unflinching and steady, even when his eyes locked with hers.

Petite, even in heels, she had a creamy olive complexion. A wealth of inky-black curls cascaded over her shoulders and her eyes were equally dark.

She looked at him as if she'd already judged him and found him lacking. He'd never seen her before in his life. Or had he?

He cursed the gaping hole in his memory. He'd been diagnosed with selective amnesia after his accident four months ago. Which seemed like complete and utter bull. No one got amnesia except hysterical women in bad soap operas.

With a smile, he disengaged himself from the group

around him and made his way to the mystery woman.

She wasn't coy. She stared straight at him as he approached, her chin thrust upward in defiance.

"Excuse me, but have we met?" he asked in his smoothest voice.

His gaze moved over the generous swell of her breasts pushed up by the empire waist of her black cocktail dress.

When he glanced back up at her face, he saw fury in her eyes.

"Have we *met?*" Her voice was barely a whisper, but he felt each word like the crack of a whip.

Before he could process her response, she nailed him with a right hook. He stumbled back, holding his nose.

One of his guards stepped between Rafe and the woman, accidentally sending her to one knee. Her hand flew to the folds of her dress.

It was then, as she cupped her belly, that the realization hit him. She was pregnant.

Her eyes flashing, she turned and ran down the marble hallway.

Rafael ran after her. He burst from the hotel lobby, and saw two shoes sparkling in the moonlight, twinkling at him.

He blew out his breath in frustration and then shoved the pair of sparkly, ultrafeminine heels at his head of security.

"Find the woman who wore these shoes."

Will Rafael find his mystery woman?
Find out in Maya Banks's passionate new novel
ENTICED BY HIS FORGOTTEN LOVER
Available September 2011 from Harlequin® Desire®!